MAN DOWN

Mark Pepper

RED DOG
UK

Published by RED DOG PRESS 2021

First Edition

Hardback ISBN 978-1-914480-83-6

Paperback ISBN 978-1-914480-81-2

Ebook ISBN 978-1-914480-82-9

www.reddogpress.co.uk

For Tina and Carl,
With Love and Respect

Chapter One

'OH, BLOODY HELL…'

Something was happening with the fare he'd just dropped off. He had watched her wander into the small park and sit forlornly on a bench before he'd edged his vehicle up the road to wait for his next job to come through. She had refused to be taken all the way to her house, despite his insistence. You could only insist so much with these people; he didn't know them. Hers was a daft decision for several reasons, but daft decisions came thicker and faster as the night wore on and the booze went down. It was gone midnight now, officially Christmas Day. Too late to be sitting alone in deserted parks, even in well-to-do neighbourhoods, and bloody cold with it. Yesterday's snowfall was now crusty hard.

The two youths had passed his car in silence, save for their crunching footfalls. Dark-clothed and hooded, they were the kind of people he denied entry to his car even if they had a legitimate booking. It was fashion profiling, but it had kept him largely unscathed over his five years in the job. He had no clue if they were local rich kids dressing *gangsta* or the real thing. And had they carried on walking, he wouldn't have cared either way.

In his rear-view mirror, he'd watched as they appeared on the screen of his back window, moving further away from his car. *Walk on, just walk on…*

But they had abruptly halted and looked to their right, and he knew what they'd seen. Slowly, they had moved off the pavement into the park and disappeared from sight.

'Seriously, lads, it's Christmas. Give me a break…'

Driving away was not on option. Matt Spiller was the sort who could beat himself up at the best of times and for no good reason, so potentially abandoning a damsel in distress would have plagued him.

He shifted the Audi's auto gearbox into reverse and allowed the car to creep backwards, its quad exhausts burbling gently, clouding the frigid night air. Drawing adjacent to the park entrance, he stopped and watched as the lads approached her. Her gaze, previously down at the snow around her stilettoed feet, now belatedly lifted. He couldn't make out her expression, but her unaltered body language betrayed an indifference he found puzzling.

The lads briefly swivelled to look at him, suddenly becoming aware of the grumbling noise behind them. Spiller shifted the lever into neutral and hit the pedal a couple of times, hoping the roar from the big engine might scare them off. It didn't. They turned their attention back to the woman.

'Bollocks…'

Spiller pulled his red hat down low above his eyes and adjusted his beard. He reached under his seat, grabbed his tools, and switched off the ignition. Outside the car, he secreted a tool up each sleeve so they rested just inside the cuff of his white gloves, keeping them out of sight.

He trudged into the park to confront them. Hearing him approach, the youths turned around.

'Lads, you all right there?' He stopped a relatively safe twenty paces away.

'Fuck, it's Father Christmas,' one of them said, laughing, and they both moved to flank the woman on the bench, like menacing book-ends.

'In the flesh,' Spiller replied through the mouth-gap in his white beard.

'You got our presents, wanker?' said the other one, and sniggered crazily.

Spiller suspected the influence of drugs, and he could tell from their accents they weren't denizens of the posh part of town. He shook his head. 'Nope, you're on the naughty list. Do you want to leave the nice lady alone so I can get on with my deliveries?'

'Fuck off. You might not have shit for us, but we got *loads* in our sacks for this bitch.'

The lads cackled crazily, but the woman still appeared strangely unfazed by it all, randomly glancing between the three men.

Spiller groaned. 'Come on, boys, it's Christmas, the season of goodwill and all that happy shit. Just go home.'

'You go home—none of your fucking business.'

It was only going one way. Spiller knew that. They weren't put off by him. He was a little taller than them, and it was easy to see under his red smock that he was physically built, but those were not the attributes that habitually dissuaded people. Ever since childhood, Spiller had possessed a haunted look that could make the handiest of opponents think twice. He just looked… dangerous; deranged even. It was made worse by exhaustion and low moods—both of which were factored in tonight—but, even on a relaxed and balmy summer afternoon, there weren't many who would look Matt Spiller in his deep-set, dark-ringed eyes and think it the best option to rile him.

He approached ten slow paces.

The lads reacted. They reached inside their jackets, one producing a meat cleaver, the other a bowie knife. They let their weapons speak for them.

Spiller stood his ground, adrenaline pumping now and making him shake. He laced his gloved fingers in front of his abdomen, making access easier. 'Miss, I'm going to need you to cover your eyes for this. I don't want you to see what's about to happen. You won't like it.'

She spoke for the first time, and sounded slightly peeved. 'Really?'

'Yes, close your eyes now and keep them shut until I say otherwise.'

'Tosser thinks he's Jack Reacher,' said the youth with the bowie knife. 'What you gonna do?'

The woman obliged, closing her eyes, just as the lads made their move, which Spiller immediately interrupted. His fingers simultaneously flicked back the cuffs of both gloves and dropped the tools into his hands. He raised his left hand and hit the rear of the tactical torch, blinding them with its strobing white light. They yelped like they'd been thumped, and squeezed their eyes tight shut as Spiller moved in, flicking his right wrist to extend the telescopic spring billy. He swiped forehand at one hooded head, then backhand at the second, and continued until both youths fell to the snow, one completely out, the other moaning. He cut the strobing. Another quick swipe and the moaning stopped.

The woman opened her eyes and pointed to the tac-light. 'Can I get one of those? I've been a very good girl.'

'Please go and sit in my car.'

She shrugged, stood up, and tottered on her high heels uneasily through the frozen snow towards the pavement.

A FEW MINUTES later, Spiller joined her. He stuffed his tools under his seat and peeled off his gloves, which he put in the door pocket.

'Shouldn't they be white?' the woman asked, smirking. 'I thought Santa had white gloves.'

'They were.'

'What did you do to them?'

'Don't worry about it, they're fine.'

She laughed. 'I'm not worried; I couldn't give a toss. Little shits.'

'One of them had a gash on his head. He was bleeding. I wanted to check I hadn't killed him.' He started the engine and sped away down the road.

'Neat torch,' she said. 'Powerful.'

Spiller let out a sudden groan and swore.

'What's up?' she asked. 'Are you hurt?'

'No, my back. It's pounding. The adrenaline.' He groaned again, but laughed through his pain. 'Three thousand lumens.'

'What?'

'The torch—its brightness. The average is maybe a hundred. Short of a gun, it's the most disabling thing you can carry if you don't want to get close.'

A quarter of a mile further on he pulled over on a deserted stretch of road. She looked at him distrustfully.

'I need to get out of this costume,' he said. 'It's a dead giveaway if anyone saw me.' He hopped out of the car and roughly disrobed, ripping the thin, joke-shop material in his hurry to shed it, and revealing jeans and a sweatshirt underneath. He grabbed a plastic bag from the boot and stuffed it all inside, hat and beard included.

Back in the car, he added the bloodied gloves from the door pocket and handed her the bag.

'Is this my Christmas present?' she said. 'I'm very disappointed.'

'Shove it in your dustbin when I drop you off. I can't be caught with it on my way home.'

'Okie-dokie.' She smoothed a hand across the dash in front of her. 'Nice car, by the way. I meant to say earlier, but I was...' She waved a hand around to complete the sentence.

'Pissed?' Spiller said, and accelerated away.

'Uh-huh. What's your name? I like you.'

'Matthew. Matt.'

'Well, Matthew Matt, thank you for what you did back there. Got a bit of a red mist going, eh?'

'No, all pretty clinical.'

'If you say so. I'm at seven Ameley Villas.'

'I know it. So... who are you?'

'Emma.' She patted him on the thigh. 'And don't take me the long way round or you won't get a tip.'

Spiller shook his head. 'Jesus... seriously, what made you want to get out and sit in a park at this time in this weather? And what the hell was that... nonchalance? Like you didn't care what happened.'

She squinted at him. 'I had it covered.'

He snorted. 'Yeah, looked like it.'

'What's under the bonnet? Sounds like a beast.'

'You like cars?'

'I drive an M4.'

'So you like cars. It's a three litre, remapped. It'd give your Beemer a run for its money.'

'No doubt. Shit, are you The Transporter?'

Spiller glanced at her and saw her eyes were closed. He guessed she was late-twenties, and she was, for damn sure, provocatively attractive, both in looks and temperament.

'Stop staring,' she said, eyes still shut.

He did, offering no denial.

She yawned expansively. 'Stupid car for a taxi.'

'Thanks.'

'Who in their right mind uses an S5 Sportback as a frigging taxi?'

'No one—not in their right mind.'

'Must eat fuel.'

He smiled. 'But it's offset by the fun factor. I couldn't do this job in a Prius; I'd be bored shitless.'

'Yeah, I remember you saying, you're… what was it? *Not a nine-to-five kinda guy.*'

'Uh-huh.'

'Ex-military, you said.'

'I did.'

'Hmmm… so, why do you have a torch? Why *don't* you carry a gun?'

He gave her a frowning glance, but she was poker-faced. 'Unfortunately, you have to hand them back when you leave.'

'Ah.'

'And, apparently, they're illegal in this country. I don't know, I read that somewhere.'

She didn't respond, her eyelids heavy again. Spiller tapped the electric window down a few inches, inclining his ear towards the gap. There were sirens in the distance, several of them, overlapping and wailing and vying for attention.

Suddenly, at the end of the road, the ivy-covered brickwork of the detached houses began pulsing neon blue, which brightened until a liveried police van rounded the bend and came towards them, its siren silent, its roof-bar strobing. Spiller held his breath as the Transit carried on by and picked up speed, throwing its diminishing light-show off the hedges and gated properties he had just passed. He watched it miniaturise in his rear-view mirror and then take a bend out of sight.

'Fuck me…'

She patted him on the thigh again. '*Way* too tired.'

Two more turns and Spiller arrived at Ameley Villas. He drove through an archway into the small estate of new stucco townhouses and detached properties, arranged in a circuit around a communal garden with a pointless hump in the centre. He pulled up outside number seven, one of four three-storey townhouses. On the driveway was a pale blue BMW M4.

He switched off the engine, and his passenger's drunken snores took precedence. He crossed his arms and stared at her crumpled form. Dark, tousled hair, her once-pristine make-up now smudged vulnerably; skirt hitched a little too high from her slouching, revealing a flash of skin between hem and stocking; the short, fur-collared coat gaping at her crop-top-covered cleavage.

The snores ceased with a grunt. 'Stop staring,' she said, then opened her eyes and peered at him. 'How much do I owe you?'

'Forget it.'

She unclipped her handbag and threw back the flap to retrieve her purse, from which she withdrew two tenners. She rolled them and placed them in the Audi's cup-holder.

As Spiller watched the plastic notes expand inside the receptacle, he caught a glimpse of something in her bag that made him stutter in his refusal. 'It's fine, hones–'

Emma quickly closed the bag and clipped it shut, and was so deftly out of the car and onto the gritted pavement that it was hard to believe she had a single tot of booze inside her.

'What the hell was that?' Spiller said, but the slamming door cut his enquiry in half, at least as far as she was concerned. He leaned across the central console and grabbed the door release, pushing the door open. 'Hey, you need to take this,' he said, grabbing the bag full of his incriminating Santa outfit.

She paused before turning around and returning to the car. Before she reached the open door, Spiller pulled the spring billy from under his seat and shoved it down inside the corner of the bag.

'Take that as well. It's five miles home. I can't get pulled over with that. Dump it all under some crap in your dustbin.'

Her mouth distorted disagreeably as she deliberated. Then it fell back into position as she grabbed the bulging bag. As she did so, he placed a hand gently but firmly on hers and pointed at her handbag, making her freeze momentarily, her breath no longer clouding the air.

'That's what you meant about you having it covered, is it?' he asked.

She yanked her hand from under his, taking his bag with her. 'No idea what you're on about.'

He straightened up in his seat and she slammed his front door a little too harshly before mouthing *thank you* and blowing him a kiss. Ever the—albeit quite lecherous—gentleman, Spiller watched her safely through her front door before starting the engine.

As he completed the circuit and exited beneath the archway, a few heavy flakes of snow began to fall.

'White Christmas,' Spiller said to himself, then shook his head slightly at the events of the evening. 'Well… for some.'

AS HE PUT more distance between himself and the enigmatic Emma, Spiller began to wonder if he'd really seen the thing he thought he'd seen. At the time, it had sure as hell looked like the butt of a small pistol, or, less sinisterly, possibly the handle of a stun-gun. Now, though, his mental projection seemed out of kilter with his earlier conviction. He could only conjure a black shape that could have been a make-up case or a boxy purse or… anything that wasn't a gun. And it had been lurking in the dark of her handbag, lit only by the Audi's courtesy light, glimpsed by a mind fuelled by stale adrenaline and the dread of being apprehended. And why *would* a young woman out on the town be packing a weapon like that? It was certainly a persuasive deterrent against the unsavoury elements that infested the night-time world Spiller inhabited, but would an evidently bright and affluent individual risk the hefty legal implications of carrying such a piece of hardware, if she even knew where to source one?

Equally mysterious was her lackadaisical attitude in the face of what might have been a physical, even sexual, assault. It was as though she was beyond caring, but even the most mortally depressed individual would baulk at an attack of that nature. If harm were to be suffered, it would be self-inflicted, not hijacked by a couple of scumbags.

So *did* she have a gun in her bag? Was her response to the situation engendered by self-assurance rather than self-loathing? The knowledge that, one way or another, by her hand or Spiller's, she would emerge unscathed?

His mind was tumbling into turmoil a lot quicker than normal. He wanted to get back home and off the streets ASAP, but the snow was coming down so fast that his progress had been considerably slowed and his headlights lit a wall of descending flakes that made his fractured mind feel he was constantly lifting into the air. He felt queasy with it all. An unbroken twelve-hour shift was bad enough with his perennial tiredness, but the violent end to his evening and the disorienting weather added layers he could barely tolerate.

The severity of his reaction to the hooded youths increasingly bothered him. Not putting them down in the first place—that was a necessity—but what he did to them afterwards. It had seemed logical in the moment, and there was certainly a justification to it, and it wasn't really the act *per se*, rather the potential ramifications should he be caught. His use of force had gone from reasonable and necessary to highly gratuitous, and that had altered the legal optics.

The derestricted dual carriageway that took him the last couple of miles to his home was an oasis of speed in a desert of thirties. It was always a good opportunity to open the Audi's pipes. There were no GATSOs along the verge, nowhere for a police car to hide out, and no point in an ambush at this time of night. The cops had better things to do with their time. Indeed they did.

The weather should have put paid to a quick blast that evening, but as he joined from the slip road, he found his boot gaining a familiar leaden weight. He heard the aftermarket induction kit under the bonnet suck in a lungful of cold air, and the heavily tweaked engine came alive. The sparse tyre-fall of a nascent Christmas-Day morning meant the road surface was a uniform white, but Spiller was following a straight line with all-climate tyres. Besides which, he didn't really give a crap. He had reckless flashes like this; less nowadays, but still far too numerous for his health.

As the Audi broke the seventy limit, he thought again of his last fare. He had to wonder if he'd been wise to leave all the damning evidence with Emma, someone whose moral compass he knew nothing about. Perhaps she would awake remorseful in the early hours, thinking her saviour had gone too far by battering the youths, not even knowing what else he had done. Then she would call the cops and hand over the plastic bag.

The Audi lost its grip and the steering went light in his grasp. The excessive speed of his car was suddenly and bizarrely countered by a slowing of brain-time. Spiller felt himself gracefully spinning. How many times he didn't know, but it seemed like it was taking forever and there was no loss of momentum with each revolution through the slick snow. He tried as much as possible to steer into the spin, but to no avail. There was a whooshing sound from the tyres and an angry snarl from an engine he belatedly decided he should disengage from his right foot. He had a vague expectation that an impact was imminent, either with the central barrier or the nearside embankment that would no doubt flip his car on its roof, but the expectation was strangely devoid of any distress.

He came to a standstill on the hard shoulder, perfectly aligned with the inside lane but facing the wrong way. It looked like the neat ending to a stunt-driver's trick. Through the falling snow he could make out the haphazard skid marks in the yellow glow of the carriageway lamps, the hidden blacktop revealing itself in random swirls, but the evidence of his misadventure was so quickly filled in again that a less sane man than he might have wondered if it had happened at all.

The engine was still burbling, and, for the second time that night, Matt Spiller experienced an adrenaline dump that made him groan like he'd been caught by an unexpected and unusually painful orgasm.

'Oh, *Jesus…*' He began laughing hysterically.

The police Range Rover that pulled up facing him a minute later had its blues fluttering back and forth across the roof-bar and inside the front grille. Spiller switched off his ignition. Before the snow laid down an impenetrable curtain across the glass, he lifted a hand and waggled his fingers at the two officers facing him, then thought that was probably what a pisshead would have done, so he let the snow cloak him from their view, and waited.

Spiller weighed up his situation as best he could. Had the cops seen him spin out? Had they been following? *Had* Emma called them? And what type of cops were they? Regular or Traffic? The latter, the white-caps, would view his balletic driving style very dimly indeed. It was their *raison d'être*.

Shortly, there was a tap at his window. He dropped the glass two inches, but even that let in some bulbous flakes on a chill waft of air. The cop wasn't hanging around in the cold any longer than he needed to. He tapped the window again to indicate a wider gap was required. Spiller lowered it halfway. The cop gave him the once-over and a quick glance around the car's interior— probably looking for empty bottles or cans—before making the inevitable request.

'Do you want to come and take a seat in my car, pal?' A demand couched as a question.

'I bet you say that to all the boys,' Spiller retorted with a reckless abandon he couldn't seem to control.

'*Now.*' The officer pulled open Spiller's door.

Spiller raised his window, then stepped out into the snow and saw it was worse than he'd thought. This guy wasn't a Regular or even Traffic; he was Armed Response, with a pistol attached to the upper thigh of his black combat trousers. His fear of Emma's betrayal loomed large.

After being ushered into the back of the Range Rover and sealed, read *locked*, inside, Spiller watched the cop jump back in the front passenger seat and ruffle his scalp to dislodge the flakes before they could melt. He looked to be in his late twenties, a good-looking lad, skinhead haircut notwithstanding. There was an unpleasant fug in the vehicle, a mix of sweat, old takeaways and flatulence.

'Sooooo…' said the cop behind the wheel as he turned around. 'Good evening, sir.' The driver was older, a touch of grey at his temples and several lines etched across his brow.

'Good evening. Happy Christmas,' Spiller replied.

'We'll see about that. First off, sir, why is your vehicle facing the wrong way?'

'I spun out. I was driving too fast for the conditions and I lost it. I'm a knob, I know.'

'Well, we like that kind of honesty, don't we, Paul?'

'We do, Sarge,' said Paul, who went back to muttering into his lapel mike, requesting information, and receiving the feedback silently via an earpiece.

The sergeant behind the wheel wasn't finished, though. 'Did you fall asleep? After a long shift? You look a little jaded.'

Spiller smiled. 'Oh, that. No, don't worry about it; I always look like this. Listen, I'm sober, taxed, insured, licensed, the lot. I was just a bit too eager to get home to my wife and kids.'

'You nearly didn't.'

'No, and that lesson is now learned,' Spiller said, trying to multitask between speaking to the sergeant and listening to Paul's end of his conversation.

Paul offered his superior an almost imperceptible shake of the head, which Spiller assumed meant his details had come back clean.

'Good,' the sergeant said, 'but I'm going to have to ask you to blow into something for me.'

'No problem.'

The sergeant had a dig around in his door pocket before turning and handing Spiller a party horn. The mouth-piece was green and the curled-up end was patterned with holly and berries.

'Seriously?' Spiller asked, but both cops just stared at him.

Under the expectant gazes of the strangest law-enforcement officials he'd ever met, he put the piece of festive nonsense between his lips and blew hard. The paper horn unfurled with a raucous squeal and then crackled back into a tight hoop. He offered it back to them.

'How was that for you, Paul?' the sergeant asked his cohort.

'Lacked commitment.'

'Again, please, sir, and keep blowing until I tell you to stop.'

Spiller took a deep breath and blew hard on the horn for a second time.

'Keep going keep going keep going keep going keep going keep going, that's enough.'

The horn collapsed back into itself, and Spiller offered it to the sergeant.

'Your gift, sir. Paul—thoughts?'

'I'm feeling a lot more festive. Good effort.'

'Agreed. Happy Christmas, sir,' said the sergeant. 'Now, stop driving like a dickhead—you have a wife and kids.'

Spiller obeyed with a nod, and Paul let him out.

Being released from his five-minute incarceration into a snowy Christmas-Day morning was akin to being reborn. Spiller couldn't believe how terrified he'd been, how horrified by the prospect of his lost liberty. He gulped in the freezing air as a parched man would imbibe at a desert well.

Once safely ensconced in his snow-laden car, Spiller started the engine and hit the wipers, which strained to swish the snow from the glass. Then the armed cops accommodated his departure by straddling their vehicle protectively across the inside lane as he manoeuvred to face the correct direction, and home.

Chapter Two

SPILLER AWOKE THREE hours after falling asleep, which was two hours after he'd got in bed and eight hours after getting back home. It was nine o'clock. Another insomniac night, although his cursed wakefulness had a definite cause this time, not just the free-floating mind-garbage that usually blocked his path to slumber. He had watched TV for a long while before heading to bed; his usual nocturnal diet of brash, bearded Americans turning old wrecks into classic customs. It was rare for him to catch an episode he hadn't seen at least once before. He knew his mind would need to compute things at some point, but he'd scheduled a little escapism and a few beers first.

The beer hadn't helped him sleep. There was a sweet spot where it occasionally did, but mostly he just drifted off around dawn through utter physical exhaustion, his mind finally kowtowing to his body. Over the years he had tried everything to overcome the problem. He had changed his working hours, his eating habits, his bedtime, his alarm call, meditation, alcohol, pills and potions. He could always knock himself out with a high enough dose of pills or booze, but both led to hangovers that never seemed worth the extra few hours of dreamtime. So he'd accepted the situation as a part of his existence. He got on with his life and functioned adequately enough when he was awake. He just barely slept.

The moment his head hit the pillow, his thoughts had turned to the question of his continuing liberty. Whether the authorities would be able to identify him was dependent on several issues.

Firstly, the local network of council-installed cameras made criminal behaviour on the streets an increasingly risky proposition. It wasn't about tracking the person to the scene; it was about focusing on the scene, then tracking the perpetrator back to their point of origin. The park last night was in a residential area where Spiller had never noticed any council cameras, but many of the surrounding properties would have their own private systems. These would be focused on their own driveways, though, so would only catch the sides of cars passing in the road.

The second thing would be the satellite tracking of his vehicle by the taxi base he paid his weekly "track" to, which enabled him to access the jobs they put out on the system. For the system to work efficiently, the data-head in the car needed to know exactly where each driver was to allocate the nearest job. The base would be able to map the route of any of their vehicles over an entire shift, should the police ask for such evidence. Thankfully, Emma had booked directly with him, and he always disconnected the data-head on off-book journeys.

And the third and biggest issue was Emma herself. A young woman he didn't know from Eve, who not only had a story to tell but also a bag full of items that proved its credence.

The temptation to drive to her house and demand the return of his belongings was almost overwhelming, but it was Christmas Day. If she was at home, she would certainly soon have visitors for the day, if there wasn't already a boyfriend on the scene. With the holidays, Spiller knew the bins would not be collected for a few days yet, so the articles would either be stored ready to throw out or already pushed down beneath the detritus. Either way, Emma would have several days to mull over the incident and possibly have her conscience pricked against a tinselly backdrop of goodwill to all men—even potential muggers and sexual predators.

But this was a problem for another day—the next day. Boxing Day or no, he would need to venture along to her house and deal with it.

For now, Spiller had to wish his wife and daughters a happy Christmas. So he had to get ready. They were due for lunch at his in-laws' at midday, so he would barely have any time with them if he didn't leave soon.

Of the lies he had told the police last night, the one that had truly pained him was about driving home to his family. He hadn't driven home to his family in more than six months. The place he lived in was not a home, it was accommodation. It was a small flat that served the purposes of a separated man who had his kids round for a day every couple of weeks. His wife was still his wife, but that was more to do with avoiding the issue than there not being one. At some point they would divorce. He accepted that; perhaps when their youngest was mature enough to know this wasn't just mummy and daddy having a little tiff, although he suspected six-year-old Sophie already had the smarts to know it, certainly at some intuitive level she couldn't yet articulate.

SPILLER WAS OUT of the house by ten o'clock, his car boot full of poorly wrapped presents. The roads were quiet, so the journey took less than fifteen minutes when, on any other day, it would have taken forty-five. Last night's snow was melting fast under an unseasonably warm sun.

He arrived to see his wife, Helen, leaving the front door of his erstwhile home with Sophie. He jumped out of his car and ran to them.

'*Daaaaaaaaad!*' Sophie yelled, excitedly jumping up and down on the spot.

'Hey hey hey, what's happening?' he said to Helen, knowing his tone of voice was loaded with the peeve he felt.

'I'm due at my parents,' she responded, continuing to usher their daughter towards the street while picking up a large Santa sack that bulged with gifts.

'Soph!' he said. 'Come here, sweetie.'

Sophie ran in for a big hug. 'Happy Christmas, Dad!'

Spiller glowered at his estranged wife over his daughter's shoulder, then straightened up. 'You're going for lunch, Helen, not breakfast. It's not even ten-thirty. And where's Sammy?'

'Dad, did you get me a puppy?'

'I didn't, sweetie. The shop had sold out of puppies. I did get you a wolf, though, and they assured me he doesn't eat little children unless he's *very* hungry. He's in the car.'

Sophie made a fake-miserable face at one of her father's lame jokes. 'Oh, *Daaaaaad.*'

Helen turned and let Sophie back in the front door. 'We'll be in in a minute, darling.'

'Why would you try and leave before I got here?' he asked.

'You're late. You said nine-thirty, so I thought you weren't coming. I know what you're like with sleep.'

'Exactly. So you could have given me a bit of wriggle-room, and you must have known I'd not just *not* turn up.'

Helen said a word: 'Sorry.' Then she went back in the house, dragging her Santa sack behind her and leaving the door ajar.

Spiller looked skyward, closed his eyes and inhaled deeply, blowing out a lengthy breath in a forlorn effort to calm himself. When he looked down, he saw he was being watched. Sophie was at the window of the front living room, next to a Christmas tree, her expectant smile not quite dismissing the sad pinch of her eyes. He gave her a Mr Bean grin and the thumbs-up, and went back to his car to retrieve her gifts.

GATHERED TOGETHER IN the front room, Spiller was reminded of times past, although *gathered* seemed the wrong word as it was just the three of them, and he was fairly sure a gathering required more than three people, and a family gathering at least required the presence of all the closest family members.

'Helen, where's Sammy?'

She took a moment before responding, like she was hoping a better answer might present itself. 'She's not here.'

Spiller waited for her to expound. Sophie's hands had been poised above her mound of gifts, but they now dropped to her sides as she slouched back on her heels, realising the present-opening was not so imminent. Spiller stared at his wife.

'Sammy's got a boyfriend,' Sophie announced, trying to spur things along.

'Oh. Okay. Since when?'

'She's seventeen,' Helen said.

'I know how old she is.'

'Two weeks,' Sophie obliged, absently picking at a loose end of Sellotape on one of her dad's boxes.

'Oh,' Spiller said. 'Helen, are you telling me a boyfriend of two weeks has managed to lure our daughter away on Christmas Day? Who's she going out with? Justin Bieber?'

Sophie giggled. 'You don't know who Justin Bieber is.'

'Apparently I do, and I have all his stuff.'

'Are you suggesting I'm at fault for letting that happen?' Helen asked.

'Name one of his songs,' Sophie urged.

'What do you mean?' Spiller said to his daughter.

Sophie eyed her father, unsure if that was an answer or a question, and not wanting to fall into a dad-trap.

'Matt!' Helen said. 'Are you blaming me? I didn't just let her walk out this morning, you know?'

The implications of that took a couple of seconds to sink in. 'You mean…'

Sophie chirped up helpfully again. 'We've not seen her since yesterday.'

'*What?*'

Helen stood up and held the door open for him. 'Kitchen,' she said.

Sophie wilted. 'Can I watch telly?'

SPILLER SAT AT the kitchen table while Helen put the kettle on and prepared some coffee.

'In your own time,' he said.

She angrily flicked at the kettle, stopping its soft roar. 'What do you want me to say, Matt? What should I have done? Lock her in her room? She's seventeen, she goes to college, she has a life of her own. What am I meant to do? What would *you* have done?'

They were all good points. He had no idea what he'd have done. He plonked his elbows on the table and cupped his forehead with his palms.

'Have you spoken to her since yesterday?' Helen asked.

He shook his head. 'Couple of days ago. She sounded fine. I said I was looking forward to seeing her today, and she said the same. Said she couldn't wait. That's what's odd. Why would she choose a new boyfriend over us? Why would he even let her? Any decent guy would insist she spend time with her family today. And surely *his* parents wouldn't think this is right.'

They both let the elephant in the room tramp around for a few seconds.

'Unless...' Helen said.

'Unless he's not a boy. Unless he's a man who stopped spending Christmas with his parents years ago.'

'Shit.'

Spiller felt nauseous. Like any father, he'd never relished the prospect of his eldest daughter hooking up with a proper boyfriend, with everything that entailed, but he'd resigned himself to it happening. This, though, was not that. If they were right, this was a whole different parental horror story. This was a guy, within a matter of days, having such a sway over their daughter that she could abandon her family on Christmas Day.

'Do we call the police?' he asked.

'And say what? She's got a boyfriend and she's been gone one night. What are they going to do?'

'Aren't you worried?'

'Course I'm bloody worried. But this is what kids from dysfunctional families do.'

Spiller winced. 'Jesus, is that what we are? Dysfunctional? Helen, we're separated; we're not the fucking Lannisters.'

She didn't respond.

'How's Sophie taking this?' he asked. 'Her big sis not being here?'

'She deals with it like she's dealt with everything: in a mature way I can't even begin to emulate.'

Spiller smiled, and felt tears well so quickly that one managed to sneak out. 'Yeah, she's an amazing kid. Helen, make yourself at home—sit down.'

She did so, but said, 'We should go back through. Sophie...'

'What are we going to do, Helen? Have you called her this morning?'

'Duh, *yeah.*'

'I'll try.' Spiller pulled out his mobile, but the call went to voicemail. 'Sammy, it's Dad. Where are you? Call as soon as you get this, please. We're worried. And... Happy Christmas. Your little sis misses you—'

At that moment, Sophie burst into the kitchen and rather undermined her father's assertion by happily shouting, '*Presents presents presents PRESENTS!*'

'Love you, Sammy,' Spiller said, and ended the call. 'Come on, kiddo, let's go and unwrap that wolf.'

Sophie gave him a look. 'Dad, you did not get me a wolf.'

'I did, it's in that box—the wolf-shaped one.'

'Stop winding her up,' Helen said amiably as they all headed for the front room, where Sophie had paused *Despicable Me.*

'Oh, she knows me. Don't you, Soph?'

'Yes, you're a very silly man.' Sophie settled behind the mountain of gifts she had collected into one teetering pile while her parents had been in the kitchen.

SPILLER WORKED THE remainder of Christmas Day. It was always a pleasant change, ferrying happy families to and from their relatives, rather than transporting puking pissheads around. There was usually some distance work involved as well, although the fares dried up earlier than on a normal day.

That morning, Helen had ushered him out of the house as soon as Sophie had completed the big unwrap. He had left with six pairs of Minion socks, which at least meant Sophie had chosen his gift, not Helen. The already-strained atmosphere had been exacerbated by Sammy's absence, and especially the unknown reason for it. He had tried calling her numerous times since, to no avail. It had felt like he was waiting for a cancer diagnosis, desperately hoping he was worrying about nothing, but quietly convinced the signs were dire. Every time his mobile rang, his heart sped up, but it was always just another private booking.

He called Helen at midnight to check, only to be gruffly informed she would *obviously* call if she heard anything. They discussed again whether to involve the police, but decided they would wait until the morning. It still felt odd not ending a call to his wife with "I love you". Mostly their calls were terminated by one or other saying "fine" and hanging up.

Last night's business with Emma was fading fast in his mind, superseded by his current preoccupation, but also by the logical assumption that no news was good news. The more time that passed, the less likelihood there was that she'd call the police or that the police had managed to catch a glimpse of his car registration on CCTV. Although... the severity of the situation rather dictated in favour of a prolonged enquiry, so he realised it was still early days. For that reason, his desire to regain possession of the items he had left with Emma would not abate.

The cops weren't waiting at his door when he returned to his flat that night. But he slept little, as was his wont.

Like Christmas Day, Boxing Day was also a relatively agreeable time, another round of conveying decent people between pleasant places, unfortunately interspersed with the inevitable prat or two, but such was life.

Spiller managed to make it to seven p.m. before the urge to call on Emma overwhelmed him. He unplugged his data-head, entering stealth-mode, and headed towards Ameley Green.

A quarter of a mile from his destination, an incoming phone number appeared on the Audi's media screen. Spiller tapped to answer. 'Hello.'

'It's me,' said the irate female voice.

He recognised who it was. 'Emma! How was your Christmas?'

'Cut the shit and come and get me.'

'Be outside in sixty seconds. And bring my bag.'

'What? You're *here*?'

'Yes, I know it's the taxi drivers' cliché, but I really am just around the corner.'

The Audi's tyres crunched through a few frozen remnants of snow as he approached her house. Emma was ready for him, standing on the pavement, arms crossed.

'Well, you're a bleedin' nutter, aren't you?' she said as she got in and settled next to him, slamming the door.

'How so?' he asked, knowing how so, but really hoping she didn't.

'Drive.'

Spiller stared at her. 'Where's my bag?'

'Safe. Drive.'

'Bag.'

Emma jabbed him in the arm with a rigid forefinger. 'I just watched the news.'

Spiller squinted at her as though he had no clue where the relevance lay, but his brain had worked out the likely answer even before he said, '*Okaaaay*...'

'You cut their thumbs off.'

'Ah.'

'You cut their fucking thumbs off. What the fuck...'

Spiller shrugged. 'What do you want me to say? I did. It's done. They won't grow back.'

A yelp of laughter escaped her; a horrified sound, but not quite absent of amusement.

'Our thumbs separate us from the animals,' he explained. 'They didn't deserve them. And, on a practical level, they're certainly not going to be holding machetes again, so the world is a safer place.'

She was shaking her head. 'No, no, I get the warped rationale behind it, I'm just wondering how your mind works. What went on in your head that told you to do it?'

'You really don't want to know what goes on in my head. Could you *please* go and get my bag now?'

'No, I'm keeping it.'

Spiller felt a red mist start to billow. But it wasn't a dangerous red mist; it was the sort that comes from impotence. The anger of knowing she had the upper hand and he would only make matters worse by trying to raise his status above hers. He inhaled audibly, and slowly blew out through pursed lips.

'What do you want?' he asked.

'I want you to kill someone.'

Spiller didn't know what to say that would appropriately encapsulate his... what? What was it he felt? Amusement? Bemusement? Disbelief? Horror?

His silence riled her. 'You've got nothing to say to that? People ask you to kill someone every day?' She snorted to reinforce her disgruntlement.

'So, you're keeping my bag so you can blackmail me,' he said, his flat inflection making it rhetorical.

She stared at him, which was answer enough.

'What makes you think I'm up for something like that?'

She smiled crookedly and waggled her thumbs.

'There's a big difference between a thumb and a life,' he said.

'Oh, now you want to get all precious about this, eh? Give over.'

They sat in silence for a few moments, the air laden with tension.

'Well, go on,' he said. 'Who? Why?'

'I'll pay you,' she said, starting to appear a little daunted by the enormity of her own gall. 'I mean, I don't know how much... you know... people charge.'

Spiller laughed. 'I'll Google it, shall I? *How much for a contract kill in the UK?*'

'Fifty thousand,' she blurted. 'I'll give you fifty grand.'

Spiller abruptly stopped laughing. 'You need to get out,' he said, more because the amount she was offering was genuinely interesting. Fifty grand was a lot of money to him. It was a hell of a lot of hours taxiing. There was persuasion in that amount of money.

'You've killed people before, haven't you? When you were in the army or whatever?'

'I could have been a cook, for all you know.'

'You weren't though, right? Although it would explain your skill with a knife.'

He used his most winning smile to try and defuse her intent. 'Listen, this is getting silly. I did a bad thing to those lads the other night, but they were asking for it. This is different. *I'm* different—to the way I was in the past. Okay? I don't want to go back.'

Something about her demeanour suggested he'd broken through, then she trashed his notion by prodding him hard in his arm again. 'You are going to kill someone for me. I am going to pay you fifty grand for doing it. And then we will never see each other again. Either that, or I take your bag of bloody goodies to the police and you go to prison anyway.' She got out of the car, pausing at the open door, letting in a rush of cold air to chill the interior and further freeze his soul. 'You've got a couple of days to think about it,' she said, then slammed the door on him.

Spiller sat there, stunned. The big engine growled away in front of him, venting a sound he similarly sensed within him.

Chapter Three

THE LAST PEOPLE Spiller wanted in his life were the police, but he called them anyway. He didn't ask Helen's permission and didn't see why he should; Sammy was his daughter as much as hers. Perhaps they were having a quiet day because they said they would send a car to Helen's house within the hour. He signed off from work and headed over there.

As he drove, Spiller sensed his mood degenerating into a familiar spiral. It felt like he was being sucked down a plughole. To a certain extent, his mind was always circling a dark drain. It had been like that for many years; since childhood, really. As he'd got older he had become more adept at avoiding that final descent, usually managing to drag his thoughts back and up and plug the drain before it happened, but, plugged or not, it was forever beneath him, just waiting to open up and pull him in.

Three cars arrived outside Helen's house in short order.

Spiller's was the first. He manoeuvred the Audi into a tight parallel park opposite the front door and had just switched off his ignition when a liveried Hyundai pulled up, taking a spot ten metres down the road. Spiller watched as two uniformed officers emerged, one male, one female. He was waiting on the pavement by the gate in a pool of light thrown down from a lamppost when the coppers approached the house, the female carrying a black folder embossed with a silver crest. She appeared to be fortyish. The male, with sergeant stripes on his chest epaulette, was maybe early thirties. They were all poised to utter their greetings when the third vehicle arrived.

The exhaust note from the red Nissan Skyline put Spiller's Audi to shame. It almost hurt the ears. The male driver, vaguely outlined behind tinted glass, came to a halt right next to them. Undeterred by the officers' presence, if not in defiance of it, he roared the engine a couple of times as his passenger climbed out, then he quickly sped away down the street.

Spiller stared at his daughter. His relief was immense.

'Hi, Dad,' Sammy said meekly. She moved close to him and stood there, waiting for him to hug her. Spiller slowly wrapped his arms around his eldest, and Sammy reciprocated with the tightest hug he'd ever known. He looked apologetically at the officers as Sammy's hug tightened even more and he heard the front door open and a relieved squeak from his wife. He let his daughter go, but she kept on hugging him.

'Sammy, come here, darling,' Helen said.

Reluctantly, Sammy loosened her embrace, let go of her father. 'Sorry, Dad,' she muttered, before shuffling up the steps towards her mother. Spiller watched as Helen gently ushered her indoors and closed the front door, sealing the three of them out.

The female PC—Carnaby from her name-badge—spoke first. 'Mr Spiller?'

'Yes.'

'And that was Samantha?'

'Yes.'

'Do you still want us to come in?'

'Uh… I don't know that there's much to say. I mean… she's back. Sorry I wasted your time.'

Spiller expected that the officers would simply say their farewells and be on their way, but they stood their ground, and he suddenly wondered if Sammy had been only their first order of business.

But they weren't lingering for him, for his crimes, Spiller could see that. There was something in their demeanour that spoke of awkwardness. Carnaby turned and looked up the road in the direction of the recently departed Skyline, then glanced at her colleague, who was obviously deliberating quietly with himself.

'What's up?' Spiller asked. 'Who was that? Do you know him?'

'Might be best if you come and sit in our car,' said the sergeant, name-tagged Enright.

Spiller's second invitation to sit in a police vehicle in two days, but this one scared him far more than the first.

'We can talk in front of your daughter, if you like,' Enright said. 'And your wife, obviously, but...'

Spiller shook his head and started to walk past them towards their Hyundai.

ENRIGHT TURNED TO face him while Carnaby met his eyes via the rear-view mirror.

'I'm not sure we should be telling you this, Mr Spiller, but if it was my daughter, I'd certainly want to know.' He glanced at Carnaby, who nodded minutely in agreement.

'Who was that in the Skyline?' Spiller asked.

'His name's Callum Ward. He's known to us. *Well* known to us. Your daughter's in serious bother if she's started knocking about with him.'

Spiller's heart was racing like he was on meth-amphetamine. 'Go on. What's he done?'

Carnaby answered: 'It's more like what's he *not* done. He's spent over half of his twenty-eight years locked up. He's probably the nastiest bastard within a hundred miles.'

'He's twenty-eight?' Spiller asked, realising that probably wasn't the most pertinent bit of information he'd just received.

'You need to get your daughter away from him,' Enright said. 'Or I'm afraid this won't be the last time you call us.'

'He's...' Carnaby began, searching for the right description '...not the best boyfriend material.'

'How's she in danger?' Spiller asked. 'Is he going to get her in trouble or is he going to hurt her?'

'Likely both,' Enright said. 'Have they been together a while?'

'Few weeks, I think,' Spiller replied, and knew Enright was asking to determine if Sammy might already have suffered at her boyfriend's hands.

'She seemed very sad,' Carnaby noted, revealing her verdict on the matter. 'That was a long hug you got.'

The officers let Spiller stew in his thoughts for a while, until he asked: 'Will he let her go?'

They answered by saying nothing.

'Thank you. I appreciate the warning.' Spiller got out of the car and spoke to them through the open passenger window. 'You can't do anything, can you?'

'Not until *he* does something,' Carnaby said, then smiled feebly. 'On the bright side, given his form, he's probably going to get himself locked up again pretty soon. It's a matter of time with everything he's into.'

Spiller shook his head. 'I'm not inclined to wait.'

IT WAS A sign of Spiller's state of mind that the rushed footsteps behind him as he neared the house had him swivelling ready to throw a punch.

Sergeant Enright held his hands up, smiling crookedly. 'Hey, it's only me.'

'Sorry... bit stressed.'

'I just wanted to say—off the record—be careful with Ward. I'm not warning you off as a copper; I'm not telling you to leave things to the police because there really is nothing we can do at the moment. I'm just saying, if you're thinking of doing something yourself, be very careful. He's a nasty bit of work.'

Spiller wondered if he was being tested on his intentions, so decided a non-committal response was in order: 'Thank you.'

Enright nodded and took a card from the pocket of his stab-vest. 'That's me. Call if you need any help.'

'I will, thanks,' Spiller said, and Enright returned to his car.

Spiller looked at the card. Sergeant Alfie Enright. He took out his wallet and slipped it between two ten-pound notes.

In the few seconds before he reached the front door, Spiller had decided not to let Helen know what the coppers had told him. She had every right to know, probably needed to know, but he felt a foreboding—the fear of a series of events potentially soon to unfold, about which it was best Helen knew as little as possible. His mind had raced ahead to the worst-case scenario of having to kill Ward, and Helen needed plausible deniability, both of the event if it happened, and the knowledge of why her husband may have been culpable.

Helen had left the door ajar for him. He entered, passing the front room where Sophie was glued to one of the *Despicable Me* movies.

'Hi, Dad, are you wearing my socks?'

He backtracked a few steps. 'No, I'd never fit in your socks, they're too small. You've got them on; I can see them on your feet.'

She scowled. '*Daddy.*'

He hitched up his trouser legs to show her the Minions. 'Yes, darling.'

She laughed at him. 'You look silly.'

'Thanks, that was the idea, was it? To make me look silly?'

She nodded, grinned, and turned back to the TV.

'I'm cutting you out of the will,' he told her.

'Whatever.'

In the kitchen, Helen was waiting for him, seated with a cup of tea.

'That girl is six going on sixteen,' Spiller said.

'You called the police.'

He shrugged, took a seat opposite her.

'I was about to,' she said. 'I couldn't have waited another day. Do you want a drink?'

He shook his head. 'Sammy upstairs?'

'Getting a shower.'

'Did she say anything?'

'Just sorry. I didn't want to push her. Not yet.'

'Why didn't she answer her phone?'

'He took it off her.'

'Christ.' He looked around the room. One corner was out of commission—had been since they'd split. It was awaiting a new washing machine, new cupboard units. Capped-off pipes and crumbling masonry around gaping holes. He'd been remodelling when their bickering had reached a crescendo and she'd told him to leave. She'd not called in a professional to finish the job and had warned him off doing so. Perhaps she was leaving it as a permanent reminder of the mess he'd left behind, both literally and emotionally. Shit, like he needed a visual aid. She'd even left his box of tools and materials lying there.

He pointed to the mess. 'Why don't you let me sort that out?'

'You've got the cash for new units, new appliances?'

'I can get it.'

'I thought not.'

More hurt than angry, he said, 'I would give you my last pound coin if I thought it would make your lives easier.'

She softened. 'I know you would, Matt. We're okay.'

'Let me deal with it. I'll work extra hours.'

'I'm earning, Matt. We're not destitute. I'll sort it out.'

He nodded. 'So, how are we going to deal with Sammy?'

'Gently. Very gently. Whatever's going on, we don't want to come on strong and send her straight back to her boyfriend. In fact, I'd rather have a quiet word myself first.'

'Why? She talks to me. You know how close we are.'

'And you know how much she hates to upset you.'

Spiller thought about it and nodded. He'd always told his girls they could tell him anything and he wouldn't be cross. But cross and upset were different, and his daughters could read his feelings with great ease. Helen, on the other hand, had a dispassionate side she could muster for anyone, including her daughters. It was a front, but it allowed for difficult conversations to take place in an atmosphere of relative objectivity. He knew she'd be the best one to speak to Sammy initially. Especially bearing in mind the information he'd gleaned from the cops about her boyfriend, which would launch him into any conversation like a missile fit to explode.

'Okay,' he said. 'But please don't let her see him again for the time being. Even if you have to lock her in her room.'

'I won't.'

Spiller knew his expression was doubtful.

'It's okay, Matt, we're on the same page. I don't like this any more than you do. Whoever that guy is, he already has way too much influence over our daughter.'

'I'm going to say goodnight to the girls,' he said.

HE COULD HEAR the shower running as he climbed the stairs. On the landing, he inclined his ear to the bathroom door. Sammy was doing a sterling job of submerging her sobs, but he could hear the odd little squeak.

'You okay, darling?' he called through the door.

'Yeah.'

The sob was in her voice. It was heart-breaking.

'You sure?'

'I'll be okay.'

'Mum says he took your phone.'

'He gave it back. I've got it.'

'Good.' He'd told Helen he would take a step back for the moment. He had to do that, for all their sakes. 'Okay, sweetie. I'm always around if you need to talk.'

'I know. Love you, Dad.'

'I love you too.'

He backed away from the door and popped his head into Sophie's room, having heard her scurry up the stairs earlier. She was sitting on her bed and jolted as she noticed her dad's face appear. Her hand had darted behind her back and she looked guilty.

'Whatcha got there, Soph?'

'Nothing.'

'It's obviously something. Don't make me put on my Felonious Gru X-Ray goggles.'

She giggled, but her amusement quickly faded as she sheepishly produced a yellow tube with red lettering.

'Gosh, a Sherbet Fountain. I didn't know they still made those.'

Sophie gave a shameful shrug.

Spiller eyed her. 'Mum didn't get that for you, did she? She doesn't like you having too much sugar.'

Sophie shook her head as tears welled.

Spiller went over and squatted down. 'Hey, it's okay. Where did you get it?'

'Sammy. It was in her bag.' She started snivelling. 'I only took it because—'

'It's okay,' he cut in. 'You know you should have asked, but it's okay.'

'Sammy's sad,' Sophie said, quietly blubbering. 'I heard her crying.'

Spiller stroked his daughter's hair. 'She's fine. She's just tired. Don't worry.'

'Sorry, Dad.'

'It's okay. Just pop it back before she gets out of the shower.'

A smile replaced the frown. 'I will.'

He kissed her forehead and straightened up. 'Right, I have to go.'

'Dad...'

'What, sweetie?'

'Is grandad retarded?'

Spiller burst out laughing. 'Well, I've always had my suspicions.'

Sophie was referring to Helen's father, Craig, who she and her mum had spent Christmas Day with, and who had always disliked his son-in-law for his career choices and had made no bones about displaying that pique. It was the one good thing to have come from the separation—Spiller didn't have to see that total arse ever again.

'I think, sweetie, that you might mean *retired* rather than retarded.'

She looked puzzled, convinced of her initial description.

'When someone stops work when they're older, they retire,' Spiller explained. 'So we say they're retired.'

Sophie made a face like she was still certain he'd got it wrong rather than her, until Spiller pointed at the Sherbet Fountain again.

'I'll put it back,' she said. 'Love you, Dad.'

'Love you too.' He kissed her and retreated from the room.

When he got back to his car, Spiller did some Googling on his phone. Callum Ward had made the local news over the years. It seemed he'd drawn up a bucket-list of crimes at a young age and had been ticking them off with aplomb ever since. There were periods when his name wasn't in the news, but those were evidently while he was being cared for by Her Majesty's Prison Service. Spiller found his heart palpitating at the thought of his daughter spending one single minute in his company. It wasn't just the threat of violence towards her, it was the possibility of her being implicated in his next criminal endeavour, and of her becoming forcibly hooked on his current drug of choice—drug crimes having been a persistent feature of his court appearances.

Life could change so damned quickly. Two days ago he hadn't been intending to kill anyone. He'd been a regular guy driving a taxi, unhappy with his lot but immeasurably better off than most people in the world. Now, he desperately wanted to kill one person and had been asked to kill another. On the latter, he decided he'd just have to bide his time. Hopefully, Emma would come to her senses and simply not get in touch again, although that still left the possibility that she'd hand his bag to the cops anyway.

He keyed the ignition and manoeuvred away from the kerb. There might still have been some decent fares that evening, but he wasn't in the mood, so he kept his data-head switched off and headed back to his flat.

THE NEXT MORNING at ten o'clock, Spiller was woken by a call from Helen. He'd been properly asleep for maybe three hours. He didn't quite know what to make of the information imparted by his wife. He had a dinner invitation that evening. He was to be at the house by seven o'clock, where they would be joined by Callum Ward. Helen had invited him for a get-to-know-you meal. She had spoken with Sammy and had apparently decided the best approach was to meet the situation head-on. However it had happened, Sammy had fallen under Ward's spell and was not to be dissuaded from seeing him again.

Short of locking her in her room, there was no way to ensure an end to the relationship, so Helen had decided they should at least try to mitigate it by becoming a concrete fact in Ward's mind. It didn't make much sense to Spiller, and he suspected she was also flying blind. Unless they were to chaperone their daughter on every date, simply meeting Ward would not make her safe in his company. But Spiller supposed that, as far as clutched straws went, it was a reasonable gambit, so he acquiesced.

With his night written off, Spiller ventured out early to earn a few quid. He disliked working days. They were safer than nights, but the fares were generally short-distance and the heavier traffic hurt his effective hourly rate. And people usually didn't tip. Pissed people tipped. If they didn't run off, they tipped.

Spiller took very unkindly to runners. The dickheads who did it didn't know, but it was an act of theft known as *making off without payment*. They thought it was fair game, evading a taxi fare, but it wasn't. Not fair, not a game. Some of them had found that out the hard way.

Spiller had never encountered a daytime runner. Now, it seemed he was about to experience his first one. Only, it wasn't really a runner. It was... more of a *Zimmer*.

The old biddy he'd collected from the nursing home and taken to the local store was making off without payment, although *making off* suggested some haste, and of that she was thoroughly incapable. She looked ninety-plus, but she was perfectly in charge of her faculties. She was stooped in accordance with her advanced years, but if she'd been straightened out—by a steam-roller perhaps—Spiller guessed her height would be maybe five-ten. Her accent was incredibly fine; royally posh. She reminded him of Mrs Richards from *Fawlty Towers*.

The entire fare had been a proper pain in the arse. At the outset, he had waited patiently for her to zimmer towards his car, then he'd helped her in and loaded her frame into the boot. He'd then driven through sluggish traffic to the nearest shop, helped her out, handed her the frame, and watched her shuffle into the building. She had emerged ten minutes later with a bulging plastic bag hanging on the frame, which clacked from the bottles of booze he'd spied her purchasing. He had helped her back into the car, put her frame in the boot, and re-joined the dawdling afternoon traffic. On the bright side, she had offered him a piece of fudge, which he had politely declined, not knowing at the time that confectionary was to be his only recompense. Back on the driveway of the nursing home, he had helped her out, re-attached her gnarled fingers to her Zimmer frame, and watched as she started to inch her way back to the entrance. The whole thing had taken over half an hour. For barely five quid. Which he anyway wasn't about to receive.

'Uh…' Spiller uttered as she slothed away from him. 'Aren't you forgetting something?'

'I don't think so, thank you,' she said haughtily.

'My fare. You owe me a fiver.'

'Thank you!'

Spiller was stumped. He normally chased after runners, but how to chase someone he'd overtake in two seconds? He'd once rugby-tackled a guy to the ground as he fled, but in this instance that would be hard to explain to the coroner.

He walked three paces and blocked her path. She stopped zimmering, briefly looked up at him, then shuffled left in an effort to loop around him. He stepped in her way again, and she started to make another laborious detour.

'You owe me a fiver,' he reiterated.

'I shall drop it into your taxi office.'

'Really? Where's that, then?'

'Yes, where is that?'

'In town, opposite McDonald's.'

'Then that is where I shall leave it for you,' she said, having managed to side-shuffle into a position where she could once again make a beeline for the entrance.

'What's my driver number? Who are you going to leave it for?'

'Yes, what is your driver number?'

'Thirty-five.'

'Then that is the number of the driver I shall leave it for. Thank you so much.'

'And how are you going to get there?' Spiller asked, immediately wishing he hadn't.

'I shall summon a taxi-cab.'

He nearly swore, but instead blocked her path again, causing her to begin another protracted evading manoeuvre.

'I can do this all day, you know,' she informed him.

Spiller cursed, then noticed something: she didn't have her shopping bag. He grinned and headed back to his car. For a brief moment, she seemed elated by her victory, before she noticed her mistake.

'Oh, *fack*.'

Hopping back in the Audi, Spiller spotted her bag full of booze in the rear footwell. It was more than a fair exchange.

'Stop!' she squealed. '*Thief!*'

He dropped the window. 'Not nice is, it? Bitch.'

WHILE AMUSING, THE Zimmer Incident—as it would henceforth be known in local taxi folklore—was but a brief distraction from the weighty matter of Callum Ward. As the minutes ticked by towards their evening meal, Spiller found himself contemplating more and more how he could kill the guy and get away with it. Probably not in front of his wife and daughters, although he couldn't rule out any scenario should Ward become problematic during their meeting. One thing he did know: the police had provided plenty of motivation. People like Ward could not be given the benefit of the doubt, not when his daughter's safety was on the line. To protect his own flesh and blood, Spiller had to accept that a mess might need to be made of Callum Ward's.

Back at his flat, Spiller laid out a few of his weapons on the bed. He had built up quite a stash over the years. Replica guns; knives: flick, stiletto, butterfly; a rigid telescopic baton; a spring billy; a monkey-fist; a kubotan; and, most seriously, a pepper spray and a 400,000-volt stun-gun flashlight. It was amazing what a person could buy on eBay in the early days. He had taken them all out taxiing at various times over the years but had latterly settled on his tactical torch and the spring billy, which was unfortunately now in Emma's possession. He had frequently considered getting rid of the stun-gun and pepper spray as they were classed as Section 5 firearms, but he'd never had the heart to throw them away. And now he was thinking he'd made a wise decision.

He cleared away all but the stun-gun and kubotan. They were small enough to secrete about his person. He would wear an old denim jacket with large inside pockets and have one in each. With two hours to go, he lay down on the bed to see if he could grab forty winks. He didn't think he would, with all that was running around in his head, but he would be better-served later on by a more rested mind. Doubting his ability to fall asleep, he did just that, soundly, and for considerably longer than forty winks.

BY THE TIME Spiller had woken up and got his shit together, he had barely half an hour to reach Helen's house. And, this time of the evening, that was fifteen minutes short of the journey time. Thus, it was a testament to the leaden nature of his right foot and a taxi-driver's knowledge that he managed to arrive at Helen's only five minutes late. Ward's Skyline was already parked outside. Spiller swore, then found a spot further up the street, parked, and ran back to the house.

Helen opened the door to him and whispered, 'You're late,' although she didn't look irritated. In the same low tone, she told him, 'He's been here ten minutes.'

'Sorry. What's he like?'

'On the face of it, very pleasant. Come in.'

The kitchen smelled of Bolognese sauce and garlic bread, and Spiller noted a simmering pan of orange gloop and a packet of spaghetti sitting next to an empty cast-iron pot. Ward was seated at the kitchen table with a glass of lager in front of him. He was on the same side of the table as the stove, where Helen got back to working on the meal.

Ward stood up as Spiller entered, and offered his hand and a beaming smile. 'Mr Spiller, I'm Callum.'

Spiller felt instantly disarmed. The guy did indeed seem nice. He had a slight local accent, but nothing Spiller would have considered scummy. His hair was short and Eminem-blond, and there was a white NY baseball cap on the table and a black puffa jacket hanging over the back of his chair. His clothes, despite being the *de rigeur* sports outfit of the chavvy drug-dealing underworld, at least looked expensive. In fact, Spiller reckoned just one of Ward's trainers would have cost more than everything he was wearing, or had worn that whole week. They shook hands firmly.

'Matt,' Spiller said, slightly nonplussed. 'You can call me Matt.'

'Matt, great to meet you, thanks for the invitation.'

'Oh, that was my— That was Helen's idea.'

As he stood opposite Ward, Spiller took the opportunity to assess the man physically, and quickly concluded they were very similar in height, weight, and build. They would be evenly-matched in a fight, and that was a bit of a bummer. If things were to go south, Spiller would need to get the jump on him. Facially, Ward appeared to be what the police had said he was. Beneath the smiles, Spiller saw features that could harden in a heartbeat. Ward sat down again.

'Where's Sammy?' Spiller asked Helen.

'Upstairs, just finishing her make-up. She'll be down in a mo.'

'And Soph?'

'Playing in her room. She ate earlier.'

Spiller nodded. 'Okay. Is there a beer in the fridge for me?'

'Help yourself.'

Spiller turned his back on them both and delved in the fridge for a can. There was a good selection in there, plus a bottle of wine. He tore off a Coors and sat down opposite Ward, cracking the can and taking a slurp.

'Use a glass,' Helen said. 'We have a guest.'

Ward laughed. 'It's okay, I'm usually a can-man myself; I don't mind.'

She smiled at him. 'But I do. Matt—glass.'

Spiller obeyed, taking a beer-mug from the cupboard and decanting his lager into it. He sat down again.

Ward raised his glass. 'Cheers.'

'Uh, yeah… I suppose so.'

They both drank.

'Look,' Ward said amiably, setting his glass down. 'I know why I'm here. We should get that out of the way. I know I'm a few years older than Sammy. I know—'

'Eleven,' Helen interrupted. 'Eleven years older.'

'Well, yes. If we're counting.' He gave a short and gracious laugh.

'Parents do,' she replied, turning back to the cooker to give the sauce a stir.

'Okay… I mean, are you asking me to stop seeing Sammy? Is that why I'm here?' By the end of the sentence, his expression had leached any sign of social niceties.

Spiller opened his mouth to speak, but was cut short.

'Matt, get Callum another beer.' Helen tore open the pack of spaghetti and lifted the heavy pot onto the stove using its two handles. 'And flick the switch on the kettle, please.'

Spiller nodded and turned back to open the fridge. His eyes kept going to the knife block on the countertop. He was ready to strike, but he needed to provoke a negative reaction from Ward that would justify giving him a jab with something. Probably the best way to do that would be to answer Ward's question by forbidding him from seeing their daughter again.

'About seeing Sammy,' he said to the interior of the appliance. 'To be honest—'

The clang from behind him was both dull and deafening. Heart hammering, he swivelled, expecting to see Helen picking up the cast-iron pot she'd evidently dropped.

But the pot was not on the floor; it was hanging by a handle from one of Helen's severely-clenched fists. The thing that was on the floor was Callum Ward. Spiller took a step back and looked beneath the table at their guest. Ward was out cold, and it took a stupidly long moment for Spiller to add two and two, because the four on the floor really didn't make sense.

He gawped at her incredulously. 'Did you just hit him with that?'

She was visibly shaking, but her nod was big enough to show through.

'Helen, what the fuck… I thought we were going to talk to him.'

'*That cunt hurt our daughter!*'

Spiller held a finger to his lips and pointed at the ceiling.

'They're both out!' she yelled. 'I sent them to friends for the night. He fucking hurt our beautiful daughter, Matt.' She burst into tears and dropped the pot on the floor.

Spiller went to her. 'Hey, what d'you mean?' he asked, but knew enough to know exactly what she meant.

'Last night, I walked in on Sammy after her shower. She's covered in bruises and fucking cuts and all sorts! Like he's been using nail clippers on her! Bits of her skin are missing!'

'Christ. Is she okay?'

'*Of course she's not okay!* And she never will be as long as this piece of shit's still breathing! *And* he was stashing drugs with her!'

'*What?*'

'After you left, I heard Sammy shouting at Soph. I went upstairs and it was all to do with a pack of sherbet. Only it wasn't fucking sherbet. She'd taken it from Sammy's bag.'

Spiller went faint and wilted into the chair Helen had just removed Ward from. Jesus. Little Soph could have overdosed.

'*And* she said you'd seen it! You'd seen it in her fucking hand!'

Spiller matched her volume. 'I didn't know what it was! It didn't say fucking Crack Fountain on the side!'

As if by silent agreement they both instantly calmed down. The seriousness of the situation would not be well-served by hysteria and they both knew it. Now the room was quiet, they could hear something that wasn't. Ward was beginning to moan quietly.

Helen stooped and picked up the pot.

'What are you doing?' Spiller asked.

'I'm going to put the pasta on—*what do you think I'm doing?*
I'm gonna crush his fucking skull.'

'God, I have *never* heard you swear this much.'

'*That's* what you're taking from this?'

'Helen, I want him dead as much as you do, but you can't kill
him in the kitchen. You hit him with that again and break his
skin and we'll have his DNA all over the place.'

Ward's moans were growing louder. His eyes were shifting
behind his closed lids.

'Well, *Matthew*, unless you've got a better idea, I'm gonna give
him another whack or he's gonna wake up and then it really will
get messy—for all of us.'

Spiller dipped a hand in his jacket and pulled out his stun-
gun.

Helen looked at it. 'Why do we need a torch?'

He didn't answer. The weapon crackled as the current visibly
arced between the prongs. He bent down and jabbed it against
Ward's thigh for a few seconds, making him shake. When he
broke contact, Ward was still moaning.

'It hasn't worked!' Helen said. 'Give him a longer blast, knock
him out!'

'They don't knock people out; they incapacitate. Here.' He
gave it to her. 'I've got some tow-rope in my boot.'

Helen peered at him. 'Rope? *Rope?* Unless you're gonna hang
the fucker, so what?'

Spiller spoke as softly as possible to her. 'We tie him up, call
the police.'

'We need to kill him, Matt! For what he did and for what he
could do! You want him getting up and walking around again
after what I've just done to him? Never mind how he might
retaliate; all he has to do is deny everything and then *I'm* the one
in court for twatting him over the head.'

'I know, and that's exactly the problem. We kill him, we go
to jail and our daughters end up in care.'

'Only if we get caught.'

'Everyone gets caught.'

'Bullshit. Plenty of people get away with murder. They're called cold cases; murders that never get solved.'

'Yeah, I've seen those documentaries, but that's when it's a stranger; when the police don't know exactly who to speak to.'

She stared at him for a moment. 'Why would the police look at us?'

He ignored the question. 'Helen, they already know what a scumbag he is. With what Sammy tells them and the drugs he left with her, they'll be able to lock him up again.'

He didn't need to see her accusing eyes to know he had just screwed up. Boy, had he dropped a bollock. He'd known it the second the words were out.

'The police *already* know what a scumbag he is, do they, Matthew? They'll lock him up *again*, will they?'

'Um… I'm going to get the rope. Just zap him again if he starts moving.'

Luckily, Helen was so furious she couldn't speak to interrupt his swift exit from the kitchen.

SPILLER MADE SURE to saunter across the street to his car, like anyone would who was enjoying a lovely family meal with their daughter's new boyfriend. He wanted desperately to run, but you never knew who might be curtain-peeking. At the open boot, he stuffed the tow-rope into a supermarket bag, wondering if it was maybe too thick to tie tightly enough. He had some cable ties in his toolbox in the kitchen. Maybe they'd be better. He slammed the lid down.

'That you, Matt?'

Spiller turned to see his next-door neighbour, David, standing outside his house. A few years Spiller's junior, they'd been doorstep buddies when he lived with Helen. Long chats if they bumped into each other coming or going, but nothing more. Their paths simply hadn't crossed on those occasions when he'd dropped by to see his daughters since the split.

'Hey, David, how's life?' Spiller said, scrunching over the top of the bag to conceal its contents.

David came out to him and shook his hand. 'I should be asking you that. What happened? I thought you and Helen were forever.'

Spiller gave a shrug. 'Well, you never know what goes on behind closed doors, mate.'

'Who's your visitor?'

'Pardon?'

'The prat with the rorty exhaust.' David nodded towards Ward's Nissan Skyline.

'Oh… uh… friend of Sammy's.'

'And you let her have friends like that?'

'She's at that age, mate. Not a lot we can do.'

'I guess. So…'

David was clearly in the mood for a chat, but Spiller made an apologetic face. 'Sorry, I need to get back inside. Things to discuss. We'll catch up one of these days, I promise.'

David offered his hand again. 'No worries. Take it easy.'

'Yeah, you too,' Spiller said, and headed back across the street at a pace he deemed correspondent with a desire to talk divorce rather than tie up a local drug lord.

THE SIGHT THAT greeted his return to the kitchen was such a done deal that there was no point getting angry. It stopped him in his tracks and made his jaw drop cavernously, but there was no undoing it, so it struck him there was nothing to be gained by questioning it.

Helen looked at him with a comical expression. 'Oops.'

'*Fuuuuuuuuck.*'

The picture on the kitchen floor was still developing. He'd done enough DIY in his time to know how long it took to stop creeping, and it seemed like it still had some way to go. Ward was twitching, but Spiller couldn't see that continuing much longer and reckoned the creeping would outlast it. It was just the body having a final little tantrum against the inevitable.

Spiller was mesmerised as he watched the creamy substance billow slowly from Ward's mouth and nostrils, merging into one bulbous, ballooning mass that threatened to swamp his face completely. It was like watching Joseph Merrick turn into the Elephant Man in super-fast-mo.

'*Fuuuuuuuuuck,*' he said again.

Helen giggled maniacally.

As the pace of the creeping slowed, Spiller stepped towards his wife and gently took the canister of expanding foam from her. The nozzle was still drizzling. He set it down in the corner of the room where his other tools were.

Uncertain what words, if any, were appropriate, he stared at Helen from across the room. Her face was now impassive.

'He had to go,' she said. 'It's our daughter.'

Spiller nodded, and realised why he'd not been annoyed when he entered the room. She was right: killing Ward was the only way to ensure Sammy was safe from him.

Ward lay still now. The foam was hardening.

'You okay?' she asked, seemingly indifferent to whatever answer he may give.

'Wow, when did you become Lady Macbeth?'

'What are we going to do, Matt?'

'Don't know. I need to think.'

'And why didn't you tell me you knew about him?'

'I didn't want to worry you. I was trying to figure out a way to handle it myself. I didn't know he'd already hurt her.'

'But you knew he could?'

Spiller didn't respond.

'Jesus, Matt…'

'Shall we call the police?'

Helen guffawed. 'Are you joking?'

'They know what he's like. I'll say I did it. I'll claim self-defence. I plant a knife in his hand and say he came at us.'

'Right. And you just happened to have a tin of expanding foam in your hand, eh? That might work for Jason Statham, but you ain't him. I mean, who the hell uses expanding foam as a deadly weapon?'

'Apparently you do, my sweet.'

'Oh, fuck you! You know what I'm saying. No one is going to believe *that* is anything other than premeditated. Especially with a lump on his head the size of an egg. A fucking moron could work out the sequence of events.'

Spiller held his hands up in surrender. 'All right! Fair point! I did say I needed time to think. Give me a few minutes, will you?'

They sat opposite each other. After a moment, Helen swore softly.

'What?' Spiller asked.

'Sammy will certainly expect us to call the police. She begged me not to, but she's going to know something's wrong if we don't.'

Spiller thought about it. 'And we'll have to tell them Ward was here tonight. I bumped into David outside and he asked about Ward's car. Once they start investigating his disappearance, they'll be looking at us pretty closely.'

'Why would they do that? You ignored me earlier when I asked. Why would they look at us, Matt? Why?'

Spiller grimaced at the recollection. 'When I spoke to the police… I might have suggested I was about to take matters into my own hands.'

She stared at him for a moment. 'You penis.'

Chapter Four

IT TOOK TEN minutes of deep thought to come up with a plan. They had to get Ward and his Nissan Skyline far away from the house—that was obvious. But Spiller couldn't be seen getting into it, either by David or the various CCTV systems on the surrounding houses. And, even if Spiller could covertly get Ward into the boot and himself behind the wheel, carting him away in a car with a nick-me exhaust was too risky. All it would take was a bored copper.

After agreeing the plan with Helen, Spiller went back out to his Audi and grabbed his tactical torch and his leather driving gloves.

As decoys went, Spiller reckoned it was pretty good. The first stage involved Helen going next door to borrow a corkscrew from David. Spiller would then time his exit from the house to coincide with David standing on his doorstep during a brief exchange with Helen, because they needed David to see Spiller leaving. Or, rather, they needed him to see Callum Ward leaving.

The problem of removing the real Callum Ward from the house would be dealt with later on. In the meantime, they decided to drag the body down to the cellar and leave it hidden out of sight behind some storage boxes. Before doing so, Helen placed a couple of plastic bags over Ward's grotesquely bulbous head and taped them at the neck to make sure no loose hairs could be tracked out of the kitchen and down the cellar steps.

Once dumped below, Spiller stripped Ward of his outer clothing and trainers, shed his own garments, and got into Ward's. As he'd earlier assessed, Ward had a very similar physique. He made sure he had Ward's mobile phone, wallet, and car keys, then ventured back upstairs. He was greeted by Helen, who handed him the NY baseball cap, which he pulled low down above his eyes.

She regarded him and shook her head. 'You need to lose the stubble; Ward doesn't have any.'

'David's only going to get a brief look.'

'So it's best the person he sees looks nothing like you.'

She was right. He headed upstairs to the bathroom and found his old razor and some shaving foam, and quickly removed the shadow from his face. As he was leaving the room, Helen ushered him back inside. She was holding an aerosol can.

'Whoa, woman, keep that away from my mouth.'

Unsurprisingly, she didn't smile at his joke. Instead, she started shaking the can furiously, making the agitator rattle.

'What is that?' he asked.

'White hair spray, left over from Halloween.' She grabbed a towel and draped it around his shoulders. 'We need to colour your visible hair.'

'Okay.' He removed the hat.

Helen doused his hair across the back and sides with noxious-smelling white powder, then let it dry. He replaced his hat and admired his new look in the mirror. *'Hi, my name is, what? My name is, what? My name is—'*

'Dim Shady. Listen, can we just do this?'

Helen showed Spiller into Sammy's bedroom, where he retrieved the Sherbet Fountain Ward had left with her. He took it downstairs, wiped its surface, pulled on his gloves and placed it inside a small freezer bag which he zipped shut. It was a huge risk taking it with him, but the more evidence the police found to link Ward to drugs, the easier it would be to conclude the whole thing was gang-related.

He put on Ward's puffa jacket, stuffed the bag in the pocket and got the car keys ready in his hand. They moved to the front door. She gave him a plastic bag containing an old pair of his trainers—all part of the plan. They both stared intently at each other.

'I love you,' Spiller said.

Her fingers paused on the handle. 'What? Really?'

'Yes.'

'No, I mean *now*? Now is the time for endearments, is it?'

'Sorry.'

'I love you too, Matt, but that's not what's lacking and you know it, and this absolutely isn't the time to talk about what is.'

He blew a sigh, both nervous and frustrated. 'Okay. You know where to meet me and when.'

She nodded.

'I can't call you,' he said.

'I know.'

'I can't take my phone in case they decide to trace my movements at some point, and I can't call you from his.'

'I know, I know, I know. We agreed everything.'

'Just making sure. I'm hoping to be with you by ten at the latest, but it could be later. If I'm not there by midnight, I'll have been pulled by the cops and, with that sodding exhaust, that's a real possibility.'

'Just try and stay off the gas as much as you can,' she said.

'Of course. And remember to bring my clothes. And don't bring your mobile.'

'Roger that.'

They both took deep breaths. Then she opened the door and went outside, leaving it ajar. He put the snick on it, then listened as she descended the steps, walked down their path, along the pavement, up David's path and his steps, and rang on his doorbell. After a few seconds, the door opened and Spiller heard David's delighted voice betray the excitement he felt seeing the next-door-neighbour he'd always wanted to shag.

'Helen! How are you? Don't you look gorgeous tonight?'

'Oh… thanks. Yeah, I'm good, David. I was just wondering—'

'I spoke to Matt earlier.'

'Yeah, he mentioned. Sorry, would you have a corkscrew I could borrow?'

And that was Spiller's cue. From behind the door he spoke a little louder than necessary so his audience would catch it all.

'You're not seeing Sammy again, so you better get used to it!'

He pulled the front door firmly behind him as he stormed out of the house so it banged noisily, as though someone inside had slammed it on him. He raised a middle finger rearward as he went to the Skyline. He beeped the car as he approached and slipped in quickly behind the wheel. He fired up the engine and manoeuvred out from the kerb, hitting the accelerator angrily for effect.

AS MUCH AS he wanted to be rid of the car and get back home, Spiller knew he couldn't take a direct route to the hills. It occurred to him as he drove the first few hundred metres in the Skyline that, if this were his vehicle, he'd have fitted it with a tracking device. If such electronics were lurking in some secret nook, a direct route without stops would suggest only one viable explanation for its final resting place: that Ward had become so depressed by his chat with Sammy's parents that he'd decided to drive into the middle of nowhere and kill himself. And how likely was that scenario?

So, Spiller headed into town and out the other side to a council estate whose reputation was well-known and well-deserved. Although he was sure there were many decent people living there, his years of taxiing had taught him to avoid such areas if he wanted to keep his health, nightly takings and vehicle intact. He drove to a lane on the outskirts of the estate that petered out on wasteland once cleared for further development that had never happened. The estate's CCTV network was purposely indiscreet to discourage delinquency in public areas, but this area fell outside the coverage. It had become an illicit dumping ground for those who couldn't be bothered driving the couple of miles to the council tip.

He parked the Skyline and killed the engine. The possibility that a police patrol might happen upon him was terrifying. There could be no innocent explanation for his spray-haired impersonation or his presence behind the wheel of a car that didn't belong to him. But, if the vehicle were being tracked, he needed to place it for a while in a spot where something unsavoury might have occurred.

He took out the freezer bag containing the tube of drugs, and removed Ward's trainers. He opened the door, dropped both shoes outside, and sprinkled some of the white contents on them. He put on his own trainers, got out, opened the boot and placed one of Ward's shoes in the back right corner, along with the depleted tube.

In Spiller's ideally-envisaged world, the following would happen: the police would trace the Skyline to the estate, find one shoe coated in drugs, then later discover the other one lurking in the boot. Conclusion: a drug deal gone awry, Ward killed, bundled into his own boot, then dumped.

As Spiller cruised out of the estate, he passed a gathering of shady youths who eyed the car. He imagined it was familiar to them. He inclined his head slightly to the right so the peak of the NY cap hid more of his face. Behind the smoked glass, the blond hair would still be obvious, and that was perfect.

Heading out of town, he breathed a sigh of relief.

Then his heart nearly stopped.

The blue that lit the inside of his car and bounced off the surrounding buildings was enough; there was no need for a siren. Adrenaline flooded his system. He contemplated putting his foot down, but he'd seen how those escapades ended on the documentaries. More units join the chase, then the helicopter goes up. He decided to play it by ear. He'd not broken any laws—at least not that the copper behind might know about. Perhaps he could hand over Ward's driving licence and bluff it. If not, he would plant his foot hard down and take advantage of the Skyline's superior power.

He pulled over, leaving the engine grumbling. The police car followed suit. He could see in his rear-view it was single-crewed. The officer got out and approached. Spiller lowered his window and was about to ask what the problem was when the cop spoke.

'Oh,' was all he said.

Spiller looked up at him, still hoping the cap would hide his true identity; he imagined all but a rookie officer would know Ward's face.

'How are you, Mr Spiller?' the officer asked.

Spiller looked him full in his deadpan face. It was Sergeant Alfie Enright.

'Uh… good… thanks.'

'Good. You drive safely.'

Spiller didn't know what to say, so he said nothing, but it would have been redundant anyway as Enright about-faced and went back to his vehicle. Spiller watched in his side mirror as Enright got in, stopped the blues, started the engine, pulled out and drove past the Skyline and away down the deserted road.

'What the fuck just happened there?' Spiller asked himself.

He didn't know, and it didn't matter. He'd just been handed a stay-out-of-jail card. He could muse over the whys and hows at his leisure, but right now, he had to capitalise on the situation and get the hell out of town.

HE WAS ON the motorway within five minutes. Ten minutes later, he looped off onto the by-pass and headed towards the countryside. The by-pass turned into an ascending A-road after fifteen minutes, and then came the B-roads that twisted through the dark hills, which turned out to be not so dark under the layer of snow that clung to them ever more thickly with the increasing elevation. At least the roads were clear, the ploughs of Christmas morning having barged aside the snow, now a mottled brown from the grit and muck thrown up by the passing tyres.

The idea was to get to a place that lacked any surveillance. No CCTV, no ANPR. Drive deep into the wilds. It didn't matter that the car would probably be found the next day. It was only important that no one saw who got out of the vehicle or where that person went.

Spiller knew the hills and their trails from his youth. A good part of his recreational time as a youngster had been spent hiking all over the place with his parents. They had been great role models, paragons of health, at a time when exercise had not been the focus it was today. Unfortunately, their efforts hadn't been rewarded with huge longevity, both dying in their sixties within a few weeks of each other while Spiller was in the Middle East.

The car park was deserted, as he'd expected. He had ventured down a winding track to reach it, creeping slowly through a depth of virgin snow that threatened to stop the vehicle dead. No one had been daft enough to come here since Christmas. In the summer at this time in the evening, people might have been returning to their cars after a day out, but this was deep winter and bitterly cold. Spiller parked the Skyline in the corner of the area, as far out of sight as he could, and killed the engine and the lights. The relative silence that greeted him was wonderful. All he could hear was the wind in the trees. Ahead of him was the dark expanse of the reservoir, extending unseen into the distance. It was a monstrous stretch of water.

As he contemplated, something struck him like a bolt of lightning: he felt great. He'd battled depression for years and could trace it all the way back to his childhood. Not that he'd experienced anything traumatic—he'd just been a generally miserable bugger as a kid, and the ageing process had only ripened those feelings. Despite the events of the evening, he felt more alive and worthwhile than in years. Only it wasn't despite, it was thanks to. Tonight had shaken up his staid existence. Much like his lashing out in the park to protect Emma, Ward's grisly demise had awoken something primeval and elemental in him. Remove the fear of discovery and there wasn't a whole lot he felt bad about.

A whole lot? Fuck all. The last time he'd properly felt as vital was six years ago in the Gulf. If he'd been able to call Emma at that moment to accept her proposal, he'd have done so.

He put Ward's mobile in the glove box and got out of the car, locking it. There was a huge temptation to search the vehicle to check for any weapons—he liked weapons—but it was best such items, if they were present, were left for the cops to find.

He made a mess of the snow all around the car, shuffling back and forth from driver's door to passenger door to boot, every which way, then a similar snow-shimmy to the water's edge. There was no snow where the reservoir lapped at the pebbles that encircled it, so his tracks ended there, his direction of travel now obscured.

He activated his torch, but dropped its intensity so he'd be less visible. The route around the reservoir to the rendezvous point was approximately two miles. He began walking, his feet clacking the stones against each other. The dim pool of light from his torch vaguely lit the way, bobbing left and right with his motion. His breath was heavy and dank, clouding the frigid air as he soldiered on. After twenty minutes, he stopped and launched Ward's car keys as far as he could into the water.

With a mile to go, he broke from the shoreline. He crossed the reservoir path and headed up a track, negotiating the now rugged terrain, climbing upwards. Without the benefit of his local knowledge, he'd have been lost in minutes, swamped by a landscape made seamless by winter. But, less than an hour after leaving the Skyline, he was nearly at the rendezvous, high up on a hill, distantly overlooking the water.

Spiller surveyed the remote pub car park from the trees on the periphery. There were half a dozen vehicles. It wasn't the sort of place a normal person walked to on a freezing December night. The picnic tables were empty, save for a layer of snow, like icing on a row of sliced cakes. The pub sign swung with a creak atop its lit wooden pole, adjacent to the deserted B-road that wound its dual ways back to civilisation. The Fawn Buck. Now, there was a name to play with after a few too many pints.

He skirted the car park, staying among the trees. Fifty metres down from the pub, he came to a drystone wall that bordered the road. He crept along just the other side of it, low and out of sight.

He shortly arrived at a small lay-by: the rendezvous. He was shivering now, trembling in waves. The sweat from his arduous ascent from the reservoir had dried into a freezing cloak on his skin. The bulky puffa jacket was a triumph of style over function.

When Helen arrived ten minutes later, he was shaking uncontrollably. He saw headlights approaching, then the car slowed, and he knew it had to be her. She steered the Peugeot 308 onto the half-moon of snow-covered gravel. He popped up above the wall and gave her a wave. She dropped the window.

'Clothes, quick!' he shouted in a quivering voice.

'Change in the car!' she said.

'I'm filthy!'

She climbed out with a bulging plastic bag and handed it across the wall to him, then quickly got back in to escape the chill. Spiller changed out of Ward's outfit into his own clothes and some clean footwear, stuffing the dirty attire back in the bag.

'Water!' he yelled across the wall to her.

Helen threw a plastic bottle through the car window, which hit him in the face. 'Shit, sorry!'

He bent over and poured the water over his head, rubbing at the back and sides of his hair where the white spray was. He continued until the milky liquid cascading onto the ground turned clear. He left the bottle where it was and clambered over the wall with the bag, which he chucked in the car boot. Helen already had the heating on full blast when he jumped in the passenger side and sealed himself off from the cold. It was instant bliss. She handed him a towel, and, as he rubbed at his scalp, she swung the Peugeot onto the road in a U-turn and accelerated away.

'Enjoy your little walk?' she asked.

'Delightful.'

'Any problems?'

He thought of Sergeant Enright's weird traffic-stop, but said, 'No, all good.'

'Just the dead body to dispose of, then.'

He gave her a sidelong glance. 'Yeah, just that.'

They drove in silence for a few minutes. At least, they didn't talk. The car heater was making a racket as it pumped out a sickly, fuggy heat. Spiller was starting to lose the shakes, so he turned it down a notch.

The incident with Enright had been playing on his mind since it happened, but had been all tangled up with the other concerns he'd had in making good his escape to the wilderness. Now that was over and he was beginning to catch his breath, he was able to extricate the episode and try to make sense of it. Only it didn't make sense. Not unless Sergeant Enright didn't give a crap about the law and blatant skulduggery, but... that didn't make sense.

Spiller decided it was one of those things you just had to slot away in the brain's *what-the-fuck?* folder. It was a folder that had gained a good few files that night already.

Helen eased the car around the bends, taking it nice and gentle as they descended from their hilltop rendezvous. By design, the route back was completely different to the one Spiller had taken to the reservoir. It would only be the last few roads that matched—if anyone saw the need to check the Peugeot's registration against a recorded image.

'I was thinking...' she said.

'What?'

'Maybe we don't need to get rid of him.'

'*What?*'

'We could say we asked him to finish off the kitchen and, you know, he slipped and impaled his face on a can of foam.'

Spiller smirked. 'Right.'

'That could be his epitaph: Here lies Callum Ward. Shit at DIY.'

'Yeah, I'm fairly sure the church wouldn't allow that.'

BEFORE THEY ARRIVED back in camera-land, Spiller decided it would be a good idea to shift onto the rear seat and lie down out of sight. He was playing the worst-case scenario that Helen's car would at some point be looked at and any surveillance of it scrutinised. If that were the case, it would look odd that she'd departed the house alone and returned with him, when he'd apparently arrived and not left.

Getting in the house unseen was helped this evening by something that usually pissed Helen off: the lack of an empty parking space along the street. When this happened, Helen would reluctantly drive down the narrow ginnel at the back of the terraces, open the rickety wooden gates, and reverse into the lower yard that the cellar door opened onto. Tonight, the inconvenience was perfect, and it justified what might have otherwise appeared like a spot of suspicious parking. The back yard was utterly private, the shape and arrangement of the buildings at the rear being such that no one overlooked the area.

But what was good for Spiller getting into the house unseen was even better for the clandestine removal of their unwanted guest.

Once inside the cellar, Helen was hit by the giggles. It was, Spiller hoped, borne of hysterics rather than amusement, but, either way, it was oddly infectious.

'Helen, stop,' he said, starting to convulse. 'This isn't funny.'

'We're Bonnie and Clyde,' she spluttered, and cackled harder.

They laughed together for a short while, but it was the longest time in years. When they quietened down, Helen looked at him, and he'd have sworn he knew that glint in her eye.

'God, I am so turned on,' she said, confirming it.

Before he could respond, she moved closer to him and went for his belt buckle as she planted her open mouth on his.

Spiller thought it was the best sex they'd ever had. They were all over each other like ravenous teenagers, tearing their clothes off like people only did in the movies, trying every position and then some, oblivious to the chill in the cellar and the proximity of the man they had just murdered. The old sofa he'd been meaning to dump for two years came in very useful.

They climaxed together, their previous intimacy allowing them to match each other's escalating passions.

As they dressed, Spiller watched his wife's demeanour change, like the cold had suddenly seeped into her bones. In the throes of sex, he'd thought he might ask afterwards if the act had meant something more than the physical, but he could see now that it hadn't.

'Let's get him in the car and away from here,' she said, pulling her fingers through a tangled bit of hair.

'Yep.'

Helen went outside and opened the hatchback and laid out some plastic sheeting Spiller had bought for decorating but had never used. She held the cellar door open as a gloved Spiller lifted Ward's head-bagged, near-naked body under the shoulders and dragged him outside, then hefted him awkwardly into the

Peugeot's boot. He could feel the rigor mortis in the limbs he had to bend into a compliant shape to fit. With the body cramped in, Spiller covered it with a couple of old blankets and gently closed the hatchback.

'Now what?' she asked.

Spiller dithered. Admittedly, this part of the plan had lacked specificity. If he'd been listing bullet-points, this one would have read "dump body". The basic necessity was to get into the hills again. Should the police check, local cameras would pick up his exit from the neighbourhood, but they would lose him as he ventured off-grid, searching for the remotest spot he could find.

'Well?' Helen asked.

'I don't know. Do I just dump him or do I try and hide who he was?'

'You mean… what? Remove his teeth and set fire to him?'

Spiller nodded.

'You want to get to somewhere really dark, then start a bonfire?'

'Fair point.'

'I meant, do you have somewhere in mind?'

'I think so. It's in the middle of nowhere. A winding road you wouldn't normally stop on. There's a wall with pretty much a sheer drop over the side into dense woods. I don't think there are any paths nearby.'

'People hike off paths.'

'It's a dangerous area,' he said, getting peeved. 'And I can't think of anywhere else, so unless I'm just going to drive around for hours with a corpse in the boot, it'll have to do.'

'Okay, but *you're* not going to be driving anywhere.'

'What? Why not?'

'I took you off the insurance.'

'So what? If I do get pulled, I think the cops might be more bothered by the body in the boot than my lack of insurance.'

'The point, *you divvy*, is that they'd definitely search the car if you're an uninsured driver.'

'Oh. So…'

'We both go, but I'll drive.'

'No way,' he said. 'One of us has to stay out of this as much as possible. We can't both get nicked. Think of the girls.'

She did, and nodded quickly. She handed him the keys. 'Don't get caught.'

He smiled facetiously. 'That's my last bullet-point.'

'What?'

'Never mind.'

THE PEUGEOT WASN'T top-spec, so lacked built-in sat-nav. Spiller had no clue if such devices secretly stored a car's whereabouts, even switched off, but was glad he didn't have to worry about a Big Brother sitting on the dashboard. As before, he left his mobile phone with Helen and set off for the hills. The presence of Ward's body curled up behind him was palpable. His eyes kept checking the rear-view mirror, not so much for tailing cops, but in case Ward suddenly appeared there, staring accusingly at him like murdered people did in horror movies.

As he neared his destination, his confidence soared. Was he *en route* to the perfect murder? Ignoring the file marked "Sergeant Enright" in his *what-the-fuck?* folder, he certainly couldn't think of anything that would easily link them to Ward's disappearance. If asked, David would attest to seeing Ward leave the house; Helen had later gone for a drive alone—perhaps after an argument with her hubby; and he had apparently never left. This second trip might look a bit odd, but, without forensics, anything the cops found would be circumstantial at best. Ward had come for dinner so there might be evidence of his presence, but nothing any casual house guest wouldn't leave behind. The boot of the Peugeot would need to be cleaned, but there was no blood or fluids back there. Likewise the cellar; a hoover and a mop would do it.

The geographical isolation he sought came at a price. With less traffic since the snowfall of Christmas Day, the road surface became increasingly treacherous as its dimensions narrowed and its path snaked tighter. Spiller had to slow to a crawl at times, terrified of a slide that might end his trip in the worst possible place. Yet, even his mere presence in that location on such a night was fraught with peril. Should a police four-by-four roll up on his rear bumper, they would no doubt want a word.

The spot he'd visualised was fit for purpose, exactly as he remembered. Only a fool would pull over on such a bend on such a winding road. Tonight, Spiller would have to be that fool.

There had been no car headlights in his rear-view mirror for fifteen minutes, so he guessed he was as safe as could be, although the curves and contours of the terrain meant there might be a vehicle two minutes behind and he wouldn't know. And a car could be coming towards him at that very second. Still, he had to seize the moment.

He stopped the car close to the drystone wall and jumped out, leaving the engine running. He popped the hatchback and threw the blankets off the corpse, then quickly dragged it over the tailgate, propping it against the wall. Actually, this was going to be a damn sight more difficult than he'd thought. The wall was higher than optimal. It was a great shield to what lay beyond, but getting Ward into that beyond would not be easy. It took Spiller several attempts and too many minutes to get him lodged on the snow-topped wall. Once there, Spiller was able to hoist his legs upwards so his body had to go with the momentum and tip backwards. The disruption took several stones off the top, and Spiller listened briefly as the dead weight of the objects crashed down the other side through the steep undergrowth. It took five seconds for the sounds to cease, which meant he'd achieved a good drop. He slammed the boot and hurried back behind the wheel, and set off on another circuitous return to civilisation.

All that was left was the disposal of Ward's muddy outfit, and the blankets and sheeting. He'd dump them tomorrow. He'd had enough tonight and didn't want to fall at the final hurdle, getting nicked secreting it all in a wheelie-bin at the back of some shop. There was plenty of rubbish in Helen's cellar that needed to go to the tip. He could collect it all tomorrow, so he wasn't seen suspiciously disposing of just one bag.

Driving back, he started to think about Helen. She'd always had a spine, but her attack on Ward, and the manner in which she'd sealed his fate—literally—made him wonder if he'd ever truly known her. He'd always believed he'd kill for his kids, or die for them, but she'd not hesitated. Where he had dallied, suggesting the police deal with the pan-assaulted Ward, she had gone right ahead and filled his throat and facial cavities with builder's foam. It had a clinical quality he had to admire, but it was a bit bloody scary knowing the mother of your children was something of a homicidal loon. However, he knew she'd made the right decision, given the failure of the legal system to punish the country's scum adequately, and a failure in this instance would have put them all—especially Sammy—in possibly mortal danger. His reticence hadn't been based on any moral qualms, rather the possibility that the girls could be deprived of their parents by the courts.

An hour later, Spiller carefully reversed the Peugeot into the lower yard and up to the cellar door. Helen was waiting for him. He climbed out through the hatchback, taking the items he intended to dump.

'Everything okay?' she asked. 'You got rid of him?'

'No, I brought him back. I might have him stuffed as a warning to Sammy's future boyfriends.'

'Ha ha. What are you going to do with that lot?'

He grabbed a black bin-bag and shoved everything inside, then tied the top. 'I'm going to come back tomorrow morning, get rid of some of this rubbish down here, plus this bag. If anyone asks, we had an argument about the state I'd left the house in. You went out for a drive to cool down, and I decided to do something about it. Hence my return tomorrow to clear out all this shit.'

She thought about it. 'So, you do that before the girls get back. Then I call you and tell you Sammy's been hurt by Ward, you come back and we call the police together.'

'Yep, that's the plan. Shit.'

'What?'

'Did Sophie hear anything of what went on last night? Between you and Sammy?'

Helen shook her head. 'No. She heard Sammy crying, but I just said she was sad she missed Christmas with us.'

'Okay. Will she lie for us?'

'Sammy?'

'Yes. Who else?'

'About what?'

'Exactly *when* you found out what he'd done. She'll have to lie. She can't say she told us *before* this evening. That's motive. She tells us. We invite him round. He disappears. How's that going to look?'

'Uh... not great.'

'No. Which means we also have to tell her Ward was here tonight. When the cops realise Ward's missing, they'll be back to see us and they absolutely cannot be the first people to tell her he was here. She has to be primed. She hears that out of the blue, it's going to set off a ton of alarm bells.'

'But... if we tell her he was here tonight, then ask her *not* to tell the police she told me yesterday what he'd done... she's going to wonder why—even before the cops come back and tell her he's gone missing.'

Spiller's head was swimming. 'Bollocks.'

Helen contemplated. 'But how else can we play this?'

'Okay, but we're not saying we invited him for dinner, right? At least we can say he just popped round to see her, but she wasn't in.'

'And what if he's told people I invited him? What if the police pull the phone records? I got his number from Sammy's mobile, but I called him on mine. How would I explain that to the police?'

'Do phone companies record calls?' Spiller asked.

'I don't think so, but just the fact that I called him.'

Spiller dumped himself on the sofa on which they'd earlier found some temporary common ground. 'Shit.'

Helen perched on the arm-rest, laid a hand on his shoulder. 'Okay. How about this? We tell the police she told me last night, but she begged me not to call them—which is true. I *didn't* tell you, which is also true. I then invited him round, hoping we could persuade him he was too old for her. He got in a huff and stormed off. You went home. Then I call you tomorrow morning and say I have something to tell you about Ward, what he did to Sammy. She comes back and we all talk, then we make the call. That way, she doesn't have to lie about anything.'

Spiller was incredulous, and imagined the cops would be the same. 'A loving mum invites their kid's abusive boyfriend for a friendly chat after he's been beating her up? Really? You don't call the police *immediately*?'

'Well… what if you told me what the cops had told you—that he's been in prison—and I just didn't trust them to take care of it, and thought, you know…'

'What? That a guy who tortures women would give a flying fuck what a woman thinks? Helen, the moment you tell the police you knew what he'd done, that's motive. Then all this looks premeditated—him coming here tonight. I thought we wanted to avoid that. And what's Sammy going to think of us?'

Helen shrugged, resigned and exhausted. 'Matt, it is what it is. We give them half the truth; it's better than a total lie. It helps our credibility. And it means Sammy can't be compromised. The police will tap David for his CCTV and see Ward apparently leaving the house. They can think what they like about my shit parenting skills. They need proof and we didn't leave them any. I'm not going to crack under pressure. Are you?'

'No.'

'Good.'

He nodded, sat for a moment before heading upstairs to the kitchen, leaving Helen to lock up downstairs. He grabbed his mobile phone and car keys and left the house, making sure to look back at the building so the neighbours' CCTV would catch his face.

Chapter Five

ANY HOPE SPILLER had of avoiding a double-whammy shit-show was dashed the next morning. He had barely slept a wink, it was seven o'clock, and he was waiting for the kettle to boil. His mobile rang and he recognised the number.

He'd been kidding himself that Emma would simply fade into the past as a bad dream. He'd thought that one man shouldn't have to deal with two wholly crappy situations at once. He'd envisioned some glorious parallel universe where he'd reach the end of today without a call from her.

'Fuck,' he said after he'd pressed to answer.

'I heard that.'

'You were meant to.'

'So?' she asked.

'What?'

'We should meet.'

'I anticipate being quite busy today,' he replied, thinking of all that would ensue at Helen's house once the police were involved over Sammy's injuries.

'You can taxi tomorrow,' she said.

'I'll call you later.'

'Don't fuck me about.'

'I'll call you later or you can do your worst.'

The line was quiet as she thought about it. 'Okay. Later.'

He ended the call, then shifted his morning routine into overdrive. He skipped the coffee, his morning ablutions, jumped into his clothes, grabbed his stun-gun, and left the flat.

He was outside Emma's house half an hour later. Her BMW was on the drive, and he pulled the Audi onto the pavement behind it to block any exit. He called her number.

'I'm outside,' he said when she answered.

'I can see. What are you doing here, Matthew? You said you'd call.'

He peered up at a front window and saw her peeking under some blinds at him. 'I want to come in and talk.'

'You shouldn't be here.'

He knew that. Establishing a traceable connection between them was a ploy. He wanted them to be linked beyond her Christmas-Eve taxi ride. He wanted to make her scared to move forward, knowing the police would look at all communications prior to a serious crime.

'Two minutes,' she said, and hung up.

The front door opened slightly, and Emma's resentful face appeared in the gap. Spiller got out and hurried up the drive and quickly inside. He closed the door behind him as Emma retreated along a white hallway into a stark and modern kitchen that smelled of proper coffee. He followed her. She was wearing a loose set of pink silk pyjamas that somehow managed to cling to all the right places as she walked, and was unfortunately arousing. She turned to him as she reached the kettle on the sideboard. She looked very different to the other night, all glammed up and daubed in war paint. There was a vulnerability to her now that he'd not thought possible.

'Stay there,' she ordered as he crossed the kitchen threshold.

He stopped, and momentarily felt he wanted to give in to her, kill for her, do anything for her.

'Why did you come here?' she asked, then answered her own question with a statement: 'You're trying to mess this up, aren't you? Make sure you're seen here so I'll let you off the hook.'

Spiller smiled an admission. 'I just want my stuff back. Then we can pretend we never met.' He put a hand in his jacket pocket and closed it around the stun-gun, and noticed her focus briefly flick down from his face to his hidden hand and back up again.

'Why can't you just do what I want?' she said.

He shrugged. 'Well, I had to dump a body last night and I'm trying to keep it to one a week.'

Emma grinned facetiously. 'Funny. What's in the pocket? Another of your taxi toys?'

He was about to lie, but he'd brought it for a reason, so decided to fess up. 'Stun-gun.'

She nodded approvingly. 'Cool. And you brought it to force me to hand back your bag of bits, did you?'

He didn't answer.

She laid a hand on the chrome knob of the drawer next to her. 'Want to know what's in here?'

'I'd guess teaspoons considering the proximity of the kettle.'

She laughed briefly. 'You'd guess wrong. You remember that thing you thought you saw in my bag the other night?'

Spiller had to work out the implications. He knew what he thought he'd seen, but why would she use his suspicion as a threat unless she knew what that suspicion was, and how could she know unless he'd been right?

'Take out the stun-gun and put it on the counter,' she said.

He obliged. 'You're telling me you have a gun in that drawer?'

'Did you think you saw a gun the other night?'

'I wasn't sure.'

'But now you are.'

He shrugged.

'That stuff you left with me,' she said. 'You're not getting it back. Not until you do what I want.'

Spiller raised his hands, palms towards her, and, as unthreateningly as possible, breached the threshold to take a seat at a glass-topped table. As he did so, Emma slid open the drawer a few inches, but not enough for him to see inside. Anyway, he wasn't up for a tussle.

He looked at her, a pleading in his eyes. 'I am the very last person you want involved. You don't understand my situation.'

'Meaning?'

'You think I can do this and not draw any heat, don't you? For you or me. But you're wrong. And you need to trust me on this.'

She scoffed at him. 'That's crap. If the police knew it was you the other night with those lads, you wouldn't be here now, you'd be locked up.'

Spiller shook his head slightly, smiled weakly. 'Not what I'm talking about.'

Emma pushed the drawer to and stared at him. He let her. He'd have sat there for hours waiting for her to speak. He was talked out, worn down, done in. If she couldn't see how broken he was, she was a fool who deserved to have him screw up her life.

Eventually, she came and sat opposite him, defusing the tension. Neither had a weapon to hand, and her trust in him was humbling.

'What's wrong?' she asked.

He heaved a sigh. 'I wouldn't know where to start. And you wouldn't believe me. Just... please understand that I'm not the man for the job. And whatever this person did to you, killing them won't make you feel any better. It'll destroy you.' He glanced around the room at the expensive fixtures. 'You seem to have a nice life. You should cherish that.'

Her attitude suddenly bristled. 'You have no fucking clue about my life, Matthew. What? You equate a nice house with happiness? You can't be that naïve.'

'So, you're not happy—I can see that. But you can always be *more* unhappy.'

'Could I? My sister is dead and the person responsible is walking free. Any idea how unhappy that makes a person?' She regarded him venomously.

'No. Thankfully not. But let's remember one thing, shall we? You're the one who crashed into my life, not the other way round. I saved you from God knows what that night in the park. You say you had it covered, but if you did have a gun that night, I still saved your arse by making sure you didn't have to use it. I don't owe you. You owe me. Just get my stuff.'

Emma bowed her head then stood up quickly, scraping the chair legs across the tiled floor. Their eyes met for a moment before she turned and left the room.

While she was gone, Spiller considered peeking in the kitchen drawer, but he really couldn't be bothered and she was back soon enough that she'd have caught him doing so.

She had his bag of Christmas-night goodies in her hand. 'Here,' she said, holding it out to him. 'Take it and fuck off.'

Spiller stood up and received the bag. 'Thank you.' He went to retrieve his stun-gun and shoved it in his pocket, then faced her. 'What are you going to do?'

'None of your business and why would you care?'

'Let's say I do.'

She deliberated for a moment. 'I'm going to walk up to him and kill him.'

'How exactly?'

'What? You don't want to kill him, but you'd like a consultative role? Fuck off.'

At the second time of asking, he took his leave.

AS SPILLER HEADED towards Helen's house, he started to feel incredibly sorry for Emma, to the point that he almost felt compelled to call and tell her he'd do it. There was a frisson between them he'd not experienced since the day he first met Helen. It was no doubt unreciprocated by Emma given the probable fifteen-year age difference, but, *damn*, it was potent. Despite his best efforts, her clinging silk jim-jams—and what lay beneath—filled his mind's eye as he drove, making his journey one that he could barely recall by the time he pulled up outside his wife's house.

Helen must have been waiting at the window because she opened the door before he could knock.

'The girls back?' he asked.

'No.'

Without further discourse, he went upstairs to dump the stun-gun. It was extra risk he didn't need to carry around with him. He opened the attic hatch and lowered the metal steps and climbed up. There, just beyond the boarding that ended under the descending pitch of the roof, he tucked the weapon under some fibre-glass. He then went down to the cellar and collected up some of its detritus, including the Ward bin-bag. It was the first of four trips he would make up and down the stairs as he filled the boot and back seat of the Audi.

THE LOCAL TIP was on restricted hours over the festive period. He hadn't thought about that until he arrived, so was very glad it was open at all. It was busy. With limited council refuse collections, people were becoming their own bin-men. At the gate, a yellow-coat with a clipboard flagged him to a halt. Spiller lowered his window.

'Just doing random checks, sir. Where have you come from today?'

Spiller wasn't in the mood. 'What?'

'The use of this council facility is for local residents only. Do you have anything with your home address on it?'

'No.'

'Can I ask where you live, sir?'

'Sure. The Outer Hebrides, but there was a bit of a queue up there so I thought I'd nip down here.'

The yellow-coat stiffened, but must have seen something in Spiller's eyes that made him step back. 'Next time,' he said, and waved the facetious bastard through.

Spiller negotiated the one-way system past the various dumping stations for books, clothes, TVs and tyres, and up a slope to the semi-circular lane that gave onto the main amphitheatre of shit. As one car pulled out of a space, he pulled in. As he got out, the mountainous heap of black bags made him smile; it was due for removal. Later today or tomorrow, the JCBs would roll in, cradle up the crap and load it all into container trucks that would head straight for landfill.

He proceeded to empty his car, hurling it all over the concrete wall into an ultimate oblivion.

SAMMY RETURNED FIRST. Parental pleasantries were exchanged on the doorstep, then Sammy was ushered into the front room where the door was closed. She clearly knew from their expressions that a serious conversation was imminent. She could barely meet their eyes.

'Mum told you,' she whispered to the carpet.

Spiller stepped in close. 'Just now. Can I hug you? I don't want to hurt you... you know. I hope I didn't on Christmas Day.'

She answered by bursting into tears and throwing her arms around him. If his embrace was painful, she didn't show it. Probably she didn't care. His eyes welled up uncontrollably as he thought of the injuries she'd suffered that he'd been unable to prevent. He didn't ever want to let her go.

'I'm so sorry,' he said.

'You didn't know.'

They slowly broke apart, then she received just a brief hug from Helen. Spiller assumed she'd delivered Sammy enough hugs to last a lifetime the night she'd seen the marks on her daughter's body. Helen directed Sammy into an armchair, then she and Spiller sat on the sofa, bolt upright.

'You didn't tell your friend anything, did you?' Helen asked.

Sammy shook her head.

'We need to call the police about this,' Spiller said.

'You can't.'

'It's okay. He won't hurt you again. I promise he'll never hurt you again.'

'How can you know?'

It was a fair question and one he'd expected, but one that couldn't adequately be satisfied without a confession.

'Please trust us,' he said, and looked to Helen, who nodded at Sammy in agreement.

'You'll be okay,' Helen said. 'We fixed it. He ca—'

Spiller slightly shifted his leg so his foot pushed hers; a cue to shut up, which she did. While they needed Sammy to believe she was safe, their wording had to be cautious. "Will not" rather than "cannot". The latter had implications.

Sammy appeared not to have noticed her father's subtle physical dig, too wrapped up in her ongoing concerns.

'He said he knew where Soph went to school,' she explained. 'If I left him. That's why I stayed. That's why you can't call the police. He may not come after me, but what about Soph, or you two? I don't want you getting hurt because I did a stupid thing. I'll just go back to him. He'll lose interest in a while. He'll find someone else.'

'Don't be stupid!' Helen said, overlooking the impossibility of her returning to him, and more annoyed by her willingness to do so.

'We warned him off,' Spiller said. 'He got the message, I promise.'

Sammy scrutinised her father, then her mother, silently requesting elucidation, but posed the obvious question before they could respond: 'You spoke to him? When?'

'I did,' Helen said. 'Yesterday.'

Sammy appeared fairly horrified by the intervention. 'And said what? Stop thumping and cutting my daughter? Yeah, I'm sure that's gonna stop him. Have you any idea what sort of a person he is? Now he knows I told you, he's going to beat the shit out of me.'

Helen was shaking her head. 'No, he won't, he won't...'

Sammy's focus turned to her father, imploring his input. 'Dad, please tell mum that a quiet word from her is fucking useless.'

'Please don't swear,' Helen said.

'We didn't have a quiet word,' Spiller corrected. 'It was a bit of a shouting match.'

Sammy gawped at him. '*You* talked to him as well?'

'We had him round for dinner,' Helen said flatly.

Sammy screeched with laughter, but only for a second. She clocked her parents' expressions. 'You're serious?'

'I invited him,' Helen said. 'Last night. Not your dad. We argued, but he saw the light. He won't bother you again. It's over. So, now we call the police and you......... what?'

Spiller understood why his wife had stopped talking. The look on Sammy's face. It was an ugly blend of the worst emotions: fury, resentment, disappointment, astonishment, but most of all, betrayal.

Suddenly, Sammy shot to her feet. She snatched at her sweatshirt and pulled it up to reveal her bare midriff, darkened and bloodied by punches and cuts, then yanked down her jogging pants to reveal the same. Spiller winced at the first sight of her injuries. Her eyes opened like taps, gushing tears as she screamed at her mother.

'*How?* You saw these fucking things on me! How could you not call the police? How could you ask him round here—to our fucking house! What sort of mother are you? If it was my daughter, I'd have fucking killed him! You weak, pathetic—'

'*I did!*'

'*Bitch!...* what?' Sammy calmed down as she stared at her mother.

Spiller felt his heart skip a few beats, then do a crazy little dance in his chest. He glanced at Helen, who didn't seem to need to catch up with her words. There was no hint of a *faux pas* on her face.

'Helen...'

'*What?* She wants to call me out on being a bad mother? Fuck her.'

Sammy gasped. The tears ceased like a safety valve had been twisted shut. 'Mum...'

Helen directed her gaze at Spiller, but the venom had a different target. 'She's big enough to hang around with drug-dealers, she's big enough to hear the truth.'

As though in a trance, Sammy pulled up her pants and lowered herself back into the armchair.

Helen pointed at her daughter. '*You* put us in this situation, my girl. You don't get to throw the blame on me.'

Sammy turned her eyes to her father. 'Dad?'

There was a big question in that one word, and he answered with a simple nod.

'You killed him?' Sammy asked her mother, seeking further confirmation.

'No one does that to my daughter.'

There was evidently so much spinning inside her young head that Sammy couldn't verbalise any of it. She leaned back and the cushion enveloped her shoulders like a soft hug. She stared unfocused into her lap.

'You must have a lot of questions,' Spiller said. 'But now's not the time. And it may never be the time. You can't know the details. For our sake, you can't. Just know that I'm every bit as involved. It's not just your mum. So, what you choose to do from this moment will determine if you continue having us around. Do you understand?'

A barely perceptible nod.

'We don't blame you. Whatever your mum says, we know you just made a mistake. We've all made mistakes. This is a big one, but we can move past it. But you need to do something for us. I mean, apart from the obvious; apart from not telling the police we did it.' He smiled, but no one was looking.

'I'd never,' Sammy whispered.

'I know. Sammy…'

She looked up.

'When the police come, you need to tell them what he did, but you also need to tell them you only told us this morning. Both of us. They can't know either of us knew before last night. The story is, we invited him round to ask him to leave you alone because he's too old. He wasn't happy and left in a bad mood.'

'What if they don't believe you?'

'We… we've got that covered, don't worry. Don't worry about anything. The only lie you have to tell is *when* you told us what he'd done to you. And that was this morning, just now. You don't need to act. You can cry, scream, be traumatised, just as you are now. But you have to lie about that one thing.'

'She will,' Helen said, looking with renewed love at her daughter.

A bulb seemed to light in Sammy's head. 'Dad…'

'What?'

'Why would you call the police about him now you've told me what you did?'

Spiller and Helen looked stupidly at each other.

Sammy explained to her dumbass parents: 'If you don't tell them what he did to me, they won't come. But, even if they do, the most you say is that you had him round and sent him on his way.'

Spiller realised they'd been so locked into the idea of a police visit that neither had noticed the game-changer of Helen's confession to Sammy. They grinned at each other, but both instantly sensed a grin was inappropriate given the overall situation.

'Good spot,' Spiller said.

'Sorry I was horrible,' Helen said.

'I made you do a horrible thing,' Sammy replied. 'I get it.'

They all sank into their cushions. They were spent. Spiller noticed that Helen's hand was lightly touching his, but, rather than edge away, she moved it over a couple of his fingers. He smiled to himself.

'I can't believe you did this for me,' Sammy said after a minute.

'All your mother,' Spiller said. 'And I'll stand up in court and say that.'

They all laughed, and the break in the tension was palpable, but it didn't take more than a few seconds for their amusement to dissipate, with Sammy's expression turning puzzled.

'Should we be reacting like this?' she asked her parents.

Spiller recalled the previous night—the inappropriate sex in the cellar.

'I don't know,' Helen said. 'I don't think there's a rule-book, but... I know what you mean.'

A ring on the front doorbell announced the return of the blissfully oblivious Sophie. They could hear her chattering away to her little friend on the doorstep.

Helen broke the faint hand-contact she'd established and rose to her feet. 'Sammy, pop upstairs and make sure Soph can't see you've been crying. And keep those marks hidden away from her.'

Sammy got up and they both left the room together—Helen heading to the front door, Sammy up the stairs. Spiller was left alone. He listened to the parental chat outside, and Sophie's forlorn request that her friend be offered a reciprocal visit, starting now. Helen made an excuse about having relatives to visit, and Spiller smiled as he recalled Sophie's malapropism about her grandad being retarded. Sophie was heard to patter past the room and scurry up the stairs as Helen bid her little friend's mum goodbye. Any other day he would have called Sophie in for a big hug and a silly joke, but this was a day like no other, and he feared there could be many more such days ahead. Their trajectories had pinged off into uncharted space.

Shortly, Helen popped her head around the door. 'Do you want to spend some time?'

'With?'

'Us. As a family. Unless you need to work.'

He shook his head. 'I'd love to. What do you have in mind?'

'I don't know. A movie? Maybe a board game?'

He smiled. 'Sounds lovely.'

IT WAS LOVELY. Until about four o'clock.

Spiller had managed to keep weighty matters from his mind for most of the afternoon, distracted by the giggles of his daughters as they blatantly cheated their way through the board game *Sorry!*—strategically jumping their counters too many moves ahead to knock their parents back to their start circles. Helen seemed to be equally diverted, but it was hard to tell. Similarly Sammy, although they all three physically stiffened each time a car door was heard to slam in the street, only relaxing a couple of minutes later in the absence of a knock at their door.

The door-slam at four o'clock was different. The noise was no different, but the powerful exhaust note that preceded it made Spiller's ears prick, and he sensed something portentous besides, enough to break from the game and move casually to the window, stretching and yawning to mask the move.

'*Daaaaaaad,*' Sophie said. 'It's your go.'

'You take mine. Just need to stand up a while.'

She obliged, sensing another chance to set back her dad's progress around the board.

Spiller peeked through a gap in the curtains, hoping his sense of foreboding was as bogus as his daughters' decimation of their opponents. Across the street, bathed in the porch-light of a neighbour's front door, a well-dressed man was knocking, a white Maserati parked nearby. Even in the gloom, Spiller recognised it as a Quattroporte. The door opened and a brief exchange took place before the neighbour pointed across at Spiller. The man started to turn, but Spiller pulled the curtains tight shut before he could be seen. He swivelled to Helen, who was already eyeing him. The tense set to his mouth spoke volumes. Sammy looked at her mother, then traced her gaze to her father's worried face. Sophie was too engrossed to notice.

The doorbell soon rang, swiftly followed by a couple of fist-thumps. After a few seconds' inactivity from Spiller, Helen and Sammy, Sophie pointed out the obvious.

'Dad, someone's at the door.'

He went to answer it.

The man standing outside was vaguely familiar, but in a way Spiller knew he'd never fathom without some help. He looked approximately thirty years old, hair neatly parted and slickly swept back in an old-fashioned style.

'Sorry to bother you,' said the man. 'Are you Mr Spiller?'

Rather than appear wary, Spiller made an effort to smile. 'That's right.'

'Okay, I wasn't sure. Your neighbour seemed to recognise the name when I asked.'

Obviously not the cops, then, Spiller thought. The cops knew where people lived. He waited for more, and primed himself to not overly react to anything.

'My name's Dominic Ward,' the man said.

Spiller narrowed his eyes like perhaps the name meant something.

'My brother's Callum.'

'Okay.' Spiller hoped his calm expression was the visible duck to the frantic, submerged paddling of his brain. It was instantly clear that Dominic Ward knew of his brother's relationship with Sammy, and Spiller deemed it smart to state that truth rather than have him feel he'd wheedled it out. He spoke again before Ward could say anything else, stepping outside and pulling the door to behind him as he did so.

'If you've come here to speak on your brother's behalf, there's no point. We told him: he's too old for our daughter. She's only seventeen, for God's sake.'

'You called him?' asked Ward.

Spiller suspected he was being tested. 'No. He was here. We told him to leave her alone and find someone more his age. He wasn't happy, left in a bad mood. If you're here to plead his case, forget it.'

Ward smiled slightly. 'I'm not. Can I come in for a few minutes, please?'

Spiller tried to imagine what an innocent man with nothing to hide would do, but it was a stretch, so he shrugged, stepped back inside the hall and indicated for Ward to enter. Spiller led him past the front room and into the kitchen, where he closed the door and offered him the chair his brother had last night been clanged out of. Spiller remained standing.

In the light, the initial out-of-reach resemblance became more apparent, but it was only in the eyes. Ward was shorter than his deceased brother, and appeared a few years older. He was in an expensive suit, cloaked by an overcoat. He looked more like his brother's legal representative than his sibling.

'I know,' Ward said. 'Only our mother can tell us apart. Different milkmen, as our dad likes to joke.'

Spiller conjured a polite smile. 'So, what can I do for you?'

'My brother's missing. He vanished immediately after he left here last night.'

Spiller said nothing. The conversation in the front room seeped through the walls and he wished he was in there still, only magicked back five years with the hindsight he had now.

'His car has a tracking device,' Ward said.

So, Spiller had been right, which meant he was indeed being tested. Tested on the doorstep about how they'd been in contact, and tested now by the false assertion that Ward had gone missing directly after leaving the house.

'One of his associates tried calling him last night but couldn't get through,' Ward said. 'He contacted me and asked me to track Callum's movements.'

'Modern technology, eh?'

Ward peered at Spiller suspiciously.

'So, why the big fuss if your brother doesn't answer his phone of an evening?' Spiller asked, feigning ignorance of Callum Ward's nefarious career choice.

Ward appeared to debate whether to respond. 'My brother's a bad lad. Between you and me, I did try to get him to break it off with your daughter. I could see she's a good kid from a decent home. She didn't belong in his world.'

'And what world would that be?'

'You say my brother left in a bad mood,' Ward said.

Spiller nodded.

'You told him to leave your daughter alone.'

'We did.'

'And what did he say?'

'Not a lot. Got pissed off, got up and left.'

'Describe his mood.'

'I met your brother for fifteen minutes. We talked, he left. I didn't know him. I'm not a shrink.' Spiller moved to the door and opened it.

His visitor took the hint and stood up. 'You say fifteen minutes. The data says his car was outside for more than an hour.'

'Don't know. Maybe he took a walk before driving off.'

Ward nodded slowly. 'Yeah, maybe. Don't you want to know where the car was found?'

'Honestly? You could tell me the foot of Beachy Head and I wouldn't give a shit.'

Ward regarded him sourly. 'Well, that's not very Christian of you.'

'He was too old for our daughter and, by your own admission, he was an arsehole. I don't care where he went; I only care that he doesn't come back here.'

'Well, *someone's* going to come back here,' Ward said.

'Oh?'

'His car was found in the hills, parked beside a reservoir. Empty, except for his mobile phone. So I've obviously had to call the police. And they've taken a keen interest, given Callum was known to them. They're recovering his vehicle right now. And, as this was his last port of call before disappearing, you'll likely receive a visit in the near future.'

'He drove straight from here to the hills?' Spiller quizzed, embracing the peril in posing such a question. 'I upset him that much, did I? Big lad like that went away and jumped in a lake because of me?'

Ward wavered. 'You know, however Callum earns his money, he's still my brother.'

Spiller nodded. 'I get, but that doesn't give you the right to infer shit.'

'What did I infer?'

'You being here is an inference in itself.'

Ward offered his hand facetiously, which Spiller didn't accept. Then Ward ambled past into the hall, but very quickly grasped the door handle of the front room and nipped inside.

'Oi!' Spiller yelled, pursuing him.

In the front room, Helen and the girls had abruptly stopped playing *Sorry!* and were looking at Ward, who smiled affably.

'What the—' Spiller began.

'Hello, Sammy,' Ward said. 'I met you briefly a week ago.' He extended his hand.

Like her dad, Sammy did not reciprocate. She looked at her mum.

'Who the hell are you?' Helen said. 'And how dare you just barge into our living room!'

'How are you?' Ward said to Sammy, ignoring everyone else.

Spiller watched helplessly, not knowing whether to intervene and drag him outside. It seemed the natural reaction, but perhaps

Ward was looking for Spiller to demonstrate how a potential threat to his daughter manifested itself. So he held back for the moment.

Sammy managed a smile. 'I'm well, thank you.'

'Callum didn't hurt you?'

A momentary hesitation preceded Sammy's denial.

The thrust of Ward's question was clear to Spiller: he was seeking a motive for the disappearance of his brother at their hands. Spiller was just about to grab him when he spoke again.

'Dominic Ward,' he said to Helen. 'Barrister-at-law.'

'Good for you,' Helen replied.

Spiller stayed his hand. A barrister. Seriously?

Ward turned to Spiller, delving in his coat pocket, seemingly sensing an aura of doubt. He offered a business card for verification.

Spiller took it, tore it in half, dropped it. 'Get out of my fucking house.'

'*Daaaad,*' Sophie ticked him off.

'*Now.*' Spiller grabbed Ward's sleeve and led him into the hallway to the front door, which he pulled open. 'And don't come back. I mean it.'

Ward stepped outside. 'You know, the police are the least of your worries.'

'What's that mean?'

Ward seemed to deflate, like he didn't relish what he was about to say. 'I may have taken a different path in life to my brother, but we grew up with the same people on the same estate. His friends were my friends. And I still know them. Christ, half of them have me on speed-dial. They're going to want to know what happened to Callum.'

'And you're going to send them my way.'

Ward jabbed a finger lightly at Spiller's chest. '*I'm* the only reason they're not here right now. They were looking over my shoulder when I checked my brother's route. I was the one who stopped them coming here to talk to you.'

'Why?'

'Because they're not the best talkers in the world—not when they smell a rat.'

'*A rat?*' Spiller said. Christ, how badly he wanted to point out the detour he knew the Skyline had taken.

'I practise criminal law, Mr Spiller. I defend people I know are guilty. I've defended my brother in the past. I can sense when people have something to hide. And *you*... you're hiding something.' He jabbed a finger towards Spiller again, but it was quickly encircled in a tight fist.

Spiller so wanted to snap the digit in his grasp, but instead just held it firmly with the threat of breakage inherent in his steely grip.

'That's assault, Mr Spiller.'

'Not yet. Believe me, you'll know if I assault you.'

'Let go.'

He couldn't keep it in. 'Are you seriously telling me your tough-guy brother got so upset that he drove straight from here to the hills to top himself? Pull the other one.'

Ward yanked his finger out of Spiller's loosening grip. 'He... did stop off somewhere.'

'So, what's your problem with us? And if you thought your brother might have hurt my daughter, why would you give a shit if he's disappeared. Sounds like good riddance to me.'

'He's my brother,' Ward said simply.

'He was a twat.'

An accusing stare from Ward. '*Was?* Past tense?'

'Yeah, last night. He was a twat. And probably every night. That's why I kicked him out.'

Ward stepped out of reach and shook his head. 'Sure. My brother's never been kicked out of anywhere in his life. He's the one who does the kicking.'

'It was a metaphor,' Spiller said lamely.

Another shake of the head, this time loaded with disdain. 'Woeful.'

'What?'

But Ward turned and walked, beeping the remote on his Maserati from afar, and Spiller was left to figure out the woeful part for himself. The quad exhausts burbled as Ward manoeuvred out from the kerb and slowly set off down the street.

Spiller stood there for a few minutes, considering. Woeful. It was an apt judgement, on pretty much everything. His entire life. And it wasn't just his life. He'd had a woeful impact on his family, their emotions. But this was a whole other level. Now, fresh negativity was inbound from sources both known and unknown. No doubt the cops would be paying him a visit, but there was an argument for pre-empting that moment because the other people Ward had predicted would visit were likely to be highly *un*predictable. Essentially, a threat had just been made against Spiller and his family. It had been couched as a warning, but it amounted to the same thing.

He shut the door and closed out the world.

There'd been a time when life had been good, when things hadn't been so complicated. But he'd been unable to feel the goodness in what he had, and his mood had trashed it. Now it was too late to reclaim it. All the component parts were still there—they were sitting in the front room, a wall away from him—but they were skewed and twisted and irrevocably damaged. Even little Sophie, although she didn't know it yet; no way would her innocent childhood remain unblighted by this.

Helen came out to him. She held his hand. 'Hey…'

'I don't think we're safe,' Spiller said quietly.

'We'll be fine.' She led him into the kitchen and shut the door. 'He knows nothing.'

'Ward's car had a tracker. He knows he was here last night. And he clearly suspects his brother hit Sammy, which would be reason enough for us to react.'

'We'd have called the police,' Helen reasoned. 'Ninety-nine out of a hundred parents would have called the police.'

'But we're the one percent and he knew something was up. He knew I was lying.'

'No BAFTA for you, mate.'

'Very funny. Only it isn't. Because he's not the one that bothers me. He won't act without proof, and neither will the police.'

'So?'

Spiller pulled out a chair and sat heavily. 'So... he suggested his brother's associates might want a word with us.'

Helen took a chair opposite him, shifted an empty coffee cup to one side. 'You didn't go straight from here to the hills?'

'Course I didn't. I did what we agreed.'

'So, that's got to be reasonable doubt, hasn't it? Even for a bunch of Neanderthals. The tracker must show him stopping off at the estate.'

'It did,' Spiller said. 'He admitted that.'

'So, anything could have happened. A drug deal gone wrong? A vendetta? Why the hell would they think it's us?'

'They shouldn't.' But Spiller was thinking about Sergeant Enright's traffic-stop.

Undaunted by a lack of that knowledge, Helen became more confident of her ground. 'If we call the police now, say we've basically been threatened, get them to check David's CCTV, ask them to confirm to Ward's brother that he left here in one piece... we're sorted.'

Spiller looked dubious.

Helen carried on: 'Ward's brother can pass that info to his associates and they'll have no reason whatsoever to come here. Matt, what's up?'

'Something... odd happened last night.'

'You think?'

'No, I mean... you remember the cops who showed up the other day when Sammy came back?'

She nodded.

'One of them stopped me last night.'

Helen's lips pursed to form the letter W but her brain seemed to not know the most appropriate question.

'I'd just come off the estate,' Spiller said. 'He knew the car. It was a routine stop.'

'Fuck. Did he recognise you?'

'Straight away.'

'*And?*'

'And he sent me on my way.'

Helen was shaking her head slightly. 'He didn't know it was you. He can't have done.'

'He called me Mr Spiller so I'm pretty certain he did.'

Her lips formed an unspoken interrogative again. She suddenly grabbed the coffee cup and took it to the sink, where she scrubbed at it with a soapy pad like Lady Macbeth worrying away at a phantom blood stain.

'Jesus Christ,' she muttered. 'Jesus...' Then she turned to face him. 'He didn't ask you anything?'

'Nope. Gave me a little smile and told me to drive safely.'

'You had white hair! You were dressed like a chav gangster!'

Spiller shrugged. 'He wasn't interested.'

She dropped the mug in the sink and Spiller thought he heard it crack.

'Well, he bloody will be now,' she said. 'Ward's a missing person now—at the very least.'

'I'm wondering if he's in with them. You know... on their payroll. Maybe he didn't deal with me last night because he knows they *will*.'

As though she hadn't heard, Helen picked the mug and its detached handle out of the sink and dropped them through the bin's swing-top.

'Helen...'

'Call the police.'

Chapter Six

AS SPILLER HAD expected—and hoped—the coppers who showed up three hours later were detectives. Briefly dismissing the thought that Sergeant Enright was in cahoots with Ward's mob, he'd considered calling him, vaguely thinking the combination of the card he'd been given and the strange waiver last night might amount to a bent cop who would turn a blind eye, or, better still, make it all go away. But, even if Enright were a bent cop who was open to a bit of vigilantism from the general public, he was still just a sergeant. He didn't have the power to shut down a misper case, much less a potential murder, and nor would he have sufficient clout to stifle any objections from Dominic Ward or his brother's scumbag associates.

So, Spiller had asked to be put through to CID.

A DS and a DC turned up; Madden and Goodrick. The DS was carrying a black zip folder. They introduced themselves on the doorstep, and the absence of the word "Inspector" in their titles was reassuring. Spiller hoped it signified a lower level of interest. The sergeant was female and black, maybe fortyish; the constable was male and white, late twenties. They offered perfunctory smiles as they were invited into the house. Spiller led them into the front room, which had been vacated by Sammy and Sophie who had been sent upstairs to watch TV. Helen was sitting stiffly on the sofa, ready for action.

Spiller indicated the two armchairs opposite the sofa. They both settled on the edge of their seats. Spiller sat beside his wife, not bothering to ask if they wanted anything to drink. Goodrick extracted a black notebook and biro from his inside pocket and poised the nib over a fresh page. Madden unzipped the folder and riffled though a few bits of paper. As she did this, Spiller quietly observed the DC, whose eyes scanned the room, taking in the décor. They lingered for a few seconds on a framed photo above the fire, among the compulsory family shots. Spiller saw Goodrick's eyes pinch. It pictured him during his time in the Gulf. Desert-pattern uniform, comms headset, holding an SA80, a demolished Afghan hut behind him. If Goodrick had anything to say about it, he kept it to himself.

Madden perused a piece of paper then looked up at them. 'So, I think I'm caught up as far as this goes. I spoke to Sergeant Enright and PC Carnaby earlier, who explained they'd previously visited this residence in relation to worries you had about your daughter, Samantha.'

Her expression requested confirmation, but Spiller was still fazed by the innocuous mention of Sergeant Enright; he really was keeping schtum about things.

'That's right,' Helen answered.

'You were concerned about her relationship with Callum Ward, yes?' Madden said.

Spiller shook himself and responded. 'We didn't know his name then. We just knew our daughter hadn't come back for Christmas. It was the officers you mentioned who identified him.'

'Oh?'

Spiller had a horrible moment. Had he just dropped Enright in it? After Enright had protected him? 'Uh, well, they knew his car and just said we should be on our guard, you know, maybe he wasn't the best boyfriend material. We were extremely grateful for the warning.'

Goodrick was taking notes as they spoke.

'And your daughter turned up safe and sound in the presence of the officers?' Madden asked.

Spiller nodded.

'Was she okay?'

Helen answered: 'Sad about missing the family Christmas. Otherwise fine.'

'Good. Is she here? In case I need to have a chat?'

Helen nodded. 'Upstairs.'

'Okay,' Madden said. 'So... today. What happened?'

Spiller heaved a sigh. 'Callum Ward's brother turned up. Dominic. Said his brother had gone missing, his car had been found in the hills, the car's tracker placed him here before he drove to the hills, and he wanted to know what had happened.'

'And what *had* happened?' Goodrick asked.

Helen jumped in again. 'We asked him round. Just him and us. Not the girls. We told him he couldn't see Sammy any more. He was too old for her. He got annoyed and Matt had to tell him to leave.'

'And he went quietly?' Madden asked.

'I wouldn't say quietly,' Spiller answered. 'He was shouting a bit, swearing. But, I mean, he left. It didn't get physical, if that's what you're asking.'

'And you called us because Dominic Ward suspects it did get violent?' Madden asked.

'He said his brother's *associates* are going to think we have something to do with his disappearance, even though he admitted that the car's tracker shows he left here and went somewhere else before heading off to the hills.'

'I understand,' Madden said. 'We have spoken to Dominic Ward, who did provide us with the vehicle tracking data you mentioned. While I can't disclose the exact route taken following the departure of the vehicle from this residence, I can confirm an extra stop was made before it arrived at its final destination, and CSI is combing that first location as we speak. In light of the fears you expressed over the phone, we've asked Dominic Ward to make it clear to his brother's associates that we are fully investigating and will take a very dim view of anyone whose assumptions jump the gun.'

'That's good,' Spiller said. 'Thanks.'

'You should talk to our neighbour,' Helen chipped in, and pointed. 'That side. His name's David. He saw Ward leave. Callum Ward, I mean. I was chatting to him on the doorstep when Ward stormed out. And he has CCTV.'

'We'll do that,' Madden said, and Goodrick made a note. 'Would it be okay if we spoke to Samantha now?'

'Is that necessary?' Spiller asked.

Madden smiled without warmth. 'I won't know until I talk to her.'

'Alone?' Spiller asked, and knew he shouldn't have.

Madden peered at him. 'Would that bother you?'

Spiller was thinking of a response when Madden spoke again. 'As Samantha is not yet eighteen, she would need a responsible adult to be present. You're both welcome to stay in the room. Is she fully aware of what's happened?'

'Yes, I'll get her,' Helen said, but it was Spiller who quickly stood up and left the room.

He climbed the stairs slowly, not really wishing to reach Sammy's room, and not sure that anyone would describe either of her parents as responsible adults. He hadn't wanted to be left alone with the detectives in case he said the wrong thing— again—or seemed too nervous, but he also didn't want to be the one to tell Sammy she now had to lie like Pinocchio if she wanted to keep her murderous parents out of prison.

Sammy was hovering on the landing. She'd been eavesdropping.

Spiller gave her a little hug. 'How much of that did you hear?'

'Enough. What do I tell them?'

He ushered Sammy into her bedroom and pushed the door to. 'Don't panic. Just what we said. They have no reason to suspect us of anything. Remember, they're only here because we asked them to come. Just be pleasant with them. Be yourself.'

She looked puzzled. 'I don't know who that is.'

'The person you were before you met Callum Ward.'

SAMMY ENTERED THE front room in silence. She didn't greet the police and they didn't initially greet her. She claimed the seat her father had vacated beside her mum, while Spiller perched on the arm of the sofa. Once settled, the cops switched on a couple of smiles for her.

'Hello, Samantha. Happy Christmas,' said Madden.

'Thanks. And to you.'

'How are you?'

Sammy nodded before saying, 'Good.'

'You're not worried about your boyfriend?'

'Ex,' Sammy said.

'Your parents ended your relationship, is that correct?'

'I suppose.'

'And, were you happy for it to end?'

'Callum was too old for me—I can see that now.'

Madden studied her for a few seconds. 'Was it just the age difference?'

Spiller was agonisingly close to jumping in but knew it would seem too defensive.

'What do you mean?' Sammy asked.

'I'm just wondering if anything Callum Ward... *did*... bothered you.'

'I know he wasn't about to apply to join your lot any time soon.'

Both detectives let slip genuinely amused laughs. Spiller smiled, but hoped his eldest wasn't getting too cocky. It wasn't a good look on a seventeen-year-old, especially not one with life-changing information in her head.

'No,' Madden said. 'You're right there.'

Goodrick spoke: 'Have you any idea, even the faintest notion, why Mr Ward might have disappeared? Did you see him argue with anyone when you were together?'

Sammy was shaking her head to it all.

'Did *you* argue with him?' Goodrick asked.

'Me?'

Spiller had grown rather unfond of Goodrick since he'd sat down. He hadn't said much, but his ability to multitask, to transcribe the conversation while simultaneously casting a suspicious eye around the room, had grated—especially the continual return of his focus to Spiller's war photo, as though that was a crime in itself. But Spiller preferred the quietly watchful Goodrick to the inquisitive version.

'Where are you going with this?' Spiller asked.

'With what?'

'This line of questioning. My daughter's the victim here, not the suspect.'

The detectives looked directly at each other, like a choreographed moment in a dramatic dance piece, and Spiller felt nauseous. What the hell had he just said? His brain turned to marshmallow.

Madden peered at him. 'A victim? In what way?'

Thankfully, Helen stepped in. 'You don't think a seventeen-year-old schoolgirl in thrall to a twenty-eight-year-old is a victim? Shame on you.'

But Madden was not to be dissuaded. 'Mr Spiller? How is your daughter a victim in all this?'

'I think my wife just explained, didn't she?'

Goodrick was back to his scribbling, only this time he seemed to have more to jot down than the verbatim content of their exchanges. Spiller looked at him, watched his hand shifting back and forth across the page. Then he looked at Sammy, who seemed to have physically shrunk into the sofa, staring down into her lap.

Spiller stood up. 'I'd like you to leave. I invited you; now I'm asking you to leave. You've upset my daughter. We can't help you. She can't help you. As I said to Dominic Ward, I don't give a toss where his brother is; I only care that he doesn't come back here. Or that his arsehole mates don't. Can you make sure that doesn't happen, please?'

Goodrick ceased his note-taking. A clearly peeved Madden looked from Spiller to Sammy. Madden put her hands together in front of her chin, as in prayer, and starting tapping her fingertips. Spiller was about to repeat his request when she spoke.

'Samantha, could you stand up for me, please?'

'Sammy, stay where you are,' Spiller said.

Madden stood up. Goodrick followed suit.

'Samantha... Sammy,' Madden said. 'Please stand and lift up your top slightly for me. Just so I can see your abdomen. My colleague will leave the room if you prefer.'

Helen's hand found Spiller's. He hadn't been about to remonstrate, but her simple touch had told him not to. Had Sammy remained seated, he may have objected again, but, with tears brimming, she obeyed the detective's gentle order, and Spiller understood this was his daughter's moment of catharsis. So he let it happen.

Spiller looked away and down at the carpet.

Shortly, Madden said, 'Oh, Sammy…'

Sammy's parents started to weep.

FOLLOWING THE REVELATION of Sammy's wounds, much was left unsaid, on both sides. Naturally, neither Spiller nor Helen had offered a confession of their crimes, and, when asked, Sammy had dutifully lied, saying she had only shown her parents the injuries that morning, denying a potent motive for a possible dinner-date ambush the night before. Sammy could have lied and said she'd not told them at all, but her parents' reaction had been sorrow rather than shock, and that implied they knew already. Whether the detectives believed her, Spiller didn't know, although he accepted it would be a stupidly gullible copper who'd take any assertion at face value, and neither Madden nor Goodrick struck him as such.

Spiller had asked how they'd known Sammy might have been hurt. Even had Enright and Carnaby not warned him, he could have worked it out—it was obviously Ward's MO—but he wanted to appear ignorant of Ward's violent history. Madden had taken photos of the injuries, but warned that Sammy would need to be interviewed properly at the station later that day, examined by a police doctor, and have official photographs taken should she want to press charges, which Sammy agreed she did. Both coppers had praised her for being brave enough to do so.

In truth, a lot was said. But the obvious challenge never came. Even if Sammy had only shown her parents the injuries that morning, why would they have called the police just to report Dominic Ward's visit? Why were the attacks on their daughter not worthy of mention? In Spiller's head, the answer was obvious: because the attacks were now moot because the attacker was now dead. He hoped he was gracing the detectives' hypothetical thought processes with suspicions they'd never form, but he reckoned they were too healthily sceptical not to think this.

Madden and Goodrick had left their contact cards, then left the house, only to knock on David's door, exiting twenty minutes later and heading to their car. At least Spiller's Ward impersonation seemed to have passed muster.

Or, suspicions firmly formed, they were allowing him the luxury of delusion. Off they'd go, apparently none the wiser, leaving the poor Spillers to recover, but secretly determined to expose the sham of their fragility.

Chapter Seven

THE NEW YEAR came and went, and the world went back to work. Spiller had not stopped. In between shifts, he spent a lot of time with his wife and daughters and slept over every night. It was a safety precaution. He took Sophie's room while she bunked with her mum. Sammy's wounds faded away, at least physically. With resilience Spiller hadn't foreseen, she carried on as normal, but he could sense a shadow cloaking her. She didn't smile or laugh as much, but he thought it was more than that. She seemed to have dulled inside. No one spoke about Ward. No one said not to; the conversation was simply too big to be had so it was never begun. Like an *omertà*, the three who knew said nothing.

For Spiller, it felt like he was wandering through an episode of *The Twilight Zone*; a strange tale in which the protagonist had the sense something terrible had occurred but was forced to live the lie of a regular life until the horrors revealed themselves. But the real terror was in the waiting, waiting for the revelation that would end the pretence of that regular life.

For days it didn't come.

The day before it did, Spiller decided he had to follow up on the brief exchange he'd had with Helen the night of the murder. They were in the front room watching the news. The girls were upstairs. He muted the TV.

She looked at him. 'What?'

'You said you still loved me. The other night as I was leaving to dump Ward's car. I said I loved you and you said—'

'I remember.'

'So?'

She thought. Spiller watched her thinking.

'Has there been anyone else?' he asked.

'Well, I had a pretty good shag the other night.'

His face dropped before he clocked her crooked grin. 'Oh...
right.'

'Are you better?' she asked. 'Your moods?'

He shook his head. 'No. But I cope with them better. I'm on
more of an even keel.'

'Are you?'

'Well... present circumstances notwithstanding, I reckon...
yeah, I'm doing better.'

Helen regarded him seriously, but fondly. 'You're not, Matt.
It only feels that way because you have no one to bounce off
now. I was a sounding board. I was... like a wall in a squash
court. Your mood hit me and came back to you, so you whacked
it towards me again and again and again. You only cope better
now because you've lost the wall. Your moods don't rebound on
you. So you actually feel better. Less guilty. About the effect
you're having. Am I making sense?'

He nodded reluctantly.

'And *I* feel better, Matt. Without you. I don't wake up each
morning wondering which Matt I'm going to find lying next to
me. I don't worry that I'll have to explain to Sophie that Daddy
doesn't mean to shout, he's just feeling sad today.'

'I wasn't well,' he said simply.

'You're still not well. It's just not... amplified any more. By
us.'

Spiller felt his tears well, and wasn't that proof positive her
point was valid? He was throwing it out there and it was coming
right back at him. He started to feel sour.

'I don't know, Helen, I'm sure there was something we said
to each other once about *in sickness and in health*. Did you not say
that to me? Or did you interpret that as just physical health? I'm
assuming you wouldn't have left me if I broke my leg. You'd
have waited for that to heal, no?'

'Yes,' she said patiently, like a kindergarten teacher to a child.
'But some things don't heal, do they? They keep on hurting. And
hurting everyone around.'

His eyes defocused on the TV screen and blurred with
moisture.

'I know you love us, Matt. You'd never raise a hand to any of us. But... you used to get angry. It wasn't just sad. And it might not have been anger directed towards us—I know that. I know it was all directed inwards—and I know Sammy sort of understood, but Sophie certainly didn't.'

'I know.'

'So you know why you can't come back.'

He rubbed at his eyes. 'God, I'm bored. I am so desperately bored. That's the problem. I used to do something exciting, then it stopped.'

'But that exciting thing is what messed you up.'

'I know, but now I can't make sense of... the hum-drum.'

'We're the hum-drum, Matt. Me and the kids. We're everyday life. That's what family is. If you can't embrace that...'

He could. And he couldn't. He could embrace that as a part of his life, but not its entirety. There had to be more.

'Helen, I know family and love are the heart of life. I know that. But, what's the heart for if not to keep the rest of the body alive? And that's the problem. There's no... rest of the body for me. I do a job I hate. I don't even get to the gym any more I'm so knackered because I can barely sleep. I'm bored shitless, just... ticking off the days until someone nails my box shut.'

'Aren't we enough?' she asked.

'That's not fair. I just explained. Life is more than sitting at home with the fam. Jeez, I don't even have any mates.'

She laughed. 'Matt, you're not unsociable because you have no friends; you have no friends because you're so antisocial.'

'I have Gibbo. He's a mate.'

'He's a colleague. You park up together and bitch about life when there are no jobs on the system. When was the last time you two went out for a pint?'

'Never.'

'There you go.'

Spiller was beginning to feel anxious. He got this low-grade panic whenever the world conspired against him and he couldn't fight back, and this felt like that. Helen was right about everything. He was stuck. Mentally, emotionally, he had stalled years ago and he couldn't self-administer a jump-start. The only spark he'd felt for years was Christmas Eve, separating the scrotes from their thumbs, and then the whole scramble to get rid of Ward's body. But it was hardly something you could turn into a hobby. *What do you do to have fun, Mr Spiller? Oh, you know, a bit of vigilantism on the weekend. Keeps the juices flowing.*

He could feel Helen's sidelong look of pity.

'Matt, you had ev—'

He held up a palm and she stopped instantly.

'You've never understood me, have you?' he said. 'You've never... you've never *seen* me.'

'What the hell does that mean?'

'Doesn't matter.'

'No, you don't say cryptic shit like that and leave it hanging.'

'Okay. You've always judged me by your own standards. But they're not standards. You didn't set them for yourself; they're who you are. You don't understand depression because you don't feel it. Well, bully for you. But that's not a choice you've made. You think it is, but it isn't. You think you're so much stronger than me because you don't get down, but that's just the way you're wired. You think I'm weak. But how would you know what strength is if you've never had to fight to be strong?'

'You think I don't fight? You think my life's easy?'

'No... I don't. This is it: you don't understand what I'm trying to say. Helen, you are built to cope. You've never suffered depression. You don't even think it exists. You think it's the word weak people use to excuse how pathetic they are. It's an illness, Helen, every bit as bad as cancer. It kills people. I fight every day just to get out of bed, to move through each day. It's a struggle of epic proportions but I do it. You know why? Because I'm strong. I hate a lot about me but that's something I do like. Because there are lots like me who just go under.'

She at least gave him the courtesy of considering his words for a few seconds.

'You're saying *I'm* weak?' she asked. 'Because I'm *not* depressed?'

His shoulders sagged. He shook his head. 'No. I'm saying you're not tested like I am.'

Helen squinted at him, still puzzled. Too puzzled to even get annoyed.

'It doesn't matter,' he said, and meant it.

'How great is my life, Matt?'

Spiller wished he could jab at the worms now crawling from the can he'd cracked open. She really hadn't understood.

'Ever think about that? While you're wallowing in your own misery. I'm a single mum. I work in a phone shop doing odd shifts to fit in with my child-care, and I can only do that because the boss fancies me so he's willing to make allowances.'

'Your boss fancies you?'

'Shut up, Matt. I've got an estranged—some might say *strange*—husband who could be a great man if he could only get his shit together, and now I have one daughter who's been abused and another I'm paranoid about bringing up unscathed. I wanted to fly aeroplanes.'

'*What?*' He smiled gormlessly.

'Yeah. My dad was willing to fund my training, but only one of us could be away and your job came first, so my dream went on hold, which means it got binned. And now it's too late.'

'I didn't know,' Spiller said. 'Why didn't you say?'

She regarded him like he was daft.

'I'll look after the girls,' he said. 'Go and do what you want. It's not too late. I can taxi any hours. I can be there to look after the girls while you go off and train. I want you to do that.'

She was shaking her head, tears welling. It was mention of the girls. She could never cry for herself. She wasn't wired that way.

With sorrow absent in her voice, she said, 'It is *way* too late.'

SPILLER MOVED BACK to his flat that night. Entering his austere accommodation was worse than before. Spending time with his family, despite the warped reasons for that sojourn, had been special, and made his return to seclusion feel far more desperate. It felt like a prison cell, and that made him want to run out screaming because prison still seemed a strong possibility. But his last conversation with Helen had made staying with her an even less attractive option. He had destroyed her life, her hopes. She had given up her dreams only to watch his turn into a nightmare that had engulfed them all. Earlier, she hadn't asked him to leave. He had left because he couldn't allow the negativity erupting from his every pore to bounce back at him.

He played with his guns for a while. He stripped them down as far as he could, oiled them and fixed them back together. All were fakes, but a couple were closer to the genuine article in that they dismantled into their component parts. A Colt .45 1911, a 9mm Beretta 92, a 9mm Browning Hi-Power, a .357 Magnum. Fairly standard sidearms, nothing exotic. He'd owned them since his late teens, a time when no one bothered if a kid walked into a model shop and bought a replica gun that wasn't painted orange. It was a bit sad, he realised that, but they connected him to a time when he had carried one everywhere for months, and that was a comfort.

A little later he tried to sleep, failed, so went out to earn a few quid. He had missed the pub tip-out, but in a few hours the airport runs would start and would carry him through to the beginnings of rush-hour, when he would clock off to avoid the jams and the sodding Zimmers.

He made good money that night. Sometimes the jobs fell that way, a series of trips linking nicely with little driving in between, all £20 fares. Other times you were never in the right place at the right time, piddling fares of a few quid each, interspersed with long waits and miles of travelling to the pick-up.

It was a good night.

Until 5am.

Spiller was on auto-pilot at that time in the morning. He could travel miles without registering a single event. The radio was on low, a little background chatter to lessen the isolation. Human voices, singing, chatting, vainly trying to make him laugh; it all linked him to a species he felt detached from, but could not deny.

It was the frown his subconscious had stamped on his face that alerted him. It wasn't the details conveyed by the news report, it was his expression, twisting his features, that switched off his auto-pilot and brought him back to himself.

The B5464. A warning about a diversion, provided to people who were mostly still asleep and unable to take advantage. The B5464. Something about that road. He knew it. He snapped himself aware, listened to the end of the traffic alert, telling him the highways agency had closed the road and diversions were in place, in response to what the police were describing as "a serious incident".

Spiller pulled over. The alert had ended and the weather was being broadcast, but that road, the B5464...

He felt his body pulsing. Exhaustion, but with a layer of dread woven in.

He opened the maps app on his mobile phone and located the road in question.

'Shit.'

SPILLER STAYED IN bed until lunchtime, dozing while monitoring the hourly bulletins. He gathered nothing new. He hoped it was merely a car accident, but the road closure was consistently referred to as an "incident", which suggested otherwise. He checked online sources every so often, but details were limited there too. He wondered if Helen were listening to the news at the phone shop, thinking the same, but he hadn't made her aware of the exact route that night, so she'd maybe not have cottoned on anyway. For the first few hours, the news came via the traffic bulletin.

Then, at midday, it was promoted to the headline story of the news itself.

A body had been found.

It had to be Ward. How likely was it that two bodies had been dumped along the B5464? Spiller swore at the certainty, but, perversely, entwined with his fear was a strand of delight. The life he most hated, the one where nothing interesting ever happened and that seemed to have resumed, wasn't likely to continue, and that was aberrantly thrilling.

Spiller popped a couple of ProPlus, swilled them down with a large mug of tepid coffee, and headed into town.

THE SHOPPING PLAZA where Helen worked was a shithole. It had been a "precinct" before the council had got all posh and ripped up the gum-pocked grey paving stones, replacing them with colourful brick blocks that contrasted even more sharply with the discarded "chuddy", as it had been called in Spiller's youth. What the council hadn't managed to replace were the natives of the town, highly populated by spotty school-leavers who dragged their multiple snot-nosed offspring behind them while they all munched on Greggs and McDonald's. There were probably some nicer people milling about, but Spiller liked to focus on the negatives.

Every shop had a sale on, including the one where Helen worked. It was busy inside, full of people taking out contracts they couldn't afford just so they could boast the latest gadget. He caught her as she was about to pop out for lunch. More accurately, he caught her manager catching her before she popped out for lunch. Spiller stopped in the doorway as she left the staff room at the rear of the shop, and saw a man with a paunch in an ill-fitting suit subtly grasp at her hand. She gently but firmly eased away from him with a pleasant goodbye. Clearly, this was the guy she'd mentioned who had a crush on her. But what Spiller was seeing was workplace harassment of a woman who needed her job—and the flexibility it offered—too much to remonstrate properly.

He stepped back outside and waited for her to leave the shop. 'Helen.'

She flinched as he spoke. 'Jesus, Matt, what are you doing here?'

'We need to have a chat.'

'About?'

He inclined his head to her ear. 'Ward.'

Helen froze, looked at him. 'Is it bad?'

'I'll tell you over a sandwich. I'm buying.'

THEY SAT ON a metal bench next to a solitary leafless sapling, a token piece of nature among the concrete and brick. Icy gusts funnelled through the plaza as children pushing children passed by. It was too cold to eat outdoors, but this wasn't a conversation to be earwigged. Spiller told Helen what he'd heard on the news, and his almost certain conviction that it could be only Ward who they'd found.

She was pissed off. Through a mouthful of ham sandwich and chattering teeth, she told him, 'I'm very tempted to say you had one fucking job to do.'

He shrugged. She launched her barely eaten lunch into a nearby trash bin; probably more disgust at him than dislike of the taste.

'How could they have found him?' she asked. 'You said it was in the middle of nowhere, no stopping places, impossible to hike nearby.'

'I didn't say impossible; I said unlikely. And we didn't have a lot of options that night, if you remember. But, to respond to your facetious bloody comment, yes, I did have one fucking job: to dispose of the person *you'd* just fucking killed.'

She was quiet. Spiller took a bite of lukewarm pasty. The cold of the metal bench was unpleasant under his thighs, despite his thick coat. Both of them were shivering, but they remained seated.

'What do we do?' Helen asked.

'Nothing. Deal with whatever comes our way. *Who*ever comes our way.'

Would that be the police, Ward's brother, or his cronies? Or all of them? It was an obvious question that didn't need airing. But Spiller did want to ask something.

'Is it okay if I come back and stay with you and the girls?'

She nodded instantly, looked at the trash bin. 'I'm still hungry.' She got up.

'Do you want me to get you something else?' he asked.

'No, I'll go. You should go home and get some sleep; you look horrendous.'

'Oh, ta.'

'Be at the house by four-thirty when I bring the girls back.'

'Sure.' He finished his last morsel of pasty, scrunched up the paper bag and chucked it towards the bin, missing.

'Do we tell Sammy?' Helen asked.

Spiller had thought a lot about that and still couldn't decide. 'What do you think?'

'I say no. Not until we absolutely have to.'

'And if that's ten seconds before the police barge in?'

'She knows not to say anything. Nothing's changed since we told her.'

'She'll see it on the news. It'll go national.'

Helen cursed. 'I don't know. We'll talk more later. It may not even be him. We have to wait for a name.'

They looked at each other for a few seconds. He wanted to give her a hug and suspected she needed one, but she turned and walked away a split second before he could make the move.

Spiller reckoned he had ten minutes. A few minutes for her to reach the butty shop, buy whatever, and return to her place of work. Ten minutes was enough. It wouldn't take long. He set off briskly for the phone shop.

AS INSTRUCTED, SPILLER was outside the house by four-thirty. It was fully dark. He still had keys, but felt it would have been presumptuous to use them as though his invitation was anything more than a necessity. He had slept fitfully for a couple of hours, then packed a bag to last him a week. He assumed the police might take longer to pay them a visit—gathering evidence and all that—but anticipated Dominic Ward *et al* would not choose to wait. A week would encompass the most threatening time.

Having no inkling that her dad had left the previous evening after a tiff, Sammy no doubt assumed he'd simply gone out taxiing last night. She and Sophie gave him hugs on the pavement as Helen unlocked the house. He asked a lot of fatherly questions about their day as they headed indoors.

'Are you coming back, Dad?' Sophie asked, looking at the holdall he'd set down in the hallway. Spiller hoped she didn't attempt to peek inside. Along with his clothes and toiletries were his favourite taxi toys and the replica Browning.

He smiled at her. 'For a while.'

'For good?' she said, like she hadn't heard.

'Have you got much homework?'

'A few sums. Sammy says she'll help.'

'Phew,' Spiller said. 'Cos I'm a bit thick.'

Sophie laughed and scurried upstairs with her schoolbag.

'Wash your hands!' Helen called after her.

Sammy followed her sister, but with a trudge more than a scurry. Halfway up, she stopped, turned, and came back down. She looked at her parents with a kind of pleading, and silently indicated they enter the front room. Door pushed to, she gave them a half-smile.

'I don't want to worry you but… Dad, did you dump that… rubbish in the hills?'

Spiller nodded.

'They may have found it. It was on Google.'

Spiller and Helen exchanged glances. 'We know,' he said. 'I heard this morning.'

'Oh,' she said. 'Okay.' She kissed them both and left the room.

Bemused, they looked at each other. '*She's* bothered about *us*,' Spiller said.

'You've got some very strong women in this family. I'll make some dinner.'

Spiller was left alone. Implicit—at least to him—was that the man of the family was not strong. His eyes scanned the room and settled on his Gulf photo. His brain began to fog up. His consciousness retreated back inside his head and he found himself peering out through gaps in the container that carried him about. He was perfectly still. It was like a meditative state, instantly entered without him even trying. It wasn't the first time. Uninterrupted, he could stay like that for an hour or more. He wondered if it might be the precursor to a breakdown; the engine stalling before being condemned to the scrapheap. Or maybe it was his battery auto-recharging so he could keep moving forwards.

Fifteen minutes later, he hadn't moved. He had a vague sense that standing still wasn't his top priority, but it felt so nice. It was Sammy who disturbed his reverie.

'Dad?'

'Hey, Sammy.'

She frowned at him. 'What are you doing?'

'Thinking.'

'Oh. I thought you might have come upstairs to… you know… chat.'

Ah. That was his top priority: his daughter. 'Sorry, darling, I know we should have talked more about it but…'

'I didn't want to before.'

'Are you okay?'

'They've identified him. It's online.' She sat heavily on the sofa, like her legs wouldn't support her any longer.

'Shit. Sorry,' he said, but wasn't sure what for. As his wife had so ineloquently pointed out, Sammy was the one who'd chosen to hook up with a scumbag. And his wife had been the one to deliver a fatal overdose of builder's foam. All he'd done was clear up their mess. Still half-away with the fairies, he grasped the arm of the chair and lowered himself into it.

'*Dad!*'

Her urgent tone snapped him out of it. 'What?'

'It wasn't real until now. It was just a weird thing mum said. I knew you weren't lying but… while he was just missing, it didn't seem real. That she could have done it.'

'You know… I think the best thing to do is dob her in. We'll provide alibis for each other. We may even get a reward.'

She managed a slight smile in response. 'What do we do, Dad?'

'Wait. Be prepared. And always deny. We did a good job that night, sweetie. I mean, covering our tracks. Unless they find some damning proof, we just deny. People get caught because they confess. If we don't confess, we'll be fine. And we shouldn't need to confess. Confessions are all about guilt and your mum and I don't feel guilty. We were protecting you. We'd do it again.'

'Please don't,' Sammy said.

He smiled. 'Love you, darling. I'm so sorry this happened to you.'

'I should have known. I did know. I had a big red light flashing in my head the whole time, but...'

'You're young. It was exciting. I understand. Who wants a boring life, eh?'

Sammy laughed briefly. 'Me. Now.'

Spiller nodded. 'Yeah.'

A boring life wasn't to be. Not for Spiller. Never for Matthew Spiller. Helen barged into the front room holding her mobile phone with a look of seething. She presented it to him, but she appeared on the verge of shoving it down his throat.

'Mum?' Sammy said, panicking.

'It's not about you, Sammy, don't fret. Read that text, Matthew.'

His full name—he was in the shit. Spiller had the vaguest notion what it might concern, but, like many things in his life, he'd not really anticipated this moment happening. He read the message to himself.

'Out loud,' she said.

'Mum?'

'Don't come into work tomorrow,' Spiller read. 'I will send you your P45 and pay you up to date. No notice is required, given the circumstances. Ask your husband.'

Helen snatched the phone back. 'Let me guess: you went back to the shop while I went for something else to eat and you threatened my manager.'

'I didn't really threaten him; I was actually very nice. I just asked him to stop pawing you.'

'That was *not* your business. I've dealt with him for nearly a year. I was handling it. It was under control. Don't you think I'd have belted him if he ever crossed the line? You seriously think I'm some pathetic little woman who needs protecting? After what you've seen me do?'

Spiller was shaking his head slightly to it all. 'I didn't threaten him.'

'It doesn't matter! You *think* you didn't threaten him, but you have no idea how angry you look, even when you're smiling. I bet I'll be sent a dry-cleaning bill for his fucking trousers.'

Sammy sniggered.

She stared at her eldest. 'It's not funny, girl. That job paid our bills. How do I pay the mortgage now? You think this idiot's gonna cover it? He can barely pay for the fuel for that stupid car. I earn more than him. *Earned.*'

Spiller's momentary desire to challenge his idiot label passed without being verbally aired.

'Like we didn't have enough bloody problems,' Helen added.

'Can't you claim unfair dismissal?' Sammy said.

'Oh, good idea. Just as the police may be thinking your dad's involved in Ward's death, let's open a civil case and have my boss accuse him of threatening behaviour.'

Sammy huffed. 'I was only asking.'

'What about your dad?' Spiller said. 'I know he never really wanted to help out much financially while we were together in case I got my grubby little mitts on it, but he knows we split. Surely he can help. He's got pots.'

Helen didn't respond.

'Helen?'

'It's gone,' she said.

'What? What's gone?'

'Everything. He spent it. Blew it.'

Spiller chuckled. 'Don't be daft. What did he have? Half a mill? What does a seventy-year-old blow half a mill on?'

'Roulette, blackjack, poker, online slots, you name it.'

He knew from her expression it was true. 'How? He wasn't like that. When did that start?'

Helen shed a tear. 'My mum doesn't know exactly, but... we can make an educated guess.'

'Go on...'

'He's been losing his marbles for months. Dementia. Mum didn't think to check the accounts until now.'

Spiller now fully understood Sophie's question about whether her grandad was retarded. It wasn't the most politically correct description, and it wouldn't have been technically accurate even back in the day, but it did make sense. Sophie had noticed the change in her grandad and had applied a playground insult, not knowing the finer points of either modern language etiquette or medical diagnosis.

'Half a million?' Spiller said. 'Jesus...'

'More,' Helen said. 'He's racked up some credit-card debt as well.'

'Is their house okay?'

'It's safe. He'd have needed mum's input to re-mortgage or whatever so... it's fine. But she'll need to re-mortgage anyway to pay off the cards. She's going to apply for a power-of-attorney.'

They both seemed to notice Sammy's presence in the room at that moment. She was quietly snivelling. Helen approached the sofa and Sammy stood up to receive a big hug. Spiller guessed Sammy would have been aware of her grandad's decline—much like Sophie—but not the financial impact. That part would have been kept from her.

'When did you find out?' Spiller asked.

Helen released her daughter, who dumped herself back onto the sofa again. Helen sat next to her and held her hand.

'Christmas. Mum said she'd been looking to organise a big holiday for them both while there was still enough of my dad left to enjoy one. But there was no money. He said he didn't know what had happened—who knows if that's true—so she checked their online history and it was obvious. I don't know...

how someone that messed up can still operate a computer, set up gambling accounts.'

'I suppose it comes and goes,' Spiller said. 'Good days and bad days.'

'And which were the good days? The ones when he was bright enough to know how to drain a lifetime of savings?'

The single tear Helen had shed had been just that: an aberration. A tear for her mother, probably for the man her father had been, but too close to becoming a self-pitying stream that she'd felt the need to staunch the sorrow at its source. Now the anger returned.

'So you can see, *Matthew*, how your intervention at my place of work has royally stuffed us.'

He did see that. He nodded. 'Sorry.'

'You'll get another job, Mum,' Sammy assured. 'We'll be okay.'

For Spiller, though, the issue had suddenly become larger than the household payments. He'd always relied on the fact of Helen's future inheritance to offset his guilt at not earning much. Not for himself, for the girls. An only child, Helen would inherit everything; the cash, the shares, the house, and the girls would be sorted. Not mega-rich, but comfortable. Not anymore.

He suddenly thought of the fifty grand Emma had offered for the hit. But even that was missing a zero. Spiller's consciousness fell back inside his head again. He involuntarily powered down. A system overload.

After a couple of minutes, he was dimly cognisant of Sammy standing up and leaving the room. Helen following, switching the light off as she went, leaving him in darkness. Closing the door. A shout upstairs for Sophie to come down for dinner. Scampering feet down the stairs. But no invitation for him.

It was okay. His current state required scant energy. He stayed there, perfectly inanimate, for three hours.

Chapter Eight

THE TIMER FOR the Christmas-tree lights clicked on at eight o'clock. Spiller, eyes blankly unfocused, jumped slightly at the interruption to the gloom. The lights danced around the fake green needles in a hypnotic pattern that threatened to bring back his stupor, but he knew it was time to go out and make some money.

Only, it wasn't, because he couldn't leave the house, because he was there to protect his family. But he had to because he was—thanks to his dumb-ass machismo—now the only bread-winner. *Crust*-winner. His tummy growled and he decided to check if there was any dinner left over in the kitchen.

The kitchen was deserted. He could hear a TV on upstairs and pictured the three of them cuddled up on a bed, Helen in the middle, an arm around a daughter each side. He'd never felt so alone. He looked in the fridge, grabbed some cold pieces of breaded chicken off a plate and munched through them so quickly they formed a bolus in his gullet that became almost immobile and incredibly painful. He stood there, eyes pinched against the agony of the slowly descending lump of poultry.

He wondered idly if that's what it felt like to have a malignant mass in his throat, and, not for the first time in his life, mused how easily he thought he'd accept such a terminal prognosis in a consultant's office. Others might gasp, cry out, well up, clam up, but he imagined he'd just respond with a stoical "okie-dokie" before getting on no differently with whatever was left of his life.

The ring on the doorbell made him smile. Something was happening. Whatever it was, it was better than nothing. And if it was David, sneaking by to see how his fuckable next-door-neighbour was faring on her own, he'd get a smack in the face for his concern.

As Spiller walked down the hallway, he heard the TV volume increase upstairs. Helen clearly didn't want her daughters to hear what might be about to occur.

He opened the front door to a red-eyed Dominic Ward. Ward looked at Spiller with a mix of animosity and pleading, the latter counteracting any threat that the former might have induced in him. This was a man who wanted answers. Spiller stepped outside and led Ward away from the house and onto the pavement.

'Did you hear?' Ward asked, his words clouding the air.

'Yes. I'm sorry.'

'Are you?'

Spiller considered for a second. 'No.'

'I want to know what happened,' Ward said. 'I just need to know what happened. I won't pass anything on to the police, I just need to know.'

Spiller didn't believe him. 'I don't know. Even if I did know, why would I tell you?'

'Because I think you're a good man underneath it all. I think, if you did something, it was to protect your daughter. I know he hurt her.'

'How?' Spiller asked. Had the police told him? Were they allowed to pass on that type of information?

'Because he always did. There was always a moment when I knew he'd hurt them. They changed. All his girlfriends. It was more obvious in some, but I could always tell when it had happened. Your daughter was amazing. She hardly let on. But it was in her eyes. A flicker of fear before everything she said and did, like she was always having to vet if she'd set him off. But it was never her fault. It was him. He was just... a sadist.'

'And you stood by and did fuck all.'

'I never saw it.'

'Doesn't matter. You knew it was happening—you just said.'

Ward stared down at the pavement. He gently swiped the toe of his expensive shoe back and forth in the light frost that sparkled under the streetlamp. 'Sorry,' he said.

Spiller assessed his remorse to be heartfelt, but perhaps it was a cunning charade. Perhaps he was miked, the police listening in.

'I can't help you,' Spiller said. 'I understand you're in pain, but why would I help you even if I could? Did you help my daughter? You could have warned her off the first time you met her. You're responsible. *Culpable*, isn't that the word you people use?'

Ward looked up and met Spiller's accusatory gaze with one of his own. 'Morally, maybe, but you're legally culpable, Mr Spiller. I know the police think Callum left here and went to the estate, which means you weren't the last people to see him alive, *but*... I spoke to some kids on the estate who saw him that night, driving. And they didn't think it was him. They said it looked like him, but it wasn't him.'

Spiller scoffed. 'Like one of those weird dreams, eh? It *looked* like you, but it *wasn't* you. Fuck, do me a favour. You're taking the word of some stoned *yoofs* who have nothing better to do than stand on a freezing street corner. You of all people should know what a reliable witness looks like.'

'They knew my brother. They said it wasn't him.'

Spiller clapped his hands in false jollity. 'Well, case closed! You'd better call the police, hadn't you?'

Ward smiled slightly. 'You just keep on missing the point. The police are not your problem. Like last time, I'm here *instead* of my brother's colleagues. They are positively champing at the bit to make your acquaintance. Word has spread about Callum's visit to the estate that night and no one has any clue what it concerned. No whispers of a clandestine meeting, either criminal or romantic. Someone would have known something and someone would have said. But no one has. Couple that with eyewitness accounts that say it wasn't even him behind the wheel, and suddenly you and your wife *are* the last people to see him alive.'

Spiller was genuinely flustered. 'The police—'

'Are the least of your worries! How many times do I need to say that? I'm trying to give you the chance to explain what happened so it *can* be dealt with by the police. All it would take to have Callum's people knocking on your door is a word from me. I tell them you did it, you did it. They want someone to kill. They wouldn't care if it *wasn't* you.'

'It wasn't,' Spiller said. 'I can't help you.'

'You mean you won't help yourself. But that's okay. Just don't say I didn't make the effort.'

Out of answers, Spiller resorted to type. Snarling, he leaned in, so his forehead rested lightly against his adversary's. To his credit, Ward didn't recoil.

'Go away,' Spiller said.

Ward stepped back and beeped the remote on his Maserati. He laughed raucously, his sorrow making an ugly exodus from his normally implacable demeanour. 'You're such a dunce,' he said.

'You're not the first to think it; you won't be the last.'

'You're putting your whole family in mortal danger.'

'It's my family,' Spiller said, like that was a cool answer.

Ward turned and headed back to his car, but stopped in the middle of the street, adjacent to Spiller's Audi. Spiller watched as he stared at it, then proceeded to make a slow circuit around it, perusing its features. At the rear of the car, he halted again, staring down at something.

Spiller went over. 'What? You sussing out where to stick a bomb? You're a bunch of low-grade pill-pushers; you're not the IRA.'

'Quad exhausts,' Ward said, like a bulb had burst blindingly alight in his head. 'Bet those make a mighty rumble.'

Spiller sensed a precursor, so said nothing.

'You know who of my brother's crew would *really* like to meet you?'

Spiller waited.

'A couple of his younger *aficionados*. They came back from a night out at Christmas with only sixteen fingers between them.'

A sickly panic sluiced through Spiller's chest, nauseated his stomach, before filling his legs with a dread that made them feel leaden. His back started pounding. He feigned passable ignorance despite this.

'Sounds about right for a human. Although I expect most of your brother's mates play the banjo, so I wouldn't rule out an extra couple of pinkies or a few webbed feet.'

'No, Mr Spiller, that's *all* they had. *Sans* pollex.'

Spiller made a face. 'What?'

'Absent their thumbs. Someone cut them off.'

'So what?' Spiller said.

'So, the person who did it had a big car. Noisy exhausts, they recalled.'

'Like you, me, your brother, and a thousand other petrol-heads in the area. So what?'

'Well, they weren't too clear about the night's events—understandably so having also been bludgeoned nearly to death—but one of them did say he thought the car had private-hire plates on it.'

'Right,' Spiller said. 'Anything else you want to pin on me? Nine-eleven? Lady Di? JFK?'

Ward laughed. 'I've been reading too much John Grisham, haven't I? Yeah, it's probably that.'

Spiller wanted to punch this man until he died. But not with the neighbours' CCTV watching. Impotent to act, he turned and walked away.

HELEN WAS WAITING in the hallway. Spiller closed the front door as the Maserati blasted past the front of the house. He leaned back against the door, then sank slowly to his haunches, cradling his head in his hands. The warmth of the nearby radiator was blissful, so homely. The TV was still on loud upstairs, set by Helen to drown out their conversation.

'What happened out there?' she asked.

'I have so fucked up,' he said into his palms.

'Tell me something new.'

He looked up at her. 'That was Dominic Ward. We're in danger. We need to get out of this house. Go somewhere no one knows us. Out of this country.'

'Sounds lovely. Where are you thinking? Our villa in Marbella? The house in Cap D'Antibes? Maybe Lake Como?'

'Helen…'

'No, this is a special kind of delusion, even by your standards. Tell me, where do we go and what do we use for cash? Forget the interruption to the girls' education…'

Spiller wasn't really listening. Somewhere, not far away, someone had fifty grand with his name on it.

Helen snorted at a thought. 'And what will the cops think of us leaving the country just as Ward's body turns up? Bloody hell, think, Matt.'

'Well, we at least need to go to a hotel tonight. Somewhere safe.'

She lowered herself against the wall to his level. 'What was said outside?'

He closed his eyes. 'Ward's people are coming. They wanted to come before, but he stopped them. I think he's going to step out of their way now. Probably he'll *tell* them to come.' He paused. 'What money do we have? Collectively?'

'I have savings. From my work and whatever my mum and dad gave me over the years. Maybe fifteen thousand. You?'

'Couple of grand, but plenty of available credit on my cards. Maybe ten. And we have equity in this place. What? Thirty? Forty?'

'Closer to thirty. But moot unless we sell the place.'

'Or re-mortgage.'

She laughed. 'With you on your chronically under-declared taxi earnings and me now out of work?'

'Shit. So… we sell.'

'That takes months. I'm assuming the upshot of your conversation with Dominic Ward was fairly time-sensitive?'

He buried his face in his palms again. She had fifteen grand. He could rustle up maybe twelve if he put ten of it on the tick. So that was twenty-seven. But he could turn that into seventy-seven with a phone call. It wasn't a fortune, but it would buy them time. They could come clean to the police about Dominic's threats and go into hiding with the cops' blessing. It wouldn't need to look suspicious.

'My money was meant for the kids,' Helen said. 'It's even more important now my dad's dosh is all gone. I don't want to spend that on a few weeks in a hotel. It's not like I wouldn't still have the mortgage and bills to pay. We'd blow through it in no time. Then what?'

He reached out a hand to her, which she accepted. 'I can get some more. Quite a lot more.'

'How?'

'Probably best you don't know.'

She just nodded, which Spiller found oddly upsetting.

'I'm going to call Sergeant Enright,' he announced.

She snatched her hand away. 'Like hell! With what he knows about you?'

'Exactly why I need to talk to him. If he'd told anyone it was me in Ward's car that night, I'd have been arrested by now. He's not said anything, and that makes him an ally.'

'Or too scared to let his bosses know he let you go for a sneaky joy-ride, now the owner of that car's turned up dead. Maybe that's all that was.'

Spiller thought about it, shook his head. 'No way. I had blond hair, I was impersonating Ward. He knew I hadn't just gone for a spin without insurance. And you think he'd bury that when it could help solve a murder?'

'Whatever, Matt. But, promise me, if this goes sideways, you and you alone take the fall. The girls can't lose us both.'

She was right. His involvement was set in stone. Enright had seen him.

He nodded. 'Let's pack some bags.'

SOPHIE WAS TERRIBLY eager about their little adventure, so her sister and parents had to act equally elated. She was simultaneously excited to be missing school and keen to know the reason. Sammy explained that they used to do the same with her when she was young because it was so much fun, which wasn't true on either count. They drove to a chain hotel in the city where conferences and wedding receptions were held and people met to have affairs. It was bright and colourful and warm. They booked a family room for a couple of nights, not seriously thinking it would be resolved in a mere forty-eight hours.

While Helen got the girls settled, Spiller went down to the bar with his mobile phone and Sergeant Enright's contact card. A few businesspeople, two smooching couples. He ordered a lager, found a corner table, and tapped in the digits. Enright answered with a simple 'hello' on the third ring.

'Sergeant Enright?' Spiller checked.

'Yes.'

'It's Matt Spiller. We need to talk.'

'I agree.'

'Just you and me?'

'I'm off duty. I'll come alone. Tell me where you are.'

Spiller obliged, and, thirty minutes and two more lagers later, Enright strolled into the hotel bar in an old fur-collared leather flying jacket, with a blue baseball cap pulled low above his eyes. He spotted Spiller and came straight over, by-passing the allure of the gleaming beer taps and back-shelves of exotic liquors. He dragged a chair to Spiller's side of the table and sat down, making their meeting appear distinctly covert.

'Hello, Matthew.' He held out a hand. 'What's the crack?'

'I might ask you the same,' Spiller said, shaking his hand.

'The other night.'

Spiller nodded.

Enright shrugged. 'You may want to just take the pass on that.'

'Okay. But you know what happened today? With Ward?'

'Of course. Why? Would you like me to arrest you?'

Spiller recoiled slightly in his chair. 'God, no.'

'Then take the pass.'

Spiller's eyes flicked to the bar, to the young bartender, who was giving them sidelong stares as though he suspected they were about to exchange nuclear launch codes.

'You look like some famous actor trying not to get recognised,' Spiller said, indicating Enright's headgear.

'Yeah, well, it's probably best I'm not seen talking to you—for obvious reasons.'

The bartender arrived at the table and stood to attention. 'Can I get you a drink, sir?' he said to Enright.

'I'm fine.'

'You need to order something, sir.'

'My friend's drinking,' Enright said.

The bartender loitered, unsure how to rid his domain of two men he clearly deemed unsavoury.

Without looking at the bartender, Enright pulled out a small wallet and flipped it open to reveal his warrant card. 'I don't need to order anything.'

'No, sir, you don't need to order anything,' the waiter replied, and retreated to his spot behind the counter.

Spiller smiled as Enright put his card away. 'Shit, did you just Jedi mind-trick the barman?'

'Ha! I wish. That'd be a neat trick for a copper, eh? Why am I here, Matthew?'

Spiller leaned forwards in his chair. 'Well, I wanted to check we're okay about... you know, but... looks like we are. The other thing is that I've had two visits from Ward's brother.'

'Dominic Ward.'

'Yeah, him. The first time was a fishing trip, but this evening he made it very clear he thinks I topped his brother.'

'Which you did.'

Spiller gave him a stony look. 'No comment. Anyway, he has no proof, but I think he's going to tell Ward's people I did it. They're on the warpath and I don't know if they'll target my family as well.'

'You're all here?' Enright asked.

'Yes.'

'Wise move. Have you told DS Madden?'

'Not yet.'

'You should. And explain why. Although she won't be the lead any more, now it's a murder enquiry.'

Spiller downed the remains of his third lager.

'What does Dominic Ward think he has on you?' Enright asked.

'He says some kids on the estate saw the person in Ward's car that night and didn't think it was him. Plus, he just thinks I'm lying. He said that even before the body turned up. And... there's other stuff.'

'Such as?'

'He thinks I did something else.'

'Such as?'

Spiller took a moment. 'Never mind. What's the deal with you, anyway?'

Enright paused, clearly weighing up whether to pursue his enquiry. 'How so?'

'Well... *this*. Especially considering *that*.' Spiller pointed.

Enright touched the small gold crucifix visible in the V of his sweater.

'Are you religious?' Spiller asked. 'You must be.'

'Not really. I'm okay with God; not religion.'

Spiller understood the distinction. 'Well, I wouldn't be too sure he's okay with you.'

'I think God wants goodness on this earth. *Bad men need nothing more to compass their ends than that good men should look on and do nothing.* John Stuart Mill, 1867.'

'And the law? The thing you swore to uphold?'

'I believe I'm complicit in the law being broken if I can prevent it, but don't. That can involve pre-emption.' Enright laughed. 'Anyway, you're playing a dangerous game of Devil's Advocate here, Matthew. You really don't want to give me a crisis of conscience.'

Spiller paused. 'So... is that it? The age-old battle? Or is there something personal?'

Enright's mouth twisted like he was debating whether to answer. 'My dad was in the RUC during The Troubles.'

'And?'

Enright absently pinched his crucifix, and Spiller surmised RUC may have turned into RIP.

'That was a gruesome way to die,' Enright said, not without a hint of admiration.

'Ward?' If innocent, Spiller wouldn't have known the manner of death. 'I wouldn't know. I don't think it's been on the news yet.'

'Course not. Still don't trust me, eh?'

Spiller gave a slight shrug, but the mention of Ward's demise had twanged an unpleasant chord deep in his subconscious. It was a tip-of-your-tongue type of thing, but a fleeting taste, like déjà vu.

'I'm sorry he hurt your daughter,' Enright said.

'Thank you.'

'Good riddance to a piece of shit.'

'Yep.' He swilled down the last of his pint. 'Tell me, how did they find the body?'

'Routine maintenance by the council. Just checking their drystone walls, apparently. Someone must have wondered why so many stones had fallen off the top. Peeked over and must have seen something.'

'Damn.' Spiller waved to the barman for another drink. 'You okay?' he said to Enright.

'I'm good, thanks. Early start.'

Spiller and Enright waited in silence for the bartender to bring over the lager. They both watched a young woman in the highest heels totter to the bar and place an order. When Spiller's drink arrived, half of it disappeared within three seconds of it hitting the beer mat.

'You should go easy,' Enright said.

'I'm not driving.'

'You need to keep a clear head. One ill-considered word from you and you're stuffed.'

Spiller symbolically pushed his drink to the far side of the table. 'What are they thinking?'

'CID? Not sure. There's a limit to what I can glean, being in uniform, but I am mates with DC Goodrick—the other detective you met—so I can tap him for some info. He knows I have an interest in the case as I was your first point of contact.'

'Okay.'

'But do me a favour and don't call the number I gave you again.' He pulled out a pad and pen, scribbled a number and handed it to Spiller. 'Call me on that if you really need me. It's a burner.'

'*You* have a burner phone?'

'I know—me. A cop who's letting you get away with murder.'

Spiller glanced at the surrounding tables to see if anyone was eavesdropping. 'Do you know if they're looking at me for it?' he asked.

'I refer you to my previous answer: don't know. I wouldn't get too excited that they're not knocking on your door yet, though. They won't make a move until they're pretty sure. Otherwise the CPS won't bite so they'll just have to lock you up then let you go. Having said that, for murder, they could keep you for up to ninety-six hours and just keep grilling you.'

Spiller was getting pissed off. 'Can you please stop talking like you know I did it? I haven't admitted anything to anyone, least of all you.'

'Fair enough. We can play it like that if you want. But it bothers me you're getting all fractious inside five minutes. How would you fare after another ninety-five hours and fifty-five minutes? Matthew, you'd better get used to the idea of people accusing you of murder. It may not happen, but you sure as hell better accept it could. You need to steel yourself.'

Spiller reached across the table to retrieve his pint, which he quickly polished off. He set it down and peered at Enright. 'Are you going to help?'

'Haven't I already?'

'I mean... get Dominic Ward to back off, and Ward's people.'

Enright laughed. 'I'm a dodgy copper, not the Illuminati.'

Spiller swore under his breath.

'I told you: tell DS Madden. You have her number?'

Spiller nodded. 'She and Goodrick gave me their cards.'

'Madden will pass it up the chain and hopefully someone will have a word with Dominic again and warn off Ward's crew. The last thing anyone wants is more violence. If you tell them you've been threatened, they'll act.'

Spiller made a face. 'But then... Dominic will have to share his suspicions with the police.'

'If he hasn't done so already. Listen, there's no shortage of suspects here. Callum Ward was a nasty bastard. In and out of prison for years, multiple crimes to his name, plenty of enemies. If there's no hard evidence to the contrary, they'll be looking at the underworld, not some fine citizen like yourself, and this'll end up another cold case.' He squinted at Spiller. 'There isn't any evidence to the contrary, is there?'

Spiller wondered again whether he could trust Enright. He gave the minutest shake of his head rather than say anything out loud that could be recorded.

'Good.' Enright offered his hand.

Spiller grasped it, but Enright's grip tightened and didn't let go. He pulled Spiller into the table and leaned in close. Spiller could smell stale coffee on his breath.

'Don't let me down, Matthew. I'm risking my job, my *liberty*, to save your arse.'

'I know. I owe you.'

'I don't need you to owe me; I need you to be discreet.'

Spiller nodded.

Enright stood up. 'Call Madden. Now. Go upstairs and call her. You can't just disappear from your house. It doesn't look good.'

Spiller rose so he could peer down on Enright, at least physically. 'I get it. Thank you for everything.'

After Enright left, Spiller had another beer. He wasn't going to call Madden that night. She likely wasn't working and Enright had been right about his intake of booze: he needed to have a clear head, especially when conversing with people who were on high alert for the slightest hint of guilt. He went back upstairs, kissed his sleeping daughters and climbed in bed beside a wife who was awake but didn't offer a word. Spiller assumed a sound night's sleep was more important than knowing what he and Enright had discussed, although how on earth anyone could sleep under these even partially known circumstances he simply couldn't fathom. Maybe she'd popped a pill.

For Spiller to sleep, he'd need to dose himself so heavily he'd probably die. It was a morbidly attractive option but, despite his lowest moods, he'd never understood how any parent could dump their depression on their kids and destroy the rest of their lives. The end of one person's anguish was only the start of others'.

Given a few hours to quieten, his boisterous mind finally began to surrender at three a.m. He could sometimes sense it happening, like a lucid dream, the overlap of conscious into subconscious. It was nice to be aware you were falling asleep, especially when it felt like a skill he lacked. *Aaaaahhhhh...*

He was bolt upright in bed in an instant, an expletive rending the quiet room. His eyes were round and wide, the revelation of his deep mind having pulled them out of shape. The thing Enright had said about Ward's death. The thing that had been quietly nagging.

'Fuck,' he said again.

Beside him, Helen stirred. 'What? Bad dream?' she muttered.

He checked the sleeping forms of his daughters in the murk. They were still.

'Did we chuck the foam?'

She rolled onto an elbow to raise her head. 'What?'

'The can. The foam. Did we get rid of it?'

'Of course we—' She faltered. 'You went to the tip.'

'But did I take it? I don't remember taking it.'

'You chucked it all in a black bag,' she said.

'That was the other stuff. The clothes, sheets, blankets.'

They both fell silent. Spiller tried to replay the events of that night. He recalled taking the can off her and... what?

'Fuck, I put it back in the corner,' he said finally. 'With my tools.'

'I put the nozzle down his throat,' she said. 'Shit. DNA.'

Spiller was already off the bed and clambering back into his jeans. The girls slumbered on. As he got dressed, he realised he didn't feel too chipper. His head was muzzy, his stomach queasy. The booze earlier.

'I'll have to get a cab,' he said to her, pulling his house keys and wallet from the side zipper of his holdall, but leaving his mobile. He knelt down by the bed. 'Is there anything else? That we missed?'

Helen let her head thud heavily on the pillow. 'Christ, I don't know.'

Spiller grabbed the hood of his sweatshirt, pulled it over his head and left the room.

Downstairs in the lobby, he passed reception and wandered out onto the deserted streets. Ten minutes away from the hotel, he flagged down a passing cab. He climbed in the back and gave the driver an address—several roads away from the one he wanted.

THE NEGLECTED GINNEL behind Spiller's house was too noisy, at least for three-thirty in the morning. Under his feet, icy puddles gave way, broken glass cracked, twigs snapped, gravel crunched, paving squelched. With a black hoodie concealing his identity, he was an emergency call waiting to happen. One peek from a neighbour, the police would be there in minutes. It was the cops' graveyard shift; plenty of time on their hands.

He entered the back yard, squeezed past the Peugeot and let himself into the cellar. He was home. Nothing to call the cops about now. A man in his own house. The suspicious figure in the alleyway? *No idea, officer, but thanks for checking.*

Spiller quickly headed up the stone steps into the kitchen and through to the hallway to cancel the alarm. It had a 30-second delay. He'd never tried to reach it from the cellar in time before.

Back in the kitchen, there it was. Even in the dark, the can of foam was the first thing he saw, sitting proudly next to the other bits of DIY paraphernalia—the only item that had proven useful since he'd dumped it all there months ago with such good intentions.

He picked it up and unscrewed the long nozzle of clear plastic filled with hard yellow. He pondered a moment, then lit one of the gas hobs, slowly feeding the nozzle, DNA-end first, into the blue flame. While the plastic melted onto the cooker, the dead foam inside it set alight with a caustic stench that made Spiller's eyes water. He started coughing as he moved it in the circle of fire, trying not to let the liquefied substance fall into the gas jets and clog them. Finally, he dropped the last bit onto the centre cap so the heat of the metal could deal with it. He switched the gas off. The kitchen reeked in a way that felt positively injurious. He opened the windows and wafted with a dish towel.

The can itself was not a problem. He could throw that in any wheelie bin. It was a standard product, available in all good retail outlets. It was nothing incriminating. Circumstantial perhaps, but not incriminating.

He sat down at the kitchen table and waited for the air to clear. If the police did visit in the morning, there couldn't be even the faintest whiff of anything acrid. He laid his head on his arms on the table and closed his eyes.

Ten minutes later, the caustic gunk had cooled on the cooker top. He grabbed a knife from the drawer and began to scrape it off, but quickly stopped.

A sound in the ginnel. A faint sound of the sort he'd earlier made himself. If the windows had been shut, he wouldn't have heard it. He peered over the windowsill as two dark-clad and hooded figures came though the yard gate and stopped by the back of the car. Something in their hands. He ducked down before they looked up but his heart nearly stalled as his brain settled on the identity of that something.

Petrol cans.

'Shit.' Spiller had a knife in his hand but it was for paring and way too small. Crouching, he moved to the drawer and quietly selected a large carving knife instead. He waited, straining his ears. Soft footsteps moved past the car and stopped at the cellar door, one floor directly beneath the kitchen window. He swore again. Had he locked the cellar door? The creak of it opening told him no. He crept to the door that led down to the cellar, straightened up and waited. One hand on the door handle, ready to pull, and one gripping the knife. He listened.

The intruders shut the door behind them, a faint clunk signalling its closure. Clandestine male whispers, difficult to discern, to put an age to. He pulled the door ajar. Flashes of torchlight in the cellar.

'Here?' one said softly.

'Upstairs. It needs to spread quickly.'

'Undo my cap for me.'

A moment while the man must have obliged. Spiller wondered why the other one couldn't have done it himself. Maybe his gloves were too bulky.

'I want to light the match,' said the first man.

'I know.'

Spiller heard them pad through the cellar to the foot of the steps. His grip tightened on the knife. On the one hand, you could call it fortuitous, arriving only minutes before an arson attack. On the other... well, it looked like his bloodletting days weren't yet over. He thought of Alfie Enright—what he'd have made of this. Spiller the Avenging Angel.

Their footfalls were light, but he gauged their progress up the steps. He stepped back from the door, poised himself, adopted the optimal stance. The door opened slowly towards him and, when the gap was sufficient, he launched a kick straight at the first man, whose shocked intake of breath came too late to translate into a defensive or evasive manoeuvre. Spiller's trainer caught him on the sternum and drove through hard. The man flailed his arms forwards, dropping the petrol can, but there was nothing to grab onto, and nothing but his accomplice behind to halt his rearward momentum, and nothing behind *him* to prevent the inevitable. Both men tumbled back down the stone steps, flipping and flopping, limbs intertwining, until they ended up in a pile on the cellar floor, one on top of the other, a painful yelp from one of them. The petrol cans landed heavily, vomiting fuel from their open necks.

Spiller hit the cellar light at the top of the stairs and rushed down after them. He stopped on the second step up, out of reach of their feet or fists, although it appeared at least one of the four arms was incapable of working properly, much less inflicting damage. It belonged to the man who'd cushioned the other man, who was face down on his accomplice, moaning. The arm was bent at the elbow in a way that went far beyond double-jointedness. Fortunately for him, he'd been knocked out by the fall so couldn't feel the injury. Or maybe he was dead, but Spiller merely mentally shrugged at the thought. The gravity of their intentions was billowing like a blown nuke in his mind. The reek of petrol filled his nostrils. It had burst out of the cans and saturated them both. Petrol they'd brought to ignite, in a house that they had no way of knowing didn't contain the sleeping forms of his wife and daughters.

Spiller was incensed. He reached into the pockets of the man who was face down and rummaged about, pulling out a box of matches. The man tried to reach behind and grab but Spiller tugged away.

Then the man rolled off the other one and lay on his back on the fuel-soaked stones of the cellar floor. His hood slipped back off his head as he did so, and Spiller's mouth fell open in disbelief as he found himself staring at the bleeding face of Dominic Ward.

Ward shuffled away from Spiller on his bum, dragging a stream of fuel with him on his coat tail. He leaned his back against the old sofa. Spiller thought he'd maybe bust a leg with the way he winced and didn't attempt to stand up. Both cans were still losing their contents in little gulping sounds.

'Some fucking barrister,' Spiller said. 'Who's this twat?' He nodded to the unconscious youth, but he had his answer without Ward responding. The leather of the youth's gloves was flat where his thumbs should have been, both of them empty. *Sans pollex.* This was the one who'd needed help to unscrew the cap.

Spiller rotated the handle of the carving knife in his fist, making the blade glint under the bare bulb on each turn.

Ward grimaced. 'You killed my brother.'

'Yeah, I did.'

The admission had to sink in—for both Ward *and* Spiller; the implications of his confession.

Ward's pained expression gained a pleading. 'Let me out of here and I'll make it all go away. I'll say I was wrong... that I know who really killed Callum. A rival gang. There'll be a tit-for-tat hit and you'll be in the clear. They'll believe me.'

Spiller was shaking his head. 'But I don't.'

'Matthew...'

'You came into my house prepared to kill my family. That's equal payback, is it? Three innocent people die for what I did? And what did I do? Kill a piece of shit sadist who was brutalising my daughter.'

'It wasn't meant to kill anyone, this was just a warning. I just wanted you to tell the police what you'd done.'

'Fuck off, I heard you. You said the fire had to start upstairs, so it would spread quicker.' Spiller stepped over the inert thumbless form, shaking the box of matches. 'Do you smoke, Dominic?'

'No.'

Spiller removed a single match from the box. 'No? You'll be smoking soon. Probably about an hour from now. Well, *smouldering*. Once the fire brigade puts you out.'

Tears sprang in Ward's eyes. 'Matthew... I have kids...'

'So do I.'

Standing in a pool of petrol, aware of the danger he was in himself, Spiller rasped the match along the strike-side. The match flared into life. Ward whimpered.

Chapter Nine

SPILLER SAT IN the comfy chair of their hotel bedroom until dawn banished the worst of the gloom from its curtained interior. He watched his wife and daughters sleep peacefully and his heart ached with the burden of love he felt for them. And it did feel like a burden at times. He loved them so much it hurt. He doubted he was alone in thinking this. There was no greater joy than loving a person unconditionally, and no greater pain than the fear of losing that love.

He couldn't take his eyes off them. For hours. He focused on the sheets that covered them, the rhythm of their breathing. How different would that night have been had they stayed at home? Would anyone have heard the break-in in the cellar? They never alarmed the house at night. Would anyone have been awakened by the crackle of the fire as it crept up the stairs? Or would the smoke have marked them all for the mortuary before any of them knew the house had been violated?

He was delirious in his tiredness. He couldn't work out if he'd done the right thing. He felt like a sociopath being lectured on the rights and wrongs of a moral dilemma and not even understanding there was a dividing line between the two. It didn't compute. It was all just one big mess in his head.

Helen awoke just after nine. The girls slept on. He told her it had all gone to plan. A taxi taken a mile from the hotel, the drop-off several streets away from the house, better to conceal his trail. A simple disposal by fire of the evidence. Then the return trip the whole way on Shanks's pony. It had taken him two hours to walk back, but better that than place the return journey on the records of a local cab company.

As Enright had suggested the previous evening, he then placed a call to DS Madden. He and Helen went into the bathroom, so they didn't wake the girls. Spiller sat on the bath-side, Helen on the closed lid of the loo. He tapped the numbers from the card Madden had given him into his mobile. Helen urged him to put the call on speaker.

She answered quickly. 'DS Madden.'

'It's Matthew Spiller.'

A pause. 'Mr Spiller... how are you?'

'Yeah, good, thanks. I just wanted to let you know that I took my family to a local hotel last night after Dominic Ward upped the ante with his threats against us.'

'Right.' Madden left a long pause.

'What?' he asked.

'We need you to come to the station.'

'Why?'

'You heard the news about Callum Ward?'

'Yes.'

'Okay. Well, I'm not in charge of the case any more, Mr Spiller. My guvnor wants to talk to you.'

'About Ward?'

Another pause, longer this time. 'There was an arson attack on your home last night.'

Helen squeaked. 'Shit,' she said, loud enough for Madden to hear.

'Sorry,' Madden said. 'Sorry, Mrs Spiller! I didn't really want to pass this information over the phone. And, don't worry, it was attempted arson; it failed. But things went, uh, quite awry for the arsonist.'

'How so?' Spiller asked, but he was thinking just one thing: *Arsonist? Singular?*

'It's all a bit strange,' Madden said. 'The circumstances. You need to come into the station. City centre, please. You need to ask for DCI Bartoli.'

'Okay,' Spiller said. 'Thanks. Is lunchtime okay?'

'I'll let him know.'

Spiller ended the call.

Helen was staring hard at him. 'Matt?'

'Hey, I have no idea. I got there, got rid of the... thing. Came back.'

'How can someone fail to set a house on fire? How stupid do you have to be? Petrol, match. That's it. *Whoof.*'

Spiller shrugged.

'I want to come,' she said.

'And I want you to come, but you need to stay with the girls, and the more you're kept out of this, the better.'

She appeared to be in pain just thinking about it. 'God, Matt. Someone tried to kill us.'

Tears welled in her eyes, but Spiller knew the tears were angry more than fearful. He stood up, briefly considered his next move, leaned down and kissed the top of her head. She didn't flinch; possibly she didn't even register his touch. He guessed she was harbouring thoughts of revenge. She'd killed a man for hurting one of her daughters; Christ, what would she do to redress an attempt to cremate her whole family?

'I'm going to get a shower,' he said.

Seemingly in a trance, Helen rose to her feet and left the bathroom, closing the door behind her.

Spiller sat down again on the bath-side. He could never let her know about last night. She'd have dropped the match, for damn sure. Maybe she wouldn't even have bothered getting clear before she did so. And when he'd struck the match last night, he'd also intended to use it. He'd planned to get to the cellar door and throw the match in before running away.

But he hadn't. He'd quenched the flame in the palm of his hand and given Dominic Ward an almighty kick in the head instead. Then he'd dragged his senseless form by the collar and draped him over his unconscious mate again. He'd run upstairs, leaving his trainers at the top of the steps to avoid tracking petrol through the house. In the kitchen he'd collected the can of foam, the crusty remnants from the cooker-top, shoved them in a plastic bag, then moved to the hallway where he'd set the alarm and hurried back down to the cellar, picking up his trainers on the way. He'd waited. The timer on the alarm had silently counted down and re-armed the house. The open cellar-door had told the system something was amiss, that the contact was broken. The alarm had begun to wail in discordant waves, shredding the frosty night air. He'd watched both men at the foot of the steps for any reaction to the noise, but they'd lain still. He'd gone through the back yard and into the ginnel, where he'd picked up a rock and hurled it at one of David's upper windows, smashing it. Spiller had needed the cops to show up quickly, and while his neighbour might have ignored an alarm, he wouldn't have dismissed glass all over his bedroom floor. It had taken just five seconds for a light to illuminate. Spiller had run, tossing the plastic bag in a wheelie bin three streets away, before slowing to a walk he'd tainted with a phony weave of inebriety whenever a vehicle passed by.

Spiller knew he'd taken a risk and it may have monumentally backfired. He hoped Madden had just been vague in her message, or perhaps he'd misheard, but he felt a twisted dread in his stomach that arsonist *singular* was right. One of them had snuck away. Which one, though? He'd anticipated the certain fact they'd say he was there, but he'd really believed they'd both been caught as he'd had to duck into a garden within three minutes of leaving the scene as a police van had sped past, blues flashing. He'd not expected either would have come round in that time. Unless... one of them had been faking. Shit—because he was positive the thumbless one didn't have a clue from the moment his head hit the floor.

He cursed his flawed thinking. It would have been the easiest thing in the world to set them on fire. Possibly the right thing, given their intentions. But Spiller hadn't wanted the scrutiny that two more deaths would bring, especially when they'd have been irrefutably tied to his house. Leaving them alive, he'd avoided the accusation of motive because, while people did sometimes fall downstairs, they usually didn't spontaneously combust, even with petrol and matches on their person. Would the cops have believed in a rogue spark theory? Doubtful. And... it was the family home. It was the place where he'd watched Sammy and Soph grow up, where he'd shared a life with Helen. He couldn't burn it all down, make his girls homeless. How would they get another mortgage with him on a pittance and Helen now out of work? And that was assuming the insurance ignored the stench of a barbecued rat and paid out.

So he had decided on the sensible option.

And Helen would have fucking murdered him for it.

AFTER HIS SHOWER, Spiller threw last night's clothes into a full bath of hot water and tipped in all the complimentary sachets and mini-bottles he could find. After grabbing a couple of hours' sleep and clothed in a fresh outfit that didn't whiff of petrol, he headed to the police station to meet DCI Bartoli. Helen said she'd take the girls out for something to eat.

Bartoli reminded Spiller of an ageing Mafioso, right down to the accent. His silver hair was slicked back, not a strand out of place. As Spiller was buzzed through from the front counter, Bartoli extended his hand with a hearty smile.

'Good of you to come in, Mr Spiller. Can I call you Matthew?'

Spiller shook Bartoli's hand, and his knuckles were fairly crushed by the grip. 'Sure.'

DS Madden was waiting further down the corridor, next to an open door.

'Please, this way,' Bartoli said.

'Where in New York are you from?' Spiller asked as they walked.

'Bayside. You know the city?'

'Not really. I visited once. What brought you here?'

'Exchange program ten years back. Cop-swap, you might call it. I came to see how you folk maintain order without guns—'

'We don't,' Spiller interrupted.

'Ha! So, I met my wife here and the rest, as they say...'

They reached the room. Spiller shook the hand of DS Madden, and they all went inside. It was a "soft" interview room and Spiller felt reassured they hadn't felt the need to haul him down some stairs to the business area of the station. It reminded him of the hospital relatives' room where he had twice received news of his parents' passing. A plug-in diffuser was open too wide, giving off a sickly-sweet aroma. Above the frosted glass that obscured the lower half of the windows, Spiller could see the room faced an internal courtyard where police vehicles were parked.

'Take a seat, Matthew,' Bartoli said, indicating a boxy, blue fabric chair. 'Just so you know, you're not under caution and you're free to leave anytime. I just need to straighten a few things out in my mind.' He and Madden settled opposite Spiller in identical chairs. A bright bar of sunlight lay diagonally across the room, but came and went with the passing clouds.

Madden smiled at him. 'How's your wife taking all of this, Matthew?'

'Shocked, obviously, but… well, we're both just happy we weren't home last night.'

'Yeah, I bet,' Bartoli said, 'Although, if you're gonna have someone break into your home, you'd want him to be a frickin' moron like last night, huh?'

Spiller smiled obligingly.

'DS Madden apprised you of the situation over the phone, yes?'

Spiller looked at Madden. 'Vaguely. Someone tried to burn our house down.'

'In a nutshell,' Bartoli said.

'So, what's he saying?'

'Nada.'

'Oh. DS Madden said things had gone wrong for him, so I was assuming you'd caught him. He's going *no comment*, is he?'

'In the most convincing fashion. He's dead.'

Spiller felt his face go slack. 'Hey?'

Madden spoke: 'Apparently, he fell down your cellar steps before he could set light to anything. The post-mortem will tell us more.'

'Wow,' said Spiller. 'Any idea who he is? He's got to be linked to Ward's gang. I told you Dominic Ward had threatened us.'

As Bartoli mulled how much information to disclose, Spiller prayed he'd say the dead man *was* Dominic Ward.

'He's known to us,' Bartoli said. 'He has priors.'

Priors. So, not Dominic Ward.

Bartoli rose and proceeded to pour himself a cup of black coffee. 'Detective Sergeant?'

'I'm fine, sir, thanks.'

'Matthew?'

Spiller shook his head.

Bartoli stood in the bar of sunlight, interrupting its route across the room. He sipped his drink.

'So…' Spiller prompted.

'Yeah, so… the dead man… no thumbs. Christmas Eve. An attack. Two youths. Four… what would you call it? *Thumbectomies?* Hacked off by a mystery assailant in a Santa suit. Who drove a powerful car. According to their statements. Loud tail-pipes.'

'Santa was serious about his Naughty List this year,' Spiller said.

Bartoli grinned. 'It could be. I'm sure that's it. So, back to last night—and this is what I need to clear up—it looks like he entered your property with two canisters of gasoline—petrol, sorry—and as he was heading up to your kitchen, he missed his footing and fell backward. Meantime, your security system is going nuts, so your neighbour calls the cops.'

Spiller nodded. 'Okay. Pretty bloody inept, but what's your concern?'

Bartoli resumed his seat. 'Your neighbour dialled 999 because someone hurled a rock through his bedroom window. And that doesn't make any sense to me. Unless the arsonist threw the rock before he entered your property, but why would he do that?'

Spiller shrugged. Bartoli's attitude was really starting to grate. 'No idea. Tell me… you didn't used to drive an ice cream van, did you? Bartoli Ices, no? That not you?'

Bartoli let his heavily hooded eyelids droop in contempt. 'Your basement door was unlocked—no forced entry.'

'One of us obviously forgot to lock it. Not a huge mystery. Was that all? I'm free to go, right?'

'Of course,' Bartoli said. 'Would you like to go?'

Spiller stood up. 'You need to charge Dominic Ward.'

Bartoli looked quizzically at Madden. 'Do we need to do that, Detective Sergeant? In the absence of any evidence?'

Madden didn't respond to what may or may not have been a rhetorical question, but Spiller sensed she felt sorry for him. She rose and opened the door to the corridor.

'Sit down, Matthew,' Bartoli said. 'We need to have a chat about Callum Ward.'

Before Madden could close the door again, a suited figure passed by in the corridor, limping badly, moving very slowly, supported by a stick. He glanced in and nodded to Bartoli.

'Hi, Angelo,' Dominic Ward said.

'Dom,' Bartoli said.

'Christ, he's right here!' Spiller said. 'He's in your police station. Someone have a word with him, for fuck's sake!'

Madden moved to block Spiller's exit from the room as Ward hobbled out of sight towards the door that led to the public enquiries desk.

'We have,' Bartoli said. 'That's why he's here. He denies making any threats.'

'Oh, well, your job's done then, isn't it? You asked. He said no. Case closed. It's not like he's a mate or anything, is it, *Angelo?*' Spiller gave them both a withering look.

Bartoli closed the door. 'Mr Spiller, I strongly resent your insinuation.'

Madden intervened. 'We know a lot of the briefs who come in here, Matthew.'

'Jesus, doesn't it bother you that my daughter was tortured by Callum Ward or that someone just tried to toast us in our sleep *immediately after* Dominic Ward threatened us? Nah, let's not bother with such trivialities, eh? Let's instead focus on who did society a favour by topping a nasty drug-dealing bastard.'

'Yes, let's talk about that, shall we?' Bartoli said placidly. 'Although I can't recall explicitly stating he'd been murdered. Maybe I did. Maybe you just made an assumption. Anyway, tell me about the night Callum Ward died.'

'Tell me what night he died and I will.'

'Let's assume it was the night he attended your house as a dinner guest.'

'Well, my wife's not much of a cook but he survived the spag bol and left.'

Bartoli smiled at the joke.

'You know all this already,' Spiller said. 'DS Madden took a statement.'

'Call me an old cynic, but I tend to not automatically believe the things people tell me.'

'And the evidence of your own eyes? If you've checked the neighbours' CCTV, you'll know full well he left. I know you spoke to my neighbour David. He saw Ward leave, for God's sake.'

'He saw *someone* leave.'

Spiller didn't respond.

'You say Callum Ward ate with you, then left. Data from his vehicle's tracker has him at your house for around an hour, yet Dominic Ward asserts you say his brother left after only fifteen minutes.'

'I never said that. He was with us for an hour. We ate, we argued, he left. The tracker confirms it, so does our neighbour.' Spiller looked at Madden. 'Any chance you could get a patrol car to watch my house for a few days? Can you people at least do that for me? So no one else tries to destroy it.'

'I'll speak to uniform,' Madden said.

'Matthew...' Bartoli sighed '...why did you call my detectives to your house to report Dominic Ward's alleged threats against your family but *not* to report the injuries his brother had apparently inflicted on your daughter, Samantha?'

Spiller kept quiet. Words had failed him. Here was the challenge he'd feared from Madden and Goodrick, only now it was directed at him by a seasoned pro, and the missing person it *had* related to was now a body in the mortuary, constipated by hardened foam.

'Matthew?'

'Am I free to go?'

'One more thing. Did you drive here?'

'Yes.'

'Where are you parked?'

'One of the bays, couple of streets away.'

Bartoli extended an open palm. 'Okay, I'll find it.'

'What?'

'Keys. I'm impounding your vehicle.'

'On what grounds?'

'Officially, it's a murder enquiry. Unofficially, I'm pissed off with you.'

Spiller looked at Madden. 'Can he do that?'

She nodded. 'PACE, Section Nineteen, general powers of seizure.'

'Shit. Well, can I get something out of the boot first? It's only a couple of kilos.'

'Ha! You should do stand-up,' Bartoli said, not unamused. 'And no.'

'Son of a bitch,' Spiller muttered as he dug in his pocket for his keys and handed them over. 'Now can I go?'

Madden looked to her boss, who gave a slight nod. She opened the door for him.

BY THE TIME Spiller reached the pavement, Ward was out of sight. He glanced left and right. Then he heard the familiar burble of a quad exhaust and he ran towards the sound. He rounded the corner in time to see the four-door Maserati nosing out of a parallel bay onto the street. He moved briskly in front of the car to halt its progress. Two uniformed officers on their way to the station slowed their walk to monitor the situation, but Ward reversed back and killed the engine. With difficulty, he got out and beamed at Spiller.

'Hello, Matthew!' he said cheerily.

Spiller played along to get the officers to move along. 'Demonic! How the devil are you?'

'Good, good,' Ward said, and they shook hands, which was sufficient for the officers to regain their pace and turn the corner.

Spiller crunched the hand in his grasp. 'You don't *look* too good,' he said, still maintaining his smile for appearance's sake. Ward's left temple was bulbous, his eye bruised and nearly closed from the kick Spiller had delivered.

'Let go before I beat you with my stick,' Ward said.

'If the end of that stick leaves the ground, it's going straight up your arse, mate.'

Ward left it where it was and Spiller let go of his hand.

'How did you explain all this?' Spiller asked, referring to his injuries.

'I said I got blind drunk when I heard about my brother and fell down the stairs.'

'Keeping it close to the truth, then.'

'What were you doing last night, Matthew? A little bird tells me you all moved out to a hotel, so what were you doing back at your house at that time? Forgot something, did you? From the other night with my brother?'

'Why are you so concerned? He was a wanker who hurt people.'

'I agree. But that's what the law's for: to deal with people like my brother. You should have called the police.'

'Says the guy who just tried to barbecue four people.'

'You took the gloves off, Matthew, not me. You set the tone.'

'Fuck you. I'd never hurt innocent kids.'

Ward leaned arrogantly on his stick and smiled. 'You should have dropped the match. Fatal error.'

'Don't I know it, but I'm not done with you. I wanted to let the police deal with you last night. You'd have been bang-to-rights, all drenched in petrol like that. You'd have been disbarred, you'd have gone to prison, had your arse destroyed on a daily basis. I liked that idea far more than burning my own house down, even with you in it.'

'Such a shame the only other person who can place me at the scene expired,' Ward said, and smirked.

But Spiller saw more in that expression than the gratitude for a lucky break. 'You...'

Ward raised a hand to his face, placing his palm across his mouth like he was about to cough, but then used his thumb and forefinger to squeeze his nostrils closed, before removing his hand and releasing a cough that turned into a laugh.

Spiller knew what it meant. 'Really? Two peas in a pod, you and your late brother, eh?'

'Unfortunately for you.'

'But I suppose you did me a favour. It's just you I have to deal with now. Because I can't have you walking around—not after last night.'

'Likewise,' Ward said.

Spiller seethed at his adversary's flippancy. He waited for a pedestrian to pass, then swept his foot in an arc to catch the base of Ward's wooden support. He immediately turned and walked away, hearing the thump of a face hitting a car wing, and a yelp. He carried on, turned the corner back towards the entrance to the station. He had a bone to pick.

As he marched up to the door, he was met with a familiar face leaving the station.

'Mr Spiller,' the uniformed Enright said formally. He subtly caught Spiller's sleeve and spun him. 'DC Goodrick told me you were coming in. Walk with me.'

As he was now facing the same direction as Enright, Spiller obliged, and walked alongside him.

'I'm not a hundred percent on what's happening,' Enright said, striding away from the building, 'but I know there have been some developments. Last night? Your house?'

'Uh-huh.'

'So, what are you doing confronting Dominic Ward outside the police station? I saw you from the rec room. I might not have been the only one. You have to be careful.'

'He was there last night,' Spiller said.

Enright stopped. '*What?* At your house? Christ alive...' Then it dawned. '*You* were there?'

'Someone in there is telling him stuff. About the case. He knows we're at a hotel.'

'Walk,' Enright said. 'It's pertinent, Matthew—that you're so convinced he means you harm you moved out of your home. They'll have told him that. Bloody hell, don't get all paranoid. This isn't some big conspiracy. They won't have said *which* hotel.'

They soon turned onto the high street, and Enright's presence carved a straight line through the shoppers. Spiller hauled his posture ram-rod straight and strode like he was a plain-clothed cop.

'Why did you go back to your house?' Enright asked.

'I just needed something.'

'Like what?'

In a gap between pedestrians, Spiller said, 'God, I am in so much shit. I should have torched them both last night. I had the chance. I'll have the whole bloody lot of them after us now.'

'Send your family somewhere safe. Another city. Or, better still, put them on a plane.'

'For how long?' Spiller asked desperately. 'Until the Ward clan all die of old age?'

'Get them away from here and we'll figure it out. Call my burner.' With that, Enright veered off down a side street.

Spiller stuttered to a halt like his batteries had suddenly expired. He looked to the edifice next to him: a pub. He'd never been one to think troubles were solved by booze, but an hour or so nursing a pint alone in the corner of a pub lured him like a remission from a deadly disease, so he went inside.

Standing at the crowded bar with a fresh pint, he realised he didn't need any time to mull things over. He knew his next move. It had been lurking, straining to be released, like a rock in a catapult. Now he let it fly and off it went, hurtling towards the front door of a townhouse in Ameley Green.

Spiller abandoned his full pint and left the pub.

Chapter Ten

SPILLER DIDN'T WANT to tell Helen he'd lost his car. It sounded a bit careless. It also denied the only remaining breadwinner in the family the means to earn a crust. He could always rent a taxi, but they weren't generally very nice, and whether he'd even have the time or inclination to work over the next few days or weeks was debatable. Besides which, recent events had made him question a lot about his life, especially the *temporary* job he'd taken years before. He'd spoken to a lot of drivers who'd only taken the job as a transitory measure after a redundancy and were now decades in. He felt he needed to break the cycle, and perhaps this was the moment to do that.

He got online and booked himself a hire car. It was a one-litre petrol Ford Fiesta, in black, cloth seats, alloys. Bit boring, but it was new and clean and didn't have council plates front and back. An hour later, he was picking it up from a city centre depot, and soon after was heading towards Ameley Green. Weather-wise, the day had turned out pleasant. Not just sunny, but warm, like spring had shouldered winter aside for a few hours.

Spiller had thought he'd need to drop a note through Emma's letterbox, but her BMW was on the drive. Parked across from her house, on the other side of the central green-space, he now wasn't sure how best to make contact. With what he was about to suggest, the less direct communication, the better. That meant no knocking on the front door and no phone calls. But as he wasn't telepathic and he was in a desperate rush, he got out, walked around the pavement, and knocked on her front door.

The apparition that appeared a minute later bore scant resemblance to the young woman he'd last seen only a few days prior. He'd never seen someone look so ill and still be upright. She was in an old baggy jogging suit, her hair unkempt, face drawn and pale and lacking any trace of make-up. He momentarily wondered if she might have mascara smudged beneath her eyes, but realised they were just exhausted.

'Jesus, you look awful,' he said.

'Fuck you,' she said, and shut the door on him.

He knelt down and spoke through the letter box: 'I'll do what you want.' Then he stood up and waited. He could see through the frosted glass that she had stopped moving, his words having halted her shuffle away from him. She stayed like that for fifteen seconds, then slowly half-turned so she could reach the door handle. The door opened slightly.

'Emma?'

But she had ambled away into the front room, where he heard her dump herself into a chair with a painful exclamation. He stepped inside, shut the door behind him, and followed her into the room.

The living room echoed her kitchen, all clean lines, fresh paint, simple yet expensive furniture. Emma reached for a mug of something that was steaming on a table beside her cream leather armchair. Still unbidden, Spiller sat down on a matching sofa.

'What's wrong?' he asked.

'Just ill. Flu or something. Or nothing. Stress. I get like this at times. Psychosomatic.'

He didn't need to ask the cause.

'So you'll do it,' she said, staring into the yellow liquid.

Spiller nodded. 'If you still want me to.'

'I couldn't do it. I tried. He drinks in a local pub every night. I waited outside.' She shrugged.

'With the gun? You do have a gun, right?'

'Yep. He walked straight by me, didn't remember me from court. Just went on his way. And I… I couldn't do it. Next day I woke up like this. I've been waiting two years. Then I couldn't follow through, so everything went to shit inside me.'

'Two years?'

'Of a four-year sentence. For killing my sister.' She looked directly at him for the first time. 'Why the change of heart?'

'I need the money. It's complicated.'

'And why should I trust you?'

'Well, that's your call, isn't it? You asked me, remember? I didn't volunteer. If you can't trust me, forget it.'

'No, I just... I don't know anything about you. You could be a fraud. Some saddo who tells people war stories when he's never been near a gun.'

Spiller pulled his mobile phone from his inside pocket. He opened the gallery and swiped through to a series of shots, then went over to her, perching on the arm of her chair. He held the phone and showed her. Half a dozen photos of him in the desert, armed and in uniform, various grim backdrops, some on his own, some with buddies.

'Okay,' she said. 'Good CV.'

He closed the app.

'Go upstairs to my bedroom. Under my bed. There's a hard case. Bring it down to me, please.'

Spiller guessed what was in the case. He went upstairs, found her bedroom, found the case, brought it back down, handed it over, but she pushed it back at him.

'You can use that,' Emma said. 'If you want. Or you may have other ideas.'

He unzipped the case to reveal a Sig-Sauer P238 micro-compact, .380 auto calibre.

'Bloody hell, this isn't your usual black-market weapon. Where the hell did you get this?'

'A friend.'

'Who knew your intentions?'

She shook her head slightly. 'This was a couple of years ago. He's just very protective.'

Spiller snorted. 'Not really. You get caught with this, you're going to prison—that's nailed on. Whoever it is put you in serious danger.'

'Well, not any more. Take it, use it—or don't—but dump it when you're done.'

He sat down with it. He dropped the mag, thumbed out six rounds into the open case on the coffee table, then expertly field-stripped the weapon to show her he knew his stuff. He reassembled it, worked the slide a few times, reloaded the mag, and clicked it home.

'Seems fine. I was wondering if it might be deactivated, but it's live.'

'Will you use it?' she asked.

'Not sure. Tell me what you know about the target.'

She heaved a sick and weary sigh. 'His name's Jeffrey Poole…'

Spiller listened as she proceeded to brief him. Poole still had a Facebook page, redundant going on two years, but plenty of photos for a positive ID. Then he heard the reason for her unabated ire, and he understood why she viewed Poole's debt as only negligibly paid. And he wondered again how he'd managed to refrain from dropping a match on Dominic Ward. He'd have lost the house, but the score would have been settled, a major problem erased. Perhaps he was more peaceable than he thought. Next to Emma, whose homicidal hatred had not been diminished by two years, he was Mother Teresa.

'The money,' he said when she stopped talking.

'I said fifty thousand.'

He nodded.

'I can't do fifty thousand.'

'You need to. Or this doesn't get done.'

'I could do twenty. Ten now, ten after.'

'No way,' Spiller said. 'The risk is bigger than twenty. Fifty or I'm walking.'

'Okay,' she said quickly.

He squinted doubtfully. 'You can *get* fifty, yes?'

Emma didn't reply, just pushed herself out of the chair and ambled like a geriatric from the room. He listened to her painful progress up the stairs. She returned a few minutes later with a weighty Waitrose plastic bag and handed it to him.

'That's twenty grand. It's all I have in the house.'

'All you have in the house?' Spiller said, bemused. 'That's more than most people have in the bank.'

Emma flopped back into her chair, panting from the effort of mere ambulation. 'Well…'

Spiller pulled apart the plastic handles and peeked inside at the rubber-band-bundled notes. 'The other thirty when it's done, right?'

'When I have absolute proof.'

He nodded, his attention returning to the contents of the bag. It was fascinating. How easy it had been—perhaps because she was so ill. He zipped up the gun case and added it to the bag, folding over the excess plastic to halve its size.

'You better do this,' she said.

'I will.'

'I mean it. I've asked you to kill Poole. Don't think I won't ask someone to kill you.'

Spiller smiled. 'They'd have to get in line.' He stood up. 'And you'd have to shake that money tree you obviously have in your back garden.'

'Remember, I have some serious shit on you,' she said, giving him a waggling double thumbs-up, as though a visual reminder was necessary.

'I think we have shit on each other after today, don't you?' He moved to the doorway and stopped. 'You get well, Emma.'

'I'm trying. Time-frame?'

'Soon.'

SPILLER DROVE STRAIGHT to the storage locker he rented jointly with his taxi mate, Gibbo. It had been Gibbo's locker originally, used to store far too many electrical items for Spiller to think they were legit. Laptops, mobile phones, headphones, related goods, all boxed up, plus piles of expensive trainers. Spiller had needed some space after moving his belongings out of the family home to his cramped flat, and Gibbo had been low on merchandise at the time, so had some square metres available. Spiller bunged him a few quid every week to contribute, but the direct debit was in Gibbo's name, so it was the safest spot to hide the Sig. Whether he would fess up to the weapon should the police launch a raid on Gibbo's Dark Argos was a question that niggled slightly, but was best not answered. His moral compass was already spinning like it was in a magnet factory.

The fact that the storage building resembled a prison, with its bright corridors and locked blue doors, wasn't lost on him.

Spiller let himself into the unit and unstacked his corner, taking boxes down and pushing them out into the corridor. At the back was a box of clothes he hadn't worn in years and maybe never would. He pulled the cardboard flaps apart and pushed the bag of cash and hardware deep down through the musty items. There was a temptation to keep hold of the gun to protect his family but, with the eyes of the police already on him, the possibility of being caught with it during a Ward-related search was too risky.

As he was leaving, after piling his boxes back up, he spied a rather natty pair of Reeboks and made a mental note to ask Gibbo how much he'd want for them.

BACK AT THEIR hotel room, Spiller found Helen and the girls sitting on the double bed with their bags packed at their feet. Sammy was playing a game on her mobile phone while Sophie watched. Sophie glanced up and briefly greeted him before returning to more important matters. Sammy stared at her father and absently handed the phone to her little sister, who took over. An agitated Helen was spinning a ring on her third finger, but Spiller saw it wasn't the gold band he'd slid on there all those years ago. He gave a nod in the direction of the corridor, and both Helen and Sammy stood up, which made him hesitate.

'It's a bit late to start sugar-coating shit, Dad,' Sammy said. 'Mum told me.'

'Told you what?' Sophie asked.

'It's okay, sweetheart,' Helen said. 'Nothing that concerns you.'

'That sounds horrible,' Sophie said.

They all looked at her, puzzled.

'Shit with sugar on it.'

'Soph!' Spiller said. 'Language.'

'She said it!' Sophie cast an accusatory eye at her sister before returning to her game.

The three of them filed out into the corridor and closed the door.

Spiller spelled it out: 'The guy who tried to burn down the house is dead. He fell and cracked his head.'

'That's a good start to a poem,' Sammy noted.

'Sammy, this isn't funny,' Helen said.

'Oh, I'm sorry. Would someone like to tell me how I'm meant to react to all this? Please, I mean it. What's the proper reaction? Murder, arson, what are the rules?'

'Keep your voice down,' Spiller said in a harsh whisper, then was struck by a thought. 'Anyway, why the hell are the bags packed? This isn't over.'

'The girls need their education,' Helen said. 'They need a normal life. We can't live like we're in witness protection. I'm not having some lowlifes dictate how we live.'

'They don't want to dictate how we live, Helen; they want to dictate how we die. That person last night didn't know we weren't there. Dominic Ward's still calling the shots, so that's not the end of it.'

'I want to go home,' Helen said.

'And if he comes knocking? With some mates?'

'We invite them in for some spag bol.'

'Oh, good plan. You start frying off some onions while I nip down to B&Q for a trade pack of expanding foam, eh?'

'Crap. I can't listen to this,' Sammy said. 'This is *insane!*' She pushed back into the room and tried to slam the door, but the slow-close hinge wouldn't allow it. She growled into a scream and barged against the door with her back until it shut.

'I want to go home,' Helen repeated. 'I'm *going* home.'

'That's utterly reckless; it's not just you, it's the girls. They could have died last night. We all could have.'

'Then do something about it, Matt. Grow a pair. Sort out Dominic Ward.'

Spiller weighed her meaning. 'Sort out.'

'Do. It. Yourself.'

'Yeah, that's what I thought you meant.'

'Think of the Ward brothers as a Gorgon, Matt. I got one head, you get the other, then it's done.'

'Fairly sure the Gorgon had three heads.'

'Well, this one doesn't. That's my point. One more and it all dies. The rest of the gang won't give a crap. Someone will take over who's not personally involved and won't care that the gang needs a name-change. They'll probably be glad. More for them.'

Spiller thought of the hit he'd promised Emma. 'My diary's pretty full on that front, dear.'

Helen didn't understand and made a dismissive face. 'Oh, just do it, Matt.'

'I can get some money,' he said quickly. 'I've *got* some money. And I'm going to get some more. We just need to get away. To the sun. Like we always said we would. Start afresh.'

'*We?*'

'As a family. I'm better in the sun, you know I am.'

'Everyone's better in the sun, Matt. It's warm. Who doesn't like a holiday? Come on…'

'I don't mean that. I mean, when I was abroad I felt different. Shit just lifted.'

'Because you loved the job.'

'It's more. My head clears. The darkness… just goes. Helen, can we at least try? As a family? Go somewhere sunny. We can rent for a while, see how we feel. If we don't love it we just come back.'

'And if I don't love you?' she asked.

'You do—you said. What? Are you saying you don't?'

She appeared to debate, then shook her head. 'I can't have this conversation right now. This is not a time for hearts and flowers. I can't even think beyond the end of today. I just want to go home, Matt. And I want you to make it safe for us to do that. Understand?' She pushed past him and disappeared back into the room.

Chapter Eleven

SPILLER HAD A plan. He'd had lots of plans over his lifetime and several hadn't, if he was honest, gone entirely according to plan. Still, it wasn't how many times a man was knocked down; it was how many times he got back up. He'd read that somewhere, most likely in a psychology-of-achievement book. It made sense. Everything in those books made sense. But he'd realised it was mostly crap. He'd read a bunch of them when he was younger, by a long line of charlatans from Napoleon Hill onwards. All that *conceive, believe, achieve* bullshit that set its naïve believers on the road to crushing disappointment. *What the mind of man can conceive of, and believe in, it can achieve.* Oh, Mr Hill, nicely played, you made a fortune with that one line. Of course some people made it. But they were the lucky ones. Right place, right time. Then they went on to write books about how they conceived, believed and achieved, and it worked for them, so it must be a *duh duh duuuuuh*... Universal Law. But what about the thousands who conceived and believed and didn't achieve? Did they fail because they didn't believe hard enough, didn't try hard enough? That was a bitter pill, and it had taken Spiller years to sick it back up and realise the truth. How many people in the world were *genuinely* suffering? Bombs falling on their heads; dying of malnutrition; swept away in floods. Didn't they desire to get out of their mess a damn sight more than some silly first-world wannabe craved a slice of fame and fortune? So, what did this so-called universal law say about them? That they were too weak-minded to kick their plans into motion? That was cruel, and not a little racist. It wasn't universal if it only covered the developed world and mostly white people.

Still, one saying he did agree with was that people who failed to plan planned to fail. A man had to have a plan. And Spiller's was to rustle up as much cash as possible and literally dump it in front of Helen as a *fait accompli*. She couldn't deny the plausibility of an escape to the sun when the means to its attainment was right there in front of her. Could she?

Spiller had reluctantly driven his family back home and settled them in before heading off to the storage unit. Sophie, who knew little about cars, had been impressed with Dad's new one; Helen and Sammy less so, considering where his old one was. Frankly, he was pissed off with Helen, and during the journey to the unit, he'd realised he wasn't even sure he really *wanted* to jet off with her anywhere, hot or not. She seemed to have a screw loose. Perhaps it had always been, bobbling about in its allotted spot just waiting for a jolt to bump it right out. Or maybe the enormity of Ward's cruelty to their daughter had simply blown a previously secure fixing from its hole, ripping off the thread that held it in place. He didn't know. People puzzled him, and age hadn't helped. He was no more able to understand people now than when he was ten.

But Helen had taken the responsibility for their daughters' safety into her own hands, so he decided she could bloody well take something else into her own hands. This whole situation wasn't his fault. She'd killed Callum Ward, not him.

Inside the storage locker, he dug out the Sig-Sauer and put it in his pocket. It was compact enough not to appear too bulky in the outline of his coat. He also grabbed the trainers he liked, as he needed to visit Gibbo anyway as part of the plan.

BEFORE HEADING TO Gibbo's, Spiller swung by the house. He found the girls in the front room watching a *Spiderman* movie, like they didn't have a care in the world. Sammy pointed to the carpet when Spiller asked where her mum was.

In the cellar, Helen was mopping the stone floor. The petrol had evaporated, but its stench was fiercely present. The cellar door was open to air the place out. She had lined up a bunch of cleaning products for later; colourful containers with spray nozzles, although Spiller doubted their combined contents would make much impact on the pungent atmosphere. She saw him descending the steps but carried on with the ablutions. He waited for a few seconds on the last step, but she seemed to have no intention of pausing her work.

'Oi!' he said.

She stopped, looked at him. 'What?'

'How serious are you about defending your family? This house?'

'Deadly. What a stupid question. Have I not shown that already? Jesus…' She started to mop again.

Spiller checked back up the steps to make sure one of the girls wasn't hovering at the kitchen doorway, then took out the pistol. Helen briefly glanced at it, made a scoffing sound, and carried on mopping.

'Helen…'

She stopped again. 'What?'

'I need to go somewhere tonight. You need protection.'

'Whoop-de-doo. How is one of your replicas going to solve anything, Matt? Who's going to believe it's real? Then what do I do? Throw it at them? Just give me that stun-gun you had or one of your noxious sprays. I don't need a stupid toy.'

'It's not,' Spiller said, checking over his shoulder again.

She looked at the weapon for several seconds. 'That's real? It's tiny.'

'It's a micro-compact. Three-eighty calibre. It's like a nine mil only shorter, less powerful. But still perfectly lethal.'

Helen looked at him, lowered her voice. 'You have a real gun? Matt, what the hell? Where did you get it from?'

'Doesn't matter. But if you're going to stay in this house with Dominic Ward still on the warpath, this stays within easy reach. But not so the girls can find it.'

'Oh, right, I was going to leave it in Sophie's toy box.'

'Helen, you either deal with this or we go back to the hotel. I'd prefer the latter, but you're being so damn stubborn I didn't know what else to do. Are you prepared to use this if you have to?'

'Yes.'

He stared at her. 'Shit, I don't want you to have it. I want you to go back to the hotel.'

Helen approached and gently took it off him. She reverently turned the carbon-steel pistol over in her hands, and Spiller saw a glint in her eyes and possibly the slightest smirk trying to tug at the corners of her mouth. Yup, screw-gone.

'So dinky,' she said. 'I just pull the trigger, right?'

He took it back from her and dropped the mag out. He intended to give her so much spiel that she'd get scared and overwhelmed and want nothing to do with it.

'It's single action, meaning you can't just pull the trigger on the first shot. You need to pull the slide back to cock it before you can fire it, but after the first shot you just keep on pulling the trigger as the slide automatically blows backwards on firing, ejects the shell casing, and rams forward again, loading the next round until the gun's empty. This latch locks the slide open when there are no more rounds left in the gun. Don't, whatever you do, pull the slide then try to de-cock it. If you fumble and the hammer drops, it'll go off. This is the safety. People often carry them cocked and locked, but it's too risky for your purposes. You only pull the slide back if you fully intend to use it. If you do, the gun will be ready to shoot and extremely dangerous. If you then find you don't need to fire it, because, I don't know, the person's run away, don't try to de-cock it like you see people do on TV. Press this button to drop the mag, then remember to pull the slide back to flip out the round that's already chambered. Only then should you de-cock it—when it's completely empty.'

She nodded keenly, like a job applicant being shown a tricky bit of equipment. 'Okay, got it. How many bullets do I have?'

Spiller's regret at showing her the gun was epic. 'Six. Shit, Helen, you really want this? If you're caught with this, you'll get a mandatory five years *minimum*. And that's if you didn't shoot anyone. And, believe me, I'll deny I ever saw it.'

Unfazed, she put her hand out. 'So gallant. Give.'

He handed it over.

'So, where are you going tonight?' she asked. 'Are you off to kill Dominic Ward?'

'No, someone else.'

She sham-smiled. 'You're a hoot.'

'Aren't I?'

'Well, the sooner you sort him out, the sooner you can take this back from me.'

'I know. Anyway, you won't need it. The police should be checking on the house; I asked if they would. Shit, Helen, can you *please* just take the kids and go back to the hotel? This whole situation is crazy. You shouldn't have a gun. You're not a gangster.'

'But I have killed one,' she said quietly. 'Our world changed that night. For the moment, this is the new normal. Was there anything else?'

SPILLER LIKED GIBBO. He was nearly twenty years younger, but he reminded Spiller of himself in his mid-twenties. More accurately, Gibbo was the genuinely happy-go-lucky chap Spiller had always aspired to be, but never had been. He'd always felt chirpier in Gibbo's presence, like the young man was a guru of the art of what-the-fuck, and Spiller could never absorb enough of that joyous outlook. Because he couldn't; he was pretty much impervious to joy. He could identify when it was happening—like in the presence of his daughters—but it only really clung to the surface, never quite managing to sink in.

Like Spiller, Gibbo favoured nights. He preferred the buzz of pub pick-ups to the tedium of long, slow crawls through daytime traffic so some geriatric could raid Asda's stock of Werther's Originals. He also said he got a lot of sex working nights. Spiller doubted he earned very much at times.

Spiller left his car outside his flat and walked to Gibbo's. It wasn't far. Gibbo lived at his parents' house, with the excellent bonus that they were never there. They'd gone to Florida some years back and had seemingly never had the heart to kick their only son out of their UK home so they could sell it. In reality, it was a small terraced house, but the area was such that estate agents called them mews properties and asked for silly money, which they got. Spiller thought it odd how a ten-minute walk could bump up house prices that much. Snobbery came with a hefty premium.

Gibbo's Lexus ES 300h was on the short driveway. The satin silver car was a year old, and it was by far the best vehicle the cab firm had on its books—unless you liked vulgar, souped-up cars like the Audi. The boot of the Lexus took up half the pavement because of the piddly frontage. Some of the residents had commandeered these areas for their vehicles as "off-road parking".

It took a few minutes for Gibbo to answer the door. He was wearing only boxers, which probably meant someone else inside wasn't wearing anything.

'All right, buddy?' Gibbo asked with a big grin, before answering his own question. 'Course you're not, you miserable fucker. Come in.'

Spiller stepped inside and followed his mate into the front room. Gibbo's parents would have wept at the state of their old house. It wasn't wrecked or particularly dirty; it was just so bloody untidy.

'Take a seat,' Gibbo said.

Spiller tried to spot somewhere to sit, so Gibbo helped by pushing a load of papers and files off the sofa onto the carpet.

'Just doing my taxes,' Gibbo explained. 'Arseholes fined me a ton last year.'

'You were doing them last time I popped in.'

'Was I?'

Spiller nodded, settling on a bare patch of cushion. 'That was in August.'

'Yeah? Well, what can I say? They bore me. Coffee?'

'I'm fine, I need to ask you a favour.'

'Sure.' Gibbo sat on the arm of a leather wingback chair.

'Could you put some clothes on, mate? My eyes are level with your tackle.'

'Is that the favour?'

'No.'

Gibbo shook his head. 'No. I'd only have to take 'em off again when you leave.'

Right on cue, a young lady entered the room in nothing but an oversized vest, which hung low showing cleavage and gaped wide, showing side-boob.

'Your accountant, I presume,' Spiller said quietly to his mate.

'Hello,' she said to Spiller, then turned to Gibbo. 'Any bread? I fancy some toast.'

'Help yourself.' Gibbo indicated the kitchen. 'Sorry, buddy, this is... uh...' he began, and clearly wished he hadn't.

The young lady offered her hand to Spiller. 'I'm his eleven-thirty from The Plough.'

'Fine pub,' Spiller said, trying not to think of the last thing her palm had grasped. As she headed into the kitchen, Spiller looked at Gibbo with a wry and approving smirk.

'Shoot—what can I do for you?' Gibbo said.

'I need to borrow your car.'

'Do what? Jeremy Clarkson wants to drive a hybrid car?'

'Of course I don't. I don't *want* to drive a hybrid car. Mine's out of commission. Jesus, do I want to drive a hybrid car...'

'I gotta say, you're not really making me want to lend it to you. Anyway, when do you need it?'

'Tonight. And maybe tomorrow. Not sure.'

'I'm working tonight, buddy.'

'No, you're not,' Spiller said, then whispered. 'You're leaving *her* just so you can go out and earn a few quid? Are you insane?'

Gibbo shrugged. 'Fair point. How much?'

'How much what?'

'How much are you going to pay me?'

Spiller thought about it. 'I'll obviously cover you putting me on the insurance, and I'll pay for my fuel.'

'Well, that's a sweet deal for you, isn't it? What about my lost earnings? I have bills to pay.'

Spiller smiled, but was now feeling quite irritated. Gibbo's banter had always been a welcome relief; right now it was exasperating. 'No, you don't. You live rent-free. And we just established you'll be going back to bed as soon as I leave.'

Gibbo cackled. 'All right, buddy, I'm just joshing. But I will ask to borrow your car at some point. You know, return the favour.'

'Well, that's not happening,' Spiller said, and laughed. 'You want to go from ten brake horsepower to three hundred? You'd kill yourself.'

The young lady padded back in with a plate of toast, which smelled very inviting to Spiller. More inviting, though, was the direction she took out of the room and back up the stairs, and the revealing flash of breast as she passed by. At that moment, Spiller thought of Emma and felt enormously jealous of Gibbo, the lucky bastard. His uncomplicated life, his easy finances, the simple sex.

Gibbo stood up, and Spiller suspected there was the beginning of an erection tenting his boxers.

'Keys are on the table, buddy,' Gibbo said quickly, heading for the door, 'under all that shit. Remember petrol, not diesel. I'll stick you on the insurance in a… later. You know… give me half an hour?'

Spiller was left alone. He heard Gibbo's steps speed up as he climbed the stairs, then the slam of a bedroom door and a whoop and what sounded like a plate hitting the floor. He briefly wondered if he was meant to sit there, listening to them bonk, awaiting official permission to drive the Lexus. Then he realised he could be there for hours, and that in all likelihood Gibbo would never get around to calling his insurer; it had taken him over five months to get going on his tax return.

So, he rooted through the detritus on the coffee table and found the keys to the Lexus. In the current scheme of things, driving uninsured ranked very low. As he headed down the hall to the front door, the young lady upstairs began to moan. Gibbo—lucky bastard. And, damn, he'd forgotten to ask about those trainers.

Chapter Twelve

THE VILLAGE OF Twilbury, where Jeffrey Poole lived, was on the very outskirts of the area Spiller would venture to when taxiing. Local clients would occasionally call from there, requesting a return journey, and the fare was worth the trek, but there was always the risk that they'd called several firms, jumping in the first cab that showed up. It was a lovely little village, settled in a geographical dip off the beaten path. Twee beyond belief, and made even more so by some leftover Christmas lights in the windows of the boutiques that lined its short and cobbled high street. A cobbled high street—that said it all. Branching out of the village were several ascending lanes lined with beautiful houses.

According to Emma, Poole's favoured haunt was a pub, The Drapers Arms, at the foot of one of these lanes, a hundred metres from the barely beating heart of the village.

Spiller drove Gibbo's Lexus along the high street. Apart from the soft pounding from the cobbles, his sub-thirty speed made the car practically silent, its electric motor offering a stealth-like quality that wasn't lost on its driver. He spotted the pub. It lacked a car park, so he pulled up a little way along the road, facing the direction he knew Poole would take to get home. As he cut the inaudible motor, it began to snow. He angled his mirror so he could see the pub's front door, and waited.

The snow reminded him of the night he'd performed what Bartoli had termed his "thumbectomies", and the night he'd driven Ward's car to the reservoir and trekked around it and up to The Fawn Buck to meet Helen. What was it with snow and nefarious activities? The thought of what he did to the youths on Christmas Eve made him uncomfortable. He'd given in that night to a part of his character he'd long tried to disown. Emma had called it a red-mist attack, but it had been far worse. He could battle a red mist. It had been a black shroud that night, and it had cloaked his better nature to the extent of a sociopathic disassociation from even the vaguest of moral codes. He didn't think he *was* a sociopath. He'd managed to refrain from cremating Dominic Ward. Surely, his desire to protect a building wouldn't have entered the equation had he been a sociopath. Right? And did sociopaths love their kids? Did they truly love anything? Or even know what love was?

Spiller soon switched the motor back on to activate the heating. He'd taken Gibbo's car to create a little evidential distance. A silver saloon taxi, mostly covered in snow? Who'd even recall the make of it? And whereas a private car idling for a while outside a pub might have drawn suspicion, a taxi wouldn't earn a second glance.

The driver's display told him it was 10.41pm. According to Emma, Poole would always leave at approximately eleven o'clock. Spiller suspected her knowledge was the result of far more than one night sitting outside the pub. He guessed, since Poole's release from prison, she'd spent many nights surveilling the place, itching to use the gun but not willing to destroy her own life in the process. Then she'd met a nutcase taxi driver. The possibility of Poole's death—and by another's hand—had become real. She'd pushed him to do it. But he wouldn't, so she'd again tried herself. And she couldn't. Which had made her ill.

Now, here he was, the plan finally in motion. She was about to hear the news she'd long awaited, and he was about to reap a handsome reward. He placed his gloved hand over the revolver in his coat pocket, felt its shape. It was only his .357 blank-firer, but it was enough for the plan to work.

The warmth in the car was lovely, *sooooo* relaxing. Before he could properly resist, heavy eyelids thwarted him.

Spiller was awakened by the opening of the passenger door. It was still snowing. Flakes wafted inside with the chill. He swore as he realised he'd been asleep. He checked the clock: 11.15pm. Bollocks. What an amateur.

'Just up the road, please, driver,' said the man, settling next to him. 'I'd walk, but in this weather…'

'I'm booked, mate,' Spiller said, as he turned to his unwelcome passenger. 'Oh.'

Jeffrey Poole didn't look or sound drunk, but many habitual drunks didn't. They learned to live with their boozing and moderate its effects, so they never completely teetered into a stupor because that would be a disaster—not being able to drink any more.

As Spiller gawped at his target, Poole's expression twisted. 'Just drive, will you? Don't judge. I've had enough.'

Spiller feigned ignorance. Now he had the man himself in the car, he didn't want to lose him. 'What are you on about?'

'You're all the same, judging me. Staring, whispering behind my back; well, I'm *sick* of it.'

'I don't know you to judge you, mate. I'm not local. Check my plates.'

Poole's bloodshot eyes pinched with uncertainty, then the courtesy bulb winked out and left the two men sitting in the dark, the glow of the streetlamps obscured by the layer of snow on the windscreen.

'God, I'm sorry,' Poole said, 'I thought…'

'It's okay. Just up the road?'

'I'm so sorry,' Pooled repeated. 'I've had an appalling time lately and I… I'm sorry. I'm meant to have done something awful, but I didn't, and I can't tell anyone and the whole village thinks I'm a disgrace.'

Drunk and vulnerable, sir? Then roll up, roll up! Step inside Matthew Spiller's Mobile Confessional. Just the price of the fare, sir. Offload your most personal secrets to a complete stranger, safe in the knowledge you'll never see them again.

'What?' Spiller said. 'Why?'

Poole physically slumped in the seat like the fight had left him. Spiller saw the anguish in every premature crease on his face. He was fifty but looked seventy.

'People think I killed a girl. I spent two years in prison. I've not been out long. But I didn't do it. I didn't. But what's the point? Who's going to believe me?'

'I will,' Spiller said quietly.

'I think I'm just going to sell up. Go somewhere no one knows me. Screw them all. What have I got to lose? Sorry, driver, it's okay, I'll walk.' He grabbed the door release, but Spiller laid a gentle hand on his arm.

'It's okay, mate. Tell me about it, then I'll take you home.'

'I'm sure you've got better things to do than listen to my sob story.'

Spiller shook his head. 'I haven't. And it doesn't sound like a sob story at all. It sounds terrible. What the hell happened?'

Poole stared Spiller in the eyes, assessing him, but Spiller thought it wouldn't have mattered what he saw in his eyes; here was a man willing to listen to a gross injustice.

'I can't tell anyone,' Poole said. 'I can't. Not round here. It would only make matters worse.'

Spiller waited rather than prod.

And Poole began talking, telling everything.

'WOW.' SPILLER WAS stunned, and for reasons Poole would never know. This had thrown a spanner in the works. Actually, the works had just disappeared down a sink-hole.

'I know,' Poole said. 'I think I'll just sell up. My name will be mud around here 'til the day I die.'

Ironic, Spiller thought, considering that day was supposed to be today.

'I think I'll walk, driver. I need the air. It's not far. Thank you for listening.'

This time, Spiller let him get out of the car. The slam of the door caused a film of snow to sluice down the passenger window. Spiller hit the wipers to clear the windscreen so he could watch the forlorn figure trudge carefully up the fresh white slope.

'Shit.'

His plan had gone to shit. He couldn't kill Poole now, even if he wanted to. And he hadn't wanted to. He hadn't gone there that evening to commit murder. He'd envisioned a clever ploy whereby Poole would be made aware of the threat against him and they would work together to disarm it. Apart from the fake revolver in his pocket, he also had some vials of fake blood. Like the white hairspray he'd used the night Ward died, it was a remnant of the kids' previous Halloween. In his head, Spiller had plotted everything meticulously. He'd explain the situation to Poole, who would be only too pleased to collaborate. Emma had placed Poole on Death Row and Spiller was throwing open the cell door. Spiller would drive to the hills, briefly put Poole in the boot of the car, then start recording on his mobile as he took him out. Under his coat, Poole would already have his shirt soaked with blood. Spiller would order him to walk a few paces and turn around. Then Spiller would let rip with a couple of shots from the blank-firer. Poole would hurl himself backwards into the conveniently soft snow, throwing open his coat as he fell. Then Spiller would approach and video the blood-soaked body. As a final persuader, Spiller would stand above the head and fire another two shots. The video would not catch their trajectories, but it would be clear where they'd been aimed. Spiller would walk away. Out of shot, Poole would paint some blood on his face and head, then Spiller would seemingly decide to record the final visage and return to the body. Blood everywhere. Two to the torso, two to the head. It maybe wouldn't work during the day, but, by the light of the moon and a little spill from the car's beams, the entire scene would be vague enough to convince. He would show the video to Emma, who would pay the remaining thirty thousand, then Spiller would erase the video and smash the phone with a hammer. Poole would keep a low profile or would move house, or, hell, it didn't really matter if he knocked on Emma's door the next day— Spiller would have his money and what could she do to retrieve it? Tell the police?

Whether Poole would have gone along with it was unknown. He may have simply chosen to call the cops and get both Emma and Spiller arrested. But the way Spiller had imagined it, it was perfect.

This wasn't.

As Spiller watched Poole disappear round a bend, he was struck by a thought that made him feel really dumb. It didn't matter that Poole hadn't done it; the plan could still work. Maybe he could offer Poole a couple of grand for his part in this murderous vignette. He tried to identify the pitfalls but couldn't see any. The basic scenario was unchanged: Spiller had to fake a murder to get the rest of his money.

He'd checked the location of Poole's house on Google maps and assessed it would take him twenty minutes' walking to get there, factoring in the snow. He wanted to catch Poole further up the lane where the properties thinned out and there was less chance of a late-night dog-walker. In a far recess of his mind was the possibility that Poole would flip on him and there'd be a bona fide fight, so he didn't want anyone witnessing the car he got into.

Spiller let ten minutes pass before setting off. It had stopped snowing.

The Lexus crept silently up the hill, its traction unsure. Spiller wondered how steep the incline might become, and whether progressing in the car would even be feasible. Still, the car moved forwards.

Spiller swore again. It wasn't going to be an easy conversation to start. *Hi, remember me? I didn't mention earlier, but I was sent to kill you. Any chance we could fake your death?*

Thankfully, the overhanging trees further up had caught the brunt of the snowfall, and the tarmac was more available to the tyres. He picked up speed as he entered a fairly straight stretch of road, anticipating that, around the next corner, he would encounter Poole. He prepared to slow as the curve approached. There was no pavement at this point, just a hedgerow with posh gates every fifty metres or so, and he didn't especially want to knock the poor man down if he was just out of sight.

His slow became a sudden halt. Conversely, his heart sped up to a near-lethal rhythm while his whole system was rocked by adrenaline.

Later, Spiller would surmise that they might not have seen him if he'd not had his lights on. The Lexus would have been drowned out by the clatter of the Transit's diesel engine. He could have slipped into reverse and retreated unnoticed. He didn't like the idea of retreating, but he'd have done so if he could because some situations were just too far gone to rectify.

But they did see him.

The men in black clothes at either end of Poole's body—one going forwards, the other backwards—stopped in their tracks. The one holding the legs suddenly dropped them and started walking towards the Lexus. As he approached, he started to pull something awkwardly from his waistband. Although the two men were the ones caught in the headlights, it was Spiller who was frozen like a rabbit about to get splatted. It was too surreal. He squinted at the object in the man's hand. It was long, with a bulbous end. He wanted to think it was a simple cosh, but the man was now five metres away and bathed in light, and the object was clear to see: a pistol with a suppressor screwed into the muzzle.

That's when he realised Poole was already dead.

Rather than stick the Lexus in reverse, some instinct made Spiller hit the accelerator. The car lurched forwards as the man reacted and started to bring the weapon up.

Two things happened simultaneously: the windscreen crazed opaquely and the car hit the man. Spiller heard the subdued crack of the weapon as it discharged a round, and he could see from the outward spidering of the glass where it had struck: directly in front of his face. He had flinched and ducked—for all the good that would have done him. Somehow, the round had bounced off; probably the angle of the windscreen and the slowing effect of the suppressor. All these realisations raced through his head as he stuck the car in reverse and backed away, trying to recall how much the lane curved so he'd avoid ending up in the hedgerow. He'd only have one chance to escape. A second bullet in the weakened windscreen would easily make it through. Luckily, the snow meant the road was clearly delineated—patchy in places under the trees, but a lot easier to track via the rear-view mirror. Had it not been snowing, Spiller felt certain he'd have veered off into the side and become a sitting duck.

Fifty metres back down the straight stretch, Spiller slowed and directed the rear of the Lexus into the opening of a driveway. Momentarily stationary, he launched a gloved fist several times through the windscreen. The lamination did its best to resist, but he was punching like a man possessed and managed to bust out a hole large enough to clear a sightline. Whether he was mashing his knuckles in the process, he didn't know, couldn't feel, and didn't care. He looked to his left up the lane, but the man wasn't there.

He nosed the Lexus back onto the lane and headed down into the village as quickly as the snow would allow. The Transit did not appear in his mirror.

IF HE WAS taking positives from the situation, the fact that the bullet had skipped off the windscreen was a big one. In fact, two combined. It had saved him from being shot in the face, and it meant the damage could be explained to Gibbo as accidental, a stone thrown up by a passing car perhaps—although that would only be relevant if the horny bastard had bothered calling his insurer earlier. Either way, Spiller had to get off the road. He was currently behind the wheel of a vehicle with a gaping hole in the windscreen, which would attract the attention of any passing cop. Besides which, it was freezing driving like that.

He drove to the other side of the village and parked in the corner of the railway station car park, nose to the wall. He got out and inspected the front bumper of the car for damage. It looked fine. He found an old travel blanket in the boot and jumped in behind the wheel again, then forced it through the hole in the glass to plug it up so at least the car wouldn't fill with snow should a blizzard sweep in overnight. As he was doing this, he noticed Gibbo's dash-cam in the passenger foot-well. The crazing of the windscreen had detached the sucker, and the unit had fallen. Shit, the SD card would have captured the night's events. He leaned over, pressed to release the card, which popped out. He slipped it into his jeans pocket.

As the last train into the city had long departed, Spiller switched on the data-head, keyed the mic and called the base, hoping the operator wouldn't recognise it wasn't Gibbo.

The female operator came back: 'Seven-Two, go ahead.'

'Could you send someone to Twilbury railway station, please? I had a private booking but there's one too many. I'm taking the rest now but there's a gentleman who needs a ride.'

'Coming back this way, babe?'

'Yeah, yeah. How long?'

'Uhhh... okay, got a driver quite close. Maybe fifteen minutes. Tell the fare to stand on the street, please.'

'Will do, thanks very much.'

Spiller sat in the broken Lexus, shivering from the cold and the shock. He wanted to put the heater on, but he couldn't risk the Transit passing by and spotting the warm exhaust fumes clouding the air. Probably, they'd be long gone by now, but it wasn't worth the risk.

So... what the hell had just happened?

It was a damn good thing he didn't have his mobile, or he'd have been on to Emma, ranting and raving, effing and blinding. This had to be down to her. What was the stupid bitch thinking? Why pay him to do the job, then get a couple of goons to step in? But... he'd only said he'd do it that morning. She wouldn't have then asked more people to get involved. Or, if she had asked someone else previously, wouldn't she have called to cancel them? It didn't make sense. And those had been serious individuals. Your average Rent-a-Thug did not come with a suppressed pistol.

As he waited for his ride home, Spiller began to muse whether he could swing the situation in his favour. The bottom line was that Poole was gone. The problem? His body might never surface. Could Spiller persuade Emma he'd done the job?

Without any solid evidence? Maybe she could pop in The Drapers Arms over the next week. She'd see Poole wasn't there. She'd said he was in there every night. Would that be enough?

After ten minutes, he went and stood behind the tall wall of the car park, next to the road. There was no one about and very little passing traffic. He'd be able to hear a taxi approaching. Car and van diesel engines sounded different. He'd know if it was safe to step out. Bugger—unless they sent a Transit minibus.

Shortly, he heard a vehicle approaching and knew it was only a car. He revealed himself, saw the taxi plates, and waved it to a halt. He didn't recognise the driver. He got in the back seat to ward off any conversation.

The warmth inside was bliss. The driver inclined his head backwards. Spiller gave the address of his flat, and the car set off. He didn't say anything else, and the driver didn't attempt to start a conversation. This was his sort of taxi driver. Spiller well understood the joy of silence at that time of night. You didn't want people asking if you'd been far, when you clocked on, when you'd clock off, if you'd been busy. You just wanted to drive from place to place as though there was no one else in the car with you. Well, he did. He got annoyed when people asked the same dumbass questions they knew he must have answered a couple of dozen times already.

As they passed back through the village, Spiller slumped down in his seat. He peered just over the door panel like he'd done as a child. He didn't expect the Transit would be roaming about—the guy he'd hit would no doubt be in A&E by now—but it was better to be cautious.

'If you're gonna be sick, let me know,' the driver said.

'I'm fine. I've not been drinking. I'm just tired.'

The village was mostly dark. The Christmas bulbs had been extinguished. One pub had a light on low, maybe a few stay-behinds, and there was a restaurant similarly lit with a few people gathered at a rear table, probably the staff having an end-of-shift tipple. Spiller had always wanted to frequent such establishments, but a meal for two would have taken a weekend's wages, and a whole-family outing would have been laughable.

He knew it was jealousy, and equally knew that wasn't the best emotion to still be harbouring at his age.

As they left the village, he started to fall asleep.

Seemingly a second later, he found himself being roused by the driver outside his flat. He dug in his pocket and handed over thirty pounds, holding his hand up to the offer of change as he climbed out, still slightly unsteady from the effects of the adrenaline.

It was late, but he had to talk to Gibbo. He popped upstairs for the keys to the Fiesta, dropping off the blank firer as he did. Before he left, he called Helen, landline to landline.

'Hi, Helen, everything okay?'

'You woke me. Yes, all quiet.'

'Good. I'm heading back shortly.'

'Uh-huh.' She put the phone down.

IT TOOK GIBBO thirty seconds to respond to the ring on his bell. Spiller was staring through the leaf-pattern of the oval door glass, waiting for a light to come on, but instead heard a window opening above his head. He stepped back and looked up.

Gibbo was bare-chested, hair dishevelled. His countenance was of a man just woken rather than caught mid-shag. 'Matt?'

'Can I come in?' Spiller asked in a loud whisper.

'Why?'

It wasn't a topic he wanted to broach from the street, but he didn't need to.

'Where's my car?' Gibbo enquired, looking up and down the street. 'Buddy, where the fuck's my car?'

'Open the door, will you?'

Gibbo huffed and shut the window. A few seconds later, he opened up and let Spiller in. Gibbo had donned a shocking-pink towelling robe. He walked into the living room, leaving his guest to follow.

'So?' Gibbo asked.

'Bit of an accident. Nothing bad. Cracked windscreen. Stone or something. Anyway, it's fine.'

In the time it took to say that, Gibbo had cursed half a dozen times. 'Where is it?'

'Station car park. Twilbury.'

'Crap. Man, why didn't you call?'

'No mobile.'

'You went out without your phone? Who does that?'

Spiller didn't respond. He did that. A lot recently, and for good reason.

'Why didn't you drive? You could have driven slowly.'

'I didn't want to get pulled over. I wasn't sure if I was insured.'

'Course you were. You think I'm stupid? I phoned the insurance after you left.'

'Oh. Well, it wasn't safe to drive anyway, it's proper smashed. I had to punch a hole in it.'

'Gee-zus. Phone box?' Gibbo said. 'I know they're rare but they are out there. You could have called. I'd have sent a breakdown truck. Or you could have called the base on the radio. They'd have called me. Shit, what if it rains? Or snows?'

'I made it, uh... weather-proof. Pretty much.'

'Shit... well, you're paying for it.'

Spiller frowned. 'What? You're insured. Windscreen repairs are free. It won't affect anything.'

'Not the point. It's the principle. You broke it, you own it.'

As much as Spiller knew he was to blame, Gibbo's attitude was annoying. 'Don't be a dick. Call your breakdown people now. Get them to send someone out. I'll take you to meet them.'

At that moment, Gibbo's 11.30 from The Plough popped her dishevelled head into the room. 'Everything okay?'

Gibbo shook his head. 'This dipshit smashed up my motor.'

She tutted and went back upstairs.

'I knew I shouldn't have lent you the fucking car.'

'Gibbo, I'm not in the mood. It was an accident. Shit happens. Put some clothes on and make the call.'

Gibbo took a step forwards. 'You're such a tit.'

Spiller knew it wasn't a threatening move—Gibbo was too concerned about his pretty-boy looks to risk a pummelling—but it took every ounce of his self-control not to throw a punch anyway. Instead, he dropped the Lexus keys on the coffee table.

'Right, you can get it yourself.' He turned and headed out of the room.

'And you can get your own fucking storage!' Gibbo shouted after him. 'If your shit's not out of my locker by lunchtime, I'm taking it to Oxfam!'

Spiller left the house, slamming the door behind him. Gibbo didn't follow. He got in the Fiesta and sat there for a minute, more upset than angry. That was his one friendship in the world trashed. Then again, would a true friend have reacted like that? Spiller knew he was a twat at times, but wasn't everyone? Didn't friends forgive their friends' little foibles?

He turned the ignition and childishly gunned the sadly quiet engine a few times to wake his ex-mate's neighbours, then he set off down the street. On the main road, he found himself heading in the direction of Ameley Green, then caught himself and pulled a U-turn. He wasn't in the right state to confront Emma. He hadn't even worked out how he'd approach her. And she'd be in bed, doped up against her flu-thing. She'd be brighter in the morning and he'd feel more composed. He thought of the SD card in his pocket and mused whether he should call Sergeant Enright about the footage, but felt he'd probably pushed his luck as far as it would go where Enright and forgiveness were concerned. The Poole business was different. Poole had been punished for his crime, albeit briefly, and, as it turned out, unjustly. Enright's morality was queered, especially given his beliefs, but he had divined an Old Testament payback with Ward that was clearly absent with Poole.

Spiller returned home, let himself in quietly, and went upstairs. Helen was sleeping next to Sophie. Despite the gentleness of the hand he laid on her shoulder, she awoke abruptly, looking terrified by whom might have crept into her bedroom.

'Jesus, Matt…'

'Where is it?' he whispered.

'Top of the wardrobe.'

'Can I use your computer?'

'Why? Need a wank?'

'You offering?'

'Ha ha. Front room.' Her head fell with a soft thud onto the pillow and she was back asleep.

Spiller reached and felt around for a second before his hand grasped the pistol. He padded into Sophie's room and pulled her *Despicable Me* duvet off the bed, draped it over his shoulders, and headed down to the living room. He collected Helen's laptop case, went through to the kitchen and down into the cellar.

He settled on the old sofa, pulling his feet off the cold floor and underneath him. He carefully slid the Sig between the seat cushions next to him, removed Helen's laptop from its bag, and powered it up. He found the SD card in the base of his pocket and slotted it in.

The recordings were time-stamped in three-minute clips. It took him several attempts to find the right segment. His heart began pounding as the footage developed from a seemingly pleasant trip up a Christmas-card-picturesque leafy lane into a scene from a Tarantino movie. He watched it several times, barely able to credit what he saw as the truth. Eventually, he began playing the clip in slo-mo, freezing certain frames to try and highlight any clues. The quality was excellent, but the Transit was parked at such an angle that its registration wasn't visible. Nor were there any markings on the vehicle. It was just a white van like thousands of others. Both assailants were in dark clothes, and both wore headgear. The one who'd been left holding Poole's shoulders was sporting a baseball cap, but the dark lower half of his face spoke strongly of a full beard rather than mere shadow. The one with the gun had on a beanie hat. Spiller froze an optimal image of his face, the second before the windscreen went opaque. Slightly chubby, clean-shaven. Enough for an identifying spot on *Crimewatch* should anyone know him. Spiller stared for a long time at the face of the man who'd tried to shoot him in the face. His feelings, though, were oddly innocuous, certainly compared to the hatred he harboured for Dominic Ward. Here was a guy who'd simply reacted to a threat. There was malice, for sure, but it wasn't personal.

Spiller shut down the media player and extracted the SD card, returning it to his pocket. He closed the laptop and set it to one side, then pulled the duvet up to his chin and tight in around his body to keep out the basement chill.

It still smelled down there, like a perfume gone wrong with all the notes still vying for attention; top notes of cherry, lemon, lavender, spice, and whatever other fresheners Helen had doused over the middle note of the bleach to cover the base note of the petrol. He could smell each one in turn if he concentrated hard enough, picking specific odours from the olfactory confusion before they swam away. It was fairly sickening.

Trying to ignore it, Spiller stared at the cellar door in the gloom until all else morphed to blackness, like the tunnel focus of a man with advanced glaucoma.

Exhausted, he couldn't sleep.

Chapter Thirteen

AT SOME UNSPECIFIED time during the night, Spiller had started nodding off. He'd formulated a plan where Emma was concerned, but he wasn't too enamoured of it. In fact, like several plans of late, it was probably garbage. He was woken by noise above him in the kitchen—Helen getting the girls something to eat before school. He enjoyed listening to the family activity, so decided not to pop up and help. It reminded him of his youth, hearing his parents downstairs after he'd been put to bed. He loved the sounds they made, chattering, pottering about. There was such comfort in those sounds, knowing there were people nearby whose lives were dedicated to his wellbeing. Spiller missed his mum and dad.

He waited until Helen and the girls left the house before stirring himself. He took the gun and hid it on top of a pipe that ran along the ceiling in the front part of the cellar. He bundled up Sophie's duvet and took it back up to her bedroom, then grabbed a quick shower. While he warmed his bones, he wondered if life might ever resume its old dullness, in the same way that a man might fancifully muse on how he'd spend ten million if he won the lottery. Could he just get behind the wheel of a taxi and spend the day picking up fares? Would his troubles settle if he did that? Was he the one compounding his woes with his every imprudent move?

Whatever else he did today, he had to get to the storage facility that morning as soon as it opened. He'd never seen Gibbo pissed off before last night, so he had no idea if his resentment would carry through, but Spiller couldn't risk his belongings being dumped at a charity shop. Not when one box contained twenty grand in cash.

Half an hour later, Spiller was letting himself into Gibbo's locker, a trolley waiting in the over-bright corridor. It would take a couple of trips to empty out his goods, and they'd all need to go to his flat, which would make it pretty intolerable if he ever had to go back and live there. He first extracted the box of clothes to check the cash was still inside, which it was. He grabbed another pair of trainers and chucked them in on top. No chance of forgiveness if he stole from Gibbo, but he was only stealing already-stolen goods.

The Fiesta ended up packed to the roof. As Spiller was returning his trolley to the entrance, he saw Gibbo swing into the car park in the Lexus. He tried to get back to his car before Gibbo got out, but didn't quite manage it.

'Oi!' Gibbo called.

Spiller stopped, looked at him.

'That everything?'

Spiller gave him a simple thumbs-up, which received a middle finger in response. Spiller decided to be the bigger person, so jogged over. 'How's the car?'

'Fantastic,' Gibbo said without a smile, and looked over at the Fiesta. 'Your Audi still buggered then?'

'Like you wouldn't believe.'

'Key?'

Spiller handed over the padlock key. 'Sorry things panned out like this.' He left his arm extended and opened out his palm.

Still unsmiling, Gibbo accepted the offer. 'Me too.'

And that was it: friendship done. No hugging it out, no animosity, just a relationship with no mileage left in it. In Spiller's warped world, though, it wasn't even a solitary blip on the radar. And he imagined it wouldn't bother Gibbo much, either. He'd no doubt find solace in the loins of some randomer later on tonight. Lucky bastard.

THE DUMP OF boxes, bits and bobs made his flat appear like one of those places you'd see on a programme about hoarders. Before locking up, he stood at the threshold to his flat and stared at the clutter. At some point, he hoped he might move it all back to the family home from whence it came, but that was such a whimsical notion it made him laugh out loud.

The events of the night before still didn't make any sense, unless Emma had hired multiple hitmen. Or someone else had a grudge. He wondered who that might be, and it seemed logical it could only be another member of Emma's family. Gee, that was one aggrieved clan, if so. But it didn't seem likely. The country would be in anarchy if the victims of crime routinely took matters into their own hands. However hurt, people nearly always bowed to the system, accepting whatever passed for justice and living out the rest of their days in bitter umbrage. Even Spiller had essentially succumbed. With petrol everywhere and a match in his hand, he had opted to leave Dominic Ward in a rare state when he'd had ample opportunity to make sure the arsehole was thoroughly well done.

Venturing to Emma's house in his sensible car, and potentially being seen to visit by neighbours and CCTV, no longer fazed him. He was aware of the retrograde shift in his attitude. He felt like a man hanging onto a precipice with his fingertips, still with strength in them, but getting bored of waiting for help. His fingers ached and that was sufficient reason to let go. His sense of self-preservation was suffering. The macabre excitement he'd felt dumping Ward's body was all but gone.

He drove in silence; no music. He was beginning to enjoy peaceful journeys in regular cars. Dull though they were, it was all quite therapeutic. And, boy, did Matt Spiller need some therapy.

As expected, Emma's BMW was on the drive. He parked half-on the pavement, composed himself as much as he could, and headed for the door. He had a vague script in mind, but anticipated he might need to veer off into some serious improvisation.

Emma took a couple of minutes to answer. Her dark-cupped eyes brightened at the sight of him. He offered a nod in response. She pulled the door wide open and stepped aside to allow him in. She was still in a bathrobe and looked just as ill as last time. As he passed her, he caught a strong whiff of body odour. He entered the lounge and sat on the sofa. Emma hobbled in to join him, fairly collapsing into her duvet-covered chair. She pulled the duvet around her shoulders and gazed at him expectantly.

'It's done,' he said.

'Proof?'

'It happened too quickly. I couldn't really get what I needed.'

'You couldn't take a single picture?'

'No.'

'Bullshit,' she said.

'He's gone. Call his house, go down to his local, he won't be there. He's gone. If there's anyone who might miss him, they'll call the cops and it'll wind up on the news. I did what you asked and I want the rest of the money.'

She smiled at him then began laughing weakly, although the sound was feeble only because her lungs couldn't offer anything stronger. She looked genuinely amused to the point of hysterics. Soon, the tears were streaming down her cackling face.

'I want my money,' he said, and thought he'd probably not said anything more pathetic and impotent in his entire life.

Emma roared, her lungs seemingly accepting the need to recover spontaneously, given the volume of antipathy their sick owner needed to vent. She began wheezing and squeaking, but the laughter didn't abate. Spiller wondered if a person could laugh themselves to death. He'd seen a Monty Python sketch to that effect, but this looked like it might really happen. In a moment she'd abruptly stop, gawp wide-eyed, and expire.

'You're priceless,' she managed to utter, before the screeching took over again.

He stood up. 'Where is it? Upstairs? Under the bed?'

'Oh, my God, you're priceless. Let's give this man fifty thousand pounds for *nothing*. What a good idea. Why didn't I think of that?' She shrieked, and the tears and hilarity continued.

Spiller marched out of the room and headed up the stairs. He could hear no discernible change in Emma. If anything, she laughed even harder. She certainly didn't bother to follow him.

He dropped to his knees and looked under her bed. Nothing. He shuffled over to a chest of drawers and pulled each one out to find only clothes. He gained his feet and pulled open the doors of a couple of wardrobes and began rooting through. Zilch. He stopped still, craned his head to the doorway. Emma had fallen silent. He hurried from the room and down the stairs.

She was okay, just mopping her damp face with a flannel. She was wheezing, but still smiling.

'Where's the money?' he asked, standing over her.

'You should go on stage. You're so funny.'

'Money.'

She inclined her face up to him, now sans all trace of glee. 'There isn't any. That twenty grand was all I had in the world.'

'Now *I'm* calling bullshit. You live in this place and have an M4 on the drive and you don't have any money?'

'Any *more* money. That was everything I'd saved since I was a kid. Birthdays, Christmases, bit of excess pay at the end of the month. I don't have any more. Well… a grand float in the bank for bills. You can have that if you want, just for the laughter you've brought into my sick little life.'

Spiller took a few steps back. He looked at her for a moment, then sat down. 'This house. That car.'

'Subsidised. Very heavily. None if it's mine.'

'I don't get,' he muttered.

'I have a good job, an even better boss. He takes care of me.'

'What? Like… a sugar daddy?'

'Nothing like. He's just a very kind man. It's okay, I realise you don't understand the concept.'

He stared at her for a minute, and she reciprocated as much as her watery eyes would allow.

'Poole *is* dead,' he said eventually.

'Whatever.'

'I'm serious.'

'Well... good. If he is, then good. But I can't pay you. Even if you had proof, I couldn't pay you.'

Spiller deliberated over his next question, but asked it anyway. It didn't seem he had much to lose. 'Did you ask someone else to kill him?'

Emma's features creased in confusion. '*What?*'

'Did you?'

'Sure, I put an ad on Gumtree.' She slowly reached for a mug on the table and took a painful gulp.

'Someone else killed him,' Spiller said. 'I was there. I saw it. I got it on video. I've got the SD card in my pocket.'

'Then I want to see it.'

'Thirty grand and I'll show you.'

Emma flashed only the briefest grin; she was worn out. 'You really are something.'

He smiled back crookedly. 'You know the truly ironic thing? He didn't even kill your sister.'

'Oh, *fuck off.*'

Spiller was unperturbed. 'I spoke to him. I was in a taxi—not mine; I borrowed one. He jumped in next to me. Just... offloaded. I get it all the time. People at the end of a rough night, they're pissed and they just open up. Relationship issues, all sorts. I hear the lot. They get it off their chests, then get out. They're not going to see me again so what's it matter? Poole told me what happened. What really happened. He wasn't driving—his wife was.'

'Crap.'

'They'd been to a party. She was designated driver. At the party she found out he'd been having an affair. She quietly got blind drunk. But she hid it well. Later, she got behind the wheel and they headed home. On the way, it all came out. They had a blazing row. She was pissed, pissed off, not concentrating, and she hit your sister. He knew it was all his fault, so he took the blame. Before the cops arrived, he swapped seats with her. He got done for drink-driving, death by dangerous driving—well... you know all that. But he didn't do it.'

Emma's face had gone slack. She looked more ill than ever. 'But...'

'You wanted me to kill the wrong person.'

'So... his wife got away with it?'

'Not for long. She's dead. He thinks guilt got her. She hit the bottle while he was inside. Pills, booze, basically overdosed.'

Emma was visibly mortified.

'If it's any consolation,' Spiller said, 'I was never going to kill him. I would have tried to stage something. He probably wouldn't have gone for it, but... I wouldn't have killed him either way.'

'But you'd still have taken my fifty grand.'

He nodded. 'Troubles of my own, I'm afraid.'

She slumped deeper into her chair, pulled the duvet in around her face and bowed her head so all he could see was a patch of forehead and a nose. He couldn't see if her eyes were open. After a couple of minutes' inactivity, he wondered if she'd fallen asleep.

In those moments, Spiller had a think. If he was any judge of character, Emma's denial of wealth rang true. Hers was a well he'd already drained. But one aspect of all this was promising, potentially ripe for exploitation.

Suddenly, she raised her head, exposing a bewildered expression. 'Then who *did* kill him?'

'You're asking *me?*'

'What did they look like?'

'Couple of guys, one with a beard. Not easy to make out much more. Do you have brothers?'

'Seriously?'

He shrugged.

'One. He lives in Canada.'

'Oh. Your parents? Could they have asked someone?'

'Of course, dear Ma and Pa. I'd forgotten about those homicidal old farts. Yeah, it must have been them.' She buried her face again.

'Emma...'

She looked up. 'What?'

'Who's your benefactor?'

'What?'

'Your boss. The guy who buys you big houses and fast cars.'

'None of your business,' she said.

'Because, I reckon a man like that might very well pay thirty grand to keep his favourite employee out of prison. Shit, I reckon I could ask for a lot more. He seems to have a soft spot for you.'

Emma looked more weary than worried. 'You never give up, do you?'

'You asked me to kill Poole. And you gave me a gun. What do *you* think your boss would pay to keep you out of prison?'

'No idea. But you'd be in there with me. You took money off me.'

'Prove it. I'd just say I refused to help. I went to warn Poole, but you'd already hired someone else. I genuinely do have it all on an SD card. Anyway, my life's a bit shit at the moment. Yours looks pretty sorted.'

'Yeah, I'm having a fantastic time, can't you tell?'

'Give me his name or I'll just drop you in it anyway,' Spiller said, surprising even himself with his gall. He'd mused on whether his problems were down to his inability to stop digging, yet here he was, pulling the tarp off the JCB.

'Fine. Charles Delaney. Google if you want his number. You'll find it under Delaney Construction. Or Delaney Import-Export, Delaney Haulage and Storage, Delaney Communications, Delaney Environmental Services. He also owns a few nightclubs, restaurants, car supermarkets, that sort of thing. He's obviously not a busy man, so I'm sure he'd be delighted to hear from a lowlife chancer like you. In fact, what the hell...' Emma pushed herself to her feet and shuffled into the kitchen. She returned a moment later and offered him a business card. 'Here you go. His mobile number's on there. Do your worst. I really don't care.'

Spiller stood up and took it from her.

'But if you do get some dosh off him, can I have a refund? Really. I'm fucking skint now.'

'Uh…'

'Oh, just do me a favour and leave. And this time don't come back.'

He dithered, almost wanting to give her a hug—theirs had been an undeniably intense, if fleeting, relationship. But she flopped back into her chair and switched on the TV, so he did as instructed and left her alone.

Spiller felt bad about the twenty grand. As he climbed back in his car, he felt decidedly ungallant. He hated it when people ran from his cab without paying, and this was a twist on that betrayal of trust. He *had* been paid for a service, and he hadn't followed through. And this was rather more than a fiver denied for a taxi ride. Then again, Emma was earning good money and was being looked after, whereas he'd never been able to earn big in his job and he didn't have a boss throwing gifts at him. Given time, she'd earn it back. Or Charles Delaney would be subjected to a sob story about a failed investment and he'd make a bank transfer to cover her losses. She'd be all right.

And so would Matt Spiller, because Matt Spiller had just decided to add blackmail to his criminal résumé.

Chapter Fourteen

IF SPILLER HAD thought the Ward situation might be ebbing away, he was about to be proven wrong. In the absence of any follow-up attack, he'd hoped the tide had gone out on that particular threat, but it seemed it was only the pull-back of the water that people saw before a tsunami swept in.

Helen and his daughters were at home when he got back. The girls had clearly been crying. They both ran and hugged their dad when he entered the front room. Sophie began bawling again while Sammy quietly blubbered into his shoulder. He held them for a while before Helen urged them to sit back down and immerse themselves in the movie that hadn't really been distracting them. He looked at Helen quizzically. She grabbed his arm and led him out of the room, through the kitchen and down the steps into the stuffy atmosphere of the cellar.

'What happened?' Spiller asked. 'I thought you took the girls to school.'

'We got rear-ended.'

'Jesus, you okay?'

'Physically.'

'You call the insurance?'

'No.'

'You get the other driver's details?'

She shook her head. 'They drove off. Matt, it wasn't an accident.'

'How do you know?'

'We were stopped at lights. We were the first car. There was a big four-by-four behind us. He didn't run into the back of us, he was stopped as well. Then he edged forwards and bumped us and started pushing. I hit the brakes but he had more power. I could see a lorry coming from the left. He was going to hit us so

I just hit the gas and managed to get through the intersection. The lorry must have missed the back of the car by an inch. The girls were hysterical.'

Spiller sank onto the sofa. 'Christ... Dominic Ward.'

'Has to be.'

'Are you okay?'

'No, I'm furious. Murderously, crazily fucking furious.' She sat beside him. 'This is strike two, Matt. We can't let him have a strike three. He nearly killed us.'

'Did you see him? In the mirror?'

'It wasn't him. But he was behind it—had to be.'

Spiller nodded. 'Did you call the police?'

'No, I wanted to wait for you. But, Matt... if they can't do something, you really have to. How many times do I need to ask?'

'I know, I know.' He held her hand. 'I'm so sorry.'

'It's not your fault, Matt. I've blamed you for a lot but this isn't your bad. Sammy had the relationship and I ended it.'

He smiled at the euphemism. 'You certainly did that.'

'I'm going to take the girls to my mum's. She says dad's having a good spell so it'll be nice for them to spend some time with their grandad while he's still... Anyway, we'll have to make an excuse with Sophie's school, Sammy's college, but... Matt?'

Spiller was thinking. 'I'm wondering...'

'What?'

'If Enright can help.'

Helen shook her head. 'Leave him out of it. The more complex this all gets, the more likely he'll feel the need to tell his superiors about the other night—you in Ward's car.'

'He wouldn't. It would end his career, the fact he kept that to himself in a murder enquiry.'

'Maybe, but let's not take the risk. Just let him get on with his bobbying. What could he do anyway?'

Spiller considered. 'Yeah, not much. I'll call DCI Bartoli. He's got to do something now, right?'

'He'd better,' Helen said. 'Where is it?'

He knew what she meant. He nodded towards the front part of the cellar. 'On top of the pipe.'

'Okay.' She looked at him intently, squeezing his hand. 'Matt? Can you do what you said?'

'What did I say? I say a lot of stuff.'

'About getting us away from here. To the sun. A fresh start. Once this is all done. I really want that. I want to leave it all behind. This house isn't a home any more—not after what's happened here. I'm tired of the cold, the dark.'

Spiller understood. The winter months had always been a dreadful time for him mentally. She'd never previously alluded to any similar negativity in her own mind, but times they were a-changing.

Now, more than ever, he had to get his hands on some serious cash.

'I promise you this,' he said. 'I'll get the money or I'll die trying.'

Helen leaned her head against his. 'That'll do.'

They stayed like that for a minute before Spiller reluctantly broke contact and stood up. 'I need to call someone.'

'Matt...'

'Yeah?'

'Make your call, then go and spend some time with the girls. They're messed up. Sammy especially, as she knows this all started with her scumbag boyfriend. Just sit with them, give them a cuddle. They miss you. They've missed you for months.'

He almost opened his mouth to blame her at that moment, for kicking him out and making him feel so unwelcome in his own home, but, for once in his life, he summoned the self-restraint to set aside his spade. He smiled and nodded, and lingered, so Helen took the hint and headed back upstairs.

Tucked down in his jeans pocket, nestling next to the SD card, was the laminated business card of Charles Delaney.

SPILLER'S HEART HAMMERED in his chest. His testicles felt normal, but the audacity of his planned speech was metaphorically inflating them to bursting point. He paced around the cellar as the phone chirped in his ear. The call was answered after five rings.

'Hello, Charles De*la*ney,' the man said, the high inflection on the second syllable of his surname making it sound like a character's introductory line in a musical.

The jollity in Delaney's voice pissed Spiller off. This could be a call imparting some terrible news. How could a person summon such groundless optimism in the face of dour possibilities?

'I want to talk to you about your employee. Emma?'

'Aha! Mr Spiller, I presume?'

Spiller felt like hanging up. Another plan was fraying. 'Uh, how do you know my name?'

'Emma called after you took my card away with you. She warned me you might be making contact.'

Spiller frowned. 'And how does *she* know my name?'

Delaney chuckled briefly. 'You shouldn't give out business cards with your surname on them if you don't want people to know your surname.'

His taxi cards. They were floating about everywhere. *Doh*. She'd used one to call him on Christmas Eve.

'I want to meet up,' Spiller said, taking back the reins. 'I don't know what Emma told you, but we have something to discuss.'

'You're right: you don't know what Emma told me. And I would dearly love to make your acquaintance, Mr Spiller; I could do with a good laugh.'

'Now... you listen—'

'Delaney's, the restaurant in the city centre. Know it? Be there at one a.m. That's the one o'clock an hour after midnight. Buzz the door. I'll be waiting.'

Spiller's mouth was agape, ready to assert the scant authority that hadn't yet been pilfered from him, but Delaney hung up. He stared at his mobile. 'Arsehole.'

One a.m.—at least Delaney was taking him seriously. Customers would have left by then. They could have a decent conflab. It was a good sign. If Emma had told her boss the whole story and he'd simply not been interested in helping her, he would have said so on the call. And what did thirty grand mean to a man of his means? Petty cash. In fact, Spiller decided he'd go in at a hundred and see where negotiations went. In his head, a final figure of seventy-five seemed fair—if fair was a word you could apply to blackmail. Spiller smirked. Rich knob wouldn't know what hit him.

Spiller headed back upstairs, sensing an end to his troubles could be in sight. How excellent it would be to use one problem to solve another.

He stopped on the final step. Damn. Without knowledge of his cunning scheme, Helen would still expect him to involve the police about the car-ramming. He had to call Bartoli. And Bartoli was someone he didn't want to speak to any more than he had to. The man already had his suspicions, and this second attempt on the lives of Helen and the girls would only stoke them. You had to be pretty adamant a person had done something heinous to want to kill their family.

THE FACT THAT DC Goodrick showed up alone an hour later to take Helen's statement was both good and bad. Good because Spiller didn't want Bartoli in the house; bad because it suggested the top man didn't believe Dominic Ward was any more responsible for this than for the attempted arson. It apparently wasn't even worth a visit from DS Madden.

The Detective Constable appeared to know it. His expression was full of apology the moment Spiller opened the door to him. Sammy and Sophie had already been ushered up the stairs, their family time with mum and dad cut short.

Goodrick was shown into the front room and took a seat, opening a leatherette folder and taking out a notebook. Spiller and Helen sat opposite.

The DC smiled. 'Mr and Mrs Spiller, I'm told you wish to report an accident.'

'Wrong straight away,' Spiller said. 'And why the hell would a detective be here for a simple accident? I told your boss it wasn't an accident. Is he *trying* to piss me off?'

'Matt…' Helen soothed.

'Some scumbag gets topped and he's all over it, but *two* attempts on our lives and your boss sides with a piece of shit solicitor and sends his lackey to deal with it.'

Goodrick smiled queerly. 'Offence taken, by the way.'

'I wasn't about to qualify it. Just talk to my wife.'

Goodrick looked at Helen. 'Mrs Spiller?'

Helen recounted the incident as Goodrick scribbled, and so detailed was her description that Goodrick at the end seemed at a loss for what more he could glean. He read what he'd written but clearly saw no holes, so closed his notebook.

'Are your daughters okay?' he asked.

'What do you think?' Spiller answered.

'I'm here to help,' Goodrick said, a little peeved. 'Your wife just said it wasn't Dominic Ward behind the wheel. My guvnor could have sent a uniform, but he sent me, precisely because you've made known your beliefs about Dominic Ward, and this is potentially related to the ongoing enquiry into his brother's demise. But *if* this is down to Dominic Ward, the likelihood is he got a *lackey* to use a stolen vehicle, which we'll find torched or certainly wiped clean of prints. I will look into this, though, don't worry. I'll call Ward in again for questioning, see if there's any footage from traffic cameras at the intersection and nearby. I'll do my job. But that's all I can do. I can't produce rabbits from hats, Mr Spiller. I can't make evidence appear if there isn't any or make someone confess if they don't want to.'

Spiller knew that last bit was true, or he'd have declared his crimes when Bartoli quizzed him. He supposed Dominic Ward was only doing the same: fronting it out. He huffed his fake disdain at the detective. 'Anyway, how are you getting on with finding out who killed Callum Ward?'

'I can't discuss that with you.'

'But I'm still a suspect.'

'We'll tell you when you're not.' Goodrick stood up and directed his attention to Helen. 'If you think of anything else that may help us, just call. Do you still have my card?'

Helen nodded. 'Thanks.'

'What if you can't find out who killed him?' Spiller asked.

'Then the case remains open and suspects remain suspects.' Goodrick smiled. 'So that knock at the door could come anytime.'

'Not my door, mate. Speaking of doors...'

Helen followed Goodrick from the room and let him out, thanking him again as he left. She returned with a concerned look.

'I know,' Spiller said. 'Waste of time. No way is this getting sorted by the police.'

Helen nearly collapsed on the sofa. 'Matt, I can't cope with much more.' Her face was full of entreaty.

All the years they'd been together, he had never heard a defeatist word from her, nor seen such despair in her eyes. She had always carried him through the tough times, bolstering his crumbling confidence. Now she was the one all hollowed out.

'Leave it with me,' he said. 'Go to your folks. Try and forget about all this. I'll deal with it. I will. Give me a hug.'

Helen stood up wearily. She shuffled into his arms and they hugged for a few seconds. He could have embraced her for hours, but she broke away gently as though the prolonged contact might sap what was left of her resolve.

'Call school, college,' he said. 'Say we've had a family crisis and you've had to go away. Then go upstairs and pack a few things. I'll go and get you some cash and bring it to your folks' house. Are you all right explaining stuff to the girls? Well... Soph, at least. Or do you need me?'

She shook her head. 'Do what you need to do.'

Spiller kissed her forehead and left the room. In the hallway, he hesitated, suddenly struck by one of his mental fugues. He didn't know where to go; downstairs for the gun and straight to the law offices of Dominic Ward to end the threat for good, or out of the front door to pursue the plot to extort money from

Charles Delaney. There was no hope for him in the former option—he'd simply walk in and shoot the man—but it was the more honourable choice. The latter felt somehow cowardly, as though he was still trying to save his own skin, leaving his loved ones exposed.

He stood there, perceptually paralysed, only distantly aware that Helen was also immobile in the front room, perhaps similarly run aground. Without consciously making a decision, he turned to the front door. A wee voice from the top of the stairs halted his progress.

'Dad?'

Spiller turned to see Sophie sitting on the top stair, clutching a cuddly Minion. He grinned and pointed at her. 'Hey, Soph. That's Stuart, right?'

Sophie looked at the toy and turned it towards her dad so it's one eye starred down at him. She made him nod.

'You okay?' he asked her.

'Dad, when this is over, can we get a puppy?'

Spiller came to the foot of the stairs. 'What do you mean?'

'Can we?'

'When what's over, sweetie?'

'Please.'

'There's nothing wrong, darling.'

'I want to call him Stuart.'

Spiller gave up trying to convince his youngest that the world around her was hunky-dory. It wasn't and she knew it, but she at least believed there was a happy ending in which she got a puppy, and, for that, for her childish hope, Spiller was supremely grateful.

'Stuart,' he mused. 'Not sure it's much of a dog's name, but... okay. He's going to have two eyes, though. I am not taking a one-eyed dog for a walk. Way too embarrassing.'

Sophie smiled as one who'd heard the right answer but didn't quite believe it. 'Thanks, Dad.'

'I'll have to talk to mum first, though,' he said, knowing Helen would have caught every word from just the other side of the door.

'I know.'

She stood up and Spiller expected her to trot down the stairs for a hug. Instead, she headed back to her room. In a way, he was relieved. His kids had brought meaning to a life increasingly bereft of significance, but he wasn't certain he was really cut out to be a dad. All those months spent away when Sammy was growing up, and nary a moment's regret despite his sham protestations at the time. And all the time he'd be willing to forgo with them, even now, had his job been kinder. But, as with so many, the job had taken the best of him, chewed him up and spat him out like a spent piece of gum.

He waited for a moment to see if Helen would bother to say goodbye, but she, too, kept her distance. He put an eye to the crack down the hinge-side of the door jamb. Helen wasn't in sight. All he could spy was the framed photo of his time in the Gulf. A grinning idiot with a gun, with no clue what lay beyond. Perhaps Helen was asleep on the sofa, drained by the day's events. Or she was just waiting to hear the front door close because she couldn't bear to see his stupid mug again.

Unbidden, his hand went to his trouser pocket. The SD card. The information on it had to be kept safe. He backed away and went into the kitchen. Helen's laptop was on the counter. He powered it up, inserted the card in the slot, and sent the file to the desktop. From the odds drawer, he took the appropriate cable, connected his mobile to the laptop and transferred the file, checking it played okay. He then buried the video deep within one of the laptop's program folders, extracted the card, tore off a sheet from the kitchen roll and wrapped the card with it, then opened a food cupboard and stared inside. There was a bag of sugar at the back, and he quietly removed the impeding items to pull it out. He unstuck the seal, pushed the card deep into the sugar, bent the top back over and restocked the shelf as it had been. Good—the video was now in three places. He went into his email account and created a draft message which he left unsent, detailing what the video depicted and where the file and card were located, and headed the email: READ IF I DIE!!! At some point, should the worst occur, Helen would hopefully see it as she dealt with his affairs, although what she'd make of his capacity to insert himself concurrently into a second set of lethal circumstances...

The door to the front room was still ajar. Spiller crept by it and left the house. On the street, by the Fiesta, he looked back. Through the thin curtains, he saw the light in the front room extinguish. Then a brief illumination as the hallway light spilled into the room as the door opened and closed.

SPILLER RETURNED TO his flat, zig-zagged through the jungle of boxes in his tiny living room, and found his bed. He kicked off his trainers and curled up like a baby, and slept like one.

He awoke a couple of hours later feeling nauseous, so polished off several bowls of cereal. He packed the twenty thousand into a small rucksack and sat it beside him like a best buddy while he watched documentaries about goldminers failing to find gold, and ex-DEA agents invalidating the title of their show by digging holes everywhere across Colombia except the spots where Pablo Escobar had buried his fortune. It was uplifting seeing folk do such things. It proved how undaunted the human spirit could be in the face of continuous disappointment. At least Spiller wasn't screwing up in front of millions of people.

At eleven o'clock, he got ready. He showered to wake himself up, dressed in dark clothing, except for a sand-coloured shemagh, which he wrapped around his neck to emphasise to Charles Delaney the pedigree of the man he was dealing with. He took the bag of cash and drove to his in-laws' house, on the other side of the city. He'd always admired their property. A modest detached but in a nice suburb where folk didn't quite have enough money to be pleasant to their neighbours. A phone call brought Helen to the front door. She stepped outside.

He handed her the rucksack. 'Here.'

'What's this?'

'Twenty grand in cash. It's best you keep it. Although don't let your dad get his mitts on it.' He grinned.

'*What?*'

'You know…'

Sadly, Helen did know, and Spiller immediately wished he'd pre-considered the appropriateness of his little joke.

'You think my dad's problems are funny?'

An apology was in order but Spiller went on the offensive. 'He never liked me.'

'Grow up, Matt.' She lifted the sack in front of his face. 'What am I meant to do with this?'

'I'd just rather you had it. I'm… I'm going to try something—to get some more. It may work. If not, I may need to use that thing in the cellar and you might not see me again.'

'Okay,' she said.

He took a moment to recover from the gut-punch. 'Really? You know what I'm suggesting there, right?'

'That you could be killed or locked up.'

'Wow. And that's okay with you.'

'No. But I told you earlier: do what you have to do.'

Sophie would have loved the expression on his face at that moment—the wounded little puppy in need of a cuddle.

'That's where we are right now, Matt. What do you want me to say?'

'Uh… yeah… nothing *to* say. How are the girls?'

'Sad.'

Spiller dawdled.

'I need to go back in.' She retreated into the porch and closed him out.

Spiller stood there, his skin growing colder, but his blood suddenly heading the other way. A few seconds later, he started hammering on the glass, forgoing the niceties of the bell. Helen answered quickly, and immediately clocked the change in him.

'Hey,' he snarled in a low voice. 'FYI, I am putting my life on the line, clearing up a mess *you* made. I've held my hands up to plenty over the years. I'm a proper fuck-up and I don't need you or anyone else to remind me, but this one's on you. So don't you dare get all pissy with me, even if my jokes are off-colour. Your dad was a complete wanker to me. Never liked me, never gave me a chance, so maybe this is goes-around-comes-around. Whatever it is, fuck him. And fuck you if you don't appreciate what I'm trying to do for this family—or what's left of it.'

He watched her reeling from his words and felt no remorse at their impact. He turned and headed back to his car, but his name stopped him. She said it gently, quietly, but with an undeniable power that interrupted his grand exit. He walked back to her.

'What?'

'I do appreciate what you're doing, Matt. But if you think I couldn't do it myself, you step inside now and look after the girls while I go and get that thing from the cellar and empty it into someone's head. Because I'll do it. You know I'll do it. Seriously, let's swap roles.'

For all sorts of reasons, both honourable and ignoble, he didn't need to think about the offer. 'No.'

'Okay,' Helen said. 'Then good luck.'

SPILLER MOTORED AROUND the corner from his in-laws' house, then pulled over and stopped the engine. Holy crap, where had his wife gone? When had those pesky aliens replaced her with this lethal *doppelgänger*? She looked like his wife, made the same sounds, but the words those sounds were forming of late, and her actions and intentions... what the hell?

He squinted at his eyes in the rear-view mirror, saw the purpose in them, and tried to align the man inside with the one the world saw. He'd always known he was a serious-looking dude, and he'd undoubtedly done some serious shit, but his character had rarely been a match for the image he portrayed. It had always been a struggle. Then again, he supposed most people were the same. He'd seldom met a person in his entire life who'd matched up to their positive first impression. They'd all been flawed to some extent, some shockingly so. When he met Charles Delaney, he'd just have to ensure his façade was impenetrable. By dint of their fortunes alone, rich folk tended to lord it over paupers, regardless of their morals. Delaney could not be allowed the upper hand.

With grave and unwavering thoughts populating his mind, Spiller set off towards the city centre.

Chapter Fifteen

SPILLER ENTERED DELANEY'S restaurant shivering slightly, which wasn't a great first impression. He'd parked up nearby for a while to wait for his appointment and he'd let the car get too cold. He should have run the engine a little more to keep himself warm.

The interior of Delaney's was dimly lit with lots of reclaimed timbers and exposed brick, industrial light fixtures, and monochrome wall-hangings depicting grand architecture gone derelict. Grey blinds were dropped on the windows for privacy. The traffic noise outside was scant and muted. Delaney himself had let him in, and now beckoned him over to a corner table, where an uncorked bottle of wine and two glasses awaited. Apart from the two of them, the restaurant was deserted, although he could hear some metallic clanging in the kitchen as the staff were no doubt resetting the bowls and utensils ready for tomorrow's influx of customers.

Delaney was a solid man of short stature. His hair was thinning but looked genuinely dark, despite his age, which Spiller guessed was knocking seventy. His choice of attire—jeans and a hooded sweatshirt—was youthful, but not so much that it looked awkward. The kind of clothes a man of his years could only get away with thanks to his wealth. He slid into his leather seat and used the downward motion of a finger to indicate Spiller do the same. Spiller didn't like it. He was already being ordered around and neither of them had yet said a word. Delaney poured out two glasses of red wine, smiling all the while across the table at Spiller like he was the most welcome man on the planet.

'So,' Spiller said, getting down to business. 'You know why I'm here, so let's negotiate.'

Delaney took a gulp of wine, swilled it around his mouth, then swallowed and purred his approval. 'Elegant… velvety. Château Bélair-Monange, 2017. Do try it, Matthew.'

Spiller refused to be told what to do. 'I want some money.'

'Ah, that's what this is all about.'

'Like you didn't know.'

'Actually, I didn't. Emma only told me a Matthew Spiller might be calling about a delicate matter, and, if he did, I should listen and she trusted I'd make the right call. And if he didn't, well, it was all moot, so she wouldn't bore me with the story prematurely. I got the distinct impression she's acutely embarrassed by the whole affair. And definitely upset, especially on top of her present illness.' His smile turned into a grin. 'But you did call and here you are. Really, do have some wine, it's excellent.'

Spiller left the glass where it was. He wished Emma *had* told her boss the story. He knew it was going to sound pathetic and pitiful spewing from his own mouth, and he'd not thought how to explain it in the most persuasive way.

Delaney took another gulp, then pointedly looked at the wall clock. 'Matthew, if you have something to say, say it. I'm normally tucked up in bed by this time.'

Spiller drew in a deep breath. 'Right. In a nutshell, Emma asked me to kill a man. She gave me twenty thousand up front. Thirty to follow after I did it. But I didn't do it. And now she doesn't want to pay me the extra thirty thousand. She says she doesn't have it. And I get: I didn't do the job. But I could put her in prison—'

'And she you,' Delaney interjected.

Spiller paused, then carried on. 'And you seem to be quite fond of her to fund her lifestyle as you have, so I'm thinking you might want to step up and bail her out, and I know you can afford it. But I don't just want the thirty now. I want a hundred. A hundred thousand pounds.'

'Or you'll go to the police.'

'I'll say she tried to hire me and I refused. There's nothing damning against me.'

Delaney studied Spiller. 'I'm confused... what on earth made her think *you* could do the job?'

Spiller laid a hand on his shemagh as if to make a point, and pulled it down a little to let some air down his chest.

Delaney smiled. 'Yes, I did note the accoutrement of your desert scarf. You're ex-military, is that right?'

Spiller took out his mobile phone and cued up the images to prove it, swiping through them one by one with the screen turned towards the doubter. Delaney refilled his glass, took a thoughtful sip, then guffawed so abruptly that wine sprayed from between his falsely white teeth so that Spiller was hit by it.

'Oh, she really messed up engaging your services, didn't she?' Delaney hooted.

'Fuck is wrong with you?' Spiller said, wiping his face.

Delaney struggled to control his amusement. 'Oh, what a silly girl she is.' He burst out laughing again.

Spiller recalled the same reaction from Emma during their last encounter, and it riled him.

'Nice touch, the scarf,' Delaney said. 'Very GI Joe. So, let's review your curriculum vitae, shall we, Matthew?'

Spiller knew what was coming, so he grabbed his glass and glugged it down like it was the cheapest plonk available. He set the empty glass down with a crack on the table top.

'Matthew Ian Spiller, age forty-three. Educated at public school, dropped out of university to pursue his true vocation in life. But was that a career in the military? I don't think so. Try the Royal Academy of Dramatic Art. A tour in Afghanistan? Try Jordan, a fair stand-in for the real thing—unlike you, Matthew.'

Spiller held his hands up. 'Bang to rights. If only your gullible little Emma had thought to Google my name. She'd have saved herself a fortune.'

'Shame your movie bombed so badly, Matthew. Really. By all accounts, it was a faithful recreation of the events depicted. The critics lapped it up, but not the public, right? Which made it your last hurrah in the acting world.'

'I don't know what's wrong with people in this country,' Spiller said. 'They're embarrassed by our veterans. It's like

Afghanistan's our Vietnam. In the States, people thank veterans for their service; here, most people scowl at anyone in a military uniform. I kept the jacket from the film as a memento, but when I wore it back here people would laugh, point, openly jeer at me.'

'Maybe that was more a comment on your acting.'

'Bollocks—the film wasn't even out at the time.'

'Well... all terribly sad. But you know what's worse than laughing at a veteran? Impersonating one. It's called *stolen valour*. Real veterans hate it. I know. I know plenty of veterans. I *knew* a lot more in the old days.'

Spiller grabbed the wine bottle and emptied it into his glass. 'It's not a *thing* with me, okay? It was an innocent lie, told out of boredom. It's just acting; me seeing how far I can push a character and still be credible. I just hate the same questions night after night. *Where have you been? When did you start? When do you finish? Have you been busy?* If people are stupid enough to think those questions are preferable to a quiet ride, I unleash bullshit on them. Okay? That night I was ex-military. Big deal. Any other night I might have said I was a... retired brain surgeon or... I used to be in M16 or... Jesus, any other night I wouldn't have had a crazy woman get in who wanted to hire a hitman. I certainly wasn't stealing anyone's valour.'

'Just their hard-earned cash,' Delaney said.

'Ha!' Spiller swilled down some vino. 'Hard-earned, my arse. You've bought her a house, a car, given her a good job. It's all fallen in her lap. What's she done to earn it? In fact, yeah, what *has* she done to earn your favour?' He leered salaciously at his host, starting to feel a buzz from the rapidly imbibed booze.

'Matthew, think what you like. I don't need the physical attention of a woman less than half my age, but think what you like.'

'Sure, you're just a kind old man.'

Delaney considered his response. 'I can be. I can afford to be. And, at other times, my wealth allows me to choose a wholly less charitable path. Like when a person attempts to blackmail me after extorting a vulnerable young woman.'

'Speaking of which, how soon can you get me my hundred grand?'

'I could have it in your hands within a day if I wanted to. But I don't want to. I don't want that at all. *Boys!*'

Spiller jumped at the raised voice, then again as the kitchen doors barged open behind him. He swivelled in his chair as two men marched towards him and stood over him. One was heavily stubbled, one had a full beard, and both were taller and broader than him. They were smartly dressed in greys and blacks, as all the best bodyguards are in Hollywood movies. Spiller shifted in his chair.

The bearded one spoke: 'Do. Not. Get. Up.'

He didn't.

'Matthew?'

Spiller turned back to Delaney.

'You are going to leave here in a few minutes and go home and forget you ever met Emma. I will provide recompense for the money you inveigled from her, which you should take as the one and only kindness from me to you. Consider your brief deceit the best-paid acting job you've ever had.'

'I need the extra money,' Spiller said, against every protestation his better judgement could throw at him.

One of the men behind him knuckled his head with each word: 'You're. Not. Listening.'

'Tell that dickhead if he touches me again I'm going to kill him.'

Delaney's eye-line hopped up a little as he quickly shook his head, which Spiller imagined only just curtailed the drop of a full fist onto his skull.

'You need to quit the method acting, Matthew. You're not ex-military. You don't have the skill-set. It's going to get you in trouble.'

'I've done shit no military man's *ever* done, believe you me. And all in the past two weeks. So don't doubt I'll give every bit as good as I get if some fucking *ape* presses the wrong button.'

Delaney smiled. 'Really? That's intriguing.' He lifted a finger and indicated that the two men come around where they could be seen. Like obedient Rottweilers, they appeared at their master's side for a moment, glowered at Spiller, then backed away to perch on a couple of nearby chairs.

'Good boys,' Spiller taunted. 'Now *staaaaay.*'

'You still want me to pay you off,' Delaney said. 'Well, credit where it's due: you're persistent.'

'Your employee asked me to kill a man, then that man was killed. I think the police would be very interested in that.'

Delaney's brow lowered. 'How do you know he was killed? You said you didn't even try.'

'I didn't. Someone else did. Two men in a van.'

Delaney's protectors simultaneously flinched, exchanged glances.

'How would you know that?' Delaney asked.

'Because I was there. I watched it happen. I went to warn him about Emma, but he was already being manhandled into the back of a van. I caught it on a dash-cam.'

'Oh,' Delaney said, and drank the rest of his wine.

Spiller saw the well-built goons suddenly look fearful. The bearded man leaned in to his cohort and whispered something. Spiller caught his eye and sensed recognition, certainly coming his way, possibly somehow mutual.

'Yeah,' he said to Delaney, as he mulled the strange connection with the bearded man. 'So don't try and fob me off. Anything happens to me, that SD card goes straight to the police. Emma swears she didn't, but she must have hired someone else in case I didn't go through with it. That woman is in deep shit if you don't pay me what I—... *Fuck. Me.*'

He stared at the bearded man again. It had clicked. The recognition. The realisation was overwhelming.

'*You,*' he said to the man.

Spiller's mind's eye had placed a baseball cap on the head of the bearded man and deposited Jeffrey Poole's lifeless shoulders in his huge hands. Spiller may have been mistaken, but his body wasn't listening to reason. It launched him from his chair towards the exit. He instinctively hurdled the leg the bearded man stuck out, and threw his weight fully at the closed door, busting it open onto the street. Possibly it hadn't been locked, but he wasn't about to stop and try the handle. He stumbled as he hit the pavement, the jellied feel of his adrenaline-soaked leg muscles turning progress into a nightmare scenario where forward momentum was oddly hampered at the very worst moment. His knees connected with the paving and he sprawled onto his chest, his palms taking some of the impact, but not enough to prevent his face skidding across the stone. He felt the skin sloughing off his nose and forehead and chin, but those were inconsequential beside his greatest fear: that in the next second a large boot would come down on the back of his neck to snap it and end his life.

Instead, he heard the merciful *whoop-whoop* of a siren, the short burst the cops used to draw attention. He scrambled to his knees and crawled into the road to throw himself in front of the stationary patrol car, arms aloft and waving frantically. Even in those terrifying seconds, he was aware that his actions were a tad melodramatic. Ever the bloody thespian.

As he gained his feet, Spiller turned back to the restaurant but the men hadn't followed him outside. The door was in pieces, hanging only on its top hinge, its glass panes shattered into a thousand bits, and it dawned on him he'd just managed to bust outward through an inward-opening door. Matthew Spiller—exit stage wrong. As he surveyed the damage, the blind detached from its roller and dropped in a crumple onto the newly crystallised pavement.

He swore and sat down on the bonnet of the police car, staring at his grazed and bleeding palms and tentatively touching his fingertips to some very tender parts of his face, drawing them away sticky and red.

'You all right, mate?' said a female voice, and he looked up into the eyes of someone he thought he knew. It seemed to be the night for meeting people he vaguely recognised. He watched the other copper pull his CS spray and walk tentatively towards the restaurant's gaping entrance.

'Mate,' the female officer said. 'What happened?'

Spiller looked at her again, then at her name-tag: Carnaby.

Carnaby. Carnaby. Carnaby…

'Mr Spiller?' Carnaby said.

He nodded.

'Didn't recognise you under all that blood. I'm PC Carnaby, we met—'

'Sergeant Enright,' Spiller said. 'You were with Enright.'

'That's right.'

Spiller pointed at the officer entering the building. 'Is that…?'

'No. Mr Spiller, what happened?'

He had no clue what to say. If he even began to tell the truth, he'd screw himself. But then… would he? As he'd said to Delaney, he'd actually tried to prevent Poole's murder. And he had video evidence that Poole had been taken by others. Plus, the audio on the SD card had his voice swearing as he'd been shot at. It was one hundred percent exonerating.

Before he could open his mouth to say anything, the other officer emerged with Charles Delaney, and Spiller noted the officer's full beard and realised it equally could have been him in the video from the other night.

'Where are his goons?' Spiller asked.

'Mike?' Carnaby said to her colleague.

'No one else in there; it was just Mr Delaney.'

Carnaby looked between them. 'Would either of you like to explain all this?'

'Mr Spiller thinks I threatened to hurt his family,' Delaney said quickly.

'What? No…'

Delaney continued, and Spiller understood that the threat was being made as he spoke.

'He has this crazy notion that I'm going to go after his family if he tells you something about me, but I don't even know what he thinks I've done. The man talks in riddles.'

Carnaby gave a subtle nod to Mike, who led Delaney back into the restaurant so they could conduct separate conversations.

'Sit in my car,' Carnaby said. 'Do you need an ambulance?'

'You tell me,' Spiller said, gurning at her, then shook his head. 'I'll be fine.'

Carnaby opened the rear door and Spiller climbed in. She went to the driver's side, settled, and twisted so she could talk to him between the seats.

'So, what's going on? I know what's been happening with you and the Wards. We all do. The whole station's talking about it. No one's mourning Callum Ward. I can tell you that much. Does this have anything to do with that?'

Spiller moaned. 'Oh, God... there's no point. I know you mean well but everyone's looking at me for shit and ignoring the real arseholes in all this.'

'All what? Tell me—I'm listening.'

Their eyes met for a long moment and he sensed she was genuine, but...

'No point,' he said. 'That man—Delaney. You know him, right?'

'Of him. He owns half the city.'

'Exactly. So who's going to take my word over his?'

'What did you mean about his goons?' Carnaby asked.

Spiller inspected his palms, pressing them together before slowly pulling them apart and stretching the loose bits of skin within the stringy, congealing blood. 'Ow,' he said.

Carnaby opened the glove box and produced a packet of wet wipes. 'Here.'

'Thanks.' He pulled out a wad and nursed his palms. 'There were a couple of men in there with him, but they've obviously slipped out through the kitchen. Look, it really doesn't matter.' He handed the packet back to her and reached for the door release, but it was locked. 'Could you...'

'Hang on a mo. You just wrecked a restaurant. That's criminal damage.'

Spiller sighed. 'Fuck.'

'Give me a minute,' she said, and got out.

Spiller looked around the interior for anything usefully policey he could pinch but couldn't spot anything. A genuine warrant card would have been fun. He had a fake one from a brief stint as a detective in a TV series. DI Nat Mortlake. It looked real enough; a leather wallet that opened to show ID on one side and a fancy crest on the other. The sodding props people had taken it off him after filming, so he'd nipped into their trailer and reclaimed it as a memento, plus a police baseball cap.

Carnaby returned directly to his door and opened it. 'You're free to go,' she said as she released him. 'He's not pressing charges.'

'That's big of him.'

'And neither is he explaining very much, which makes two of you.'

Spiller patted down his jacket pockets to make sure he hadn't lost his keys, mobile, or wallet during his acrobatic exit.

Carnaby pressed a bit more: 'Bloody hell, DCI Bartoli is going to have a frigging *field day* when he hears about this. You're already doing his head in.'

Spiller couldn't help but laugh. 'Oh, *shit*, I've got a headache.'

'Get yourself to the hospital, Mr Spiller. You could have a concussion.' She pointed at his face. 'Either way, that all needs cleaning.'

'Thanks for showing up when you did.'

'Hey, pure luck. Next time, who knows?'

Spiller was about to return to his car when Delaney emerged onto the pavement with the hirsute Mike, crunching the glass underfoot.

'Fran,' the bearded PC said to Carnaby. 'Mr Delaney would like a word with Mr Spiller, if he's okay with that.'

'Sure,' Spiller said.

Carnaby laid a hand on his arm. 'Do anything daft, you're getting locked up.'

He gave her a nod and sauntered over to Delaney as Mike returned to his colleague's side. Delaney used his irritating finger of authority to indicate they move a few paces away from the cops. At a distance where they could talk softly and not be overheard, Delaney put his back to them and spoke.

'Let this go, Matthew. All of it. Emma, me, my lads, whatever you *think* you know. Understand?'

Spiller hadn't decided on his next course of action, but now it was set. 'You know what? I am heartily sick of privileged tossers like you threatening my family. You pay me my hundred thousand pounds or I swear to God I will have a *cull*. I will round you up, every threat, real or imagined, and I will put you all in the fucking ground.'

Delaney offered a condescending smile. 'Where's that from? It's one of the *Taken* films, right? You're doing Liam, aren't you? You need to work on the accent, but I'd give you a solid six out of ten on the barely contained fury.'

'Fuck you,' Spiller said, and barged past him, catching shoulders and spinning Delaney a hundred-and-eighty degrees. As he passed the police officers, he noted their expectant expressions as they awaited Delaney's request to arrest him for assault. But no one said a word.

BACK IN HIS car, Spiller realised he was too screwed to drive. The wine didn't help, but it was his battered face that bothered him more. It wasn't just scraped raw; he had a lump on his forehead like there was a golf ball buried halfway into his frontal bone. Carnaby hadn't been wrong about a possible concussion.

He burst into tears.

He'd had a lot of trouble in his teens and early twenties extracting the precise reason for his frequent tears from the receptacle of sorrowful shit that was his brain. There wasn't a whole lot spoken about depression back then. Mental-health issues were taboo. People spoke about nut-houses and loony-bins and there was no middle ground. You were either a sane, whole, and functioning part of society or you were a broken soul who got checked into Casa Crazy. The idea that a broad section of the population suffered silently in the midst of the "normal" folk wasn't exactly dinner-party conversation.

The revelation that he might be depressed had come after reading a magazine article when he was twenty-five. It had discussed the concept of SAD—Seasonal Affective Disorder—and it was a diagnosis that ticked every box. It explained everything about the winter months. People had always told him to cheer up, but he'd never been able to. He'd known it was more than the usual British grumble about the miserable weather and short days. It was like a black tarp had been dragged over his head in October and hadn't been pulled away until well into March. His mind had been darkened, his thoughts sullied. Positive events couldn't penetrate. He knew when good things were happening; they just didn't touch his heart. And once he'd read about SAD, he knew what was wrong with the rest of his year, when he started to feel better, but not so much that he could ever apply the word "happy" to his life. Matt Spiller was depressed. Seasonally. Annually. Sometimes manically. And things had only grown worse when his parents had died, his career had taken a nose-dive, and his marriage had faltered, as genuinely crap circumstances began to fuel a sense of doom and dread that had previously been purely chemical in origin.

So, his tears at that moment weren't a surprise, nor were they a mystery. They were just unstoppable.

He hadn't cried like this in two decades. The acceptance of depression in his life at twenty-five had helped. He had named an unknown nemesis, called him from the shadows and labelled him so he couldn't scurry away again like a coward evading blame. Whenever he'd appeared since then, Spiller had known. The moment those gnarled little digits had inched into the light to begin the darkening, he'd steeled himself against what was to come. It wasn't a cure, but it was a defence.

Against this, though, there was no defence. This was the outpouring for a life he deemed wasted. The face that stared back at him from the rear-view mirror, all dark and tacky and warped by anguish, was a culmination. It felt like his just desserts, the outer visage finally in synch with the inner turmoil, like Dorian Gray coming face-to-face with his grotesque portrait.

Spiller wept for an hour and hated every minute of it. He'd tried to be less self-pitying as he'd grown older. Mostly, he'd managed. Tonight was an epic fail.

When he eventually heaved that final sob from his chest, he realised something fundamental inside him had changed. He just didn't know what.

As he didn't have any good news to report to his wife, and his face would have made his daughters howl, he decided to head back to his flat. But, by the time he got there, his concern for his family had burgeoned. Delaney was a powerful man who had made a palpable and credible threat. Spiller had been offered the chance to retreat and had viciously declined. At that moment, Delaney might have been using his significant resources to locate Helen and the girls, not only pinpointing the family home but any other linked property, such as the in-laws.

Spiller sat on the sofa and belatedly Googled his new adversary on a laptop. Emma had told him a little about Delaney's sprawling empire; he needed to know more. It didn't take many links to lead him to some extremely disturbing facts.

Delaney had been a defence contractor in the eighties and nineties. He'd lived in Northern Ireland for a while during The Troubles, providing weapons, logistics, and installations to the UK government. Until the IRA had put a bomb under his car in 1994 and killed his wife and daughter, at which point he'd taken his son back to the UK, liquidated his defence-related assets, and had become a recluse, using his fortune to disappear. He had resurfaced in the mid-noughties, ploughing his funds into various business ventures, all of which had prospered even through the crash of 2008. Charles Delaney was a shrewd man, a man with powerful contacts back in the day, and there was no reason to suppose he'd let any of them fall away since then.

It wasn't a stretch to think that Delaney could have orchestrated the demise of Jeffrey Poole, maybe as a favour to Emma. He was also the likely source of her Sig-Sauer. It took serious connections to bring any gun into the country, even old Eastern European crap, but you needed to access some elite channels to get your hands on the latest US weaponry, like the Sig and the suppressed pistol used to end Poole's life. Delaney Import & Export? Perhaps that was a euphemism and he'd only faked his retirement from the arms industry.

Spiller began to giggle. It was more enjoyable than weeping, but no more encouraging. Before Christmas Eve he'd had his problems: a job he didn't like, a failed career, and a marriage heading for divorce. But that was heaven compared to all that had happened since. A scene from *Life of Brian* popped into his head. The long-incarcerated man telling the saliva-spattered Brian: "I sometimes hang awake at night *dreaming* of being spat at in the face." Yep, some people just didn't know when they were well off.

His amusement waned as his mind returned to the primary cause of his concern: the safety of his family. He called Helen.

'Are we rich?' she asked on answering.

'Uh… not quite. Helen—'

'I thought not.'

'Helen.'

'Go on.'

'I want you to pack your stuff and take the girls to a hotel.'

'Shit, not this again.'

'*Helen!* Listen to me. Drive a hundred miles and check in somewhere. Pay with the cash I gave you. Don't use your bank cards for anything and try and stick to minor roads—less cameras. And don't even call me to let me know where you are.'

Helen barked a laugh. 'Are you kidding me? Gosh, did you get us on the new series of *Hunted?*'

'Helen, you need to do this. For the girls if not for you.'

Silence.

'Will you do it? Right now?'

A pause, then, 'Yes. I assume I can't even tell my parents where I am.'

'Better not.'

'Jesus.' She put the phone down on him.

Spiller reflected on the situation. He needed to draw up a to-do list, although it would probably end up being a to-screw list. Still…

He leaned back against the cushions and closed his eyes to think. There was stuff to do right now, but, damn, he was so tired.

Chapter Sixteen

CONSIDERING THE PLACES Spiller could or should have been the following morning, his choice would have earned him an almighty punch in the face from his wife. He'd woken with a resounding conviction that his taxiing days were over. He didn't yet know how he'd substitute the job, and accepted it could well be with something he'd equally detest, but he was done with taxiing. The job he really desired hadn't changed for twenty-five years. He still wanted to act. It had been a rather love-hate relationship in recent years, given the unemployment, but he'd never mentally let go because he was more at peace when he was acting than at any other time. And he was more fun to be with. At least, he enjoyed himself more. He couldn't speak for others in his presence, but the world did get to see the elated side of his bi-polar personality.

While he'd considered his acting career to be dead in the water since the backlash against *Combatants*—as his ill-fated movie had been titled—it wasn't strictly accurate. He still had an agent and would get an interview for a poxy little part every few months, but the odds were always stacked against him. The sheer number of fellow auditionees was one thing; another was the recycling of the same old faces from series to series; but maybe the worst was the long memories of the directors who sometimes twigged where they'd seen him before, even though he'd been leaving *Combatants* off his CV. The whole situation with that bloody movie still galled him. A lead role in a major war film, and didn't everyone love a good war film? Apparently not. Not when it concerned an unpopular, politically and religiously incorrect conflict. Delaney had done his research— most critics had applauded its brutal integrity—but it was too much for some, and the public had stayed away in droves.

People loved watching series about fictional Special Forces fighting naughty brown foreigners, but the real thing was taboo. Some social media self-appointed critics had even butchered the title and called it *InCombatants*, which had been grossly unfair to the director and all involved. Still, when had social media and considered fairness ever skipped along hand in hand?

But, like most deluded thesps, despite the lingering bitter taste and all the duff experiences, Spiller still wanted to act. So he decided to pay his agent a visit. It would be unannounced, which wouldn't win him any popularity contest, but if there was one thing he was guaranteed to win from his agent, it was the sympathy vote. Spiller had spent quite some time softening his wounds with warm water so he could get the muck and grit out, as he'd fallen asleep last night without tending to them, and now they'd started bleeding and weeping afresh. Thankfully, the lump on his forehead had shrunk, but the overall visage was pretty horrible, and Billy Banbury, winner of Luvvie of the Year Award every year since 1965, would be suitably horrified.

Billy Banbury, Theatrical Agent, was everything you could wish for from a theatrical agent called Billy Banbury. In a profession where clichés thrived, he was a cliché of a cliché. He owned and wore every day the only cravats in the country that hadn't been donated to a charity shop. The collars that framed his paisley affectations were seventies-wide, and he wore a maroon or dark green velvet jacket and black flared slacks—as he was wont to call them. Mirror-finish brogues tailed the look, but topping it was a hairdo that made Donald Trump's look sane. It was dyed Elvis blue-black, and although it was sparse, some powdery substance made it look full, until you got up close and saw it sitting inside the candy-floss structure, lending it some volume. He'd also recently discovered Botox, which gave his pallid skin the flawless look of a porcelain doll, albeit a doll with the eerily incongruous eyes of a seventy-five-year-old. Blindingly-white false teeth completed the hideous countenance, but from his mouth flowed the most mellifluous tones, with every sentence begun or ended with the words "dear boy", "dear heart", "precious love", or variations thereof.

Despite the visual and aural artifice, Billy was a genuinely dear heart himself, remained even at his age an agent with clout, and had been a serious actor in his day, a fact his office walls had been forced to attest to, with its jumble of framed black-and-white photographs that featured a young Billy alongside the likes of Gielgud, Oliver, and their other mostly dead contemporaries. Either that, or Billy was a dab hand at Photoshop.

Whether or not he was gay, Spiller didn't actually know. He'd been married from his early twenties until his wife's death ten years ago, but that was often the way back then to present an acceptable image. Maybe they'd grown into companions. Or maybe Billy was just the campest straight man in recorded history.

He lived in a Victorian property, detached and set far back from a main road that was otherwise lined with terraced houses. The house, like the man inside, had refused to move with the times. Spiller reckoned Billy could have sold his plot to a developer for millions. He was still listed in *Contacts* as a "Theatrical Agent", with no reference to the TV or movie work he handled alongside the traditional repertory. He was also, Spiller had noted worryingly on his last visit, eking out the last dying breaths from Windows XP.

Driving there in his Fiesta, Spiller was still trying to figure out what had changed in him since last night. It was a huge niggle not being able to name it because it felt momentous, and he didn't think he'd be making this trip had the change not occurred. Really, he should have been heading towards Dominic Ward with the Sig in his pocket. He supposed he had a little time now, though, with Helen and the girls safely hiding out in another part of the country. But, Lordy, what she would do to his scrotum if she ever found out he'd spent a single minute of that time trying to jump-start his acting career.

Such was the state of Spiller's facial injuries that when Billy opened the grandly carved oak door to him, he received all the endearments at once.

'Oh, dear heart, precious love, what happened to you, my poor, poor boy? You look like you just returned from a lengthy sojourn in Chernobyl. Rather… gooey.'

'I fell while running,' Spiller said. No lie there. 'It's all right, Billy, once all the scabs drop off I'll still be the handsome leading man you took on all those years ago.'

'Oh, I do hope so. I'd kiss you but I'm not sure I'd be able to pull my face away.' He offered his hand instead. 'To what do I owe the pleasure?' Billy stepped inside and waved a green velvet arm in a beckoning, rotating manner towards the rear of the house, where his office was.

Spiller walked in and straight down the dark and corniced hallway, leaving Billy to follow. Billy flounced in behind him and sat in his filigreed swivel chair, revolving it 360 degrees before grabbing the edge of his desk at just the right moment. It was the oddest thing to see from anyone over ten years old.

'You are in a desperate state, dear boy. I'm so sorry for you.'

Spiller sat in the client's chair, the plainest wooden seat Ikea had to offer. It was a status thing. 'Thanks, Billy. I won't keep you long. I was just wondering if you had anything for me.'

'Well, it's very quiet this time of year, love, you know that.'

'Yeah, anything interesting in the pipeline, though? Any whispers? Anything I'd be a shoo-in for?'

Billy turned to his brick of a computer monitor and shook his mouse to wake it up. He clicked a few times and appeared to scan down the screen. Spiller couldn't see what was on it— possibly it was eBay's cravat page.

'Uhhhhh…. sorry, dear boy, old pooter's running a tad slow.'

'You still on Windows XP?'

'Actually, no.'

'Oh.'

'Too glitchy so I restored it back to ninety-five.'

'Good call. Any better?'

'If anything, worse,' Billy said, nonplussed, shaking and tapping his mouse hard on the mat.

'Santa not bring you Windows Ten, then?'

Billy laughed to indicate he wasn't about to be conned by such new-fangled nonsense.

A minute later, he ended his search. 'No. Sorry, dear heart. Nothing. But you know I'm always looking out for you.'

'It's just…' Spiller shuffled on his bum like a kid in the headmaster's office '… I could really do with a boost right now. I need some serious money. And obviously the work. You know I love the work.'

'Don't we all, dear boy? Actually…' Billy's face would have creased in deep thought had his skin been capable of movement '…I might have something.'

'Go on, please, anything.'

'My exterior woodwork needs painting.'

Spiller waited for a moment, trying to gauge Billy's intent and hoping he'd quickly burst out laughing at his entertaining gag. But he didn't.

'Seriously?' Spiller asked, his peeve written all over his face.

'Well, there is a lot of wood out there and I'd pay you well. No?'

'No, Billy. I was thinking more along the lines of your stock-in-trade. You know? Acting work?'

Billy sat back in his chair, shifting it left and right, perusing the walls of his office like he'd never seen them before, until his eyes came to settle on his desk diary. He slid it in front of him and opened it where the bookmark lay.

'Are you still driving that taxi-cab of yours?'

Spiller's eyebrows rose so high it hurt his damaged forehead. 'You want me to take you somewhere?'

'Calm down, love. This could be very interesting for you. You know the name Brett Stutz?'

'Of course. The Hollywood director.'

'The very chap. Well, he's flying in this evening to meet with Leyton. You know Leyton?'

Leyton Scrannage, ex-soap star on Billy's books, as naturally ungifted as they came, currently trying to break into the movies. Spiller nodded, swallowing on a bit of sick.

'Well, Brett's scouting for talent for an upcoming feature. It's to be filmed in Los Angeles, but he wants a Brit for the baddie role. Preferably someone unknown in the States.'

'What's the film?'

'His usual fare. Lots of gore, weird happenings. Something about a killer biker. A horror-thriller thing. I don't know. Sounds ghastly. Based on a novel from some years back, I believe.'

'So why's he looking at Leyton?'

Billy would have frowned.

'If he's looking for talent.'

Billy tittered. 'Oh, you rascal, you. Anyway, I was going to send a cab to pick him up, but... dear boy, *you* could go. Maybe there's a little something in the script for you. It's mainly an action flick, so you'd be perfect—once you stop looking so radioactive. You could introduce yourself, give him your CV. You never know. They liked *Combatants* in the States. I'm sure he'd remember you. It must be a thirty-minute drive to his hotel. Plenty of time to establish a rapport. What do you think?'

'Sure. Certainly beats painting your house.'

'Wonderful.' Billy opened a desk drawer and took out a pad of Basildon Bond. Using a Mont Blanc fountain pen, he used his laborious cursive handwriting to jot down the flight details, tore off the sheet, blew the ink dry, folded it, and handed it across the desk.

'Don't you want to put a wax seal on that?' Spiller asked.

'Tad flippant, dear boy. Now, don't be late.'

'I won't.'

'And you're categorically ruling out the decorating gig—before I call someone else?'

OUTSIDE BILLY'S HOUSE, Spiller stared at the Fiesta. It would have made a passable taxi for one evening, if he'd been picking up Joe Bloggs from the local railway station. But showing up in a Fiesta to collect a top Hollywood director would mean a lot of ground would need to be regained on the journey to his hotel. What Spiller really needed was a luxury taxi. Like Gibbo's Lexus

ES. Spiller supposed he could always head back to the rental company for an upgrade, but all their cars were explicitly barred from being used for hire and reward. If there were a crash and Brett Stutz claimed for lost earnings, the insurance would be invalid and Spiller would be personally liable. It was an unlikely scenario, but so was your lovely wife pumping builder's foam into a man's mouth, and that had happened.

Spiller really needed Gibbo's Lexus. And he really needed to clear his flat of all those boxes. So he desperately needed to make up with his pal. It had ended acrimoniously, but perhaps he could sweeten the deal, throw a bit of cash his way—not that the mollycoddled tosser needed any.

He checked his mobile for any missed calls. There weren't any. He'd told Helen not to call, so he was glad on that score, but he had wanted to see a missed call from Charles Delaney, or preferably to hear a voice message from him, panicking and agreeing to cough up the hush-money.

He pondered whether he should drive to see Emma, to at least show her the kind of man Delaney really was. His face was sufficient evidence. But Delaney would have prepped her already with some bogus tale, and, even if she did entertain any doubts about her boss, she had a lot to lose by pursuing them.

He set off for Gibbo's house, stopping on the way to pick up a bit of cardboard and a marker pen from a pound-shop to make a welcome sign for Brett Stutz.

The closer he got, the more Spiller doubted he'd be able to win Gibbo over. He'd wrecked his car the last time and left it miles away, and Gibbo wasn't desperate for money. The only reason Gibbo had lent it to him in the first place was their friendship and his libido-induced state of distraction. Now that friendship was kaput.

The Lexus was sitting on Gibbo's excuse for a driveway. The knock on the front door went unanswered. Spiller stepped back and looked up at the bedroom window, waiting to see a bare torso or perhaps some breasts. He banged on the door again, then called his mobile, but it rang out.

He turned back to the Lexus. It was pristine. Incredible to think he'd knocked a man down in it the other night while being shot at. He peered in through the tinted glass and saw the dash-cam was back in its rightful spot.

As he rapped on the front door a third time, his eyes were drawn to the wooden planter beneath the bay window, and the decorative stones that encircled the thin trunk of a burgundy Japanese maple. He checked around in case anyone was watching, then reached for one of the stones. It was light, made of plastic. He flipped it over and slid open the cover, revealing a single key. He'd seen Gibbo let himself into his house a couple of times this way, having earlier locked himself out. He wondered what excuse he could make if he used the key, only to find Gibbo had been deep asleep or had been ignoring the caller because he didn't want his coitus interrupted.

Spiller opened the door quietly, gently closing it behind him. He paused in the hallway, listening. The house was utterly silent but for the ticking of a wall clock. The lights on the alarm panel were dark. Possibly it was defunct. More likely, it was just bad security. Spiller entered the living room and shifted a few bits around on the coffee table, looking for the Lexus fob. Not there. He scanned the room. It was still a mess. It would be until the day before Gibbo's parents flew back to visit their son. In the corner was a small computer desk with three drawers. He recalled seeing Gibbo chuck things in there at the end of a shift when he'd occasionally bobbed in for a coffee.

At the rear of the top drawer, Spiller found a Lexus fob. It wasn't the one he'd used the other night—this was a spare on a different key-ring—but it would do the job.

Now here was a predicament. To TWOC or not to TWOC...

Not, apparently, such a difficult one, as Spiller found his legs walking him into the hallway, then back outside the house. His hand pulled the front door shut, then returned the key to its stone hidey-hole. That same hand then opened the door of the Lexus and his whole body slipped in effortlessly behind the wheel as though his mental quandary wasn't even happening. A wayward finger pressed the button marked "engine start stop".

The engine responded. The gear-shifter notched into reverse. Before he could say "taking without consent", the Lexus was on the road, then silently moving forwards, seemingly of its own volition, like it was stealing itself.

It was a risk taking the car hours before the flight was due, as Spiller had no idea of Gibbo's whereabouts, so no clue when he might return to report it stolen. But this had been a gift-horse that might have bolted had he come back later.

All a big misunderstanding, officer. He put me on the insurance a few days ago, gave me the spare key, so he was clearly fine with me borrowing it. Yeah, that would fly.

Spiller drove to a housing estate near the airport and parked up to wait, listening to the radio and dozing fitfully.

ACCORDING TO THE airport app, the flight was on time. After gauging how long it would take Stutz to clear customs and collect his baggage, Spiller set off for the pick-up/drop-off parking structure. Once upon a time, a person could drive up to the terminal entrance, park for a few minutes for free, and collect or dump their passengers. Now, even taxis had to pay. And if you were unfortunate enough to be there for more than an hour, it was cheaper to fly to Spain and back.

Spiller took his welcome sign on the five-minute walk to the terminal. You had to pre-book if you wanted to park right next to the terminal, and the cost of that rivalled a week's all-inclusive in Barbados.

Everyone who glanced his way just stared, some giving him a wide berth. He had the kind of injuries five-year-olds carried after a fall in a playground, except his features, even unscathed, were far from those of an unfortunate young innocent.

He placed himself where he could be seen at the arrivals door. A small moat of isolation formed around him.

Eventually, the doors began sliding open on the passengers from LAX. Spiller knew what Stutz looked like from various chat-show interviews. Tall, bald, and stubbled so darkly he could never shave it away, like Desperate Dan. Of course, he was one of the last ones out. Spiller's passengers were always the last buggers to get off the plane.

The UCLA frat jacket Stutz wore was cool, but what were those trousers? Who wore black leather trousers anymore, who didn't also have a motorbike nearby? And peeking out from under the hems were winkle-pickers so pointy and long they made him look like an inverted ice-pick. They kept kicking the trolley as he walked.

Spiller saw Stutz notice the sign with his name on it, then notice Spiller's face above the sign, then look away like there just had to be someone else there to collect him. He was about to pass by when Spiller spoke.

'Mr Stutz?'

Stutz faltered and stopped. 'Uh...'

'Billy sent me. Billy Banbury.'

'Oh... okay. You got a car?'

'No, I was going to give you a piggy-back.'

Stutz glanced at him, smiled wryly. 'Fair enough. Dumb question.'

'A few minutes' walk,' Spiller said, realising the poor man was as yet too fazed to make much sense. 'Are you okay with your trolley?'

'I'm good, thanks.'

As they walked out of the terminal building, Spiller thought Stutz was still scouting for someone else to take him to his hotel. When that seemed futile, the director struck up a conversation.

'How do you know Billy?' he asked.

'I'm on his books.'

'Ah, gotcha. An actor with a second job. Ain't that always the way?'

'Well, some people have careers. You work with them.'

'I guess. So... would I know you from anything?'

'I was one of the leads in the movie *Combatants*.'

'Jesus, I remember that. I remember *you*. That was powerful stuff.'

'Yeah, but it didn't go down well over here.'

'How many years ago was that?'

'Six.'

'And you still haven't taken off the make-up? Jeez, that's method.'

They smiled at each other, sharing the joke, and Spiller heard that mental click you had to have with any director. This could go very well, he thought.

They chatted about the film until they reached the Lexus on the second floor of the packed and bustling structure with its low, grey steel beams. Spiller opened the passenger side and let Stutz in, then pushed his trolley to the rear of the car to load his bags into the boot. The lid lifted at the remote press of the key fob and Spiller squeaked and took a stumbling step backwards.

Inside a clear zipped-up plastic body-bag was his erstwhile mate, Tony "Gibbo" Gibson. The face had a couple of extra holes in it beyond what was expected, one in the cheek and one just above the right eyebrow. The hair was matted with dried blood and cranial tissue, although the plastic was fairly clean. There was leakage, but most of what had been pushed out of Gibbo's head was obviously elsewhere. Not such a lucky bastard, after all.

Spiller quickly weighed up the volume of luggage and knew it wouldn't all fit on the back seat. There were two hard suitcases and two large metal boxes marked "fragile", possibly containing camera gear for the auditions.

With arms that felt suddenly sapped of strength, he chucked the largest suitcase in on top of his old friend, then slammed the lid before any passers-by could look inside. Then he stood there, frozen beneath the harsh spotlights, like a man pinned by multiple beams of interrogation. It wasn't one of his weird fugues; it was simply the paralysing enormity of a sight he hadn't expected, and, luckily, he had the wherewithal to know his stutter had to be brief. He shook himself and pulled open the rear door of the Lexus.

'Forgot I had stuff in the boot,' he explained as he slid the remaining three pieces across the grey leather. Stutz didn't reply, checking something on his mobile phone. The seats would be scuffed but, hey, Gibbo would never know. The door only just closed.

Spiller settled in the driver's seat and exhaled harshly, but it did nothing to ease the ton weight nestling in his chest cavity. He tried to catch his breath, which quivered audibly with the rapid beat of his heart.

'You okay, buddy?' Stutz asked.

Spiller looked at him, unable to shake the troubled expression from his face. He nodded.

'You sure? You look like you've seen a ghost.'

'Shit time right now,' Spiller said, and started the engine.

THE FIRST FIFTEEN minutes of the journey passed in silence. Spiller knew the route to Stutz's hotel, as he knew every road within a ten-mile radius, which was just as well because he was deep in thought, cruising on auto-pilot. Stutz was engrossed in his phone, so didn't appear bothered by his sulky chauffeur. Spiller *was* bothered. There was a dead body in the boot and he was wholly convinced that was down to him. No way was this a big coincidence. While taxiing was a dangerous occupation, it was all relative. It wasn't bomb disposal. Taxi drivers sometimes got attacked, but rarely killed, and never shot—not in the UK, not that he could recall.

The events of last night at Delaney's came into crystal-clear focus. The worried look Delaney's goons had exchanged when they understood the man in the taxi had been him, not the poor bastard they'd killed. Spiller had suspected the bearded one had been there the night Poole had been taken, and beardy must have recruited the other one to help snuff out the only witness. Even if the one Spiller had rammed wasn't in plaster, he'd have had a limp, and neither of them did. Spiller surmised one of them had managed to note the registration, track the car back to Gibbo, and lure him to his death with the promise of a lengthy and well-paid journey.

Why, though, return the car to Gibbo's home address? Were they so confident in their abilities that they knew it would never trace back to them? Could they be that meticulous as to have removed every trace of their presence from the car? Or did it not matter? The police could only identify a person if their prints or DNA were in the system. And Spiller knew Delaney had the means and finances to make sure his personnel were squeaky clean. Perhaps it was just the easiest option. Take the car back to where it wouldn't cause alarm. Gibbo always carried his driving licence so finding his address was a cinch. Maybe leave it there a few days to make sure the hit had gone unnoticed, then go back and fetch it before the body bloated with gas and began to leak. What had Emma mentioned about Delaney's business empire? That he owned an Environmental Services company? That meant garbage trucks, waste and recycling sites. Perhaps it was going to take them a couple of days to organise the disposal.

Spiller drove onwards, his head a muzzy mess.

A few minutes later, Stutz slipped his phone back in his pocket. A couple of minutes after that, he shifted in his seat to face Spiller.

'I gotta say, buddy—no offence—but you're fucking weird.'

Spiller bristled. 'Really?'

'You're an out-of-work actor. You got a big Hollywood director in your car who knows you can act, and you don't try and tap me for a job? What gives?'

'Shit time at the moment.'

'Yeah, you said. And you don't think I could help?'

'I need a magician, not a director.'

'Fair enough. But anyone else would be giving me a metaphorical blow-job by now, stroking my ego. Some would have offered the real thing.'

Spiller didn't know if that was a hint or just an FYI. Either way, he couldn't think of a fast enough response, so he said nothing.

'That wasn't me asking, by the way,' Stutz said, seemingly reading Spiller's thoughts.

'No skin off my nose, mate. Ask away—you ain't getting.'

Stutz gave a curt laugh. 'No skin *on* your nose. *Mate.*'

Spiller so desperately wanted to grab the lifeline Stutz was offering, although he sensed it had already been tugged back out of his reach. Shit, had he just screwed up the most important audition of his life? How many times had he been shot in the foot by his own moods? Not just in the acting. He didn't know, but he'd never been more acutely aware of the wound being inflicted in real time. Then again... he was so sick of pandering to people with power, grinning like a cretin in the hope that they'd favour him with a crumb flicked from their table, which he'd have to scurry after only to find someone else had got there before him. It wasn't like Stutz was the first player to big-up his chances of success. He'd have a star on the Walk of Fame by now if all the promises and positive noises over the years had meant anything. Stutz would be just as full of crap as all those who'd gone before. The Great I Am, lording it over the mere mortals bowed at his feet, dangling hope before snatching it away. Fuck him.

Spiller shrugged to himself. Who was he kidding? If there hadn't been a body in the boot, or a trail of them leading to this point in his life, he'd have been sucking up like a pro. Because the most imminent stumbling block was just that: making sure Stutz didn't get a peek in the boot when he retrieved his suitcase.

'Well, I hope you don't live to regret this,' Stutz said, lording it bang on cue.

Spiller gave him a vicious sidelong stare. 'You should stop talking.'

Stutz went back to his mobile phone, and Spiller belatedly realised his attitude had probably wrecked his relationship with his agent as well. Worst-case scenario, Stutz would boycott all Billy's actors in protest.

They arrived at the hotel ten minutes later. It was called the Moorside Country Hotel, even though it wasn't next to a moor and wasn't that far into the countryside. It was surrounded by fields and woods, though, and the building was old and listed, so Billy had obviously assessed it offered enough twee green Englishness for a Left-Coaster who'd only ever seen sand and palm trees.

The long driveway had been gravel when Spiller had visited a few years before, dropping people off for a wedding reception, but it was now tarmacked. It was lined with trees and illuminated posts, and the hotel had been used more than once as a location for a TV series, although nothing he'd been in. You could usually tell where filming was taking place from the small orange arrows tied to lampposts with "Base" or "Loc" on them.

The moment the Lexus stopped, a uniformed porter had already scurried down the grand stone steps and was at the boot before Spiller could even set one foot on the ground. Spiller cursed under his breath and got out, ready to spark the porter out cold if he reached a hand towards the boot release. Thankfully, he just stood there waiting, so Spiller beckoned him to the rear door and handed him the smaller case from the back seat, which he carried inside. By this time, Stutz had emerged and he was the one now loitering at the boot. Spiller stared at him, lifted out both equipment boxes, and pointed at them. Stutz pointed at the boot; he wanted his case. As he reached a hand to the hidden latch, Spiller slammed the back door and locked the whole vehicle remotely.

'Huh?' Stutz said.

'I'll bring it in,' Spiller said. 'Just go in and register, I'll bring it in.'

'Open the trunk.'

'All part of the service,' Spiller said, trying to smile.

The porter had returned and was eyeing the strange stand-off.

'Those, please,' Spiller said to him, pointing at the boxes. 'Then you're done, thanks.'

The porter's frown deepened, but he obeyed and picked up a box.

'Dude, what is your problem?' Stutz asked.

'So says the fifty-year-old wearing leather pants.'

'I go in; you drive off with my shit? Open the fucking trunk.'

Spiller dithered, unsure how to extricate himself or improve the situation. He couldn't see a way through. He gave Stutz a dead-eyed look, which visibly disturbed him.

'Please,' Stutz said.

The porter returned for the second box and lugged it away.

Spiller took a few steps to join Stutz at the boot. He cocked his head to one side and knew the expression on his face mirrored the craziness he felt inside. He'd practised lunatic looks a lot in the mirror to fine-tune his repertoire, but this was full-on, bona fide insane.

'I... need my case,' Stutz stammered.

Spiller held the key fob high between their faces and pressed the release. The lid clicked and slowly rose. Spiller never broke the stare. When the lid reached its stop, he turned and slowly grasped the handle of the case and pulled it from on top of the plastic-covered Gibbo, placing it on the ground at Stutz's winkle-pickered feet.

'Tha—' Stutz truncated himself as he clocked the residual contents of the boot.

Spiller watched Stutz's eyes move over the corpse, taking it in. His expression went from stunned to strangely pensive before he returned to the stare that Spiller had locked on him. To his credit, Stutz didn't shout or step back. He merely offered a quizzical look. Perhaps this was his way of trying to defuse a potentially fatal confrontation. Spiller remotely closed the boot lid, maintaining eye contact like Stutz was an enemy target he was laser-painting with his gaze.

'You enjoy your stay,' Spiller whispered, backing away to the driver's door. 'Good luck finding the right people.'

IN THE REAR-VIEW mirror, Spiller could see Stutz didn't move as the Lexus sped down the driveway marked "10mph". Turning out onto the main road, he suddenly identified the change in him since last night. It was hope. His relief at escaping a vertebrae-busting boot on his neck had made him realise he really wanted to live. Part and parcel of that was a resurgence of hope. That life could get better and just maybe his dreams could be resuscitated.

Only, now it was gone again, and its absence stung afresh.

More than that, he was furious at the bastards who'd ruined it for him, who'd dumped a dead body in the boot of a car that was carrying his best-ever hope of a glorious return to the big screen. Because Brett Stutz still made movies for cinema, and people paid to see them. In a world where Netflix was largely pre-eminent, Stutz remained box-office gold.

Spiller let out a livid roar that lasted until his breath failed him and his throat felt as raw as the skin on his face.

What was he meant to do now? Dump Gibbo's corpse as he had Ward's? That was... a bloody good idea. Dump it *exactly* as he'd dumped Ward's. Those pesky drystone-wall repair people wouldn't be tending to that stretch of road again for years. The police would have searched the area thoroughly by now to rule out any more evidence. And who in their right mind would dump a second corpse in exactly the same spot?

Hold on... *who in their right mind?* He wasn't in his right mind. How could he be? So, did that mean it was a good idea? He didn't know.

He pulled the Lexus over onto a muddy verge to have a think. The winter sun had been down for a couple of hours already and the lane wasn't lit, so when he killed the headlights, it plunged him into darkness. Gradually, his eyes adjusted until it didn't seem dark at all. No vehicle passed for five minutes, and he considered dragging Gibbo's body deep into the adjacent woods. But, if Stutz was on the phone to the police at that moment, he was well within the area they'd be keen to search.

Thinking of the cops, he took out his wallet, extracted the piece of paper bearing the number of Alfie Enright's burner. He had to speak to someone.

'Who's this?' Enright answered.

'Me. Matt. Spiller.'

'Oh. You okay? I hear you took a little tumble.'

'I'm fine. How much trouble could you get me out of?'

Enright laughed. 'How much trouble are you in?'

'Uh... not sure how to quantify. It's probably a world record.'

'Is it Ward-related?'

'There's that and… more.'

The line fell silent—Enright contemplating.

'Never mind,' Spiller said. 'I shouldn't have called.'

'Wait a minute… have you done something else, or are you thinking whether you should?'

'Both of those.'

'My advice: stop. Whatever it is, just stop. Have faith that—'

'Oh, don't go all Kumbaya on me, please.'

'I was only going to say that sometimes you need to let go.'

'You mean let go, let God.'

'Your words, but yes. Just see what happens. Get out of the hole you're digging. Let nature take its course. Nature abhors a vacuum. See if it fills back in. It won't if you're still in there with your shovel.'

'So… do nothing?'

'Give it a try.'

Spiller removed his phone from his ear so he could look at it. He frowned as though Enright would see. 'All right,' he said, and tapped the red button.

It wasn't the conversation he wanted. But perhaps it was the one he needed. Maybe a little faith right now would be a good thing. Doing hadn't helped, maybe doing nothing would. Let go, let God. His youthful devouring of self-help books had filled his head with similar axioms, and some publications had been religious tracts in all but name. That saying was often found in close proximity to the biblical guidance that *faith without works is dead*, usually soon after. Have faith, put in the required effort, then await your just reward. In essence, it was the same as the more secular *conceive, believe, achieve* dictum.

No one could say he hadn't been doing the works of late. He hadn't bloody stopped. The only question was, if he did stop, how would God or the Universe or whatever interpret a just reward?

Spiller leaned forwards and looked up into the night sky, less tainted in this spot by the false aurora of city lights. He wanted to see a sign. He'd always wanted that. He'd always been open to the idea of an unseen world, even since his rejection of the counselling contained within those books. And, while he'd never been religious, denouncing the man-made and divisive nature of the concept, he'd always been sneakily jealous of anyone with an honest faith that made them wake up in the morning feeling genuinely blessed and happy. Sadly, he didn't see a whole lot around him to reinforce their beliefs. Bad shit happened all the time, and religious folk seemed wholly deluded when it did. "God spared me!" says the one person to survive a disaster. So, rationally, you had to accept the converse, right?

Spiller leaned back in his seat. Nah, there was nothing up there. No golden angel descending like an ethereal Oscar statuette to save his sorry ass. Just the sky, dark and empty. He started the engine and got back on the road and headed towards the hills.

Forty-five minutes later, he found himself at the location where he'd dumped Ward. He slowed to a crawl but his foot wouldn't go all the way to the floor. The Lexus kept on creeping, past a flapping scrap of blue and white police tape stuck between two stones, past the exact spot where the wall had been rebuilt, and onwards. Then he was picking up speed and he knew where he was heading.

His best and only friend was in the boot, and he'd still be alive were it not for Spiller's antics. Gibbo deserved better than being discarded in the wilderness like a crisp packet tossed away by a careless hiker. His parents deserved to bury a coffin with something in it, rather than wondering where their son had disappeared to.

He was taking Gibbo home. He was going to leave him where he'd found him, outside the Gibson family home where he'd lived since he was a kid. Spiller thought it likely he wouldn't even get that far once Stutz had called the cops, but he would try. There, Gibbo would be discovered and his body afforded the dignity and respect it warranted.

With this, at least, he was taking Enright's advice and letting go.

Acquiescence, though, had its limits.

Emma's boss was a crook, maybe even a mobster, and his people had murdered Gibbo. She needed to know the man she was working for and to be dissuaded from her invalid opinion of him. Maybe that was vindictive, but so was shooting a man twice in the face, especially when he hadn't even been the one in the wrong place at the wrong time.

Outside Gibbo's house, Spiller parked the Lexus on the frontage and activated its hazard warning lights, then departed the scene in his Fiesta.

Chapter Seventeen

ODDLY, HAVING SPIED him from her bedroom window, Emma came downstairs and let him in. She barked a brief laugh, still slightly husky, at his scuffed red face, then left the door open, and Spiller watched a completely transformed person bound up the grey stair carpet in a little black dress that left him with the same longing he'd had before in her presence.

He stepped inside and closed the door and followed her. In the bedroom, Emma was peering in a mirror, applying the last touches of make-up. He stood where she could see his reflection, and he tried not to allow his eyes to drift down to her tightly contoured backside.

'So, what are you going to do for me, Matthew?'

'Pardon?'

'A Shakespearian soliloquy? A sonnet? Maybe some Brecht? In your own time…'

'You spoke to Delaney.'

'You sad failure of a man, and I don't just mean the acting.' She guided some vampish red around her lips, pressed them against each other, and pouted at him in the mirror before turning. 'What do you think?' She struck a pose.

He shrugged, told the truth. 'Beautiful. I'm glad to see you're feeling better.'

'Why wouldn't I be? The man who killed my sister is dead, Charlie is going to make up my financial loss, and you are going to continue driving a taxi for the rest of your miserable little life. All is well with the world.'

He sat down on the end of her super-sized bed. 'Did Delaney tell you he was dead?'

'You did,' she said, rummaging through a deep drawer of handbags and clutch-bags. She looked at him. 'Was that a lie as well?'

'No. But Poole didn't kill your sister.'

She selected a gold Dolce & Gabbana. 'So you said. So he told you. So what? This one?' she asked, presenting the clutch.

'Hardly big enough for a gun.'

She ignored the quip, lost her joviality, parked her bum on the chest of drawers. 'Why did you lie to me, Matthew? About who you are?'

'Didn't Delaney explain?'

'Boredom, right? Doesn't wash. Not considering how far you took it. And boredom sure as shit didn't make you cut those boys' thumbs off. You're a little cuckoo, aren't you, Matthew?'

Spiller smiled. 'I'm beginning to think so.'

'I'm going out. Why are you here?'

'Your boss killed Poole and he also killed my mate, the one I borrowed the taxi from.'

She peered at him, assessing. 'See… I don't really believe you anymore. It's more lies or more craziness.'

'Well, not Delaney himself, obviously. He has people to do that shit for him. The people who killed Poole saw the taxi, identified it, and tracked it back to my mate, who they also killed, thinking he was me.'

The pinch of her eyes hinted at a lingering remnant of faith in him.

'You're not sure about your boss, are you?' he said. 'You know his background, right? Northern Ireland, the military contracts, what the IRA did to his family? You, of all people, can't tell me you don't think a person can get fucked up about the death of a loved one. He's the one who gave you the gun, right?'

'All I know for sure is you're a deluded taxi driver who fleeced me and then tried to fleece my boss. That's it. There's nothing more.'

He produced his mobile phone and cued up the video he'd downloaded from the SD card. 'Come here,' he said, patting the duvet.

'Don't get frisky on me, Matthew. I know you'd like to.'

'Who wouldn't?' he admitted. 'Look at you. Just come and sit here, watch this.'

Emma pushed herself away from the chest and sat down next to him, maintaining a gap between his jeans and her bare leg. He pressed play and handed the mobile to her, standing up so she wouldn't feel so uncomfortable, and so he could gauge her facial reactions. He took the perch she'd just vacated.

Her eyes pinched tighter as the video progressed, her whole body flinching slightly as the gunshot crazed the windscreen. She watched as the video showed his panicked escape to the soundtrack of his stream of expletives.

Then her face jolted, as one who's just realised they've left the gas on and a cigarette burning in the next room. She stopped the video, slid the progress bar backwards and played it again. Spiller could tell where she was up to from the sounds. Just before the gunshot, she paused the clip, got up, and hurried downstairs. After a moment, he followed.

When he entered the lounge, the TV was already on and she was fiddling with his mobile. After a few seconds, the paused image on his phone appeared on the big screen on the wall.

It was what he'd hoped: the shooter just before he discharged the shot.

Peering all the while at the TV, Emma set his mobile on the table and stepped closer. Spiller wanted to say something, but he let her thoughts percolate on their own.

'Fuck.' She backed away and sat down, still fixated on the screen.

Spiller waited by the door, eyeing her anguished expression, her exquisite body. He waited until she spoke, but he had to strain to hear her whisper.

'I work in payroll. I know him. I'm sure I do. Maybe from the files, maybe… maybe I've seen him around. I think he works for Charlie.'

Spiller clapped his hands to break her reverie. 'Whoop-de-do! So maybe now we can get serious and I can get the rest of my money.'

She slowly inclined her head to look at him. 'This changes nothing.'

'*What?* Emma, it changes a shitload. It means I'm not such a liar and your boss is a fucking murderer. My mate is currently festering in the boot of his car. Your boss either pays me what I want or that video, your name, and an anonymous explanation linking the two, go straight to the police.'

She stared again at the image on the wall. 'I could be wro—'

'*Don't!*'

She sank back in her chair, not caring that her dress had hitched up. 'But… why?'

'You!' Spiller came and stood in front of her. 'He did it for you!'

Emma was shaking her head. 'He had no idea I felt like this. No one did. I hid it all. Why do you think I got so screwed up? I never let on. Even my parents didn't know. Of course they knew I was upset but… not like this. Why would he do it? He could never tell me what he'd done, so what would be the point? And if Poole's body never shows up, who's going to care? A missing person might make a few lines in the local press, but that's it. If you hadn't shown me that video, I'd never have known.'

Spiller sat on the coffee table. 'He gave you the gun, right?'

She nodded.

'Why?'

'I was behaving recklessly. My parents must have told him. I was hanging out in the wrong parts of town, drinking too much. I think he thought I needed protection.'

'Protection that comes with a five-year minimum prison sentence?'

'He offered—I didn't have to accept.'

'And you never questioned the sort of man he is? That he had access to a gun like that?'

She raised her eyebrows at him. 'A man of his wealth? His past? His connections?'

'Hold on... your parents? You said your parents could have told him.'

'They know each other.'

'Old friends?'

'No. They met after...'

'Your sister?'

Emma nodded.

'Met where?'

'Some therapy thing. Like a discussion group. People who've lost people. To heal, come to terms, that sort of shit.'

'Why didn't you go?' he asked, although her last comment was answer enough.

She pulled with both hands at the hem of her dress, stretching it down over her thighs as she lifted her bum off the cushion. Then she hoiked her feet off the floor and curled them beneath her. In contemplation of his question, her nose wrinkled as she gave a dismissive sneer.

Spiller understood. Help was only useful if you were in a fit state to receive it. Forgiveness was the last step. She'd been too incensed to even take the first.

'So, you only know Delaney because of your parents.'

'Yeah. Mum and Dad dragged me along to a dinner party at his house that ended up being one of their frigging hug-fests. I left, but he made contact the next day and offered me some work, and...' she glanced around the room '...all this. It's fickle, but I suppose I'm happier here than in a bedsit so... he did what he could.'

'Such a philanthropist,' Spiller said, and stood up.

'You're wrong about him,' Emma decided. 'You've... you've brainwashed me so I can't think straight. That...' she pointed at the TV '...could be any podgy bastard.'

Spiller found himself staring at a framed photo on the wall above Emma's chair, of Emma and a girl who could only be her sister. She saw his eye-line.

Spiller smiled. 'She looks like you.'

'People always said.'

'What was her name?'

'Molly.'

'She looks like a good person.'

'The best.'

He perched back on the coffee table. 'Would she want this?'

'What?'

'You working for a man who killed two innocent people because of her. Actually, because of *you* because of her.'

'Oh, fuck off. You don't get to shame me out of a dream job just because you don't like yours.'

Spiller snorted a laugh. 'If you knew anything about my life right now, you'd know my job is the least of my worries. This'll make you laugh: I have a psycho solicitor trying to kill me and my family because I topped his brother because he was abusing my daughter. The police are after me for that. Oh, and the dead brother—he was head of a gang, so I've got them on my case as well. And those lads in the park on Christmas Eve? They're in the same gang. Well, only one now; the other's dead. Don't ask. What else? I've got your boss after me and my family because I know his thugs killed Poole, and those same thugs then killed my best mate by mistake. And I just drove a Hollywood director to his hotel in a car that, unbeknown to me, had a dead body in the boot, the body of my best mate, which the director saw when I opened the boot. So the police will be after me for that now as well. So, if you think I give a shit about my job prospects...'

Emma took a moment to absorb it. 'Jesus, that's... is all that true?'

'Every last word.'

She stared at the carpet like she was searching its pile for a lost ear-stud. Then she looked up at him. 'Charlie threatened your family?'

'He did. Even said it in front of a copper. He cloaked it a bit—said I was crazy because I'd accused him of threatening my family—but up to that point my family hadn't even been mentioned.'

'What copper?' Emma asked.

'The one who turned up and stopped his thugs killing me in the street.'

She still looked puzzled.

'Ah, right. You didn't know about the police. But you did know about this.' He pointed to his face. 'You weren't at all surprised when you opened the door. How did he explain this?'

'Charlie said you were drunk, and when his waiter escorted you outside you tripped and went your length.'

'Ha! Waiter? *Escorted?* I'd recognised one of the guys from that video. He was in the restaurant with Delaney. My face is what happens when you trip at full pelt after busting *out* through a fucking in door.'

Emma slowly rose and left the room. A minute later, she returned with a half-full bottle of dark rum. She unscrewed the cap and offered the bottle, but he declined. She took three or four glugs and sat back down.

'Why would you share all that with me?' she asked. 'The trouble you're in. You know how much ammo you just handed me?'

He wasn't sure; his mouth had run away on him. 'Maybe I think you're a good person at heart who just got caught up in bad circumstances. Maybe I think we're the same. I don't know. Or maybe it doesn't matter anymore because my goose is cooked.'

She tittered. 'Man, your goose has burnt to a crisp, crumbled to ash, and is currently wafting away on the wind.'

He nodded. 'I just want you to be safe,' he said, and she didn't challenge him. 'Your boss is evil. You need to watch your back. If he suspects you know anything…'

She took another swig. 'I still can't believe he'd do any of this.'

Spiller held his hand out for the bottle. 'May as well. Pretty sure you can't get rum in prison. I should get it while I can.'

As he tipped the bottle back, his thoughts returned to the connection between Delaney and Emma's parents. Something had caused Delaney to act against Poole. If it wasn't Emma, who or what was it? The circle of suspects wasn't that wide.

'Tell me more about your folks and Delaney,' he said, handing back the rum.

'Why? You think they're in cahoots? That's ridiculous. I know my parents.'

'Really? They don't know you. You're a murderous bitch— no offence—who carries a gun in her handbag. You think that's who they see?'

'I know them.'

'*Awww*, that is so sweet. And so naïve. You know I said I killed that drug-dealer?'

'Drug-dealer?'

'The solicitor's brother.'

'You didn't say he was a drug—*fuck*, that one they just found in the hills?'

He nodded. 'Him, yes. Anyway, I didn't kill him. My wife did. I'll take the rap for it, push comes to shove, but I didn't do it. Point is, Emma, we have no clue what anyone will do when the wrong buttons get pushed. You can spend a lifetime with someone and never really know them.'

She was gawping at him, half-smiling. 'Your wife did that? Ho-lee crap. She sounds fucking amazing.'

Spiller considered a stranger's verdict on his beloved. 'Yeah, she's... something.'

'When I grow up, I want to be your wife.'

He offered an amused frown, and she clicked. They both burst out laughing. She handed him the bottle.

When they quietened, Spiller said, 'I should have tried harder to hang onto her.'

'You're not together?'

'I'm not the easiest person to live with. I... I have mental-health issues.'

'Shocker. Were you nasty?'

'Towards my family? No. I was just miserable. Ratty. I suppose I shouted a lot. Maybe I was nasty. The job didn't help; always waiting for the phone to ring.'

'Why didn't you just give it up? Forget about acting.'

'If I knew the answer to that, my dear, I'd have written a book and made a mint.'

'What's so difficult? You tried, it didn't work, you move on.'

'Like you did after your sister?'

'Fuck off, Matthew, that's different.'

'Not really. Your mind hangs onto shit. We do that. It's human nature.'

'You boo-hooing about a lack of acting is not the same as my sister being killed.'

'All I'm saying is that some crap just gets deep into your head.'

Emma stared at the frozen image on the TV screen for a moment. 'But you did all right for yourself,' she said, rewinding the conversation. 'I Googled you—belatedly. I found your CV on your agent's website. You did some good stuff. That war film was big, wasn't it?'

'Yep. Big enough to end my career.'

'That's where your army photos come from, and why you know how to strip a gun.'

He took a swig. 'We got some proper military training prior to filming, but I've always been into guns—as much as you can be in this country. The weapons guy said I shot well enough to be a marksman. I loved it. Probably missed my vocation, if I'm honest.'

'Why didn't you kill the drug-dealer?' she asked.

'Hey?'

'Why your wife? Why not you?'

Her question had sounded like a non-sequitur but it wasn't. If he was into guns and genuinely fancied himself as a hard man who could have joined the military, why had it taken his wife to end the threat to their daughter?

'I didn't know what she knew,' he said, prevaricating.

'And if you had known?' Emma took the rum from him and finished it off.

'I overthink things,' he said. 'Probably a symptom of whatever's wrong in my head. I overanalyse. I weigh everything.

The impact, the repercussions. So while I'm thinking, others are doing.'

'You bloody well took action on Christmas Eve. I didn't see a whole lot of soul-searching before you butchered those lads in the park.'

'Is there any more drink?' he asked.

'Kitchen cupboard. Help yourself.'

'Any preference?'

'Full.'

He headed into the kitchen and pulled open several doors before locating her stash. He grabbed an unopened bottle of vodka. Still mulling over her observation about Christmas Eve, he took a couple of glasses from the sink drainer and went back to her. He set the glasses down, uncapped the bottle, and poured out two large ones. Emma leaned forwards and took hers. He turned the nearest armchair to face her and sat down.

'Christmas Eve,' he said. 'I have times when I think too much. Other times I feel literally paralysed, like someone's pulled my plug. I just stop moving. I can stand in the same spot for a solid hour. It's...'

'Not normal?'

'No. But I also have these moments when I see things with incredible clarity. I know something has to be done. With hindsight, it may be the worst decision ever, but it feels like... almost like a sacred mission at the time. I had to protect you.'

'You did protect me. You already had. You'd knocked them out. What you did after was gratuitous.'

'It was their punishment. For what they wanted to do to you.' He shrugged, a blissful insight making him smile. 'I think I fell in love with you that night.'

Emma set her glass down hard on the table, like she might need both hands to fend him off. She glared at him.

'It's okay,' he said. 'You're safe. I know there's probably fifteen years between us.'

'And you stole twenty grand from me. Let's not forget that. Hardly the best way to woo a young lady, I wouldn't have thought.'

He picked up her glass and gave it back to her. 'Listen, I'm not deluded about this. Just telling you how it is.'

'Well... don't. You're an attractive older guy, I'll give you that. I'd look at you more than once in a bar. Maybe I'd even take you home. But you and I have so much baggage between us it's insane.'

He nodded, drank some. 'So... your parents... Delaney.'

She set her glass down and went into the kitchen. When she returned, she handed him a business card and resumed her seat.

Spiller read the card to himself. *Glen Whittard, D.Clin.Psy, Counselling for Bereavement and Distress*, plus an address, two phone numbers, one office, one mobile.

'That's the guy my parents saw,' Emma said. 'He runs the group where they met Charlie. Knock yourself out.'

'Thanks.'

'Just bear in mind, the last time I gave you someone's business card you ended up with a pizza for a face.' She took a gulp of vodka. 'Boy, I am way too stewed to go out now. Why are you pursuing this, Matthew? Really? All the trouble you're in, you want to make it *worse?*'

Spiller swilled some fiery liquor around his mouth, thinking. 'Maybe *because* of the trouble I'm in. You know? What difference does it make? May as well be purposeful while I can. I hear prison life's pretty mundane. Can I stay here tonight?'

'*What?*'

'I don't mean like that. I just need a place to crash where the police won't find me—at least not straightaway.'

Emma deliberated.

Spiller grinned. 'Hey, you did say I was someone you'd take home.'

'What the hell. Sure. So, what are you going to do about Charlie? About that solicitor? If you're right about their intentions, what are you going to do? Are you going to wait until they kill your family or are you going to pre-empt it?'

Spiller studied her. She was like the devil on his shoulder, the one his angel normally shouted down and overruled. Emma was lending weight to some rudimentary questions he'd always been able to reason away.

'They're safe now,' he said, and was aware that even now he was rationalising his inaction. 'I sent them away with your money. *I* don't even know where they are, so how could anyone else?'

'Twenty grand won't last long. What then?'

'That's why I was after more from your boss.'

'You wouldn't really grass me up to the police, would you?'

Spiller shook his head. 'But *he* doesn't know that. You could help, you know. Tell him you only just managed to stop me and he's got to give me the money or your life's screwed. *And...* that video.' He nodded at the frozen image. 'The cops link that face to Delaney, he's screwed as well.'

Emma grabbed the remote and blacked out the TV, then dipped a fingertip in her drink and sucked the vodka off it. Spiller doubted it was an innuendo.

'How the hell did we get to this point, Matthew?'

He looked at her intently. 'I'm not some weirdo Walter Mitty, you know. I'm not. I was just messing around with the army story. It just got out of hand. Shit!'

'What?'

Spiller snatched his mobile from the table, popped out the sim card and prised off the back to disconnect the battery. He got up and went to the window and widened two of the blind slats with his fingers.

'Chill,' Emma said.

'You think hire cars are fitted with GPS?' he said, misting the glass with his words.

'No idea. Why? Where's your Audi?'

He turned to her. 'Police have it.'

'Searching for?'

'Nothing. Nothing to find. I've got this big-shot New York detective on my case and he's frustrated he can't get me to crack. He's done it to piss me off.'

'You're wanted as far away as New York? Gosh.'

Spiller peeked out at the street again.

'Matthew, go and park it out on the main road if you're bothered.'

He offered a mock frown. 'That's drunk-driving. I could get in trouble with the police.'

Emma smiled tipsily. 'So, what are we going to do tonight, Matthew?'

'*Same thing we do every night, Pinky: try to take over the world.*'

'Ha! You are not the Brain in this outfit, I can tell you that much.'

He laughed. 'Are you hungry?'

'I could eat.'

'Let's order in. Then watch a movie. Like a proper couple.'

She regarded him sourly. 'You're not right.'

Chapter Eighteen

THEY HAD ORDERED from Nando's, watched a movie, drunk some more, and then gone to bed together and had fantastic sex. At least, that was according to Spiller's muzzy morning-head, immediately on waking, before he noticed he was fully clothed and lying on a bed alone in Emma's spare room. So cruel, his dreams. It was like the sleeping fantasies that still came to him in which he was a huge star, seated in his tux alongside the greats at the Emmys and the Golden Globes and the Oscars. He hadn't been so far away at one stage, teetering, so he'd believed, on the brink of a glorious career. But then he'd been tumbling into an abyss of anonymity, the red carpet tugged from under him. How easily fortunes could change, and how punishing the subconscious could be, rewriting the script of his life so perfectly and authentically for his nocturnal drive-in, so he'd wake in the morning with that sense of loss pounding afresh in his heart.

His mobile, sim and battery were on a cabinet next to him. He wondered if Helen might have called, so he put it back together and switched it on. The clock said 09.51. There was a missed call, so he checked his voicemail.

'Mr Spiller, DCI Bartoli. We're done with your car. Call me back and I'll let you know where you can pick it up.'

Spiller swore and quickly made his phone untraceable again. He wondered if he should take a hammer to it but, if anyone was monitoring, it might already have pinged a local tower. Was this a ruse? Was Bartoli trying to lure him into an ambush? Would he have had sufficient time to speak to Billy and identify the taxi driver who dropped Brett Stutz off last night? Had the police found Gibbo's body? Did the police move that quickly? Not according to the documentaries. He grabbed the phone bits and headed downstairs, where he could hear some music in the kitchen.

'Morning,' he said to Emma, who appeared to be dressed for work.

'Morning,' she said without a smile, gazing into the top of the toaster at the orange glow. She didn't offer him anything, and he didn't ask. Whatever connection they'd made last night seemed to have severed.

'Thanks for letting me stay,' he said. 'I'll get out of your hair.'

'Okay.'

He loitered for a few seconds. 'You in work today?'

'Lunchtime.'

He wanted to ask what her plans were vis-à-vis Delaney, but her demeanour said it all. Maintain the status quo, because she had nothing to gain by disrupting it. The toaster popped.

Oh, yes, Spiller thought. *That girl knows which side her toast's buttered.*

As Emma pinched the slices from the slots and grabbed a knife, Spiller left the kitchen to retrieve his trainers and coat from the lounge.

INCOGNITO IN HIS inconspicuous rental, Spiller did a couple of passes outside his apartment building, eyes scanning for anyone just sitting in a parked car. It all looked okay. He needed to nip into his flat to change and collect a few bits. He was heading into town later to see Glen Whittard, and he had a character to create.

There was something about this whole Whittard situation that bothered him. Firstly, why was Delaney still involved with a psychiatrist and a self-help group more than twenty-five years after the event? Not that Spiller thought a person ever completely got over seeing his family blown to pieces, but 1994 was a long time ago. And how had Emma's parents become so close to Delaney that he thought it appropriate to lavish their daughter with a brand new lifestyle?

Within half an hour, Spiller was on his way into the city, showered, shaved and suited, and with a holdall. He parked in a multi-storey and walked the ten minutes to Whittard's office building. It took him past the front door of Delaney's restaurant, which showed no signs of damage. Inside, it was business as usual, with most of the tables occupied.

Glen Whittard had a suite in a high-rise office block that could be seen from every major approach to the city. It was clad in dark glass and it towered over the surrounding structures. Spiller imagined you had to have deep pockets to afford the rent, which said a lot about Whittard's prowess as a shrink, and equally as much about how fashionable it had become for his and the younger generation to be mentally warped. My hamster died, I have PTSD; I'm a failed actor, I'm depressed. People just seemed to wallow these days, backbones flopping this way and that, upper lips quivering and chins wobbling. If this had pertained eighty years ago, Spiller reckoned Britain would now be a part of a Greater European Reich.

As the elevator rose up through the edifice, he studied his reflection in the smoked mirrors. He was alone in the box. His face was healing okay, but it would be a couple of weeks before it was properly reskinned, especially with his penchant for picking at scabs. He watched the floor counter zip through the numbers at an alarming rate, slowing as it approached floor 30 of the 50 that comprised the building.

The door slid open on a wall finished in brushed silver panels, much like the foyer. He stepped out and headed for the toilet, where he dumped his holdall beneath the paper detritus in the waste bin, then returned to the lift. From 30 he went up to 32.

A plaque detailed the occupants of that level, and whether to turn left or right.

Spiller was buzzed into Whittard's suite by an obese middle-aged woman behind a counter. She had a small desk on the other side and she looked up at him from her computer screen.

Spiller was ready. 'Detective Inspector Mortlake,' he said, holding his TV persona in front of her face. He gave her sufficient time to check the name and the photo, which was a few years old, but still recognisably him. He flipped the black wallet shut and slipped it into his breast pocket. 'I know: I look better with a full face of skin. Hazards of the job, I'm afraid.'

She smiled. 'How can I help?'

'Is Mr Whittard in? I'd like to have a word with him.'

'*Doctor* Whittard is just finishing with a client. Ten minutes? Is that okay? I'd rather not disturb a session. Ten minutes and he's on lunch.'

Spiller smiled back. 'Of course.'

'Take a seat,' she said.

Spiller sat in one of the four chairs on offer. He almost grabbed a glossy magazine off the table but thought he'd look more professional not perusing the latest celebrity gossip. The reception area smelled strongly of vanilla. The brushed metal theme continued, but the harsh illumination of the corridor had been replaced with subdued downlights above the waiting area. The smoked windows dulled the day outside, but the depth of them—almost to the carpet—offered a lofty view over the city that was vertigo-inducing. Spiller guessed Whittard didn't have much success curing people whose loved ones had fallen off a cliff.

On cue, ten minutes later, the door to Whittard's office opened and a teary-eyed man in his early twenties exited, closing the door behind him. He confirmed the time of his next appointment at the counter, then left. The secretary rose and gave a light tap on Whittard's door before entering. A minute later she emerged and left the door ajar.

'You can go in,' she told Spiller.

Whittard's inner sanctum was painted a magnolia that couldn't offend anyone. There were several framed diplomas, a crammed bookcase, a couple of willowy pot plants, a small desk in the corner of the room, a couch up against the wall, but the centre space was dominated by two comfy armchairs facing each other. It was functional and warm, warmer than Spiller would have preferred. As he entered, he felt beads of sweat pop on his top lip. He shut the door behind him.

Whittard briefly stood up and offered his hand. 'DI…?'

'Nat Mortlake,' Spiller said. 'Serious Crime Division.' He offered his wallet for inspection, but Whittard barely glanced at it.

'Please,' Whittard said, taking the armchair nearest his desk and indicating Spiller take the other.

Spiller sank into the chair and immediately wanted to shut his eyes. Damn, that was a comfy chair. He resisted the temptation and instead weighed up his new adversary. Whittard looked frail and was extremely white. It looked like he'd never been in the sun. Spiller thought he had to be mid-forties, but he had the wispy blond pate of a newborn baby. It was a strange baldness that made Spiller think he probably still got age-checked entering pubs, maybe even bouncy castles. His voice was soft, barely above a whisper, but his smile was disarming and full of confidence, and Spiller understood why people might pay top dollar to see him.

'That looks sore,' Whittard said, indicating Spiller's face.

'Yeah, that'll teach me to chase after villains rather than question witnesses, eh?'

Whittard smiled obligingly. 'So, how can I help?'

'I'm investigating a murder and I'd like to ask you a few questions.'

'Does this concern one of my patients? Because you know patient files are confidential.'

Whittard was on the ball, but Spiller had done a little Googling. 'Well, that would depend, wouldn't it? On whether disclosure is essential to protect the patient or third parties from the risk of death or serious harm or to prevent a crime.'

A light knock on the door, then in bobbed the secretary's fleshy face. 'Sorry, just nipping out for a bite to eat, Dr Whittard. Do you need anything before I go? Or would you like me to get you something while I'm out?'

'No to both, thank you, Rachel.'

The door closed again.

'A little background first, if that's all right,' Spiller said. 'How does all this work?'

'This?'

'What you do.'

'Much the same, I imagine, as your police occupational health unit.'

Spiller nodded. 'You specialise in helping people with grief and bereavement, correct?'

'Mainly. Although it's hardly a niche. People die every day. I'll never be out of work, put it that way.'

Spiller smiled. 'How exactly do you help people?'

'I listen. I can offer behavioural therapies but mainly I listen. Most patients just want to talk. Death is one of life's immutable, unavoidable facts, yet so many are ill-prepared. Even when a whole family is bereaved, oftentimes no one wants to talk about it. The people most familiar with your situation shy away from it. The funeral takes place, you may chat openly then, you may thereafter try and talk to friends, but who really wants a night out listening to someone talk about death? So it all quickly gets boxed away.' Whittard vaguely waved his hand, indicating an area above his right ear. 'Somewhere in here. It gets filed away and left for time to deal with—time being that great healer.'

'Isn't it?' Spiller asked.

'For some. Has it been for you?'

Spiller jerked slightly in his chair. 'Me?'

'I see it in your eyes. You have a personal relationship with grief. It changes people. Often physically. I knew one chap who lost a best friend very suddenly, woke up the next day and his pillow was covered in hair. Practically bald. Not me, by the way.' He uttered a self-deprecating laugh. 'Nearly all his hair had shed overnight. Even his eyebrows. What was left turned white within a week. He was only twenty-one.'

'My parents died,' Spiller said quietly.

'They do that. It's the correct order.'

Spiller winced. 'Wow. People pay you for this?'

'Part of my job is getting patients to accept reality. To face what's happened and deal with it. When did your parents die?'

'I'm not going to get a bill for this, am I?'

Whittard laughed. 'You couldn't afford me. Tell me.'

'Six years ago. They died within a few weeks of each other.'

'How did it affect you?'

Spiller considered. 'I aged ten years in a month. I'd always felt like I was stuck at twenty years old mentally. That changed. I think physically as well. You're not the first to notice the look in my eyes.'

'Any behavioural changes?'

Spiller mused, but didn't really need to. 'Anger. My fuse shortened. It's barely more than a stub.'

'Not good in your job,' Whittard observed.

'I do okay. It's not like being in uniform. That can be confrontational. I wouldn't do well back in uniform.'

'Tell me about their deaths,' Whittard said.

Spiller wasn't sure he should open up, and it certainly wasn't the reason for his visit, but he accepted he was still messed up about it and here was a guy who knew his stuff and was offering a freebie.

'I was away with the job. My dad went first. Cancer he'd hidden from everyone but my mum. He was fine when I left, but it just ripped through him in weeks. I came back towards the end, when my mum had to tell me because she knew he didn't have long.'

'Did you get to spend some time with him?'

'Not enough. And it's like he wasn't my dad. The way he looked. It still haunts me.'

'Do you resent your mum?'

Spiller frowned. 'Why would I?'

'Keeping it quiet until the end. Some people may think that wasn't her decision to make.'

Spiller wanted to object to a stranger's attack on his mum's character, but, truth be told, it was something he'd grappled with for years; only, for reasons he couldn't divulge under his present guise. He'd have been forced to abandon filming. Maybe he'd have been replaced. And maybe that would have saved his career, having someone else take over that damnable role.

'Possibly,' he said. 'Anyway, after the funeral I said I'd stay with my mum, forget the job, but she insisted I go back.'

'What were you doing?'

'Working with Interpol. I was all over Europe at the time. Anyway, I went back and within a few weeks, my mum had a heart attack and dropped dead in the kitchen. I think she died of shock... heartbreak. She'd always been fit as a flea.'

'Highly likely. The risk of a heart attack increases twenty-fold within twenty-four hours of a bereavement. The heart can actually change shape, you know? It's called Takotsubo cardiomyopathy. What did you do then?'

'When?'

'After your mother died.'

'Oh. What does anyone do? Kept myself busy, got on with life.'

'Aha! There you go: Time, deal with this for me.'

'I'm okay,' Spiller said defensively. 'I'm not flooding your room with tears, am I?'

'Unfortunately, tears are not the answer, nor an indicator. A person can cry a thousand times over the same thing and never release an ounce of pain. Did you cry?'

Spiller nodded. 'Still do. I don't think anyone ever gets over a death. It just... gets absorbed somehow. Like... a stone that rolls down a snowy slope and turns into a big snowball. The stone gets lost in the middle as the snow gets thicker around it. But it's always in there.'

Whittard raised his pale eyebrows. 'Mind if I nick that for my next book?'

Spiller turned his eyes to the bookcase, scanned it. 'You're published,' he said needlessly.

'Four times. Working on a fifth.'

'So, what about those people you can't fix?' Spiller asked, returning to the issue. 'There must be some.'

'Of course. Some people are irreversibly broken. Shattered, in fact. There's no piecing them back together.' His eyes pinched. 'You're referring to someone specific, are you? One of my patients?'

Spiller had to say the name at some point. 'Charles Delaney.'

Despite readying himself to decipher Whittard's reaction, there was nothing to read. Whittard didn't flinch. He was deadpan, impenetrable.

'No?' Spiller said. 'You're denying you treat him?'

'I won't confirm or deny. I can't. Trust is everything in my profession. I'd lose all credibility if I shared confidential information just because someone asks.'

Spiller shifted forwards in his chair but still felt too low, in physicality and status, so he stood up. 'Even when that someone is a police detective? Even when that police detective has a warrant to lawfully acquire information pertinent to a murder enquiry.'

Whittard offered a bemused smirk. 'Please, do show me.'

Google Images had given Spiller a good idea of what a court order looked like, and he was pretty nifty at knocking up fake documents on his computer thanks to his generally artistic bent. The question was whether Whittard had ever seen the genuine article before. Spiller had the piece of paper in his inside pocket, but decided not to risk it.

'I'd rather not go that route. Just tell me yes or no: is there anyone in your files you're especially worried about? Yes or no. I don't need a name; I'll draw my own conclusions.'

Whittard slowly rose to his feet and looked at his bookcase. He approached it, selected one of several duplicate copies he had, and handed it to Spiller. It was one of his own, a tome entitled *Good Grief*.

'It's about accepting bereavement. With my compliments, Matthew. I hope you find something in it that helps.'

Spiller looked at him, wryly, crookedly. 'What did you say?'

'Pardon?' Whittard's pokerfaced façade couldn't deal with his bungle, and a dull horror swam across his glazed eyes.

'What did you call me?'

Whittard recovered slightly. 'Matthew; you said Matt. Matt Mortlake.'

'I said Nat. Nat. Not Matt. And even if I'd said Matt, why would you think it's okay to call me Matthew?'

Flustered, Whittard turned back to his bookcase and began tapping in any volumes that were protruding, like a man with OCD. Spiller backed up to the door and flicked the lock. Whittard heard and wheeled to face him.

'What are you doing?' he said.

Spiller sneered. 'You know, I was on the verge of leaving. I was thinking this was just a waste of time. Then you said my name.'

'I misheard. Nat, Matt, Matthew, so what? I want you to leave. Right now.'

'You knew I was coming. You know who I am. Which means Emma told you. Or she told Delaney and he told you. Either way, I was right: you're involved.'

Whittard made a sudden lurch towards Spiller, who instinctively thwacked him in the face with his book. Whittard's fear-enfeebled legs lost their strength and dropped him to the floor, so the back of his head struck the front of his desk.

'Ow!'

Spiller stepped forwards. 'Shit, your book's great; I feel better already.' He took a pen-drive from his pocket. 'I want your files. You're going to download everything on your computer onto this.'

'Like hell.'

'Or I'll take you up to the roof and throw you off. How ironic, hey? Shrink famed for treating depression commits suicide. Or maybe I'll just beat you to death with your own book.'

'I'm not going to do it.'

Spiller hunkered down in front of him. 'And that's where we're different; because I will. I'll do it. Delaney killed my friend. And the fact someone warned you I was coming means you're somehow involved. Download your computer or I'm going to kill you.' He grabbed Whittard by the tie and lifted him to his feet, then pulled him around to his desk chair.

'My secretary will be back soon,' Whittard whimpered as he was pushed into sitting.

'Then I'll have to take her up to the roof as well, and she'll take out at least six people on the pavement so…'

Whittard caved. He took the pen-drive and stuck it in the USB slot. Spiller watched carefully as he went into his documents and began to transfer the folders.

'Some of this is nothing to do with my patients,' Whittard objected.

'I'll work it out. Carry on.'

The last folder completed its download a couple of minutes later, but Spiller dallied at Whittard's side.

'That's it,' Whittard said.

'Programs. Go into your programs.'

Whittard hesitated.

'Never mind, just shift them over,' Spiller said. 'All of them. I don't have time.'

Whittard sighed as he made the necessary clicks. Spiller watched the slow progression of the bulky folder and its data-heavy contents.

'I don't know what you hope to find,' Whittard said.

'Yeah, you do.'

'You are so messing with the wrong people, Matthew. God, you have no idea.'

'Yeah, I do.'

With the pen-drive replete, Spiller snatched it from the slot. 'Now, be a good boy and sit tight for ten minutes.'

SPILLER DESCENDED TO the thirtieth floor and hurried out and along to the toilet. He retrieved his holdall from the waste bin and locked himself in a cubicle. He emptied out his change of clothes and proceeded to swap. The suit went into the bag while he donned a pair of jeans, a t-shirt, a khaki army jacket, a baseball cap and a pair of clear spectacles. He took out a small mirror and a skin-coloured pancake of stage make-up and spread it down his nose and across his chin, concealing his injuries. It wouldn't survive close inspection, but he didn't intend anyone to get near.

From 30 he went down to 4, stepped out and smashed the glass of a fire alarm, activating a piercing siren, then he headed for the stairs. By the time he reached the foyer, he was among a stream of people exiting the building. There were three uniformed security guards on the door, clearly keen to find someone, but that someone was wearing a suit and sporting a scuffed face, and that wasn't Spiller any more. Not one of them gave him a second glance. He slipped out onto the street and headed back to the multi-storey.

Chapter Nineteen

A COUPLE OF things Spiller needed now: a computer and a gun. He needed to analyse the information on the pen-drive and defend himself against the people who were pissed off he had that information. Whittard's warning about the sort of people he was messing with had been dire. From the sound of it, Whittard presumably knew what had befallen Spiller at Delaney's restaurant, and why, but Whittard still surmised that Spiller didn't know the worst of it. That was a worry.

As with the brief reconnoitre of his flat, Spiller drove by the family home a couple of times to make sure no one was staked out. He parked around the corner and made his way down the ginnel and in the back way, through the cellar. Shit, would that place ever not reek of fuel? He stared at the old sofa he'd made love to his wife on. They had worked as a team to protect their daughter that evening, then sealed the pact with some torrid sex. Generally, it had been an atrocious night, so it was a measure of his current plight that he felt nostalgic, nevertheless. He shook himself.

In the front section of the cellar, he took the Sig from its spot on top of the pipe and slipped it into the pocket of his army jacket. Now he really would be in trouble if the police nabbed him. There was no ducking and diving your way out of possessing a firearm. He nipped up the stone steps into the kitchen and found Helen's laptop where he'd left it.

He wasn't sure where to go. He wasn't safe there or at his flat, either from the police or from Delaney. Nor from Dominic Ward, come to that. Amazingly, the danger Ward posed had paled to an inconvenience; another measure of how dismal was Spiller's current state. A hotel was an option, but expensive, and how much time would it really buy him? There were so many people on his trail, or about to be. Since the morning, he had grown ever more convinced that DCI Bartoli's message about his car had been a trap. People were closing in, and so much depended on which party found him first. He wasn't about to shoot a copper; anyone else was fair game.

Spiller took the laptop and settled on the sofa in the front living room. Let go, let God. Why the hell not? Bring it on. And may as well enjoy the comforts of home while he still could. He set the gun beside him on the cushion and opened Helen's laptop, waiting for it to boot so he could load the pen-drive.

Whatever he was searching for, he had a feeling he'd know it when he saw it.

Twenty minutes after starting his trawl, Spiller was stumped. There were numerous files of session notes, but none of the patients were named. It was Patient #3 or Patient #12 or Patient #17… Worse, the notes weren't even transcribed; they were scans of Whittard's copious scribblings which, as befitted any self-respecting medical man, were nigh on indecipherable. In certain places, Whittard had even morphed into the lost art of shorthand. The other files were concerned with the drafts of his published works and associated academic research, and Spiller's hunch that Whittard may have buried some information deep within a sub-sub-sub-folder in his Programs, as Spiller had with the dash-cam video, was also confounded.

What did strike him, though, was the split of the case notes into four different folders that did not correlate to the numbering of the patients or the dates on the files. One of the folders contained a large number of ongoing files, according to the dates. A second contained numerous files whose session dates were historic, which Spiller supposed were closed cases. But a third contained just three files of ongoing notes, and a fourth featured just half a dozen files of historic cases, and it was the separation of these latter two that made no sense. What was special about these cases?

Spiller reopened the folder of six files, then clicked the first file marked Patient #7. Oddly, squinting as he tried to decrypt the scrawled notes made them slightly more intelligible, like when you made more sense of a pixelated face by blurring your focus. But, although certain words leapt out at him more easily, the overall gist was still a mystery, obscured by poor handwriting, abbreviations, and archaic shorthand.

Then a word did jump out at him. *Molly?* Was that Molly? As in Emma's sister? Or maybe Holly?

Spiller checked a couple more files for any standout words or names, but only saw one. In a folder for Patient #19, the name Rinks. Maybe. Could have been Pinks. Or Binks. Honestly, with Whittard's hand, it could have been anything. But it did look like Rinks. And, earlier on in the notes, a reference to rape. Or could have been rope. Or... bloody anything. Spiller opened another file of session notes from the same patient and squinted through them. There it was again: Rinks.

Spiller opened Google and typed *rinks rape* into the search bar, then refined the results from *All* to *News*. There were several stories leading the results about a conviction for an attempted rape at an ice rink. He scrolled down a little and found a different story, with the news snippet bolding the word Rinks after the name Oliver. He opened the article and read it.

Six years ago, Oliver Rinks, 37, convicted of the rape of Megan Loughty, 22. Sentenced to eight years.

Spiller scrolled a little further and found a more recent article. Two years ago, the severed right arm of Oliver Rinks, newly released after serving four years of an eight-year sentence for rape, was found at a waste-recycling centre after the claw-grab loading garbage into a container lorry split the bag it was in.

And the owner of the centre where the discovery was made: Delaney Environmental Services.

Spiller opened a new tab and dropped the name Megan Loughty into Facebook. There were no results. The only UK-based Loughty was a Joe. A friend request was required to see more than the profile shot, but Spiller didn't recognise the guy, who looked to be in his mid-twenties. Nevertheless, Spiller proceeded to search for Joe Loughty on Google Images and found the same profile pic, but also a few more.

'Christ,' Spiller muttered.

There was Joe Loughty, in a pub, with his arms around an older male on either side, and Spiller recognised both of them. One was the guy with the suppressed pistol he'd rammed with the Lexus, and the other was the bearded guy from Delaney's restaurant, who he'd thought was the man in the background of the video who'd been left holding Poole's shoulders.

Now he was in no doubt. And the connection was obvious: Joey Loughty, brother of Megan Loughty, and the youngest of three Loughty brothers, two of whom worked for Charles Delaney. A further logical surmise was that the name he'd seen in Patient #7's notes was indeed Molly, Emma's sister, and that Delaney had asked the Loughtys to get rid of Poole as a favour to Patient #7, who had to be extremely close to Molly for them to seek professional help over her death. But it didn't seem likely it was Emma herself, as she'd appeared genuinely shocked by the video and had openly admitted to recognising the face of the gunman.

Spiller wondered if there was any point trying to locate any direct links to Delaney in the session notes, but realised there wasn't. He had enough already. Nowhere near enough to constitute damnable evidence in a court of law, but plenty to make sense of a jigsaw that had hitherto been a jumble. The separate folder of six historic cases also made more sense. These were special cases. And perhaps the three ongoing cases in the other folder were ones Whittard expected might one day find their way into the special folder. The big question was: in what way were they special? But only a fool would discount the relevance of the untimely fates of Rinks and Poole.

Spiller looked up from the screen and straight at the image of his acting photo from the Gulf. How pathetic that he'd framed it. Not just because it was a reminder of a merely so-so career, but more because he'd never bothered correcting visitors' misconceptions who didn't know about his past. He picked up the gun and aimed it at the image of his head. He wanted to work the slide, load a round, and pull the trigger. But what might follow from that? A second bullet into his flesh-and-blood skull? He didn't trust himself not to do it. He set the gun back down.

He so wanted to piece his phone back together and call his wife. She was still his wife. He still loved her, and he knew it was reciprocated. And his two beautiful daughters; he wanted to hear their voices. But, while he could piece his phone back together, what hope was there for his family? They were better off without him. People often said that to sound noble, to draw a protestation, but this was just him, talking to himself. It was true.

Spiller closed the laptop, took the mobile, battery and sim card out of his pocket and put them on the laptop's lid. Slowly, he reassembled it. He found Delaney's number in his call log and pressed to connect.

'Mr Spiller,' Delaney answered. 'Or should I say DI Mortlake?'

'Call me what you like. Call me all the names under the sun. I don't care. The price just went up to five hundred thousand.'

'*For what?*' Delaney almost shrieked.

'Let me run a few names by you: Oliver Rinks, Megan Loughty, Joey Loughty.'

'I don't know those names.'

'Joey Loughty's brothers work for you, dickhead. I found pictures online. And I have a video of them killing Jeffrey Poole. And I've only spent an hour on a handful of the files I took from Whittard's office. And I'm not a real police officer. So, what would a team of experienced forensic detectives make of those files, given all the time they need? You'll be in there somewhere.'

'You stole those files. They're inadmissible.'

'Okay. So the police raid Whittard's office and seize the originals legally. Or do you think he's made of such stern stuff that he'd delete it all to protect you? If he even knew how to delete it properly. Remember Shipman? He thought he'd deleted everything.'

There was silence from Delaney's end, and Spiller wasn't about to break it. It was a good sign; Delaney was thinking.

'You're a conman, Matthew. I'm not biting.'

'You're joking.'

'You think I've survived in business all this time by kowtowing to extortion? I've dealt with worse than you. I'm not biting.' He hung up.

'You're joking,' Spiller said to the dead line. 'Motherfucker.'

He thought of calling Emma then and blasting her for grassing on him, but where would that get him? She had picked a side, and, even from his point of view, she'd probably made the right call.

As he was staring impotently at the phone, it rang, and he jumped a little. The caller ID made him frown: BILLY. He let it ring out. He knew what was happening. This was DCI Bartoli acting on information received from Brett Stutz. Having failed to lure him into picking up his car, and rather than begin a manhunt, Bartoli was using Spiller's agent. Probably Billy would request he drop by the house to discuss something innocuous, and the police would be there waiting. Crap, how gullible did they think he was?

The phone rang again and Spiller answered. 'What is it, Billy?' he said gruffly.

A beat, then, 'Dear boy, why so bellicose? Are you having a bad day?'

'Yep, and I don't want it to get any worse.'

'Well, who would? Matthew, love, I need you to pop around as soon as you can. It's rather imperative.'

'I bet it is,' Spiller said, picturing a team of coppers crowded into Billy's office, all crossing their fingers.

'You really need to be here, dear boy. *Prontissimo*. All right? I'll be waiting.'

'Okay.' Spiller ended the call. He stared again at his movie photo, stood up and went and turned it face down. He felt a fugue coming on, so shook himself and went upstairs. He wandered into the girls' bedrooms, soaked up their warmth, smiled at the sweet recollections of days past. Long past. He trudged back downstairs again and made another call.

'What?' Delaney answered.

'I'm going to the police now. Right now. They're waiting for me. In half an hour, they're going to have everything I have on you. You, your knuckle-scraping thugs, Emma… you're all going to jail. And me. But that's fine. I've had enough. So, last chance on that money. Half a million. You won't even notice it.'

A pause like before, but then: 'I need some time.'

'Why?'

'It's half a million, Matthew. A lot's changed over the past ten years. Secret Swiss accounts, stashing money in the Caymans or Panama, those days are gone. You've heard of Mossack Fonseca?'

'The sparkling wine?'

Delaney huffed. 'Good Lord… I need some time to gather that sort of money, so nothing flags. Leave it with me.'

'For how long? I wasn't kidding about the police. They want to talk to me.'

Delaney exhaled noisily again, swore. 'Hide it. The information. Hide it well. *If* you get pinched and you keep quiet, I'll sort you out. I'll provide for your family. If I don't keep my word, you can give it all to the police.'

Spiller mulled it over. 'How can I trust you?'

'Ditto. We have each other by the balls, Matthew.'

'You don't have me by the balls. My balls are just dandy.'

'Your family is very precious to you, no? I know mine was to me.'

Spiller bit his lip. He could rage against another threat against his family and make it manifest, or he could retreat and collect half a million pounds for them.

'How long?' he asked Delaney through gritted teeth.

'Twelve hours. I need to speak to my accountant.'

SPILLER WRAPPED THE pen-drive in plastic and hid it in the sugar bag with the SD card. In due course, if he had to, he could let Helen know where it was. Depending on Delaney's actions, she could trash them or hand them to the police. As for the video on his mobile and buried in her laptop, who was to say it wasn't a stunt, or a clip from an amateur movie?

He perched at the kitchen table, looked at the spot on the floor where all this started, where Helen had plugged up Ward's face. There was a reckoning coming. He was in the middle of too many events to slip out unnoticed. He hadn't killed Ward, or the thumbless one who'd tried to burn his house down, or Gibbo. But he was culpable. He'd done stuff, illegal stuff, and plenty of it. Perhaps he'd run his course. As soon as Delaney saw he wasn't going to talk, his family would be relatively rich. It was blood money, drained from the corpse of his one and only friend, but it was better Gibbo's death served some useful purpose.

As though to strengthen his resolve, his mobile rang again.

'Hi, Billy.'

'Dear boy, are you on your way?'

'Just about to leave,' Spiller said. He hung up and went back to the front room to collect the gun. Maybe it wasn't the police waiting with Billy. Maybe it was Delaney's people. Or Ward's.

Out on the street, his hand poised to let himself into the Fiesta, he heard a noise that made him freeze. He looked up the street as the nose of Callum Ward's red Nissan Skyline edged out of a parking spot and waited. He couldn't see who was behind the wheel; the windscreen was tinted too dark, probably illegally so. The car just sat there, its exhaust growling, its right headlight peeking at him menacingly. Spiller climbed into his car, took out the Sig, worked the slide and snicked on the safety, then pocketed it again and got out. With both hands in his pockets, but with one directing the muzzle forwards, he walked along the pavement briskly towards the Skyline.

In the fifteen seconds it took to reach the car, Spiller decided against opening fire. No doubt the occupants were behind the failed attempt to ram his wife and kids into the path of a truck, but this was a street lined with CCTV, and, whatever the police suspected he'd done, there was no proof of anything yet. Whittard wasn't about to complain, what with the links Spiller had already exposed to Poole and Rinks. Even with Gibbo, although it looked terrible, there was no evidence against him because he was genuinely innocent. And why would a man who'd just offed his best friend use his car to pick up a fare from the airport, knowing he'd have to open the boot? No. Right now, the police had zilch, so why would he offer himself up by committing a crime in broad daylight?

As he approached, the front passenger window dropped. Spiller bent a little and checked out the occupants. He recognised the guy in the passenger seat; his bandaged thumb stumps, if not his hostile snarl, provided an instant ID. Spiller's thumb was on the safety, ready in case either one made a move.

'Matthew,' came a familiar voice from the dark of the rear seat. Then Dominic Ward's bruised face appeared between the front seats, shaded by a red Under Armour baseball cap. 'Oh, snap.' He pointed at Spiller's face and laughed.

'You've come all tooled up, eh?' Spiller said, taking a step away from the door so it wouldn't catch him if it opened suddenly. 'I don't mean weapons; I mean these fucking tools.'

They were well-trained; neither reacted, although the thumbless one's snarl became a rabid slaver.

'I see you got your brother's vulgar car back,' Spiller added.

'I inherited everything. All that my brother left behind.'

'You giving up the law thing, then? I'm sensing a conflict of interest.'

'I'll see how they jog along together for a while.'

'Were you driving the four-by-four the other day?' Spiller asked the driver.

The faintest curl at the corner of the driver's mouth answered the question.

'Well done,' Spiller said to him. 'You just joined your boss on my shit-list.'

'You're all talk,' Ward said. 'Two attacks on your family and you're just standing there, talking.'

'One dead brother and you're just sitting there, talking.'

'I'm biding my time'

'Why? Why wait?' Spiller's finger curled around the trigger. 'Make your move. Right now.'

'Still trying to get me locked up, eh? I see the cameras looking down at me.'

'So, if you're not going to do anything, what are you doing here?'

Ward smiled. 'A good barrister never shows his hand.'

'What would you know about being a good barrister? Or good, full stop. You're a piece of shit, just like your crackhead brother.'

The men up front shifted towards their doors but were stalled by Ward clapping a restraining hand on their shoulders.

'You get on your way,' Ward said to Spiller. 'We'll catch up soon enough. When the time is right.'

Spiller shook his head and straightened up. He turned and headed back along the pavement, all the while hoping he would hear them running up behind him so he could blast six .380 rounds through the pocket of his combat jacket.

Chapter Twenty

THE JOURNEY TO Billy's house was undertaken in silence. Spiller felt like he was the sole participant in a funeral cortège, where playing the radio along the route would be disrespectful. At times he thought he could hear the growl of the Skyline's exhaust, but he put that down to paranoia. He couldn't see them in his mirror, and successfully tailing a vehicle from several cars back was the stuff of spy movies. In real life, in the city, one unfriendly traffic light would ruin the pursuit.

Outside the driveway that led to Billy's house, Spiller slowed and pulled into the kerb. He looked along the privet-lined gravel approach to the large garden that fronted the property. He couldn't see anything worrying, although the drive did bend out of sight around to the rear of the house where Billy parked his own car, a pristine orange Morris Marina Coupe which he'd owned from new. Spiller suspected there could be cops parked there, or maybe they'd left their transport nearby and walked. The most worrying sight would have been a white Transit van.

He reversed across the pavement and between the terraced properties that insulted Billy's abode with their presence. The car rocked left and right as it sank into and popped out of the rain-filled holes that dotted the drive, until the boot passed the end of the fenced rear gardens of the abutting houses and came to a halt overhanging the front lawn where the drive started to bend. Spiller felt it was better to be ready for a quick exit, even if that could so easily be thwarted by a vehicle straddling the entrance. His psychological box-ticking was limited; he'd take what he could.

He got out and looked at the house across the grass. All quiet. He stuck his hand in his pocket and realised the Sig was still cocked and on safety. He'd have to be careful with that. He knew, if the cops were waiting, having the gun meant a mandatory prison term, but not having it and finding instead that Delaney's crew was waiting seemed like a worse scenario.

He approached. He knocked. He waited.

A solemn-looking Billy opened up a few seconds later. 'Dear boy...' He pulled the door wide open.

Spiller stared down the hallway that led to Billy's office. No sounds. No shrieks of *"Armed Police!"* No one obviously lying in wait. He glanced behind him. No one rushing him, no snipers hiding in the oak tree in the corner of the garden. He stepped inside. Billy closed the door, then headed down the hallway towards his office. Slowly, Spiller followed, his right hand in his pocket, loosely clasped over the butt of the micro-compact. At the threshold to the office, he halted. On the other side of the room, sitting stiffly on a chaise longue, was Brett Stutz, bearing the countenance of a man about to pull the lever on a hangman's trapdoor. Billy settled behind his desk and glared at his client.

'Matty, you fucking *genius!*' Stutz suddenly exclaimed, launching to his pointy-booted feet, and laughing so hard he was nearly instantly in tears.

Billy was also smiling now, although guardedly.

Spiller was dumbfounded, but sensed an explanation was about to gush forth, so he waited. Stutz advanced and grabbed at Spiller's right arm, pulling his hand from his pocket and nearly the gun with it. He clapped his palms around Spiller's hand and pumped it repeatedly up and down.

'Dude, you are *awesome!* I've seen some ballsy auditions in my time but that was next level! Christ, I nearly shat my pants when you opened that trunk! It was so real, and you... you... I never seen such... Christ, I can't even tell you what I saw. It was fucking *awesome!*

Spiller glanced at Billy, who was trying to maintain his cheerfulness in the face of an onslaught of cheap cursing the like of which his office had never witnessed.

Stutz wasn't done yet. 'Fuck, you just... got me. Even as I was walking into the hotel, I was thinking... *was that real?* Just fucking genius. It's like you got an advance copy of the script.

Everything I wanted from the lead character you gave me. Man, I was fucking blown away. I mean, was that a dummy in the trunk or did you get a buddy to help out? I'm guessing a dummy, right?'

Spiller nodded.

'Yeah, I thought so. You know, the real thing would have been a lot... *gunkier*. You know? More blood, brain matter, but Christ...'

Spiller looked at Billy again, who now appeared quite bilious.

'You got it,' Stutz said, finally releasing Spiller's hand.

'What?'

'The lead! It's yours! You are that man! You are *my* man!'

'Oh,' was all Spiller could say.

Stutz whooped and stepped back, looked his new star up and down, then moved in for a Hollywood hug, moaning his delirious approval as long as it lasted.

'This is the big time, Matty! You know that, right? Your whole world changes from this second. Uh... you do want the part, right?'

Spiller tried to smile, not to appear too thrown. 'Yeah, course. I'm just a bit overwhelmed. Thanks.'

'Okay, so, I'm gonna see a couple more of Billy's people now, then check out some folk across town, but... just for lesser roles, okay? You're off the market, okay? Don't you go accepting any other offers, okay?'

'Not a chance,' Spiller said.

'Look out for the contract, Billy, old bean! I'm gonna email my PA on the way to the airport later. You'll have it by tomorrow morning.'

Billy looked fondly at his client, stood up and extended his wrinkly, liver-spotted hand across the desk. 'Well done, dear boy. Sorry about the subterfuge on the phone. Mr Stutz wanted to keep you in the dark; make certain he was the one to tell you. I do wish you'd run these things by me first, though. That audition of yours could have gone horribly wrong.'

'Tell me about it.'

'Let us walk you out,' Stutz said.

On the doorstep, Spiller turned and regarded them both. Stutz clapped an arm around Billy's shoulders. It was a distinctly odd coupling, sixties British theatre and contemporary Hollywood, like something had gone terribly but happily awry with Grindr's algorithms. He opened his mouth to say goodbye but noted that their eye-lines had shifted away from him. He tracked their gaze.

Standing beside the boot of his Fiesta were the figures of Ward's driver and his thumbless passenger. Apparently, that *had* been the growl of the Nissan behind him. Shit. They both had their baseball caps on, pulled low above their eyes, but Spiller could see they were checking the house and the garden for any cameras. As though Billy Banbury would have CCTV.

Satisfied it was safe, they both started towards him, drawing out machetes from under their jackets. Spiller heard Billy squeak. The one with the bandaged hands fumbled and dropped his weapon, stooped to pick it up.

'Look at you, all fingers and… fingers,' Spiller said, and set off to meet them. As he marched across the damp grass, he shoved his hands into his pockets as though he thought he could tackle them with just a couple of head-butts.

Spiller had known this day was coming. He'd been around a few dead bodies recently, but he'd managed to avoid dealing any fatal blows. Stutz had been right about one thing: this was the moment his life changed.

Five metres apart, Spiller pulled out the Sig, knocked off the safety, took the stance his firearms trainer had instilled in him prior to filming in the Gulf, and squeezed off two rapid sets of two rounds. The classic double-tap. All heart shots. Behind him, Billy yelped. It happened so fast that Ward's men barely had time to falter in their approach. They grunted as the rounds hit, staggered a little, then fell face down on the lawn. Spiller knew a .380 was lethal in the right place, but death wasn't always instant in the torso, so he hurried to close the remaining distance between them, giving each of them a bullet in the back of the head to empty the clip and make sure.

Quickly, before Stutz or Billy could get near, he pocketed the Sig and started to drag the heavier older man towards the car. He popped the hatchback and, with a power seemingly summoned from the hellish depths of his soul, he effortlessly hoisted the body off the lawn and into the space, which he assessed was too fricking small for two corpses. On the plus side, the rental company had conveniently installed a plastic insert to protect the boot fabric.

Somewhere out on the street, a big engine roared into life and there was a squeal of rubber. As he slammed the boot, Spiller imagined a panicked Ward tearing away in the Skyline, realising that gunshots weren't good news when he'd only sent people with blades. Spiller hurried back to the lighter corpse, dragging him by one leg to the rear door of the car. He manoeuvred his head and upper back into the closest foot-well, then ran around the other side, climbed in and pulled him across, positioning his head on the mat. He scurried back to collect the two weapons off the grass, chucked them in the rear footwell and shut the door.

Before he swivelled to face his audience, Spiller had the foresight to slap a huge grin across his face, although he didn't know if they were even there still. Maybe they were already on the phone to the police.

But they were there, Stutz in the same spot, Billy cowering in the doorway. Their expressions revealed their uncertainty about what they'd just witnessed. So Spiller tipped them the right way.

'Thank you!' He beamed and took a restoration-comedy bow. Standing up straight again, he waited, smile fixed, for them to react.

Tentatively, Stutz cracked his face into a dubious smile, then started to cackle and applaud.

'Thank you,' Spiller repeated. 'I thank you.'

'Ha! The actor who just keeps on giving!' Stutz said, and bellowed, clapping harder.

'Matthew?' a still-nervy Billy said.

'Just sealing the deal!' Spiller shouted gleefully at his agent. 'But…'

'Thank you!' Spiller said again, forestalling the completion of Billy's sentence, which he imagined would have been: *You didn't even know Mr Stutz would be here.*

'Are they not gonna take a bow?' Stutz asked.

Spiller glanced back over his shoulder. 'Oh... them, nah! They're very method. Until I say otherwise, they're dead.'

'Fucking awesome,' Stutz said, then pulled Billy forwards again to give him another shoulder-hug. 'Billy, why did I not know about this guy sooner?'

A befuddled Billy shrugged.

Spiller went to the driver's side, gave a final victory wave, and jumped in.

LIFE HAD BECOME a surreal movie. One of those flicks that chronicled the most bizarre sequence of events that sucked the main character into a spiral he couldn't break free from. Whatever he tried only served to worsen the situation, and any favourable events were never that—not for long. Spiller had seen a film like that once: *Very Bad Things.* It had starred Christian Slater and appeared to be the sick forerunner to *The Hangover* movies, in which some friends head to Las Vegas for a bachelor party that becomes progressively more nightmarish.

Spiller didn't need to be in Stutz's new movie; he was the lead in his own. This particular scene would see him driving around with two dead bodies in his car, one of which was behind him for anyone on the pavement to see. He didn't know what to do with them, and, unless he could find a place where they'd never be found, their subsequent discovery would alert Billy and Stutz to the fact that they'd just watched a bit of open-air snuff theatre. Actually, he suspected Stutz may not have fully bought into this second act, but wasn't about to screw up some dream casting just because two people had died. In fact, three, because, if he doubted this second act, he probably now doubted the first.

You had to laugh, and Spiller did. Loud staccato whoops he'd never heard himself utter before and that put him in mind of an extremely worried chimp.

At the end of Billy's road, Spiller stopped at a Give Way, awkwardly wriggled out of his jacket and draped it over Thumbless Boy as best he could. He pulled the SIM and battery from his mobile, and, just as he had done the night of Ward's murder and again after finding Gibbo in the boot, Spiller soon found himself heading into the hills for lack of anywhere better to go.

Daylight was fading already, which meant he'd have the cover of darkness, and Spiller revisited the plan he'd abandoned for Gibbo's corpse, namely dumping them where he'd left Ward. Two more gangland hits by the same rivals, the bodies left in the same spot to send a message. It seemed logical. Moreover, Spiller was out of ideas. He'd have been fine if this were a movie, as he'd be a gardener towing a wood-chipper, or a butcher with a professional meat-grinder, or an industrial chemist with access to an acid bath, or maybe the foreman of a building site where they were just about to lay some deep foundations.

Still, if the bodies were discovered, Stutz would be in the States and oblivious, and Billy... maybe buy him a bumper box of cravats to keep him quiet. Although why would he want to hurt his most lucrative client? Or end his career in ignominy, his legacy forever linked to Spiller's murderous exploits?

Even in this remote, wooded area, there was too much early evening traffic. Spiller drove for an hour before pulling into a lay-by, separated from the road by a dense semicircle of trees that obscured his solitary car from passing vehicles. He killed his headlights and, before the courtesy light faded, he looked behind him. He knew a lot from a lifetime's fascination with guns, and he knew a corpse didn't bleed much once the heart stopped, and he'd put two slugs into each. The floor mat beneath the head would have to be thrown, but the chest hadn't leaked out to stain anything except the clothes he'd died in. Spiller would have to get rid of his own clothes, though. The head shots could have caused backsplatter, even if it was so faint he couldn't see it.

Spiller was too fearful to linger for long in case a police patrol used the lay-by as a turn-around and decided to check him out.

He got back on the road and drove for another hour, back and forth along the same winding route.

As he drove, he tried to assess the situation. The mounting body-count was an undeniable pisser, only mitigated by the fact that the right people were dead. On the truly bright side, however, he had just landed the lead role in a blockbuster movie to be directed by a Hollywood icon. Brighter than that, he was going to be rich off that movie alone—forget what may follow, as a circus of fickle sycophants suddenly lauded him and heaped upon him the best screenplays in town.

This pending influx of money might also unfuck his situation with Delaney, and therefore partly with Helen and the girls. If he didn't need Delaney's money to support them, the man might back off with his threats, which would just leave Dominic Ward. And who was to say he wasn't already rethinking his vendetta in light of his recent staff shortages?

Spiller decided he needed to speak to Delaney again to clear the air, and that Emma would have to be there as arbiter to prevent any more nastiness. It was doubtful Delaney would resort to violence if she was there to witness it.

When he deemed it quiet enough to do the deed, Spiller headed off towards the place where the stones had been replaced on the wall, just along from the flapping bit of blue and white plastic. He stopped the car and acted swiftly. The wind was chilly, but he trembled mostly from nerves. They'd done a good job on the wall, cheating a little with some cement, so it remained intact as the stiffening bodies briefly see-sawed over into that great recycling system known as nature. He heard them crashing down the other side for several seconds, breaking branches and snowballing the undergrowth into a noisy little avalanche until they settled and all he could hear was the wind in the trees. Spiller wiped his prints off the machetes and chucked them over as well.

Ten minutes from there, he stopped on a small bridge that crossed a lake. He took out the Sig, pulled his sleeves down over his hands and wiped the gun down, including the magazine. He got out and launched it as far as he could across the water. It landed with an unseen *plop*.

On the outskirts of the city, Spiller pulled into a retail park and purchased a complete change of clothes, shoes and all, from a large supermarket. He also bought some lighter fuel, matches, a bottle of spray bleach, and some new floor mats. In the toilets, he bundled his old gear into a carrier bag and then went back out to his car, freshly attired. From there, he drove to the housing estate where he'd faked Ward's presence the night of his death. He went to the far side of the estate, to the waste ground beyond the CCTV, doused his bag of clothes and the rear floor mats and set fire to them. His experience taxiing told him it would be the first of several fires set in that area that night, and no one would care, much less call the police or fire service.

Chapter Twenty-One

HAVING HAD ACCESS to a real-life firearm, and to now be without, made Spiller feel naked. Perhaps if Emma had provided him with more bullets, or he'd held just one back, he might have kept the gun. Empty, though, it had been useless to him, but a ballistic gift to the police if the guys in the hills were ever discovered.

How could Spiller defend himself if attacked again? If more of Ward's people came, they'd bring worse than blades, and he knew for certain that Delaney's people carried firearms. And what did he have? The most potent item was his stun-gun, but he wasn't even sure where that was. He knew he'd hidden it somewhere, but he'd done so much flitting about recently between house and flat and hotel, and most of the time he'd been in a daze. He assumed his replicas were back at his flat, but they were very likely to get him killed. Good for scaring unarmed people; even better for encouraging armed people to shoot you.

Spiller drove the Fiesta behind the house, down the ginnel, and reversed it up to the cellar door. He placed two new floor mats behind the front seats, then took the plastic boot insert inside, where he sprayed it with bleach. He took it back out, sprayed all around the back seats and in the boot, set the tray back in its place, and just hoped the bleach was strong enough to degrade any traces of blood without noticeably fading the car's interior. The rental people wouldn't like that.

He locked the car and the cellar and went up to the kitchen, where he opened a can of beans, sat down at the table and ate them cold, then promptly threw them up warm. He cleared the sink, swilled his mouth, and tried again with some toast, munching it slowly. As he did, he made his mobile active again. The moment it booted, Billy called.

'Hi, Billy.'

'Matthew…' No *dear boy*. Then silence.

'Billy?'

'Yes.'

'About earlier?' Spiller suggested.

'Yes.'

'You're wondering how I knew to set it up.'

'Indeed.'

Spiller had figured out a response. 'I knew I'd either be greeted by Brett, or the police if he'd taken the body-in-the-boot thing seriously. I bet on Brett.'

'But…'

'What?'

'It all looked…' He trailed off again.

'I'm a good actor, Billy. It was meant to look real.'

'But…'

'Billy, have you ever seen a Brett Stutz movie?'

'Good God, no.'

'There you go. What I did today is nothing compared to his stuff. Special effects are amazing these days. You were shocked. He loved it. Because he knows how it's done.'

'But…'

'What?'

'You're not an SFX man, dear boy, you're an actor. You need… what do they call them? Squids, blood packs, to fake a shooting. I saw those two men hit by bullets.'

'Squibs,' Spiller said.

'Eh?'

'They're called squibs, with a B.'

'Oh. But…'

'Billy, say what you want to say. You think I actually killed two people in your front garden, right?'

'I confess… it did rather appear that way.'

'Well… I didn't. And, Billy…'

'Yes?'

'If it was real, then two men with machetes were about to hack me to death. So I acted in self-defence, right? But I didn't

272

because it wasn't real. I faked it. And, because I faked it, you're about to earn fifteen percent of... I imagine a *lot* of money. You're going to be in clover for the rest of your life. Well... velvet.'

'It's twenty,' Billy said.

'What's twenty?'

'My commission on a feature film. Ten percent theatre, fifteen television, twenty movies.'

'Even better for you,' Spiller said. 'What do actors make as a lead in a big movie? Fifteen, twenty million dollars? Okay, so I'm unknown, so maybe I get five or ten. Even five, your end is a million dollars. Or you could throw a spanner in the works and tell the police you think I killed two people, then I miss filming and you lose a million bucks.'

'Dear boy,' Billy said instantly, 'I shall call you the moment the contract arrives. Have a splendid evening.'

'I thought so.'

The call ended and Spiller allowed himself a smile. Nice, for once, that the fickleness of the profession had worked in his favour. While he still felt vaguely upbeat, he placed a call to Helen.

'Fuck,' she answered, 'I thought you'd forgotten about us.'

'*Muuuum...*' Sophie complained in the background.

'Sorry, darling. So, Matt, are we okay to come out of hiding now?'

'Very soon.'

'Fuck.'

'*Mum!*'

'Sophie, put your headphones in, please.'

There was a pause while Helen obviously waited for their youngest to mute the parental filth.

'What's happening, Matt? Why is it suddenly safe to call but it's still not safe for us to come home?'

'How are the girls?' Spiller asked.

'As you'd expect: scared and confused. What's happening?'

'I have another phone call to make and it's going to sort everything out, I promise.'

'Why couldn't you have made it *then* called us?'

Spiller pondered on this. 'Good point. But, honestly, things are much better. I even got an acting job. You heard of Brett Stutz?'

'Who hasn't?'

'I got the lead in his new movie.'

A moment's silence. 'And this is what you call *much better*, is it? Because this is what I'd call certifiable. Shit, I know you've been deluded at times, Matt, but this is next level.'

'That's just what Brett said! About my audition!'

'Bonkers.'

'Call Billy. Go on, call my agent. I'll text you his number. Call and ask him if I'm deluded. Ask him what happened.'

Helen was quiet for a few seconds. 'I'm not going to call your agent, Matt. But if this is a lie, if this is another of your crackpot fantasies, we are done. Do you understand? You're out of our lives.'

'Okay. I'm not kidding about the job. You can even tell the girls. I wouldn't say that if I was lying, would I? I'd never get their hopes up like that.'

'All right, Matt.' She sounded like she was done arguing with his craziness.

'Where are you?' he asked, picking up a pen and grabbing a newspaper from the counter.

'Sure I can say? I thought the Deep State was after us.'

'It's fine.'

'The Addfwyn Nant Guest House. Just outside Betws-y-Coed.'

'Sounds lovely.'

'We've made the most of it.'

'Spell it for me.'

'A D D F W Y N, then Nant, N A N T.'

He jotted it down on the corner of the front page as she spoke, adding "Guest House", then drew two squiggly lines under it, and a love heart after it. 'Sit tight,' he said. 'I'll call. It may be late, but I'll call. Give my love to the girls.'

'I always do.'

He ended the call and immediately located Emma's number. It rang and rang and rang out. He tried again. The same. On the third attempt, she picked up just as he was about to hit the red button.

'What now?' she answered.

'You told Delaney I was going after Whittard, right?'

'I told him I'd given you his card. Why?'

'He knew I was coming. Whittard was expecting me. Why would Delaney warn him if there was nothing to hide? Hey?'

Emma sighed. 'I've no idea and I honestly couldn't give a bugger.'

'Well, there was something to hide, and I have it.'

Another sigh, more profound. 'Surprise me.'

'They're connected.'

'I know that. I told you that.'

'No, it's deeper. There are things I found you wouldn't believe.'

'I'm sure I wouldn't. What d'you want?'

Spiller pushed a crumb of toast around his plate. 'I need your help. I took something from Whittard and I want to negotiate with Delaney. I want you to help. Sort of... adjudicate.'

'What exactly does that mean?'

'Make sure he hears me out and doesn't kill me. You know he kills people, right? We watched the movie together. I want you to be there to make sure there isn't a sequel. I'll give you your money back if you do. You don't tell Delaney, he gives you another twenty, so you get forty.'

'I can add up, thanks. And, technically, I'd only be getting twenty as the other twenty used to be mine.'

'If you're being pedantic. Listen, twenty grand for ten minutes. Just be there while I talk to him. He won't kill me in front of you.'

'Or, if he's as bad as you think, he'll kill you, *then* me.'

'Twenty grand,' Spiller repeated.

'Jesus... when?'

'Tonight. Needs to be tonight. This all needs to end.'

'I'll ask, that's all I can do.' Emma hung up.

One last call to make. He wanted his car back. He found DCI Bartoli's card in his wallet but instead found himself on the receiving end of a call from a withheld number.

'Hello?'

'It's your Guardian Angel.'

Spiller recognised Alfie Enright's voice. 'Hi.'

'Just wanted to know if my advice worked. Did you let God?'

So much had happened since he'd been given that counsel twenty-four hours earlier, he had to work out what it related to. Okay, Gibbo. Leaving Gibbo in the boot and returning him to his driveway.

'I don't know,' he said. Then he thought of his job offer and all the dough heading his way. 'Possibly. If it did, that thing about working in mysterious ways makes a lot of sense.'

Enright laughed lightly. 'Is your family well? How's Sammy?'

'She's... I don't know. They're away. Safe, at least.'

'That's good.'

'So, have there... have you heard about any more... *weird stuff* happening since last night?'

'Such as?'

'Oh, you'd know if you'd heard.'

'Then no. I'm not aware of anything.'

So, Gibbo was still in his boot, rotting away. How repulsive.

'Matthew... whatever you're still doing, dial it back.'

'That's the plan.'

'Because this is our final conversation. No more help from me, okay? This phone is now burned. If anyone asks, I met you once outside your house the day Ward turned up with your daughter. More than that, I'll deny.'

'Understood. Thanks for checking on me.'

'Uh-huh.' *Beep.*

Dialling it back wasn't the plan. Gibbo was a big problem. He'd left the hazard lights on the Lexus flashing in the hope that someone would investigate and Gibbo would be discovered and laid to rest. He'd accepted there would be repercussions for him. He'd been added to Gibbo's insurance a few days ago and there'd immediately been a falling-out within earshot of one of

Gibbo's girlfriends. He'd anticipated being pulled in for questioning. But that was before he landed his dream acting job. Police attention now would be a disaster. It wasn't about Stutz or Billy; it was bigger than them. No way would the movie's financiers want anyone involved in their project who was linked to a murder.

Spiller wondered if he should drive Gibbo's car up to the wilds of Scotland and dump it in a loch. There had to be somewhere up there he could roll a car down a hill into some deep water. Okay, slight issue of how he'd get back. Maybe hitch, or take a bicycle and pedal to the nearest railway station.

So much hassle. 'Fuck it.' he said to himself.

Gibbo would just have to go over the wall. Why not? What difference would another body make? Dump him, drive to the estate, torch the car on the waste ground.

He grabbed his car keys and headed back down through the cellar into the rear yard.

SPILLER PARKED A street away from Gibbo's house and walked the rest of the way, and carried on walking when he reached the house as there was no point stopping.

The car was gone.

He walked to the end of the street, crossed to the other pavement, and walked back. He stopped and stared at the bare frontage of the house. Did someone else have access to the car? Another taxi driver? Had the police only just seized it? Or had it been crushed into a box by a Delaney baling press?

Spiller went back to his Fiesta, settled, and called DCI Bartoli. It rang a couple of times.

'DCI Bartoli.'

'Matt Spiller.'

'Your car?'

'Please.'

'Okay, you need to take your driver's licence over to Brinley Industrial Estate. We have a pound on Sixth Avenue.'

'Will you be there?' Spiller asked.

'Why in God's name would I be there?'

'Dunno. Maybe you like cars.'

'Cars I like. You I don't. They open at eight a.m.'

'And you're not going to be there.'

An irritated huff. 'Why? You want me to be there? You got something to tell me?'

'Nope. It's just... if you want to talk to me, I'd prefer you just say so.'

'Jeez... coupla things strike me: One, there's still something you think I need to hear. Two, whatever it is, it's bad enough that you think I'm setting an ambush.'

Spiller decided not to respond. Just maybe he'd already said too much.

'Anything else?' Bartoli asked.

'Um, I'll be going to America in the next few weeks.'

'Okay.' A pause. 'You wanna know where's good to visit?'

'No, just keeping you informed. Like a good citizen.'

'Thank you for doing your civic duty.'

Spiller laughed. 'Aren't we a couple of facetious old bastards?'

'I'll see you around, Mr Spiller.'

Spiller mused about the fate of the Lexus. More than likely, it had been destroyed. It wasn't what he'd have wanted for Gibbo, but it sure as hell served his purposes. The bottom line: there wasn't anything he could do about Gibbo now. Whoever took the car took the body. It would disappear or turn up. Either way, it was out of his hands.

EMMA CALLED JUST after midnight. Spiller was watching TV at the family home, debating whether to chase her. He'd dropped by his flat on the way back, picking up his replica Browning Hi-Power. The Beretta, the Colt and the Magnum were all seen as American movie guns, whereas the Browning had links to the European military going back to the Second World War. If he was forced to wave a gun about, it would be the most credible.

Emma told him to come to her house and she would drive them to the rendezvous, which was scheduled for one forty-five. Delaney had picked a 24-hour petrol station on the same retail park where Spiller had earlier purchased his change of clothes. The forecourt was covered by ANPR and CCTV, which Delaney hoped would make Spiller feel safe.

With his Browning tucked down his belt, just in case, Spiller arrived at Emma's house at one-fifteen and she drove them to the retail park in her M4. She was a good driver; understood how to read the road. They didn't speak to each other the entire journey. Oddly, for Spiller at least, the silence was comfortable, as though they were soul-mates who didn't need to speak to communicate. He assumed she had a very different take on the atmosphere.

She entered under the harsh lights of the station canopy at 01:37 and parked down the side of the shop, next to a car wash. Spiller looked over at the 24-hour supermarket, where a few shoppers were dribbling in and out. One vehicle meandered from the car park to the petrol station and its female owner filled up at the Pay-at-Pump. Spiller watched her watching them, a suspicious look on her face. Spiller tried to look like a copper. Then she left.

01:45 passed and Spiller began to feel agitated. He started giving Emma sidelong looks that she ignored. At 01:56, she turned on the radio, keeping it low. The DJ was playing a tune that Spiller despised. Some guy droning miserably about how he wasn't good enough. Even for a depressive like Spiller, it was incredibly irritating. The song really needed to end with a gunshot to make any sense. He wanted to check the radio station, but the display was in dark mode. He reached a hand towards the buttons and she slapped it away.

'Not your choice,' she said. 'My car.'

'Where is he?' Spiller asked.

'Not here yet.'

'State the bleeding obvious, why don't you? He definitely said one forty-five?'

She nodded.

'Shit.'

Spiller vaguely noted the start of the 2 a.m. news bulletin but was too busy scanning outside the car to pay much attention. A minute later, he was paying attention. Emma had whacked up the volume and was staring at the console intently.

'... *was apparently assaulted by someone impersonating a police officer, who stole several items from his office. After suffering a blow to the head, Mr Whittard later became unwell, was taken to hospital, but died from his injuries. Next of kin have been informed. The weather... it looks like—*'

Emma stabbed a finger at the button and ended the broadcast, then leaned away from Spiller as she stared at him.

'Christ... you killed him.'

Spiller's horror was colossal. He felt himself weaken systemically, like a nerve agent had ripped through him. His mouth dropped open but no words emerged.

'You killed him,' she said again.

'I... I didn't. He was okay. This was Delaney. He killed him. To cover his tracks. He'll have cleared out the whole place. Computers, files, everything.'

'You're telling me you didn't assault him?'

Spiller felt cold, but his face burned. 'I... hit him with a book. He banged his head, but it was... it was a tap. Really, that couldn't have killed him. Delaney did it.'

'Delaney Delaney Delaney,' Emma mocked. 'It's never you, is it? Nothing is ever your fault, is it, Matthew?'

'No, actually, nearly everything is my fault, but I didn't do this, I couldn't have done. He was fine when I left.'

'He must have had a bleed on the brain. A small one. They can take hours to develop.' She started the car.

'What are you doing?'

'Whatever happened to Whittard, Charlie's not coming. He doesn't need to. You've got nothing on him now, but he has everything on you. All he has to do is give you up to the police and you've had it. I assume other people saw you there.'

Spiller nodded. 'Going in. Security. Probably cameras. And his secretary.'

'Your best bet now is to let this go. Just pray that's all Charlie wants—to even things up so you can't blackmail him. Forget the money; keep my twenty, I don't care.'

Emma pulled away from the car wash, raced across the forecourt and headed back to the by-pass.

Spiller was still reeling. A piddling tap on the head and Whittard dies. What a fucking weakling.

'Can you call him?' he asked.

'Charlie? Why?' She put her foot down on the deserted tarmac, soon passed the ton. The streetlights zipped overhead. Flash flash flash flash... quicker and quicker.

'Find out if we *are* even. I need to know. I got a huge job earlier today. A Brett Stutz movie.'

'Bullshit.'

'Seriously. I wanted to meet Delaney to negotiate a truce. I don't need his money any more. I'm going to earn millions in Hollywood.'

Emma giggled. 'You are so warped.'

'He could have had all the files back. I just wanted him to leave my family alone.'

'Clinically deluded.'

'Will you please slow down?' he said, peering at the speedo.

Emma eased off the pedal, let the BMW drop to 80. 'I'm taking you back, you're getting your car, and then you're leaving me alone. Okay?'

'Whatever,' he said.

'No. Not whatever. You do what I say or Charlie will have you locked up or killed and I really don't care which.'

Spiller sulked for a bit. 'He can't do this to me.'

He pulled down the vanity mirror and looked at himself. Damn, did the man inside not match the image. He flapped the visor back up and slouched in his seat. Emma eased back up to a ton and Spiller realised he missed being in a car that really shifted.

EMMA SWUNG THE Beamer onto her driveway like she was determined to smash through the front of her house and end up in the back garden. She braked hard and the big callipers halted her progress with mere centimetres to spare. Spiller got out and moped around sullenly as she marched to her front door, let herself in and slammed him out.

Spiller turned and looked at his sorry little hire car. He walked towards it but carried on past and into the communal garden, between some staked saplings, and onto the mound in the centre, where he lay on his back on the frosty grass and stared up at a clear and speckled sky. He pulled the hood of his sweatshirt up around the back of his head.

'Let go, let God, my arse,' he whispered. It was cold enough that if he fell asleep there, he'd probably not wake up. He'd never been so tempted. He wouldn't have to do anything proactive. This wasn't taking pills or climbing to the top of a multi-storey or tying a noose. He just had to lie there, close his eyes, drift away.

He lifted his head and looked at Emma's bedroom window. Pitifully, he wanted her to look out, see him, and invite him inside. Into her bed. Into her.

He resumed staring at the sky. An airliner was passing high above. Where was it going? Los Angeles? Its lights winked at him, mocking him. He exhaled a slow stream of warm air, obscuring it, then he closed his eyes. The cold in the ground seeped upward into his body.

No, this was very uncomfortable. He got up and went to his car. He had a house and a flat nearby, both with radiators and duvets.

Spiller realised as he drove home that he had no choice any more. He had to let go. He wasn't sure if God or Satan would occupy the director's chair, but there was no way to steer this one way or the other. He'd lost control. Probably he'd never had any. And maybe it wasn't as bad as all that. However Whittard had died, it didn't serve Delaney to have the police haul Spiller in for questioning. In all likelihood, Delaney had already wiped the footage showing he was even at Whittard's office. This was a prime example of Mutually Assured Destruction.

He had to be optimistic. He had to believe good ol' Napoleon Hill had been right all along. Spiller had pursued fame so ardently that the universe had finally acceded and delivered it. He would get his car back, he would get his family back, Gibbo's body wouldn't surface, neither would the two beyond the wall, the police would come up empty on all their investigations, and both Delaney and Dominic would back off and forget about him. He'd jet off to LA and finally enjoy the career he'd always deserved.

On the other hand… what if Delaney was only getting started? Whittard was out of the picture, so maybe Spiller was next. Maybe his family was still vulnerable. It was pleasant to entertain fanciful and upbeat views, but in these circumstances, it was highly risky.

Spiller left his car on the street and rushed into the house and through to the kitchen. It was late and Bartoli seemed a disgruntled sod at the best of times, but…

Bartoli answered quickly, considering the time. 'Yes, Mr Spiller, how can I be of service to you?'

'I was wondering… could you send someone to look after my family, please.'

'Come again.'

'They're at the…' he pulled the newspaper towards him '…Addfwyn Nant Guest House. It's near Betws-y-Coed, that's North Wales.'

Bartoli clearly had to gather his thoughts. 'Okay, unpack that for me. What does *someone* mean, and… shit, *why?*'

'Someone with a gun. One of your armed officers. Preferably a couple of them. And… because you know I'm caught up in something.'

A longer pause as Bartoli considered the request. 'No.'

'They might be in danger.'

'Explain. I'm not deploying a firearms unit to frigging Wales at three o'clock in the morning unless I can fully justify it.'

Now it was Spiller's turn to fall quiet.

'Mr Spiller...'

'It's complicated.'

'Are people heading to that location as we speak to cause your family harm?'

'Not sure.'

'Apart from me and you, does anyone even know where your family is right now?'

'Don't know. I don't know if... I don't know what... *capabilities* these people have. If they can tap phones, listen in on conversations.'

'Are these people M15 or M16?'

'No.'

'Then I wouldn't worry. Go to bed, Mr Spiller. And, rest assured, we will be continuing this conversation tomorrow in a more formal setting.'

Spiller ended the call. Damn, had his paranoia just screwed him? He didn't want another chat with Bartoli. Not at all. He'd have to play dumb again, and Bartoli would be *so* pissed off. He'd done this a few times in his life—overthink things. He'd bolloxed a couple of dream acting opportunities early in his career by jumping the gun and getting riled rather than being patient.

It was too late now to call Helen, and what news did he have that she'd want to hear?

With the Browning still down his waistband, he made his weary way upstairs to the bedroom he used to share with his wife. He set the gun on the bedside table, stripped down to his underwear and crawled under the winter duvet. It was bliss. He could smell his wife. He pulled her pillow towards him and cuddled it, but he nodded off thinking of Emma.

Chapter Twenty-Two

THE FIGURES ON the other side of the front door weren't
unexpected. Through the misted panes, Spiller could see two
dark uniforms. Neither was wearing headgear. Clearly, this was
the posse sent by Bartoli to escort him to the station. Spiller had
dressed early in anticipation. It was just after eight o'clock. He'd
had some breakfast already; loaded up on calories to get him
through all the questions Bartoli would throw at him that he'd
refuse to answer.

It was Alfie Enright on the doorstep, which was strange after
his vow to cut all ties. Beside him was a five-foot tall female
officer with a blonde bob, and Spiller mentally applauded her
obvious willingness to take on all-comers despite her diminutive
stature. Maybe she was a Tai Chi master and could throw him
across the room with a flick of her wrist. Before Enright spoke,
Spiller remembered not to remember him very well.

'Mr Spiller, I'm Sergeant Enright. We met a couple of weeks
ago.'

'Uh, right,' Spiller said vaguely.

'This is my colleague, Special Constable Olwen. Can we
come in, please?'

'Sure, I know what this is about.' Spiller turned and headed
down the hall towards the kitchen. 'Just going to make a quick
coffee,' he said as he went. 'Need the caffeine. Your DCI is a
right bore!' He went to the kettle, pressed the button, heard them
follow in behind. He whistled randomly, as a person does when
they're trying to appear nonchalant.

'Mr Spiller…'

Spiller turned and, although Enright had spoken, he found
his eyes drawn to Olwen's face. She was trying to hide it, but she
looked devastated. He properly noticed their caps for the first
time, clutched in front of them with both hands in a way that

felt horribly portentous. An icy cold flushed through his legs. He was already grabbing for the back of a chair when Enright asked him to sit down.

Enright slowly took the seat opposite him. Spiller stared at the newspaper in front of Enright, on which he'd last night scribbled Helen's secret location.

'Mr Spiller, I'm afraid I have some very bad news.'

Special Constable Olwen sniffed as her chin began to wobble.

Even before he heard the words, Spiller knew. He felt his soul, his essence, drain out of him, taking, as it went, his strength and every good thing he'd barely, and so desperately, clung onto for twenty-five years.

'No…' he whispered.

'There was a fire,' Enright said. 'At the Addfwyn Nant Guest House. Just before dawn. Everyone inside perished. One of the vehicles outside belonged to your wife. Three bodies were found in one of the rooms and… it would appear they might be those of your family. They will need to be formally identified but… I'm so sorry.'

Olwen burst into tears.

'Donna, would you mind going and sitting in the car, please?' Enright handed her the keys and she ran down the hallway blubbering. 'I'm so sorry, Matthew. I wanted to be the one to tell you.'

A monumental fugue gripped his every atom. Spiller could think, but not move. He looked at Enright looking back at him, waiting for his sorrow or questions or fury or… something. It was like those movies where a victim is given a drug that paralyses physically without impairing mentally. Spiller had always thought that would be a disgusting way to go. The sheer helplessness.

'Matthew?'

Perhaps this was the culmination—of all those years expecting the worst. Hoping for the best, working to achieve all he could, but always falling short, and increasingly succumbing to the creeping plague of depression that ate away at any remnant of hope until nothing remained. Maybe there was no further to fall, no more grieving inside him. He'd entertained worst-case scenarios for so many years, maybe now he was simply inured to the real thing. Maybe this was the one useful facet of depression.

'Matthew, I need you to come with me.'

'Bartoli,' Spiller said.

'He wants to see you.'

'No. Not that.'

'What do you mean?'

'This is Bartoli.'

Enright made a face. 'What's Bartoli?'

'He did this. He killed my family.'

'DCI Bartoli?'

'I told him where they were last night. No one else. No one else knew. I asked for his help. I wanted him to protect them.' Spiller tittered crazily. It was the kind of noise he often made before the dam broke and out poured a flood of tears, but not this morning. His voice went flat again. 'So stupid.' Without an ounce of emotion, his automaton brain continued its deliberations.

Enright was incredulous. 'Bartoli? DCI Bartoli?'

'He told Dominic Ward. They know each other. That day at the police station. They said hello. Angelo. Dom. First names. A DCI on first-name terms with a defence barrister. They should hate each other.'

'Matthew, this is stupid.'

'He's from New York. Maybe that's where they get their drugs. I don't know. I only know no one else knew where they were. And I know Ward tried to kill my family twice before.'

'Matthew, let's go and talk to Bartoli. He'll straighten this out for you.'

Spiller rose so quickly he knocked the table into a tilt against Enright, who grabbed at his hat. The way Spiller felt, it wouldn't have surprised him had his vision been suddenly overlaid by a retinal display streaming information in red. He had a mission, targets.

'I'll get to Bartoli,' he said. 'Ward first.' He made a beeline for the door, shifting the table into Enright again, whose attempt to get up was thwarted.

'Matthew!'

Spiller stopped at the foot of the stairs, but not in response to Enright's protestations. He'd suddenly remembered where his stun-gun was. He needed it. He needed something. Behind him, he heard the metallic thwack of a police baton being extended.

'Matthew, stop!'

Spiller turned to him. 'I'm going upstairs. I need to vomit.'

Enright held still, so Spiller clambered up the stairs. Behind the bathroom door was the pole for the attic hatch. He hooked it on and pulled down the ladder.

In the hallway, Enright came to the foot of the stairs and looked up. 'What are you doing?'

But Spiller was already climbing and quickly disappeared into the dark loft. He crawled to where the boards gave way to fibreglass, and reached a hand under the coarse pink material. By the time he'd backed up and turned around on his knees, Enright's head had appeared through the hatch opening. Spiller activated the weapon and shoved the arcing, crackling prongs against his neck. Enright grunted and slid back down the ladder. Spiller peered through the hole and saw Enright's twitching form sprawled on the landing carpet, perilously close to the top of the stairs. Enright looked accusingly at the impassive face, framed by the loft opening.

Spiller descended. He stood over Enright as the man's frazzled nerves failed to override the lactic acid saturating his muscles. He moaned what might have been a swear word if he'd been capable of speech. Spiller reached down and took the yellow Taser from the hard holster on the front of his stab-vest, then delved into a couple of its flapped pockets to locate Enright's warrant card. He stepped over him and went downstairs.

He grabbed his combat jacket from the rail in the hall and left the house, weapon held out of sight. Special Constable

Olwen wasn't looking his way as he climbed into his car and set off down the street.

ACROSS TOWN, AT the law offices of Dominic Ward, Spiller kept his composure as he questioned the young receptionist on Ward's whereabouts. He guessed she'd seen enough ne'er-do-wells cross the threshold not to be daunted by his venomous, scabby mug. The fact of his family's demise still felt like a nightmare he'd woken from. It wasn't real. How could it be? Its monstrous weight was temporarily suspended by a gossamer thread of disbelief. He was being guided by the merest sliver of sanity, so fragile, yet so devoted to redressing the abuse that it was, for the moment, fully in charge.

'He's in court this morning, you just missed him.'

'Court where?' Spiller asked.

'Crown Court. City Centre. He has that big case. You'll have seen it in the press.' She beamed at him, so proud to be associated with such a high-flying boss.

'Which one?'

She frowned slightly at his ignorance. 'The Trevor Mickles case.'

It rang a bell. He tried to dig it out from the mess of his mind. 'The road-rage guy.'

'Well, that's to be decided, surely. May I inquire to what your visit's in regards with?'

'You need to use simpler sentences.'

'Sorry?'

'And you need to start looking for another job. Crown Court, right?'

Confused, she nodded.

It had been all over the news three months ago. Trevor Mickles, accused of knifing to death another driver after a minor altercation at traffic lights. With a history of violence and other serious crimes, Mickles had been released early from prison for firearms offences only a week before the stabbing. A true piece of shit, unrepentant to this day, and, you'd have thought, indefensible. Apparently not. Dominic Ward was on the case. Defender of the indefensible. The outrage at the time would have put most barristers off. Such was the public backlash against Mickles' two-fingered indifference that death-threats had been made.

The modern red-brick courthouse was a two-minute drive. Outside, Spiller saw that death-threats had turned into a few people in thick coats and woolly hats milling about with placards that read *Death Means Life!* Out of context, it wouldn't have made much sense. The police, however, weren't taking any chances, posting a couple of armed officers on the entrance, replete with Heckler and Koch G36 assault rifles. Seeing them, Spiller did a U-turn and took his stun-gun and Taser back to where he'd parked.

After a hurried return, he passed by the officers and through the large glass doors, where he was confronted by a metal detector. He joined the queue to be checked and was soon through and searching the wall signs. He'd not been in a courthouse before, but this looked busy. He doubted there'd be this many police on a normal day—there were a couple of armed officers inside as well—and he spotted a few loiterers he identified as journalists.

Spiller strutted up to one of the officers and briefly held up Enright's warrant card. 'Hi, mate. The Mickles case?'

The officer gave a rearward nod to the door he was guarding.

'Has it started?'

'About to.'

Spiller was becoming quietly frantic. If he barged in, he'd be arrested, and what was the point? How could he fatally attack Ward without a weapon? Given a few minutes alone with him, he could do it, but not when people would be jumping on him within seconds, or shooting him.

'Counsel gone in yet?' Spiller asked.

'Yeah. What happened to your face?'

'The job. You know how it goes.'

'That's why I've got one of these.'

'Mate! Long time!'

Spiller found himself being ushered along the corridor by Enright, who had a steely grip on his elbow, and fingertips dug into painful spots that Spiller assumed were pressure points. Enright barged through a set of swing doors into a quieter part of the building. He stopped beneath the overhang of some stairs.

'If I let you go,' Enright said, 'you walk with me out of this building.'

'I'm going to kill him,' Spiller said, eyes welling. He sensed he was about to lose control, that the thread was about to snap, and the loss of his family would go off in his head like a dirty bomb. He had to get a grip.

'You're not—not today. You walk with me or I call my buddies down there and tell them you're not a copper and you stole my stuff. I'll have my warrant card back, by the way.'

Spiller handed it over.

'Matthew, do you trust me?'

Spiller didn't know. His eyes were on fire with the agony of his suppressed tears.

'Okay,' Enright said. 'Put it this way: have I told anyone what I know about you?'

Spiller shrugged.

'You know I haven't, you idiot, or you'd be locked up by now. I'm on your side. I know you're hurting, but you won't get anywhere with this today. My God, you couldn't be in a worse place if you want to attack someone.'

'I'll wait 'til lunchtime. He'll go to the loo and I will tear his windpipe out with my bare hands, then stamp on what's left of his fucking neck. I just need ten seconds with him.'

'Matthew—'

'Why aren't you arresting me?' Spiller asked, suddenly appalled by the man. 'Even just for assaulting you? Fuck, don't you have any red lines?'

'I do, and I know you're way over yours, but this isn't the time. You need to walk with me. Trust me.'

It felt like a betrayal of his family to leave that place, but he didn't have a choice. He nodded.

'Don't run,' Enright warned. 'When you get outside, don't run. We go and get my Taser from your car, then you get in mine and we go somewhere.'

'Bartoli. That's fine. I'll do him first.'

'Just walk,' Enright said. 'Don't mess this up.'

THE WHOLE WAY to the car, Spiller had wanted to run. He'd wanted to run screaming through the streets in no particular direction until he crossed a road at the wrong moment and a speeding bus stopped his progress. He wanted to flee from his life, and it was testament to how much he did trust Enright that he obediently accompanied him. Was there salvation in this man? It felt like that. Was Spiller capitulating to the age-old motive for embracing a religious man? Fear and desperation.

'Where's the hobby bobby?' Spiller asked as he settled in the passenger seat of the police Hyundai.

'I told her to walk back—I had stuff to do.'

'You recovered from that zap pretty quickly.'

'I'm quite robust.'

'Sorry,' Spiller said.

'Yeah, well, don't do it again.'

'Is Bartoli waiting?'

Enright didn't respond, but Spiller quickly realised they weren't heading to the police station from the direction they were taking.

'Where are we going?'

'Dominic Ward didn't kill your family.'

'Right. And how the fuck would you know?'

'I know a lot of things I shouldn't—you know that.'

They stopped at a set of lights. The streets were thronged. Spiller watched the people pass, criss-cross, all ignoring each other, connected by the universal woes of life, separated by their personal reactions to them. Whittard had been right. They were all hurtling towards the same destination, but no one on board knew how to share their fear of the journey.

'Alfie, tell me.'

A couple of young boys crossed in front of the stationary car, one of them giving its occupants the shake of an open fist: wankers. The boys laughed. Enright ignored them. It started to rain. The lights changed and he set off.

'Alfie...'

'Fran told me about the other night. Outside Delaney's restaurant.'

'Fran?'

'PC Carnaby.'

'What did she say?'

'That you weren't making much sense. But you were scared. And very angry.'

Spiller said nothing.

'You shouldn't have crossed Delaney,' Enright said, hitting the wipers.

'Pardon? What are you saying?'

'He's a powerful man. He's been on our radar for years. Whispers, allegations, nothing comes of it. Fran said you accused him of threatening your family.'

'He did.' The rain was now pounding on the roof. 'You're saying Bartoli told Delaney, not Ward.'

Enright lifted a hand off the wheel and wagged a finger at Spiller, as if to say, *you got it.*

'Where are we going?' Spiller asked again.

'I'm taking you to his house. You're going to kill him.'

Spiller let the revelation sink in. 'You're a very bad policeman.'

'I know.'

'Just tell me where he lives. You don't need to get involved.'

'You'll never get in. It's a fortress. He has every conceivable defence: high walls, cameras, motion sensors, thermal imaging. It all went in after he moved here from Northern Ireland. You wouldn't get ten foot inside the perimeter before they caught you. In this, I can take you right up to the front door.'

'And I take on his people how? With a stun-gun?'

'Kit-bag, behind my seat.'

Spiller looked back and saw a black zipped holdall.

'Stick your hand in, feel around.'

Spiller obliged, unzipping the bag and rummaging inside. It felt like clothes in there, maybe an extra fleece, some gloves, a pair of trousers. Then his hand touched a familiar shape. He carefully extracted the gun and looked at it low between the seats.

'Glock Seventeen,' Enright said. 'Police issue, but untraceable. Certainly no link to me. You know how to use one? You should.'

'I was never in the military,' Spiller said, turning the weapon over in his hands.

'I know—you're an actor. You had some training, though, right? For that film?'

Spiller nodded.

'You just need to rack it, then it's good to go. You'll have one in the chamber, sixteen in the clip. Once you do rack it, there's no manual safety. The safety's in the trigger. So you need to keep your finger outside the guard unless you mean business. I know that's the fashionable movie look, but with this weapon it's critical.'

'Okay.'

'When we get there, there's a long drive. I'll drop you—'

'How do you know? Have you been before?'

'Google Maps. I'll drop you along the drive, you jump out. The security's concentrated on the perimeter. Once you're in the grounds, you'll be okay.'

Spiller laid the weapon in his foot-well and put his toe over it to keep it still. They drove in silence. Spiller had a lot of questions for Enright, especially now, but none of them seemed worth asking. He had provided Spiller with the only answer that mattered, and that was enough.

They left the silver and grey monoliths behind, heading out through the suburbs and into the countryside, the other side of the city to where the hills lay, onto a green plain where only the very successful or the highly corrupt could afford to live.

Chapter Twenty-Three

SPILLER COULD HEAR it had just stopped raining. He couldn't see anything, though, as he'd five minutes earlier climbed over into the back and was now keeping a low profile. He'd pushed the passenger seat forwards to its stop and was now crouching behind it under his jacket, Glock in hand. As concealments went, it was a little hide-and-seek, but it would be enough to evade the cameras.

The car turned off the lane and drew to a halt. He heard Enright's window drop, then an electronic buzz.

'Can I help?' said a male voice on the intercom.

'Police.'

'Do you have an appointment?'

'I said police, not Avon. Open up.'

Spiller heard a clunk, then a slight electric whine for ten seconds. He hunched lower. The car moved ahead slowly.

'Get ready,' Enright said over his shoulder. 'Bushes coming up. Stay hidden until you see me leave.'

Spiller pulled his jacket from over him, struggled into it, worked the slide on the Glock, and set his hand on the door release. The car came to a stop and Spiller hopped out, closed the door, and scurried straight into a bunch of dense laurels. He was instantly soaked, having dislodged the rain from the leaves. Through the foliage he could see Delaney's house in the distance, beyond some mature horse chestnuts, although *house* was a misnomer. It was an original country manor, built of grey Yorkstone blocks, six windows-wide across the front. Spiller had always detested the taxi fares that ended up at such places, where his failure to succeed was so starkly delineated. Off to the right of it was a sympathetically built, one-storey extension, mostly glass-sided, which looked like it might contain a swimming pool.

At least, he thought he could make out a couple of orange lifebelts on the wall inside.

Five minutes later, he heard a car heading back down the drive. He peeked through the leaves and saw the police Hyundai. As it passed, Enright kept his eyes straight ahead but subtly lifted his hand and offered a thumbs-up. Spiller took that to mean it was on; Delaney was in. Whatever the pretext for his visit, Enright had obviously managed to establish that one fact.

Spiller was shivering now, from the cold, the wet, but mainly from a rage-filled anticipation. Delaney was going to die for what he'd done. Any of his people who got in the way, or were even present, would also die. Oddly, even now, he still imagined he was in a movie, stalking the big boss-man who'd taken his family from him. It was a cliché, like every damn revenge movie ever made. It was the willing suspension of disbelief made manifest, the most potent refusal to cave to reality, to keep the truth hanging there by a thread. Just a few minutes more. That's all he needed.

He wondered how such a scene would be scripted by a screenwriter. Would they have him wait until dark? Would they make him creep from tree-to-tree, getting ever closer? Would they have him cosh a guard and steal his clothes? Difficult, that one; he couldn't even see any guards.

Spiller ran out from the laurels, Glock in hand, straight towards the pool-house. At every step, he expected someone would shout out or set off an alarm. He didn't honestly expect to be shot, though. This wasn't a movie, much less a Bond film with identically dressed minions patrolling with machine guns.

He reached the building and peered through a window. It was a pool-house, with rattan loungers, verdant pot plants, and scuba gear in the corner.

And the solitary figure of Charles Delaney.

Delaney, dressed in a black bathrobe, was just settling on one of the cushion-topped loungers. Beside him on a table was a mug of something. He opened a copy of the *Financial Times* that obscured all but his stumpy legs. Spiller scanned the pool-house again for anyone else, but Delaney was alone. He moved along to some double doors and gently pressed the handle down. It gave. He glanced behind him, but there was still no one around. He pushed the door inwards slightly and listened. Classical music was playing, emanating from a small black box sitting on a nearby ledge.

He stepped across the threshold into the muggy atmosphere.

There was a sudden crumpling as Delaney lowered his newspaper. He stared blankly at his unwanted guest, then lifted the *FT* up again so he could fold it nicely. He set it on the table and picked up his mug and took a sip.

'Matthew... tea?'

Spiller had watched too many movies where characters talked so much they missed the chance to act, so he quickly approached. He raised the Glock, took aim, and fired three times into his chest. The empty casings jumped one after the other from the ejection port. Delaney jolted and his head fell forwards, but Spiller knew something wasn't right.

It hadn't felt real. It was something that always pissed him off with films, that the guns showed no recoil. It was the difference between a live bullet and a blank. And he had just fired three blanks. He pulled the trigger again, aiming at the head. No recoil, no head-wound.

'Shit!' He stared daggers at the Glock in his hand, like it was acting maliciously in not spitting real bullets.

Delaney raised his head just as the two henchmen from the restaurant ran in. Stupidly, Spiller turned the gun towards them and pulled the trigger repeatedly until the slide blew back a final time and locked open. They didn't flinch. As the empty casings stopped skittering across the tiles, the two men looked at him with contempt, then slowly pulled out their own weapons, full-frame Sig-Sauers. They held them at their sternums, ready to thrust towards him.

Spiller growled and hurled the Glock at Delaney, but it missed and clattered across the floor until it hit the far wall near the arched doorway into the main house.

A moment later, from that portal, a man in a wheelchair emerged.

Delaney said, 'Matthew, meet Ronnie Loughty.'

Podgy Ronnie rolled himself along the side of the pool, then pulled a wheel back so the chair turned slightly, pointing his blocky white boots straight at Spiller. Both his legs were plastered up to the thigh, and Spiller recognised him as the gunman from the night Poole had been taken. It was gratifying to see the damage he'd done with the Lexus.

'And you've met his brother, Terry.' Delaney pointed at the bearded one. 'And my son, Alistair.'

Spiller looked at the handsome Alistair, then back at Delaney, then at Alistair again.

'You're adopted, right? This fucking Hobbit can't be your dad.'

Delaney chortled. 'He got the good genes—from his dear mother.'

'Cunts,' Spiller said. 'You're all cunts.'

In his chair, Ronnie sniggered. 'You don't look very happy.'

'No? You don't look too *buoyant* yourself, mate.' Spiller lunged at him, driving a kick into his outstretched feet.

The wheelchair rolled towards the pool edge too quickly for Ronnie to halt it. It tipped into the water, back-flipping him from his seat. Spiller heard a yelp emerge, then submerge, and watched as the weight of his plastered legs dragged him beneath the surface.

Delaney tutted. 'Terry, fish him out, please.'

Terry swore, handed his weapon to Alistair, shrugged his suit jacket onto the floor, kicked off his shoes, and jumped in. Spiller stepped to the edge. Ronnie was on his side on the bottom, flailing his arms to try and gain some lift, but getting nowhere. Terry swam down, managed to get his brother upright and manoeuvred him to the pool wall where he was able to grab onto the pool steps and start dragging himself upwards.

Alistair extended both guns towards Spiller, flicking the muzzles to indicate he should step back, but Spiller was past caring. As Ronnie's hair broke the surface, Spiller grabbed the curved rails and repeatedly stamped on his head until he let go and drifted back to the bottom, arms windmilling as fast as the water would allow, desperate mouthfuls of air bubbling out of him. Terry hardly had a chance to grab a lungful at the surface before he was forced down again to retrieve his drowning sibling.

Spiller watched. It was fascinating to see the end of a life, to know what was coming even as others railed against the inevitable. Within seconds, Ronnie stopped protesting. Terry seemed to inherit his brother's panic, doubling down on his forlorn efforts to re-float what was now literally a dead weight.

A minute later, Terry pushed himself to the surface and sucked in some air, rasping at the influx. He trod water for a moment, then screamed at Spiller. '*I'm gonna fucking kill you!*'

Spiller took a few steps back, grabbed the music machine off the ledge, and threw it towards him. Terry squealed as the box of mains power approached, but, just as it was about to drop into the water, the cord reached its limit and the box detached, splashing inert into the pool.

A growling Terry scrambled up the steps and beckoned for his gun from Alistair, and Spiller sat down on a lounger and waited to be shot.

'*No!*' Delaney barked. '*Terry!*'

Terry swivelled at the command, facing his master. 'Boss...'

'He should have been more careful! Ronnie knew the risks. You both made a mistake that night. My business with Mr Spiller is not concluded. I'll tell you when you can have your gun back. Go and get dry!'

Terry turned and stared at his brother, his body wobbling back and forth in the churned water. He looked back at Spiller, chlorinated drops falling from his furious face like tears.

'*Go!*' Delaney said.

Terry went and gathered up his jacket and shoes and left the pool-house. Alistair walked over to his father and stood next to him, guns dangling by his side.

Delaney picked up his mug and took a slurp. 'You're a revelation, Matthew. Who'd have thought you'd have such fight in you. Must be all those weeks in the military.'

Now everything had calmed down, Spiller's head was beginning to work through the ramifications of his blank-firing Glock. Enright had to have known about it. So, was he in league with Bartoli and Delaney? Where did this conspiracy end? Had Enright sent him to Delaney's so they'd kill him? If so, why wasn't he dead already?

'What business do we have to conclude?' Spiller asked. 'Just shoot me. I mean it. I don't want to live without my family.' He could feel that diaphanous thread lengthening. Thinner and thinner and weaker and weaker. He started to sob. 'Why did you do it? *Why?*'

Outside on the driveway, a car was approaching. Spiller looked through his tears to see the police Hyundai. He shifted, ready to pounce on the deceitful piece of shit.

'Nah-ah,' Alistair said, raising one of the Sigs. 'Stay there.'

Spiller watched as Enright parked, got out, and headed towards the pool-house. Enright entered, ignoring Spiller, but giving him a wide berth.

Delaney stood up, tightened the belt of his bath-robe and shook his hand. 'Alfie.'

'Charlie. Alistair.'

'Hey, brother.'

'How did it go?' Enright asked.

'Not that great.' Alistair nodded towards the pool.

Enright walked over and looked in. 'Shit. Terry know?'

'Yeah. Not a happy bunny.'

'Why?' Spiller asked them. 'Why? My wife, my beautiful daugh—'

Snap. He sank into himself and began wailing. He curled up on the lounger like a foetus, fell off onto the tiles. He bawled, he screamed, and kept asking them *why why why?*

'Why what, Matthew?' Delaney asked during a brief lull in the cacophony of mourning. 'Why what?'

'*Kill them!* You framed me for Whittard's murder. You didn't need to kill them. I wouldn't have said anything. I was done with you. You could have had everything back. All the files. You didn't need to kill my family.' He wondered whether he should crawl over to the pool and fall in and die, but that would probably be like trying to freeze to death on a mound of grass: easier said than done. He'd gag for air and push for the surface. Why couldn't they just shoot him?

'Your family?' Delaney said. 'The Addfwyn Nant Guest House, is that right?'

Spiller sobbed at the name—the memory of hearing his wife's voice dictate the address to him only a few hours earlier.

'Still in one piece, as far as I'm aware,' Enright said.

'What?' Spiller righted himself, got on his knees, dimly aware he was in a prayer position. 'You told me. You knew where they were.'

'Actually, I was just going to say they'd died in a fire. A fire can kill in a house, a car, a boat. Not knowing where they were, I was going to keep it vague. Then I saw it written down on your newspaper with a love heart next to it.'

Spiller gawped at him, his eyes screwed up, questioning. 'But... that special constable. She was in on it?'

'No, I just said we had a job to do. She never writes anything down, that girl.'

Spiller directed his pleading eyes towards Delaney.

'I don't know,' Delaney said. 'They may be dead, but, if they are, we didn't kill them. Why would I do to your family what was done to mine? Why would I knowingly inflict that much pain? I'm not like that.'

'You're lying, trying to make it worse. You sick old fuck.'

'Have you called them?'

He hadn't. He frantically dug his phone from his pocket and speed-dialled Helen.

'Matt, I've been waiting,' she answered. 'You said you'd call last night.'

Spiller wailed like a... he didn't know what. He was making a lot of new noises of late. He started crying, but good tears this time; really excellent tears.

'Matt, what's up? What's wrong?'

'You're all right? The girls are all right?'

'Yeah, we're fine.'

He wailed again. 'Honestly?'

'Yes.'

'God, I love you so much. I love you all so much. I want to come back. I want to be with you all for ever.'

'Uh… we can work on that. We… we love you too, Matt. We just want you to be happy.'

'I am happy! I am! I'll never be unhappy ever again!'

Helen sounded baffled. 'Uh… great. Can we come home now?'

Spiller looked at Delaney, who shrugged like he didn't know why he was being asked.

'Yes!' Spiller said. 'Just drive carefully.' He suddenly thought of Dominic Ward, the danger he still posed. 'But… go back to your parents' place, just for the time being.'

Helen didn't argue or sound annoyed. 'Okay.'

After hanging up, Spiller fixed Delaney, Alistair, then Enright, one after another, with a toxic stare. 'You *bastards*. Why would you do that to me?'

Delaney walked over to Spiller, dragged a lounger up close, and settled on it. Alistair poised himself to intervene should Spiller lose it.

'So you know, Matthew. So you know. What it feels like to suffer loss. So you know how you'd react. And how did you react? You came over here and shot me. Alfie put a gun in your hand and you walked in here and shot me. You didn't hesitate. Now you know why we do what we do.'

'I don't know what you do,' Spiller said.

'Yes, you do. I know you've worked out the basics. We deal with people when the legal system won't. Or when the legal system thinks it's done enough, but it hasn't. Alfie told me what you did to Callum Ward. We'd been looking at him for a while. Matthew, you got away with murder. You killed a gang leader in your own home and you got away with it. Not many people could have pulled that off.'

'Ward's brother knows I did it.'

'And can't prove a thing.'

'Only because your pal Bartoli's burying evidence to protect me.'

'Bartoli?' Enright said. 'He's not with us. I wasn't lying about that. Believe me, Bartoli wants you; he just can't get anything on you.'

'You played it brilliantly, Matthew,' Delaney said. 'That's why I thought you'd be ripe for picking. I could use a man like you. You have skills.'

'A very particular set of skills.'

Delaney smiled. 'Mr Neeson. Yes, you have skills, my friend. You behave like you're in a movie. You think like you're writing a screenplay. You work it all out, every detail, what might trip you up or catch you out. You were perfect. But then... you went rogue.'

'How so?'

'Blackmail, digging in my business, hassling Emma, interrogating Glen.'

'I needed the money. To get my family away from Ward.'

'I know, but it blinded you. You couldn't see how alike we are. So I made you see. I made you feel what I feel. So you'd understand.'

Spiller did understand. How could he not? 'I don't need your money any more. You can have Whittard's files, the dash-cam footage. I got a big film yesterday. I'm going to Hollywood.'

'Emma told me. Is that true?'

'Yes. Is she involved?'

'With us?' Delaney looked a little sad. 'More than I'd want her to be since you came along, but... no. Will you join us?'

'No. Fuck, you killed my mate. He hadn't done anything wrong. I've killed people, but they deserved it.'

Delaney sighed, straightened his back. 'That wasn't sanctioned. I had no idea about that until after you left the restaurant and the boys told me what they'd done.' He glanced disapprovingly at his son.

Spiller shook his head. 'Sanctioned? Nothing you do is *sanctioned*.'

'There will always be collateral damage in a war, Matthew. But this is why I need you. You wouldn't have done what the Loughtys did. You'd have thought it through. You'd have checked.'

Spiller laughed. 'You don't know what I'd have done. You don't know me. Did Emma tell you about the first night we met? Christmas Eve?'

'No.'

'I beat the shit out of two lads who were threatening her. I'd dealt with them, then I went back and cut their thumbs off.'

Enright inhaled sharply. 'My God, that was you?'

'I sure as hell didn't think that one through, did I? There was blood everywhere.'

'But the police took your car and didn't find anything,' Delaney said. 'So you cleaned up after yourself. You got rid of the evidence. You're good.'

'Listen,' Spiller said. 'I have never been in this position before, trying to talk myself out of a job, but, really, this isn't for me.'

Delaney looked miffed. 'But you're a natural. How you dealt with Ward, the manner of his demise… oh, bravo on that.'

'You know that wasn't me.'

Delaney looked at Enright, who looked at Alistair, who looked at his father.

'Pardon?' Delaney said.

The sultry atmosphere felt suddenly more oppressive. Sweat popped down Spiller's spine.

'Who was it, then?' Delaney asked. 'If it wasn't you?'

'Emma didn't tell you?'

Delaney smiled. 'One of the many traits I like about Emma— she's not a blabbermouth.'

Spiller looked down at his trainers. He was wearing a pair he'd nicked from Gibbo. He wasn't certain they'd like a snitch, but maybe they'd let him off the hook if they knew he really wasn't as balls-out as they thought. He raised his head and belatedly checked to make sure the red light on Enright's bodycam wasn't flashing.

'My wife,' he said, not without some pride.

No one responded for a moment, then Delaney and Enright simultaneously said, 'Your *wife?*'

Spiller gave a little shrug as if to say, *what can you do?*

'Okay,' Delaney said. 'Well, I'm bloody glad I *didn't* send anyone to kill your family. I think my staffing problems would be a lot worse than they are right now.' He glanced towards the pool as he finished his sentence.

'How did it happen?' Enright asked.

'She hit him with an iron pot, and while I went to get some rope, she… did a little DIY.'

'I think we may be talking to the wrong Spiller,' Delaney said with a smirk.

'Hold on,' Alistair said suddenly. 'Rewind…'

Delaney looked at his son. 'What is it, Al?'

Alistair stepped nearer to Spiller, but still maintained a safe distance. 'Then who *have* you killed? If you didn't kill Ward. Who did you kill?'

'Hey?' Spiller said.

'You said you'd killed people, but they deserved it.'

Spiller pointed to the pool. 'Him. And Whittard.'

'No no no, that's not what you meant.'

'Matthew…' Delaney prompted.

Spiller accepted it would only bolster his CV, but, apart from Brett Stutz's misplaced admiration the day before, he'd never commanded much kudos. It felt nice.

'A couple of Ward's people. Yesterday.'

Enright shook his head rapidly, like there was a gyroscope inside that had suddenly started wobbling and he needed to correct it. 'Wait wait wait. You're serious?'

'Self-defence, officer.'

'How?' Delaney asked.

'The gun you gave Emma. Don't worry, I chucked it.'

'And the bodies?' Enright asked. 'Where are they?'

'You know where you found Callum Ward?'

Enright's gyroscope blew apart. 'No fucking way.'

'Speaking of bodies,' Spiller said. 'What did you do with my mate?'

'We took him somewhere,' Delaney said. 'I did ask that he be handled with respect.'

'You're all heart. Can you stop hovering, Alistair? You're making me nervous.'

Delaney waved a hand to indicate his son could stand down. Alistair backed off a few paces, handed one of the guns to Enright, tucked the other under his arm.

'Anything else you want to share with the group?' Delaney asked Spiller, and laughed.

DELANEY SUGGESTED THEY all retire to the drawing room to discuss matters further, although Spiller still wanted to dispense with the discourse and put the three of them in the same place as Ronnie Loughty. The joy of his resurrected family hadn't cancelled out the horror of his previous conviction that they were dead. Nothing could cancel out that memory, nor instil in him any forgiveness for Delaney's and Enright's deceit. The only glimmer was the insight it had provided for him: that an existence without his family, even with all the fame and money Hollywood might be about to throw at him, wasn't worth having. He just hoped he could cling on to it. Even the most profound realisations tended to get trampled under the onslaught of everyday life.

Spiller was most furious with Enright. The man was so full of treachery. And hypocrisy. A police officer and a Christian? What more virtuous combination could there be? As they walked along a baroque hallway towards the drawing room, Spiller decided he had to reiterate his earlier opinion. He slowed his gait and tugged at Enright's arm, so Delaney and Alistair moved ahead of them.

'You really are a wanker, you know that?'

'From the guy who just drowned a disabled man in a wheelchair.'

'No, you really are. Making me think my family had been burnt to death.'

Delaney and Alistair noticed their fall-behind and stopped.

'We'll catch up,' Enright said to them. 'I think Matthew wants to air a grievance or two.'

They dallied, Alistair especially looking tense.

'It's okay, he needs to vent.' Enright walked a few steps and handed the Sig to Alistair.

Delaney indicated that Alistair should let them be, and they carried on.

'I do everything for the right reasons,' Enright said.

Spiller shook his head. 'You're a hypocrite.'

'If anyone does not abide in me, he is thrown away like a branch and withers; and the branches are gathered, thrown into the fire, and burned.'

'Oh, I know that. It's from The Bumper Book of Quotes to Excuse Shit Behaviour.'

'Actually, John fifteen six.'

'How about Romans twelve nineteen? *Beloved, never avenge yourselves, but leave it to the wrath of God, for it is written, "Vengeance is mine, I will repay, says the Lord."*'

Enright smiled. 'Very good.'

'School Divinity lessons. Some shit just sticks with you. You like that one, Alfie? Or doesn't it fit your agenda?'

Enright shifted awkwardly on his feet.

'Yeah, I thought so. A bit of logic and you lot clam up. I'm fairly sure that means God wants to be the one doling out the punishment.'

'You've taken the law into your own hands.'

'Yeah, but I'm not the one wearing a crucifix. Or a fucking uniform.'

Enright was quiet, and Spiller abandoned him before he could respond, trotting after Delaney and Alistair, following their voices.

The drawing room was a grand affair, like the kind the National Trust would cordon off in a royal palace. A fire was blazing in an iron hearth. Delaney and Alistair were chatting quietly at one end of a long, ox-blood leather settee. Both the Sigs were lying on a mahogany coffee table within easy reach.

'Take a seat,' Delaney told him, so Spiller remained standing.

Enright entered and grabbed a spot at the other end of the settee, and Spiller felt like he was in an audition room, ready to give them his best Shakespearian monologue.

Delaney smiled at him. 'So... Matthew. Where do you think we should go from here?'

'Well, I'm off to Hollywood. You all can carry on doing whatever you like so long as you leave me and my family alone.'

Delaney looked offended. 'I would never hurt your family. I thought we'd established that much, at least.'

'And what about what's-his-face? Terry? Am I going to have a problem with him? Because I've already got one pissed-off brother on my case.'

'Terry will do what he's told,' Delaney said. 'Especially if you fall in line.'

'Meaning?'

'Join us.'

'And I thought we'd established *that's* not happening.'

'We seem to be at an impasse, Dad,' Alistair said, eyeing the guns.

'Listen,' Spiller said. 'You want to carry on with your little *Star Chamber*, go ahead.'

Delaney chortled. 'I did like that film.'

'I bet you did.'

'The problem is, Matthew, you're in possession of some quite damaging information. The files you stole from Glen. And the video of the hit on Poole.'

Spiller's exasperation was clear in his voice. 'And you've got stuff on me! I can give you the files—I was going to—but you can't know for sure I haven't made copies. And I can't know for sure you won't one day drop me in it about Whittard. But that's good. It keeps us both in check. It means we have to trust each other. It's the only way.'

'There is another way,' Alistair said, shifting his position minutely towards the table.

'If I die, Alistair, believe me, your old dad is one hundred percent down the shitter. That information is *definitely* getting out there. I made sure of that.'

For several seconds, there was only the crackle of the fire.

Then Enright glanced at his watch. 'I need to get back out there. I am way beyond my allotted break.' He stood up, switched his radio back on. 'Please sort this out,' he said to Delaney. 'I'm exposed here as well.'

Delaney rose to his feet with a groan. 'How about this? We all regroup back here at eight o'clock tonight. Then we show Matthew what's really at stake.'

Spiller watched Alistair become instantly anxious.

Enright made a face. 'Really? You mean... the group?'

Delaney nodded. 'I don't know why, but I like Mr Spiller. And I want to trust him. Eight o'clock good for you, Matthew?'

Spiller thought about it. It was intriguing. 'Sure.'

ENRIGHT'S ATTEMPT TO curtail his further participation in the chat and thus avoid taking Spiller back to the city hadn't worked, and now he stomped out to his patrol car with Spiller lagging behind like a kid who couldn't keep up with his dad's long strides.

As Enright started the engine, Spiller asked if he'd drop him off at the police compound at Brinley Industrial Estate so he could collect his car. Enright weighed it up for a moment, and Spiller surmised he was probably working out if that would mean more or less time in the car with him.

'Okay.' Less. 'But can we not talk on the way?'

'Suits me.'

Enright drove too quickly down the driveway, past the laurels where Spiller had hidden only an hour earlier when he thought his world had collapsed in on him. It felt like a lifetime ago. The gates were already opening. Enright slowed and eased between them when the gap was barely wide enough. The wing-mirror Spiller's side clacked and flattened.

'Want me to push that back out for you?' Spiller asked. 'Sorry—I know we're not talking.' He dropped his window and returned the mirror to its proper position, then raised the glass again to keep out the chill.

Enright mumbled a thank-you and then got down to concentrating on the contours of the winding lane. The road surface was slick with the recent rain and the temperature now hovering around zero. Spiller could have made things easier for his tight-lipped chauffeur by angling his body away and gazing at the passing scenery. Instead, he slouched so half his back rested against the door post.

'What is it?' Enright asked after surviving five minutes' scrutiny.

'Pardon?'

'You want to call me more names? You want to question my faith, my vocation?'

'Asked and answered.'

'What then?'

'What makes you trust Delaney? You took that gun off Alistair like it was nothing. What if it's killed someone and now it has your prints on it?'

'Charlie's not like that. He's not vindictive. He was furious when he knew your friend had been killed.'

'Didn't look that way.'

'He was. But he's pragmatic. No point dwelling when things go wrong.'

'And why did he kill Whittard? If he's not vindictive. I thought he was important to you lot. Or was he just more… what did he call it? *Collateral damage?*'

'You killed Glen, not us.'

'No way.'

Enright shrugged.

A minute later, Spiller asked: 'How did you meet Delaney? Through this group thing?'

'No. He knew my dad back in Northern Ireland.'

'You told me your dad was in the RUC.'

Enright nodded.

'And?'

Enright drew in a long, ponderous breath. 'My dad investigated the bombing that killed Charlie's wife and daughter. He was already on the IRA's radar but this put a target on his back. They killed him six months later, shortly after the man responsible for the bombing was sent down. I was eight. Charlie helped my mum get back on her feet, looked after us. When he came to live here, we came with him. Alistair is like a brother to me.'

'And Delaney's like a father.'

'It follows.'

'And when did all this start?'

'All what?' Enright asked.

'This... Charles Bronson crap.'

Enright gave him a withering look. 'Your movie trivia doesn't help, Matthew. We're not The Star Chamber and no one's behaving like Charles Bronson, roaming the streets, looking to kill anyone who doesn't look very nice. We're organised.'

'I think my mate might have something to say about that. Oh, hold on—no, he won't. He got shot in the face.'

Enright's grip on the wheel tightened. Spiller saw his knuckles whiten.

'Carry on,' Spiller said. 'Sorry if my little home truth put you off.'

'No. Charlie can tell you tonight if he wants to. It's not my story to tell.'

It was another fifteen minutes before Enright spoke again. The fields were beginning to give way to the suburbs, the houses getting smaller and not so far apart.

'So, what are you going to do about Dominic Ward?' he asked.

'Don't know.'

A slight nod. 'We could handle it.'

'No,' Spiller said quickly. 'Not a chance. He's all mine.'

AS THEY WERE pulling up outside the fenced police compound on the industrial estate, Spiller's phone began to chirp. He answered. Enright looked at him impatiently, silently urging him to get out. Then his eyes widened as he overheard the caller's familiar drawl.

'Oh, hello, DCI Bartoli,' Spiller said, grinning at Enright.

'Where are you?' Bartoli asked. 'I need you to come down to the station.'

'Where am I?' Spiller's grin enlarged. 'Right now? You wouldn't believe me if I told you.'

Enright stiffened, offered him a pleading look.

'I'm with aaaahhh… my agent at the moment.'

Enright sank back into his seat, the start of an F-word formed by the set of his top teeth against his lower lip.

'Well, that's interesting,' Bartoli said, 'because I only a half-hour ago got off the phone with your agent.'

Spiller wanted to chuck his phone out of the window. 'Oh, right.'

'When can you come in? I think we need to continue a conversation. Then maybe start a fresh one.'

'What if I don't want to come in?'

'I'll issue an arrest warrant.'

'Give me an hour.'

After cutting the connection, it was Spiller's turn for a pleading look. 'Shit, Alfie, can you help?'

Enright smiled, enjoying the moment. 'Let's see. I'm a sergeant, he's a DCI. I'm on a fast-track promotion scheme, so I only need to gain Inspector then Chief Inspector then Superintendent before I outrank him. Can you wait ten years?'

'Knobhead,' Spiller said, and moved to get out of the car.

Enright caught his arm. 'Just don't go *no comment*, okay? That's what guilty people do. Imagine you've been given an acting role and you've got to play someone innocent. I know it's a stretch but… protest and deny, Matthew.'

IF THEY'D DONE anything at all with his Audi, other than spitefully deprive him of its use, Spiller couldn't tell. One or two bits were out of place in the glove box and various cubby holes, but it all looked generally okay. He wondered if they'd planted a tracker, then thought it didn't really matter, anyway. He wasn't going to drive it anywhere incriminating, he wasn't going to spend another day taxiing in it, and he was going to replace it once he'd signed the contract with Brett Stutz. And if his Hollywood dreams all went tits-up for a second time, it would be because he'd be heading to prison and wouldn't have much use for a car of any description.

An hour would give him sufficient time for one stop before meeting Bartoli. Leaving the compound, he directed the Audi's nose towards his agent's house.

RETURNING TO THE scene of the crime—or one of them, at any rate—Spiller parked his Audi on the street outside Billy's house and walked up the puddled drive. It was paranoid, but he didn't want his tyre tread marking the exposed areas of mud along the gravel in case Bartoli tried to backdate the evidence to fit a certain scenario.

Billy opened the door to him. 'Matthew, dear... oh, dear.' He returned to the rear of the house, leaving Spiller to follow.

'The good news,' Billy said, sitting down, 'is I have your contract. The bad news... I had the boys in blue here earlier. And then a telephone call from an American detective. Or was that you with one of your silly impressions?'

Spiller shook his head. 'What did they want?'

'They were looking into reports of gunshots.'

'Ah. And?'

Billy became the epitome of dismay. '*I perjured myself!* I perjured myself for you, Matthew. Dear boy, I broke the law! *For you!* Never... before...'

'Have you been in a position to earn a million dollars? That's why you lied, Billy. And it's okay. I had a little fun with a blank-firer and your neighbours reported it. Except no one knows where it came from so you're fine. Okay? What did the detective want when he called?'

'He said he was following up on a report from the officers. I'd told them I was an agent—one of them had a very good look, I gave him my card—and the detective had Googled me and found out I represented you. Matthew, I don't like strangers Googling me. I feel violated.'

'Billy…'

'So he asked if I'd seen you recently. And I lied! I perjured myself!'

'Don't worry,' Spiller said, and changed the subject 'Where's the contract? The one that makes you rich.'

A melodramatic sigh to expel the last of his remorse, then Billy coughed, pulled open a drawer, produced a printed document, and set it before his client.

'Sign the last page and initial all the others, please, love. You're flying out in two weeks.'

Spiller picked up the contract and began to peruse it. 'Holy shit! *Seven and a half million?*' He giggled. 'Bloody hell!'

'They did offer five, as you thought. I bumped it up.'

'Nice one, Billy—what the hell is that?'

Billy beamed. 'Oh, my new pooter. Marvellous, isn't it?'

'You know how it works?'

'Of course I do. I knew how the last one worked, it just didn't… work.'

'You've checked the contract, yes? I don't really know what I'm reading.'

'All fairly standard, dear boy. I had my solicitor run her eye over it. Signed in all the right places by them. Just you to sign now. Then it's official.'

Spiller giggled all the while he was signing and initialling. 'Can I see you send it off?' he said when he'd finished. 'And copy me, will you?'

Like a tech wizard, Billy proceeded to scan each page into a pdf document. He attached it to the return email to Stutz's PA, added Spiller's address in the cc line, then hit send.

He extended his hand across the desk. 'My dear boy, felicitations.'

'Same to you.' Spiller shook his hand and was surprised, as he always was, by how manly Billy's grip was considering his age and his dress sense. Spiller went around the desk and opened his arms out for a hug. 'Thanks, Billy.'

Billy stood up. 'For?'

They embraced, then separated.

'For standing by me. Most agents would have dumped me years ago.'

Billy's eyes twinkled. 'You've always had an edgy quality, Matthew. I knew someone would spot it one day. Although... you did make it rather difficult to ignore.'

Chapter Twenty-Four

WAITING FOR THE message to reach Bartoli that he was at the public counter, Spiller wondered where the interview would be conducted. Would it be another informal chat in the room with the comfy blue chairs? Would DS Madden or DC Goodrick be present, corralled from their other duties to provide Bartoli with moral support and to outnumber the suspect? Spiller doubted they'd be there for any other reason. Madden hadn't spoken much the last time. Bartoli sported a slightly maverick style, preferring command over collaboration. Or would Spiller be led downstairs to where the bad lads were booked in, and made to suffer the ignoble ambience of a serious interview room and be cautioned and recorded?

Bartoli entered the public area through the secure door and let it close behind him. He was wearing an overcoat and he headed towards the exit onto the street, and nodded to Spiller to follow. Spiller trailed him down the steps.

Bartoli stopped and deliberated. 'Too cold. Let's grab a coffee.'

Spiller wasn't sure what to make of this. Not an interview room of any kind, just Starbucks. He mused whether this was akin to the walk he'd taken with Enright the other day, and whether what was unknown about Enright at the time might also be unknown about Bartoli now. Did Bartoli have an agenda he had to keep off the record? *Was* he in league with Dominic Ward?

'Your face is looking better,' Bartoli said as they strolled. 'I heard about what happened.'

'Okay.'

Three minutes later, Bartoli pushed open the creaking door to a small café in dire need of renovation. It reeked of bacon and burnt oil. Not Starbucks.

'Grab that table,' he told Spiller, pointing to a corner spot. 'How do you take it?'

'Milk and sugar.'

After a friendly exchange with the proprietor, Bartoli brought the drinks over in mismatched mugs. His was black. He set them down and settled on a wooden chair that was a health-and-safety claim waiting to happen. He shrugged his coat over the back.

Spiller took a sip and raised his eyebrows.

Bartoli nodded. 'Good, huh? Reminds me of a little place off of Roosevelt Avenue. Nothing to look at but the best damn coffee in town.'

Spiller took another sip. He'd decided to take Enright's advice. He wouldn't go *no comment*, but neither would he offer anything he didn't have to, including pleasantries.

Bartoli blew across the top of his mug. 'I was at the Hundred and Ninth. Union Street, Flushing. Robbery-Homicide.'

'Okay.'

'I miss New York, Matthew. Life was simpler. My job was simpler. Of course, some cases were more complex than others, but... never so convoluted or... plain fricking nonsensical that they got under my skin. You can't do this job if it gets under your skin. You can't take it home with you. You need to have that separation.'

Spiller took another mouthful of sweet coffee.

'I'm heading back to the States,' Bartoli said. 'For good.'

'Okay.'

'I split up with my wife. She's the only reason I was here.'

'Okay.'

'*Okay?* Most folk say *I'm sorry to hear that.*'

Spiller gave an apathetic shrug. 'I know what it feels like, so I know *sorry* doesn't help. Listen, the coffee's great but I don't want to leave here stinking of grease. Can you get to the point? And if you have something to ask me, why aren't I sitting in an interview room?'

Bartoli ran a hand through his perfect quiff, mussing it so several strands dangled at his temples. 'Okay, here's what I have. One dead gang leader, to wit, Callum Ward. The brother of that gang leader, Dominic Ward, accused by you of threatening to kill your family, but no mention made in that complaint of the injuries to your daughter. An attempted arson at your house, and a cadaver, but not a complete cadaver. Missing its thumbs. A prior report by two thumbless individuals of an attack by someone who may or may not have been a cab driver. The next day, a hobbling and battered Dominic Ward. A spectacular exit by you from a restaurant owned by one Charles Delaney, who has no obvious links to the Wards. Suggestions that Delaney now also wants to hurt your family. A missing person, Tony Gibson, who's known to you, I believe.'

Spiller felt the need to respond, given he shouldn't have known this information. '*Gibbo?*'

'His parents reported him missing. They couldn't make contact, and now there's no trace of him or his vehicle, a vehicle you're insured to drive, but only as of a couple of days before he vanished.'

'Shit. I hope he's okay.'

'Course you do. It continues: Reports of gunshots, precise location unknown, but centring, it seems, on a property owned by a theatrical agent. *Your* theatrical agent. Last night, a panicked call from you requesting I send an armed unit to Wales to protect your family. And, just this morning, missing person reports filed on two of Ward's gang by their family members.'

'Okay.'

'Am I missing anything?' Bartoli restored a strand of hair that was tickling his eyebrow.

'You're the copper. Most of that stuff I didn't know. So how would I know if you're missing anything?'

'And *this* is why you're sitting in this café rather than my police station.'

'I don't get.'

'Frankly, I am not going to leave this job fucking embarrassed. I have a reputation and you are pissing all over it. Why the fuck did you call me last night?'

'Ward. Dominic Ward. You know my fears.'

'Right. Matthew, help me out. You don't want to incriminate yourself. That's okay. But, Christ's sake, give me something. On the Wards. On Delaney. You said last night you're caught up in something—quote. Let me help you get out of it.'

Spiller gave his best impression of a clueless character. Instantly furious, Bartoli stood up, his thighs catching the table and sending both coffees cascading away from him. They ended up on Spiller's crotch, and Bartoli's black coffee still held sufficient heat to make him squeal. Bartoli snatched his coat, produced a twenty pound note and handed it to the café owner, apologising for the mess, before storming out.

SPILLER'S JACKET WASN'T quite long enough to cover the stain, so he walked down the street with an awkward gait, looking like a man who'd pissed himself. On the plus side, the weather was cold enough to counter the burning coffee, although he suspected he'd still need a slathering of Sudocrem on his dick when he got home. Even more positively, it was clear that Bartoli was so overwhelmed by the strange sequence of events of late that he'd all but given up. Whoever took over might be more dogged, but would they even suspect it was all one big connected case? Bartoli didn't seem at all keen to let on to his colleagues how baffled he was.

When he got back in his Audi, Spiller desperately wanted to examine his penis but thought flopping it out only a street away from a police station wasn't the best idea.

By now, he reckoned his family would be back from Wales, so he drove to his in-laws' house. He knew he couldn't let on to Helen why he was so convinced of their deaths, as that would beg questions he wasn't ready to answer. Initially, he wasn't sure how he'd explain his outburst in Delaney's pool-house. Then it came to him.

Helen opened the door to him and he opened his arms to her. Not desperately, like he'd thought he'd never see her again; merely as though he'd taken a wander along that fabled Damascene road and now knew he could be the husband and father they'd always deserved.

'Shit, Matt, your face. Was that Ward?'

'No, nothing to worry about. Accident.'

She walked into his arms and they hugged on the doorstep.

'What happened?' she asked. 'Why were you so distraught on the phone?'

'Terrible dream. I dreamt I'd lost you. I woke up knowing you're all I need. But it was so real I couldn't shake the fear something awful had really happened.'

They parted slightly, kissed, a peck that became passionate. Then she led him into the house, into the lounge. Helen's parents, Craig and Audrey, were either end of a flower-pattern settee with Sammy and Sophie in the middle. Spiller resisted the temptation to rush over and scoop his daughters into a big, blubbering hug. The fire was set too high and there was the usual whiff of the Ralgex Audrey used for her aches and pains. The TV was on, catering to Sophie's tastes with a *Despicable Me* movie.

'Evening, all,' he said to the room.

'Hi, Dad,' Sophie said, without taking her eyes off the screen. Then she glanced at him and did a double-take. 'Dad, what happened?'

'Little accident, I'm fine.'

'Dad?' Sammy said.

'I'm fine, darling—genuinely. Soph, who are those little yellow people? Not seen them before.'

'Minions!' Craig announced, and properly noticed his son-in-law. He frowned, then smiled and slowly got to his feet, the frown returning. 'Hello...'

'Dad, this is—'

'Matthew!' Craig said. 'Matthew! So good to see you!' He grabbed Spiller's hand and pumped it. 'How are you? Your face looks sore! How's the acting?'

Spiller wasn't sure if this unusual cordiality was down to a befuddled mind or the natural mellowing of the years.

'Very good,' Spiller said. 'I'm off to Hollywood to do a movie in two weeks.'

'*Dad?*' the girls said simultaneously, eyes wide with awe.

'Wonderful,' Craig said, and resumed his seat.

Spiller nodded at the girls. 'For real.'

They both screamed and got up and hugged him.

'Well done, Matt,' Audrey said, rising. She pecked him. 'I'm very pleased for you. Your patience finally paid off.'

'Not sure I've been very patient, but thanks.'

'Tea,' Audrey said, and headed into the kitchen.

Sophie was still dancing around her dad's feet, holding his hands. 'Can we come? Can we?'

'Not sure, sweetie, you both have school.' Spiller glanced at Helen, seeking her approval, but she still looked sceptical about the whole thing. He took out his mobile, found the relevant email, opened the attached document, and found the pertinent page. He handed her the phone.

Helen read it, sank onto the arm of the settee. 'Oh, Matt...'

'Mum, what's wrong?' Sammy asked.

She shook her head. 'Nothing, it's just... so much money.'

'Dad?'

'After my agent takes his cut, around six million dollars.'

Sammy eeked in delight just as something smashed on the floor in the kitchen.

'Is that good?' Sophie asked. 'Is it more than a gazillion?'

Craig looked up as his wife entered the lounge, but quickly returned his attention to the movie. He was completely captivated by it.

Spiller went over and gave Audrey a cuddle, and whispered in her ear. 'It won't be yet, but when I'm paid, I'll help. Sorry about Craig.'

Audrey squeezed him tightly, whispered back. 'Thank you. But what I really want is for my daughter and granddaughters to be able to go home and live normally again. So, whatever you're doing that's preventing that, please stop.' She eased away and returned to the kitchen to clear up whatever she'd dropped.

Spiller understood he would never feel welcome in that house. As Craig had softened, Audrey had toughened up. And, however he was treated, it would always be the place where for years his choices were rejected, his mere presence resented.

'I can't stay,' he said to Helen. 'Things to do.' He blew kisses to the girls but decided not to interrupt Craig's viewing pleasure.

Helen led him back into the porch and shut the inner door. 'Is it over?' she asked.

'Very nearly. Honestly. The cops have given up. I just need to sort things with Ward.'

'*Just?* The man who's tried to kill us twice?'

'I'll work it out.'

'What if you pay him that cash? The twenty grand.'

'I would if I thought it would work. He's a barrister—he doesn't need the money. And twenty grand for his brother's life? Callum Ward wasn't worth twenty *pence*, but he'd take that as an insult.'

'Well, have it anyway. I don't feel comfortable holding onto that much money.'

'Okay.' He gently took her hand. 'I love you. With or without this job, that's enough. You and the girls. From now on.'

It was a brash declaration, founded on nothing. He couldn't extricate how he felt about the job from his overall emotional state, so how could he really know if he'd still be the same rejuvenated man without it? Or if, once he started working, he'd still feel miserable. There were plenty of rich and famous depressed people. How much of his illness was circumstantial? How much was hard-wired?

He kissed his wife, and was pleased it was again reciprocated.

'I'll get the cash,' she said.

Immediately she was gone, Spiller was joined by Sammy, but her earlier joy had been snuffed out like a capped candle. She spoke rapidly and softly. 'Dad, is it over?'

'Yes.'

'No more problems?'

'No,' he lied again. 'How are you?'

'Okay, I—'

'I was wondering if you needed someone to talk to. About what happened.'

'Dad—'

'You know, a professional.'

'*Dad!*' she whisper-shouted. 'You need to get rid of something. It's in the house, in the attic in my school bag. It could ruin everything. Your job, everything. I was scared to say before—mum was so annoyed and—'

'Yeah, love you too, Sammy,' Spiller said loudly to drown out his daughter as Helen pulled open the inner door.

'Yeah, take care, Dad. Brilliant news on the job.'

'Thanks, darling.'

Sammy kissed him and disappeared back into the lounge.

'Everything okay?' Helen asked.

'Yeah, yeah, she's just saying goodbye.' He took the rucksack of cash from her. 'Thanks. Kiss Soph for me, will you? And say bye to Craig and Audrey. He's...'

'Nice he finally likes you, eh?'

Spiller smiled sadly. 'Maybe I'm only likeable if your brain's addled.'

A PART OF him wanted to take the cash back to its rightful owner, but he was still pissed off with Emma about Whittard. If she hadn't shared his intentions with Delaney, Whittard would still be alive and he wouldn't be a fugitive in abeyance. He vowed, though, if he did get to Hollywood and complete the movie and get paid, he'd reimburse her.

Or maybe he wouldn't. And maybe he wouldn't bail out Craig and Audrey, either. Had they given a crap about him when he was in trouble? Had they paid his debts, even when he was looking after Helen and the girls? Craig could have made their lives much easier during some very tough times, but he'd purposely withheld financial help out of spite. Without the dementia, Craig would still be blanking him.

Spiller had a vague notion what Sammy was so scared about, but only because he could only think of one thing. Back in the house, he shot up the stairs and pulled down the loft ladder, and climbed up. Even with just the light spilling up from the landing, he spotted Sammy's backpack dumped in the top of a cardboard box. He reached an arm across, dragged the box towards him, and lifted out the bag.

Down on the landing, he unzipped it and wasn't surprised by its contents. He put a hand inside and sifted through the yellow and red tubes, counting thirty of them. Sammy must have panicked when her mum found her little sister with the pilfered Sherbet Fountain and decided that was enough trouble for one day. Sophie had tried to tell him. He recalled the conversation. She'd said "I only took it because", then he'd cut her off. *Because she has a bag full of them.*

He took the backpack down to the kitchen, slipped his hands into a couple of freezer bags to mask his prints, wiped the tubes with a wet cloth, and transferred the drugs into six separate freezer bags. Then he took Sammy's backpack up to the bathroom, ran a bath, added some bleach and dunked it, swishing it around for a few minutes. He would throw it away later, but her name was inside and he wanted that to be the only traceable thing if anyone checked. Fuck, how different his conversation with Bartoli might have been if he'd searched the house rather than merely seizing the Audi as an inconvenience. Now it was too late for Bartoli, and Spiller looked at the bagged-up drugs sitting next to the rucksack full of cash, and he pondered what to do next.

'Ah,' he said, and smiled.

Chapter Twenty-Five

SPILLER WAS ON his way to Delaney's in the Fiesta when he had a thought that made him laugh out loud. Before that moment, it had never entered his head. It was a stunning lark. It would make him late but he took a detour, heading towards Ameley Green.

'God, you're like a turd that just won't flush,' Emma said when she opened the front door.

He grinned. 'Smartly dressed turd, though. You gotta give me that.'

She eyed him from his gelled hair down to his smart black suit and his sensible shoes.

'Where are you off to?' she asked.

'*We*,' he said, extending an open palm like she might actually take it.

She sneered. 'When did you get the impression I wanted to date you?'

'We're going to a gathering at Charles Delaney's house. No need to get changed, you look fabulous.'

'I didn't get an invitation.'

'And I'm quite sure Delaney doesn't want you there, but you started all this so you can damn well see how it ends.'

'What are you going to do? Kill him?'

'God, no. Me and Chaz? Bosom buddies.' He opened his jacket so she could see he wasn't hiding anything. 'No weapons. Just me and my plus-one. Get your shoes. You can drive.'

They didn't speak to each other the whole way. As he'd expected, Emma came along willingly enough. She was too involved to want to stick her head in the sand at this late stage. She was dressed in a black office outfit, and Spiller thought they looked like they could be heading to a funeral in their matching attire. He only hoped it didn't portend the real thing. However welcoming Delaney might be, Terry Loughty had earlier watched Spiller stamp on his brother's head to drown him. Even had he been able to access all the skills of the late Glen Whittard, Terry wasn't getting over that anytime soon.

Emma parked up behind a semi-circle of cars outside the front of the house, which was bathed in the harsh beams of several spotlights. Hers was the fifth vehicle, and there was another parked in front of a double garage next to the pool-house. A concerned-looking Delaney was waiting on the doorstep with his son beside him. They both descended the steps as Emma killed the ignition, and Delaney came straight to the passenger side in time for Spiller to step out.

'What's going on?' Delaney asked, looking over the car roof at Emma, who was now giving Alistair a hug.

'Thought she might want to be clued in,' Spiller said.

'Did you? Not your call, Matthew.'

'It's okay, Charlie,' Emma said to her boss. 'I'm happy to be here.'

'You won't be,' Delaney told her. 'You need to go.'

Spiller slammed his door hard, commanding their attention. He adopted a melodramatic attitude, and a tone to match. '*She is in blood stepp'd in so far that, should she wade no more, returning were as tedious as go o'er.*'

'Please don't bastardise the Bard,' Delaney said. 'Emma?'

'I want to know what's happening.'

Delaney contemplated. 'Right! When you leave later on with information you don't like, don't complain.' He marched back to the house. 'Come!'

THE WALLS OF the dining room were lined with oak panels. Three tiered chandeliers provided light over a long, oval-ended oak table, at which were set twelve matching chairs, two at the heads, five along each side. Both head-chairs were empty, but six others were occupied, three along the far side, three along the near. Spiller spotted Enright straightaway. He was on the left, seated one down from the far end of the table, where Spiller expected Delaney would take his place. Literally Delaney's right-hand man.

'Hey, Matt!' Enright called facetiously.

Delaney and his son went to stand at the head of the table, next to Enright.

'*Dad?*' Emma said as she entered the room. 'Shit!'

'Matthew, this is Timothy,' Delaney said, indicating the guy nearest to Spiller. 'Emma's father.'

'Charles!' Timothy growled. 'What the hell is my daughter doing here?'

Emma approached. 'Dad, what are *you* doing here?'

Timothy didn't respond, glowering still at Delaney.

Emma's surprise quickly faded. 'Oh... Poole. That was you.'

'My daughter shouldn't be here,' Timothy said to Delaney.

Delaney shrugged. 'I did say. Don't worry, Tim. It's like father like daughter, I'm afraid. I'm sure you won't be able to shock each other that much. Your Emma's been a rather naughty girl.'

'Don't patronise me,' Emma said. 'Okay, Charlie?'

'Fair enough. Take a seat beside your father.'

Emma walked past her dad and left a chair empty before sitting down. She looked at the person next to her, one down from Enright, a black guy in his late thirties. He was wearing dark glasses, but there were old scars branching out from the periphery of the lenses. A white stick was hanging on the back of his chair. He extended a hand.

'Grady,' he said, and smiled. 'Your dad talks about you all the time.'

Emma took Grady's hand as Delaney settled in his chair.

'More introductions,' Delaney said.

Spiller noted Alistair remained on guard, standing at his father's side, a bulge at his hip under his jacket.

Delaney pointed to the other side of the table at a middle-aged couple who were holding hands, and a man in his sixties, all of whom shared the harrowed, drawn look of the bereft. 'Stuart and Jen. And that's Colin. Everyone, this is Matthew, a right royal pain in my arse. But a particularly talented individual. Give us a bit of Liam, Matthew.'

'No.'

'Maybe later, eh? Take a seat.'

Spiller ambled around to where Stuart and Jen were sitting and, like Emma, left a chair empty before settling, although that placed him next to Colin.

'Help yourself to drinks,' Delaney said, indicating a sideboard laden with bottles of every description. 'Grady? Refill?'

Grady shook his head. 'Where are the Loughtys, Charlie? I can't hear *or* smell them. Cheap sodding aftershave. It's okay for you mere mortals with regular olfaction. Bloody floors me.'

'Ah,' Delaney went. 'Slight hiccup. Ronnie's dead.'

'*How?*' Grady asked, as Stuart, Jen and Timothy gasped.

'How? Ask Matthew.'

Spiller chewed on his bottom lip. 'He fell in the swimming pool.'

'Artistic licence with the *fell*,' Delaney said. 'And why couldn't he get *out* of the swimming pool, Matthew?'

'Heavy legs.'

Delaney tutted. 'And what about the heavy shoe—on his head?'

'And Terry did nothing?' Timothy asked.

'He tried,' Delaney said. 'Bless his sodden socks.'

'My God,' Jen said.

Spiller got up and went to the sideboard, poured himself a large vodka, then resumed his seat.

'So...' Delaney said. 'Oh! Alfie, where's my man with the fanfare trumpet?'

'Day off, Charlie.'

'Never mind. One more introduction. You'll have to imagine the fanfare, Matthew.'

From a door behind Delaney's chair, a familiar figure emerged.

'You've got to be kidding,' Spiller said.

'Hello, Detective Inspector Mortlake.'

Spiller gawped as a resurrected Glen Whittard took his place at the end of the table opposite Delaney, who regarded Spiller's utterly confounded expression with a smile.

'Not difficult putting a fake news report on a pen-drive, Matthew.'

Spiller stared across the table at Emma. 'You deceitful bitch.'

Hearing his daughter insulted, Timothy bristled. 'Oi…'

Colin spoke up: 'Charlie, what the bloody hell's been going on?'

All eyes were on Spiller. Even Grady's black lenses bored into him. Spiller glugged some vodka. He felt like a kid who'd been hauled into the headmaster's office to face the parents of several kids he'd just beaten up.

'And where exactly is Terry?' Colin asked.

For the first time, Delaney's demeanour darkened. 'He left. I think he may be done with us.'

'Aren't you worried? With everything he knows?'

'Somewhat. But nothing I can do. And he buries himself if he buries us.'

'So, what are we doing here?' Stuart asked, leaning into the table.

Delaney let his eyes settle on each of the group for a few seconds, offering them his sincerity. 'I want Matthew to hear our stories. I want him to join us. But, at the very least, I want him to leave here knowing we're good people.'

'Why does it matter what he thinks?' Jen asked.

Delaney smiled. 'Well, for one thing, he has information that could harm us, and I can't guarantee its retrieval. Not a hundred percent. You know what it's like these days. Back-ups, the cloud. Nothing is truly deleted. Tim? Would you start?'

'You can tell him if you like. I don't need a bloody confessor.'

'Okay. Actually, Matthew, you know Tim's story already; Emma told you. Colin?'

Colin spoke evenly. 'My wife had a routine appendectomy. Routine, except the surgeon was drunk. She bled out on the table. Apparently, it wasn't the first time he'd botched an op. The profession closed ranks, just struck him off. So he went to

Canada, set up there, wrecked a few more lives. Until we caught up with him.'

Jen cleared her throat and gave the same even delivery. 'Our son was killed outside our home in broad daylight by two grown men. They wanted his mobile phone. I tried to intervene, but it was too late. My neighbour witnessed what happened. We picked out the same faces but threats were made and my neighbour lost his nerve. And I wasn't credible on my own. Then forensic evidence was quashed. The men claimed blood was transferred when they went to *help* our son. So the CPS decided not to proceed.'

Stuart squeezed his wife's hand.

Grady spoke next. 'As you can see, Matthew, I *can't* see. I was bottled outside a pub after a silly argument over a spilt drink. This was before everywhere had cameras. My attacker fled. A bit later, an elderly gent out for a stroll was robbed and killed. His throat was slashed. His wound had traces of my blood. So, the same weapon—which they never found. A doorman at the pub named the man I'd been arguing with, and I independently identified him by his voice. But, as with Jen and Stuart, the doorman retracted, so the CPS threw it out. At the time, I was in my final year training to be a graphic designer, a career somewhat hampered by my present affliction.'

'Thank you, Grady,' Delaney said. 'Alfie?'

'He knows my story.'

'All right.'

'What about you?' Spiller said, staring at Delaney. 'The IRA got your family. What did you do to them?'

Delaney's eyes pinched at the memory. 'Declan Lynch, released in July 2000 under The Good Friday Agreement after serving six years for the double murder of my wife and daughter, plus four other sectarian murders. One year per life taken. Unfortunately for Mr Lynch, I had not signed up to The Good Friday Agreement. So, in August 2000, I taught him a lesson: that if Fridays could be good, Mondays could be very bad.'

'You personally?' Spiller asked. 'Or the Loughtys?'

'This was pre-Loughty. I had some ex-military friends who owed me a favour or two. To be honest, back then, I could have ordered anything. I had the ear of the UK government at the highest levels.'

'What? The PM?' Spiller gave a doubtful look.

'Higher. Levels even the PM didn't know about. You think the Loughtys are my hired help? They're it? They served a purpose. They wanted to get involved because of their sister. I know you know about that already. Oliver Rinks.'

'What about the other brother?' Spiller asked. 'Joey.'

'Never in the loop. He's the one who went to see Glen, but it became clear it was his brothers who really needed to vent. So we tapped them.'

'And how did you two meet?'

'Me and Glen? I wanted someone to talk to when I came over here. Glen was just starting out. I knew I wasn't... *fixed.* I did want to be, but every time I read about some injustice in the newspapers, saw something on the television, it reignited all those old feelings. Still, we went years just chatting professionally. Well, me chatting, Glen listening. Then... Glen's life changed. Glen?'

'Go ahead,' Whittard said, getting up and heading for the booze.

'Glen has a severely autistic son. Jeremy. All things considered, he was making good progress. Until his carer at the day centre interfered sexually with him. A hidden camera caught the incident. It was the subject of a BBC documentary—you may recall. Anyway, the carer was slapped on the wrist, forced to sign the sex offender's register. And given counselling.'

'Counselling!' Whittard interjected from the drinks sideboard. 'For the fucking offender!'

Delaney waited to see if Whittard had more to say, but he merely shook his head and drank some whisky.

'How's Jeremy now?' Spiller asked.

'Like you give a shit,' Whittard said.

'Not so good,' Delaney answered. 'He went back into his shell and has been totally withdrawn ever since. And poor

Glen... he realised he'd been writing books full of advice he couldn't take himself. He didn't want to forgive, he couldn't move on. My therapy sessions became more like pub conversations; two fellas trying to put the world to rights. He knew I'd already put my world to rights. I'd skirted very close to the truth on many occasions. I knew I'd said enough for Glen to know I'd done more than simply talk about my pain. That's really where all this started. We spoke openly and the pact was sealed. I employed a contractor to handle Jeremy's carer, and Glen started sifting and separating his patient files. We opened a group for those we deemed most amenable to our objectives. Over the months and years we filtered out those who didn't measure up until we whittled it down to those around this table—and the absent Loughtys. At which point certain... *philosophies* were mooted.'

Spiller's eyes had been constantly flicking to Emma to gauge her reaction, and he assessed she was fully on board. She had stopped giving her father sidelong stares. Instead, her head was minutely nodding to, and approving of, all that she heard.

'Sounds like you're all avenged, then,' Spiller said to Delaney. 'There's no one else to kill, right?'

'There's always someone else to kill,' Alistair responded. 'Even if it's not personal. There will always be people who shouldn't be walking the streets.'

'Any likely candidates?' Spiller asked.

'Trevor Mickles,' Enright said. 'You were outside his courtroom this morning.'

Spiller smiled, looked at Delaney. 'You're still considering some patients, aren't you,' he stated. 'There's a folder of possibles, isn't there.'

'*Charles,*' Timothy said sternly, then shook his head.

After a moment, Delaney said, 'We need to be very careful, Matthew. If we judge incorrectly, we're finished.'

Spiller reclined in his chair, finished off his vodka.

'So, Matthew?' Grady said. 'Would you begrudge us our payback? Would you seek to have us punished for it?'

'He wouldn't,' Delaney answered. 'Matthew was here earlier and demonstrated as much. He knows about the desire for payback.'

Spiller drained a final drop of liquor and got up for a refill. With a replenished glass, he approached Grady and laid a hand on his shoulder, and the super-sensory Grady didn't flinch. Spiller met everyone else's eyes.

'You're safe,' he said. 'I'll get rid of what I have on you. You can trust me or not on that, but I promise. But... I have a glorious career ahead of me and I'm not going to risk it by joining this fucking circus.'

'Pardon?' Alistair said.

'Well, honestly, look at you all sitting there like a bunch of wannabe Judge Dredds. Any of you go out at night in a superhero costume?'

'I'd make a pretty good Daredevil,' Grady said, and sniffed. 'Vodka, right?'

Spiller looked into his glass. 'Uh...' He took a sip then set it down. 'You coming?' he said to Emma. 'Or should I call a taxi?'

Without looking at him, she held up a middle finger.

'I'll have someone drive you back,' Delaney said. 'Come, I'll see you out.'

When they were out of earshot, nearing the front door, Delaney said, 'Thank you, Matthew.'

'What for? You still don't know if I'm as good as my word.'

'I think you are. And I meant for not mentioning that Jeffrey Poole was actually innocent, and the little kerfuffle with your friend.'

Spiller stopped Delaney with an arm across his chest. 'You think two bullets in the face is a *little kerfuffle?* Fuck, you need to stop all this, you've lost perspective.'

'I apologise. Can I do anything at all to make amends? Do you need a sub until your movie money comes in? Are you happy with your car?'

'My days of taking money for the wrong reasons are over, Mr Delaney. I'm not for sale.'

'Then, can I take care of Dominic Ward for you?'

Rather than instantly dismiss the offer as he had with Enright, Spiller considered for a few seconds. Have done with it. It was an attractive proposition. But it was all too personal to sub-contract out.

'No,' he said. 'But... that scuba gear in your pool-house. Can I borrow it?'

Delaney was confused, but nodded anyway.

'Oh, and... some more bullets for that three-eighty you gave Emma.'

DELANEY'S DRIVER HELPED lug all the diving equipment onto the pavement outside Spiller's house, hurrying as there wasn't a parking spot big enough for the Mercedes Maybach, and Spiller suspected he'd been warned not to leave the £200,000 beast unattended anyway. Gratifyingly, neighbour David had heard the arrival of the V8 engine, and through his window had spotted Spiller's emergence from its sumptuous rear seat.

'Jesus, mate,' David said, coming out onto his doorstep. 'When did you win the lottery?'

Spiller barked a curt laugh, but didn't think he warranted an explanation. It was enough to know David knew his chances of shagging Helen were now vanishingly slim. Unanswered, David grunted and retreated inside.

Front door shut, Spiller regarded the scuba equipment in his hallway. By the poolside, Alistair Delaney had provided him with a crash-course in its use, and Spiller felt confident he'd at least not kill himself by strapping it on. At the end of the lesson, Delaney had returned wearing latex gloves and handed Spiller a box of fifty three-eighty calibre bullets, branded American Eagle. He'd been gone fifteen minutes, and Spiller suspected he'd had to negotiate numerous locks on several hidden doors or secret compartments. Possibly there was a subterranean shelter beneath the house, stocked with all sorts of illicit hardware. Or maybe they only existed in the movies.

Spiller took the box of bullets down to the cellar. He'd earlier stuffed the cash and drugs into the back of one of the old sofa cushions, but he wasn't convinced Bartoli wouldn't throw him a final curveball in the form of a thorough house-search. He couldn't be found with all this crap, not at this late stage when his Hollywood dream was so close to realisation. He looked around the cellar and couldn't see anywhere the police wouldn't search. Then he spotted something through the small, cobwebbed window in the corner of the back yard: Sophie's faded blue plastic rocking horse that she'd outgrown.

He went outside and brought it in. The toy was hollow, so Spiller ran upstairs, grabbed a Stanley knife and some gaffer tape from his toolbox, took them back down and cut a flap into the curved base. He pulled open the flap, pushed the cash, drugs and the bullets inside, and taped it back in place. It would be a risk leaving it outside the house, but it had lain untouched for years already, so what difference would another day or two make? He returned it to its spot in the corner of the yard.

All Spiller wanted to do now was go and lie down. It had been one hell of a day already and he didn't relish adding any more drama to it. But he'd borrowed the scuba gear for a reason and it wasn't intended for daylight use—not according to his plan.

He swore to himself and trudged back upstairs. He munched through a couple of bags of crisps, then went into the hall to set up the scuba gear as far as he could. He strapped the tank tightly to the buoyancy-control vest, then attached the tubes from the regulator set to the tank and the vest. He opened the tank valve and watched the gauge jump to full. He sucked on the mouthpiece to make sure he was getting air, then closed the valve again. He grabbed the keys to the Fiesta and began carrying the equipment outside. Once the car was loaded, he headed off.

PICTURESQUE AS THEY were during the day, Spiller was sick to death of the hills at night. It was a pleasant change, though, to be negotiating the winding inclines in a car that wasn't stolen from a dead man or laden with a corpse or two. The biggest issue a copper could have with him tonight was why he was roaming the countryside on a January evening with a boot full of scuba gear. Just short of his destination, he pulled onto the verge. He grabbed the wetsuit from the boot, discarded his clothes and wriggled into the neoprene, bootees included. Crap, it was tight. He wondered if he might die even before he got in the water, his circulation constricted, effectively crushed to death. Now the only issue a copper would have with him was why he was roaming around the hills at night wearing a wetsuit. *S&M Convention, officer.*

He arrived at the bridge across the lake at close to eleven pm. The scudding clouds meant there was scant light from the moon. He stopped in the spot where he believed he'd launched the Sig into the water. From the boot, he took the waterproof diving torch, switched it on and hurled it with what he hoped was the same force with which he'd thrown the gun. He saw the light cartwheel through the dark and arc down to disappear with a plop. He squinted to see if he could make out a glow beneath the surface, but there was nothing.

Spiller took the car around and parked it beside the lake, just off the road, adjacent to the place where he calculated the torch had submerged. There was a gate that gave onto the trees that encircled the shoreline. He opened the valve on the tank, lifted the vest and tank combo and put it on like a rucksack, then slipped through the opening with the dive bag, carefully negotiating the terrain down to the water, lighting the route ahead with his own tactical torch. He sat down on a fallen trunk and worked in its beam. He opened the bag, pulled out the fins, fin grips, gloves, mask and snorkel, pulled up the hood of his suit and made himself ready. Fin grips around his ankles, mask and snorkel perched ready on his forehead, he switched off his torch and left it on the trunk, and stood at the water's edge, fins in hand. He'd been told it was easier to put them on once he was ready to dive, as walking forwards in them was tough.

'Holy shit!' he said as the water seeped down into his bootees and up his legs. This was fun, was it? Maybe in the Maldives in

July. What he really needed was a drysuit pumped full of warm water, like those guys in the Alaskan rivers searching for gold on the TV. The deeper he got the more he shivered, and the higher the water crept inside the neoprene, edging threateningly near to his testicles, which he expected would retreat inside his abdomen and probably keep going to settle near the relative warmth of his heart, never to resume their rightful place.

A car whizzed by on the road, and Spiller stopped wading, even though he was masked by the trees. The noise of the rushing tyres faded away and he started moving again, heading further out, keeping an eye on the arches of the bridge to gauge where the torch, and hopefully the gun, had landed. A couple of minutes later, he reached the spot. The water was halfway up his thighs. He stood there for a moment, geared up like something out of a spy movie, fifteen metres out into the lake but only two feet under—in both senses.

'You're kidding… what a *twat*.'

He scanned the water, shifting left and right, forwards and backwards, but slowly, careful not to stir up any sediment on the bottom, searching for the glow of the torch.

After a few minutes, he spotted it. He delved a gloved hand into the water and retrieved it. The Sig had to be somewhere close by. He took the vest and tank off his back and stood it up in the water, then lowered his mask and snorkel and bent so his face was just under the surface, scouting the shallows with the torch. It looked like clay down there, and it was grey, so he hoped the black pistol would show up easily.

It took more than ten minutes, but he found it. He straightened up, his face numb and dripping, and checked no one had parked on the bridge to watch his nocturnal nonsense. He was still alone. He zipped the weapon inside his suit, went back to the equipment sitting in the water, swung it onto his back again, and turned to the shoreline.

Driving home, he thought of all that had happened that day. His family had died; he'd tried and failed to shoot a man in the face; he'd successfully drowned a man in a wheelchair; his family had been resurrected; he'd signed a contract that would earn him six million dollars; he'd found a bunch of drugs; he'd been introduced to a group of vigilantes; he'd seen a man he'd possibly murdered come back to life; he'd learned to scuba-dive; he'd taken a ride in a Mercedes Maybach; he'd learned he hadn't needed to learn to scuba-dive; he'd rescued a murder weapon from a whopping two foot of water.

That night he slept like the dead.

Chapter Twenty-Six

DI NAT MORTLAKE was on the job again. And this time he'd
have company.

Spiller spent the morning at the Actors Centre in the city,
recruiting. The damp-smelling basement-space had a small
coffee bar and some worn chairs, and a couple of rooms off the
common room where casting directors and agents could set up
the interviews that paid for the rent. Its main purpose, though,
was to provide a place where unemployed actors could bitch
about being out of work. The more naïve and optimistic called
it *networking*, but Spiller had long ago sussed that genuine
networking necessarily involved meeting people who could get
you acting roles, not moping about with similarly disadvantaged
folk who'd stab you in the back for one line on *Emmerdale*. He'd
not been in there for years, but he nevertheless recognised a
couple of faces out of the twenty or so. Possibly he'd worked
with them before.

The whole place buzzed with a mix of conversation and
laughter, and it made him shiver. It wasn't cold; it was just so
damn cringeworthy. The neediness permeated the room like a
cheap plug-in. Glade Desperation.

Spiller bought himself a coffee and a flapjack and sat down,
setting his leather satchel on the worn carpet tiles at his feet.
He'd seen lots of directors with such bags. He peered out from
under the low peak of a camouflaged baseball cap, weighing up
the candidates, adopting the demeanour of a person of
influence.

People came and went. He purposely caught the attention of
the more indigent characters in the room—meaning those over
forty whose time was running out—some of whom met his eyes
with tentative smiles. But he wanted to choose wisely. He had to

find the right people. They would be in there, he knew that. He knew as well as anyone the hopelessness that the fruitless passing of the years could instil, and how that constant low-grade fear could morph into a feeling of recklessness.

After more than an hour, he became focused on two people in particular. They were both older than him, and both possessed the sad visage the profession engrained in people as they aged— the look of a has-been who has never actually been. The woman had blonde hair in a swirly flyaway top-bun. The guy had grown out his mane of prematurely greying hair ready for any style or cut demanded by his next role, if it ever happened. They didn't seem to be there for any reason. There weren't any interviews taking place and they fluctuated between perusing their phones and drinking coffee, but mostly they seemed to be just idling through the day, which suggested they didn't have much to lose, like a regular job, a family life, or any sort of life. There was an empty chair between them, so Spiller got up and went over and claimed it. He beckoned them closer. They leaned in. He spoke quietly.

'How would you both like to earn a grand for fifteen minutes' work?'

The woman instantly leaned away from him, wary of the strange offer.

'Acting work?' the man asked.

'Basically. Don't worry, nothing kinky.'

The woman leaned back in to listen. Spiller opened the flap of his satchel and showed them several thick bundles of twenty-pound notes.

'Shit,' the woman said. 'Fifteen minutes?'

'If that. The only thing is... it's a bit dodgy.'

'You mean illegal,' said the man.

'Not really. I'm going to be doing the possibly illegal thing. I just want two people to stand with me and look like... police officers.'

'No way!' said the man, leaning back.

Spiller shushed him. 'You don't announce you're police, you wear your regular clothes, you don't show any ID. You just stand with me. It's all about attitude. You can't get locked up for attitude.'

The man shook his head slightly. 'I don't know...'

'It's a little joke I have going with a mate, that's all. Since school. Every January, we try and plant some old-style sweets on the other one. In their home, their office, their car, wherever we can. You know, Drumsticks, Refreshers, Love Hearts, that sort of thing. This year it's Sherbet Fountains.'

'Sounds daft,' said the man.

'First one to manage it wins ten grand from the other.'

'Bloody hell,' the man said. 'Talk about money to burn.'

'Two thousand each,' said the woman. 'And this is a non-speaking role. If anyone talks to me, I'm walking away.'

Spiller considered. 'I can do two grand. What about you?' he said to the man.

The man looked at the woman who'd just got the part. 'Okay,' he said. He offered his hand, 'I'm—'

'Smith,' Spiller cut him short. 'And you're Jones. It's this afternoon. Wear... detective clothes. You're actors—you know what I mean. Get the look right. The hair, all that stuff. Meet me outside the City Tavern at twelve-thirty. You know it?'

They both nodded.

'You're good with this, right?' Spiller said. 'Say now if you're not. I'm sure there are others here who would be.'

They nodded again, more eagerly.

'Cool.' Spiller collected his satchel and walked back onto the street.

This would be the final bit of law-breaking. Matt Spiller was done with that world. It had been a trial-by-fire introduction. It wasn't as though he'd been a petty criminal his whole life, working up to the big time. It had all happened at once. He still couldn't reconcile the man he was before that first fateful meeting with Emma with the man he was today. It felt like an aberration, a paradox of the sort you saw in a sci-fi movie, where Future Spiller entered the timeline of Present Spiller, but they could never meet up lest both of them instantly combusted.

Once this was over, there'd only be one Matt Spiller and he'd be good. Good and rich and famous.

Prior to his lurking around the Actors Centre, Spiller had staked out Ward's office, sitting across the busy road at a table outside a café, freezing his nuts off, awaiting the familiar grumble of the Maserati. He'd briefly spotted the car, which had turned down a side road, its raucous exhausts quickly fading as it descended into an underground car park. He'd then watched the still-limping Ward enter his offices carrying his briefcase and, twenty minutes later, exit and set off on the short walk to the Crown Court so he could carry on trying to keep a murderous arsehole on the streets.

Spiller still didn't want him dead. He could put a bullet in the man's head, but he wanted Ward to suffer, and there was nothing to fear from a death that came instantly. Here one moment, gone the next. Suffering came with the anticipation. But there was something worse than the fear of death, and that was the fear of a pointless life. Worse, a pointless life that followed the loss of a glorious one.

On his way back to his flat, Spiller picked up a box of latex gloves from the chemist, and a second-hand SLR camera and a silver pilot case from a Cash Converters store. Getting the props right was important. In the flat, he donned a pair of gloves and printed out a bogus search warrant. He reckoned the girl behind the front desk at Ward's office was ditzy enough that, even if she knew what the real thing looked like, she'd be so flustered by their arrival that she'd not read it. He took the freshly printed search warrant, folded it and slipped it into an envelope. He then folded a blank sheet and slipped it into another envelope, marking it subtly with a red pen. He popped them both in the pilot case, then added his fake warrant card, the police baseball cap he'd nicked years before, and a plain black one. From his wardrobe, he selected a pair of black jeans, a blue polo shirt, and a black leather jacket, and changed into them. He had to achieve the right mix of smart and casual so the baseball cap wouldn't look incongruous. As with the camo cap earlier, he needed it so his face was shielded from any cameras, but it wouldn't work with a smart suit.

From his flat, he went to the house and down through the cellar to get the rocking horse. Back inside, he used gloves to remove the drugs, bullets, and the Sig, which he'd stashed before going to bed. He wiped everything down, loaded the gun with six rounds and placed it in the pilot case, then added the depleted box of bullets and the bagged tubes of drugs. From the cash, he counted out four thousand pounds, split it and stuffed it into a couple of manila envelopes, which he added to the case along with the remaining bundles.

Crap, how much jail-time would that one bag be worth? He started shaking at the thought. He wanted to abandon the whole idea, run and hide out somewhere until his flight to LA. But where would that leave his wife and kids? He couldn't leave the country with Ward still on the prowl.

SPILLER HAD BECOME worried that the thesps wouldn't be there. Now, as he approached the City Tavern, weaving along the busy pavement, he couldn't see them. There was a couple outside, canoodling, but they were younger. Spiller entered the small lounge bar and checked around, squeezing through the liquid-lunchers in the cramped old pub.

Back out on the pavement, he swore aloud.

'Oh, hey,' said the female canoodler.

Spiller turned to them as they broke apart. It was the actors, both now with brown hair, the man's far darker than the woman's, and both styled differently to earlier. The man was in a black suit, the woman a grey trouser-suit. He stared at them, puzzled. He pointed vaguely at their hair, then noticed the woman's eyes had also turned from blue to brown. He didn't need to ask; they were in character, and, more importantly, in disguise, given the dubious nature of their employment.

'I didn't think you knew each other,' he said.

'We didn't,' replied the man, whose eyes were bright with infatuation. He kissed her again.

'Something happened,' said the woman. 'When we were waiting. We just…'

'We fell in love,' the man finished, and winked at her.

Fucking luvvies, Spiller wanted to say. 'That's wonderful,' he said. He set the pilot case on a wooden cask that served as an outside table, dipped a hand in and produced the two fat manila envelopes. 'You get these when it's done.'

'We'd better,' the woman said.

Spiller put his fake ID and the printed warrant in one inside pocket, the blank warrant in another, then pulled out the plain baseball cap and his police one. He put the plain one on, and rolled the police one and stuffed it down his belt. As he did so, the actors both produced spectacles. They laughed, as only the newly in-love can laugh, at their minds-alike thinking. They put them on and looked at each other, giggling.

'DS Smith,' he said to the woman.

'DS Jones,' she replied.

'Jesus…' Spiller handed the woman the SLR. 'Stick this round your neck. And please concentrate—both of you. I can't have you looking like all you want to do is jump each other's bones. Now, listen, my mate's a lawyer, but he's not here at the moment. I'm going to blag his receptionist, we'll go in, I'll plant the sweets, then we leave. Stay in character. You ready?'

'Yes, guv,' they both said, and giggled again.

'Fuck's sake… follow me.'

WARD'S OFFICE WAS on the first floor. The elevator was directly across the corridor. Spiller couldn't see any surveillance, but, as the three of them ascended, he dipped his face, snatched the plain cap from his head and swapped it for the police one. He handed out some gloves to his cohorts and they all put them on. When the door slid open, he marched out, followed by his troupe, and buzzed Ward's office.

'Hello?' It was the voice he remembered from the day before. The same girl.

'Police,' he said.

A moment, then the door-release clicked. Spiller blew a nervous breath and pushed. Inside, the reception area was deserted, as he'd hoped it would be at lunchtime. He felt sure there would be other lawyers in the firm, and prayed they would be out as well. While his warrant might bluff this girl, it wouldn't pass the muster of a legal professional.

Spiller set his case down, showed his warrant card and produced the correct envelope, unfolding the paper in front of her face.

'DI Mortlake,' he announced. 'We have a warrant to search the offices of Dominic Ward. Is he about?'

She looked past the piece of paper at Spiller's face, then at the other two police officers. 'I know you,' she said to Spiller. 'You were here yesterday.'

Spiller nodded. 'I was. There have been developments.'

Her eyes were shifting everywhere, struggling to take it all in, then they settled on the search warrant, which she took from him to peruse.

'Dominic Ward,' he repeated. 'Where is he? Still in court?'

She stopped scanning the document. 'Uh... yes.'

Spiller took the paper back from her, slipped it into the envelope and into his other inside pocket, in front of the envelope containing the blank sheet.

'Won't I need that?' she asked. 'To show Mr Ward?'

Spiller pulled out the rear envelope and placed it on her desk.

'About what is this pertaining?' she asked.

'Not your business, young lady,' said DS Smith in a gruff Yorkshire accent that wasn't his, but sounded like every menacing copper on TV. 'His office—*now.*'

The girl grabbed a set of keys from next to the computer, stood up and went over to one of the three panelled wooden doors off the reception area, and unlocked it.

'I'll need to tell Mr Ward before you touch anything,' she said.

Again, Spiller was beaten to the punch. 'Not how this works, love,' DS Smith said. 'Go and make yourself a nice brew and sit back down. Touch that phone, you're getting locked up. *Capisce?*'

Her head bobbed up and down in compliance. She scurried over to the coffee machine in the waiting area and busied herself.

Spiller and his team entered the office and closed the door behind them. He turned to DS Smith and whispered, '*Capisce?* Oh, very fucking Yorkshire.'

DS Smith shrugged, but won an approving smile from DS Jones.

'Just stay here,' Spiller said, and turned to survey the room. Apart from a few diplomas and certificates on one wall, and a large bit of modern art on another, it was bare of ornaments. Ward had a metal desk in the centre of the room, a modern swivel desk chair, and two chrome-framed client chairs opposite. In the corner, next to some grey filing cabinets, was a metal coat stand. There were two coats, but Spiller couldn't recall if either was the one Ward had shown up in that morning. He went and checked the pockets, but they were empty apart from some tissues. He went to the desk and started rummaging through the drawers. There was a mobile phone in there and Spiller slipped it into his back pocket, but there were no car keys. It wasn't that surprising; Spiller didn't think he'd leave his car keys unattended if they belonged to a Maserati. He swore to himself, then realised the thesps were eyeing him, waiting for him to complete the plant he'd told them about. He opened the case and took out one freezer bag of Sherbet Fountains. He pulled open the large lower drawer that contained some files hanging on tracks either side, and placed the bag at the back of it. He closed the drawer and went to the cabinets, but found them all locked.

'Are you done?' asked DS Jones. 'That's it, right? What are you doing?'

'Hang fire,' Spiller told them. 'I think I've paid for more than two minutes of your time.'

They dawdled by the door as Spiller spent the next five minutes searching for somewhere better to hide the drugs, but there really wasn't anywhere Ward wouldn't easily find them. It dawned on him as he looked around—the absence of any family snapshots.

'This isn't what you said,' DS Smith objected. 'This is completely illegal.'

Spiller contemplated just stuffing the rest of the drugs, the cash, and the gun in the drawer, but what was the point? One phone call to the cops to verify, and Ward would know the whole visit was bogus, then he'd search for whatever was missing and he'd find what had been planted. More importantly, he'd find them before the cops, then the Ward gang would have their drugs back, and a gun and a mound of cash to boot.

This was another of those Matt Spiller moments when the outcome didn't match the intention. The car keys had been vital. The goods needed to be found in Ward's Maserati when he was driving, not in his office after a phoney police raid. As a barrister, Ward would have the knowledge to drive a truck through the so-called evidence against him.

'Fine, let's go,' Spiller said, and led the way out of the office.

The receptionist was still hovering near the coffee machine, demonstrating her acquiescence, although Spiller didn't doubt she'd made a sneaky call to Ward on her mobile. He pulled open the outer door for his posse. They waited in the corridor for the lift to arrive, and Spiller felt like he was in a scene from *The Three Stooges*, so inept was the ruse. He glanced down and saw Smith and Jones were already falling out of character, holding hands and grinning at each other. In the lift, Spiller swapped hats and reluctantly handed over four thousand pounds.

'Do I get extra?' Smith asked. 'Seeing as I had lines?'

Spiller gave him a sour look. 'No. You weren't meant to speak. You were an extra, a walk-on.'

'An *extra?*' Smith said. 'I have *never* been an extra. I went to Guildhall.'

Spiller nearly trumped him by announcing his RADA pedigree, but didn't want to give anything away. Instead, he said, 'Never heard of it,' which probably irked even more. 'Camera,' he said to Jones, who'd inclined herself away from him to hide it. She tutted and handed it over.

The door opened. The moment they hit the pavement, the three of them separated. Spiller would have headed in any direction that wasn't the one they were taking, but Smith and Jones split as well, removing their glasses, Jones shaking down her hair as she hurried away into the crowds. He imagined they'd be hooking up again shortly for sex and to talk about their future. Then they'd fall out the next time one got a job and the other didn't.

Spiller retired to the coffee shop where he'd that morning spied Ward's arrival. He ordered a coffee, sat outside, and watched Ward roll up in a black cab within fifteen minutes, rushing into the building as fast as his damaged leg would allow. Five minutes later, he emerged and limped around the corner towards the underground parking. Spiller had, in the case at his feet, the means to end the threat, and was now of a mind to do just that. He was suddenly more fearful than ever. He was trying to mitigate a situation that was beyond mitigation. How many chances would he give Ward? While he preferred the option of him being locked up for the rest of his life, it was an increasingly fanciful hope. He grabbed his case and crossed the road, following Ward's steps.

There was a railed walkway down the left side of the slope to a locked steel door, which he just heard click shut. The garage itself was sealed by a four-section roll-up shutter, with a remote receiver top centre. He checked for CCTV. Nothing obvious. He mulled waiting until Ward came out, then emptying the gun into him, but he'd have to negotiate the city streets to get away and there were too many eyes watching, both robot and human. He backed away.

WARD LEFT HIS office twenty minutes later and began his limping return to the Crown Court. Spiller was shivering at his outside table again. He wondered if Ward had called the cops. But there was so much history between them now, so much both could say about the other. Did Ward need that level of scrutiny?

Spiller got up and carried his case back to the Fiesta three streets away. He locked it in the boot and settled in the driver's seat to think. Delaney had said he planned things like he was writing a screenplay, behaved as though he were a character in a movie. But how did that help if the plot was full of holes? Screenplays were a manipulation of real life, but real life couldn't be manipulated. If it could, he'd still be with Helen, they'd all have moved to LA long ago, and his parents would still be alive. Plans went awry; that's what they did. When they didn't, the deluded would revel in their ability to control fate, believing their puny strategies were working. But Spiller knew better. A person could tweak their destiny—if they worked hard. If they threw every ounce of their being into an undertaking, they might spin the bottle in the desired direction for a while. But no one could prevent that unseen boot from stamping down at random and smashing the bottle to smithereens. Certainty in life was a myth, control was a yarn.

Spiller needed help. He had another idea, but it would require Enright's involvement. He pulled out the mobile he'd stolen from Ward's office. It switched on without a password. It was juiced up and on a network, but there was no call log, no messages, nothing. It looked like a standby burner. He'd just found Enright's official number in his own mobile when it began chirping.

'Hello.'

'You've got some balls, I'll give you that.'

'Who's this?'

'That was you with the search warrant, right?'

'Shit. How did you get my number?'

'My brother copied every contact from his girlfriends' phones. In case he had to track them down if they ran away.'

'A prince among men.'

'Thanks for the little prezzy you left in my desk.'

'You're welcome. You should eat it in one sitting.'

Ward laughed. 'You stole my burner, right?'

'No comment.'

The line went dead. A moment later, the burner began to ring. Spiller swapped phones.

'What?'

'Burner to burner,' Ward said. 'So now we can speak freely. Did you honestly think you could plant that gear on me and I wouldn't notice?'

'Just proving a point: I can get to you.' It was the best he could come up with.

'All you did was return some valuable merchandise. You're an imbecile.'

'Maybe, but I'm quite a dangerous imbecile.'

Ward kept quiet.

'I'm guessing you didn't tell the gang you lost two more people,' Spiller said. 'Very clumsy. In case they haven't told you, you're on probation. They're waiting for you to prove yourself and you've made a shit old start. Three dead, all on your watch, and one of them you killed yourself. You fuck up again and I'll be the least of your worries.'

'You don't figure in my worries.'

'Good—guard down. You tell the cops about your little raid just now?'

'No. When I deal with you and your family, it can't look like payback.'

Spiller's eyes welled up. Delaney had made him painfully aware of what it felt like to lose his family. It wasn't just a fear any more. It felt real. They were alive, but his sense of loss was still strong. He took a deep breath, calmed himself.

'Remember, Dominic, when you were covered in petrol, pissing your pants and crying like a baby, begging me not to kill you?'

Ward was silent.

'You said you had family. You don't. You haven't got any pictures.'

'So?'

Spiller didn't think there was anything else to say, so he cut the connection. He pulled up Enright's number on his own mobile again, but made the call on Ward's burner.

'Alfie Enright.'

'It's Matt.'

An audible sigh. 'You don't listen. We're done.'

'I need your help with something.'

'It's my day off.'

'Perfect. Meet me at the City Tavern in town soon as you can.'

'Why?'

'And bring your ID.'

'I think I look old enough to get in a pub.'

'You know what I mean. How long will you be?'

Enright groaned. 'An hour. Do I have to?'

'You'll love it,' Spiller said.

ENRIGHT DIDN'T LOVE IT. Sitting at a small table with a Coke each in front of them and a discord of chat all around, Spiller explained his ploy and could tell his audience wasn't impressed. He could also tell that Enright's mere presence meant he was under orders from Delaney not to let the loose cannon do anything that might get him arrested, considering everything he knew and could trade for a lighter sentence.

'How many seconds did it take you to come up with that?' Enright asked.

'Bugger off. If I was so crap at this, I'd be in prison by now.'

'You raided his office,' Enright said, shaking his head. 'How was that a good idea?'

'It would have worked if he'd left his car keys.'

Enright gave a withering look. 'It wouldn't. He'd have checked his car. You said he did anyway and he had the bloody keys with him the whole time.'

Spiller felt a bit sulky. He sipped his Coke.

'But...' Enright said, absently rubbing his crucifix between thumb and finger. 'This might work. You need to check the garage first, though. Cameras, exits. You can't be caught in there. You need a way out.'

'I'll do that now. What time does the Crown Court end?'

'Usually four-thirty.'

'Okay. There's a café across the road from Ward's office. We should be in there from four in case he heads back early. Soon as we see him arrive—'

'I know,' Enright said. 'I know the crack. I've done this shit before, remember? I've been doing it for years. Call and let me know the lie of the land—if it's on. I'm going home to change.'

Spiller left Enright and made his way back to the underground garage. He loitered on the street for twenty minutes, supposedly engrossed in his mobile, before he heard the garage shutter start to roll upwards. He lowered the peak of his baseball cap, pocketed his phone, and got his fake warrant card ready in his hand. He timed his approach. He could see the nose of a black Range Rover waiting inside for the shutter to lift fully. As it moved through and up the ramp, he was halfway down it.

The driver halted and called through his lowering window: 'Oi, you! Where are you going?'

Spiller held up his warrant card and carried on down the slope and ducked under the descending shutter. As it closed behind him, he heard the Range Rover power up and away onto the street.

He surveyed the scene, turning 360 degrees as he checked the walls and ceiling. The walls were bare, and the only thing he could see above his head was fluorescent lighting and the pipework of a fume-extraction system. If there were any cameras they were cleverly concealed, and that wasn't the point of them; cameras were meant to deter. And there wasn't much need for them. There was a button beside the pedestrian door alongside the shutter, but it seemed you needed a remote to exit with a car. The garage had spaces for maybe thirty vehicles, most of which were taken. He spotted the blue Quattroporte parked towards the rear of the space. In the centre of the back wall was another door, marked as an emergency exit, with a small pane of glass in it. He hurried over. It was unlocked. He went through to find a stairwell. Up two flights and he was at street level on the adjacent street. The exit door had a push-bar mechanism. Spiller depressed it and peeked onto the busy pavement. The outside of the door was blank of handles. You could get out, but not in. He'd seen enough to give the plan a green light. He let the door shut and scanned the floor for something he could use to block the hole in the jamb so the bolt wouldn't seat. He spotted a blob of hardened bubble gum, pushed the door back open a couple of inches and tried it for size, but it was slightly too big. He began grinding it down against the breezeblock wall, sculpting it into shape, testing the fit as he went until it slotted in snugly. He stepped out and let the door close behind him, and turned his nose towards the police station. On his way, he called Enright again to add some extra details based on what he'd seen.

A SULLEN DCI Bartoli trudged slowly down the steps of the station, summoned out by a phone call to meet his least favourite person in the world. Spiller smiled affably as he approached and held out his hand, which was rejected.

'What?' Bartoli asked. 'Are you here to make a confession? I can dream.'

'No, and I don't want another coffee, thanks. You burnt my John Thomas yesterday.'

'What?'

'My dick.'

'Oh. Sue me. What do you want?'

Spiller crooked a finger and led Bartoli away from the entrance and the police footfall.

'It's not what *I* want, Detective; it's what *you* want. Which is to leave here with your head held high.'

Bartoli's mouth pouted thoughtfully, like he was doing a duck-lips pose for Instagram. 'I'm still here,' he said. 'Talk.'

'How would you like to solve the Callum Ward murder? And a couple of others.'

'*A couple of others?* Related to Callum Ward?'

Spiller nodded.

'Does that include the dead guy in your basement?'

Spiller had to rewind mentally through the past few days.

Bartoli laughed, briefly and loudly. 'Christ, you can't even keep up with the fricking body count! The guy in your basement? The arson guy? Thumbless? Remember him?'

'Ah, right. Him. No, not him. That would be a third. Same perp, though, funnily enough. So...'

'And where would I find these other dead guys?'

'Where did you find Callum Ward?'

'*What?* You're telling me—'

'Nothing. I'm telling you nothing. I'm asking a question. A rhetorical one.'

Bartoli nodded. 'Okay. And I crack this conundrum how?'

Spiller made an awkward face. 'Yeah, now that's going to involve a firearms team.'

'Oh, you just won't be satisfied 'til I deploy some weapons, will you, buddy?'

'And it's this afternoon. One chance, then it's gone. You'll need them standing by, covert, ready to go.'

Bartoli inhaled deeply, expanding his chest, then let out the longest, weariest sigh. 'Matthew, if you screw me on this, your scalded penis will be coming with me Stateside, along with your testicles, where they will be wall-mounted in my new office. So, with that in mind, you still wanna do this?'

Spiller tried to dispel the image Bartoli had conjured. 'Yep.'

'Then tell me more.'

Chapter Twenty-Seven

SPILLER AND ENRIGHT positioned themselves at a window table in the café at four o'clock. Enright had returned in a dark grey suit and smart overcoat. He had a trilby and an umbrella with him. They nursed their drinks as the light faded from the sky and a drizzle began to fall. It was perfect; Enright's hat and umbrella wouldn't raise an eyebrow. He could shield himself from prying police eyes, some of whom might be colleagues. The canopy outside the café kept the glass clear of the rain, and they both watched intently the comings and goings outside Ward's office. At four-fifteen, Enright pointed out the arrival of a convoy of four unmarked vehicles.

'Bartoli took the bait,' Enright said. 'That's them.'

The vehicles turned off onto the road where the underground parking was located.

Spiller put his baseball cap on. 'Won't be a mo,' he said, and left the café.

He trotted along the pavement until he could see down the side road. The vehicles had all pulled up on the double yellows. Their lights winked out. Spiller returned to the café.

'It's them,' he told Enright.

'I know—I said. I know what a police convoy looks like.'

At just before five, a black cab pulled up and Ward got out and entered the building.

'That's my cue,' Spiller said, collecting his pilot case. 'Don't miss him, Alfie. You've got to catch the garage door before it shuts.'

'Just go.'

Spiller hurried out, heading for the street where he'd earlier gummed up the stairwell exit, acutely aware of the Sig in his case and how close he was to some serious people with fearsome hardware who would take him down if they even glimpsed it.

Before he reached the plain steel door, he put some latex gloves on. He managed to claw his fingertips in sufficiently to gain purchase and pull it open. The rain was starting to come down hard. Inside, he dug the gum out of the hole and let the door lock. He went down the stairs and peered through the grimy wired glass of the emergency exit. A businessman was just getting in his car. As the Jag manoeuvred from its spot, the shutter started rumbling aloft. This was home-time, and Spiller knew he'd have to be careful. In the next hour, more people would be collecting their vehicles. Still, he felt relatively safe behind the door. While people could use it to egress the car park in the morning, it wasn't an option for ingress at night.

He watched the shutter descend again. He pushed the door open to check if its hinges made any sound. Quiet enough, and now he could hear the rain being thrown in sheets against the closed shutter by gusts of wind. Rivulets seeped underneath, disappearing into a grated gulley.

In the next fifteen minutes, two more vehicles were collected and taken away. Each time the pedestrian door opened, Spiller's heart palpitated and he felt nauseous. Out of all the reprehensible activities over the past couple of weeks, this made him the most anxious.

As the shutter settled back down on the concrete, the door opened again and Spiller held his breath as though the slightest exhalation might be overheard.

It was Ward, collar up, briefcase in hand. The moment his foot entered the garage, he pressed his remote, and the Quattroporte beeped twice, its indicators flashing. It was the vital window Spiller had hoped for. He had seen Ward do that before, and guessed it was a habit, disarming the car from afar, intended to give onlookers the chance to turn and clock the lucky sod who was strolling towards a motor very few could afford. Behind Ward, the door's hydraulic closer controlled its slow return, but it was way too swift for Spiller's liking. He kept holding his breath until the dark arm of an overcoat pushed through the decreasing gap and stopped its progress. The door was pulled wide again and Enright entered the garage in his trilby, lowering his dripping brolly. He spoke, but Ward was already swivelling to check who had followed him in.

'Mr Ward! Can I talk to you?'

Spiller seized the moment. With Ward's back turned, and as the opposite door clunked shut, he sneaked through into the garage and crouched behind the nearest car. The Maserati was still unlocked, but there was a chance it would auto-lock pretty quickly if no one opened it. As he scurried low behind the three vehicles between him and the Maserati, he kept an ear tuned to the conversation ten metres away, which carried to him through the echo-chamber of the garage.

'PC Enright. Here's my warrant card.'

'Really?' Ward said.

Spiller reached the rear of the Maserati and shuffled low along its left wing.

Enright laughed. 'I understand you might be cynical. Your receptionist called about a police raid she didn't think was genuine.'

'That bloody girl,' Ward said.

Spiller reached for the door handle and timed his pull to coincide with the rattle of the garage shutter in its tracks as a wet gust caught it. He opened the pilot case. The conversation by the door had lulled, and Spiller guessed Ward was scrutinising the warrant card for authenticity.

'Okay,' Ward said. 'I think I recognise you from the station, actually. You're normally in uniform, right?'

'Secondment to CID. So, what happened?'

There wasn't much room under the passenger seat, so Spiller placed just the gun and the bullets there. He firmly but slowly leaned a shoulder against the door to close it, then shuffled on his haunches so he could open the rear door.

'It was nothing,' Ward said. 'Practical joke. Some of my friends have a warped sense of humour.'

Spiller unloaded the bags of drugs into the space behind the passenger seat and pushed them under out of sight. He calculated he didn't have the time to add the cash, and, anyway, what difference would it make to the overall effect? The murder weapon on its own was enough. The cash would only be seized by the police. He leaned his shoulder and quietly closed the door.

'Well, I'll have a word with my sarge, but he may wish to pursue this.'

'I can only apologise. I'm not even sure which of my friends it was.'

'It's a serious matter, impersonating a police officer,' Enright said. 'You know that very well.'

Spiller had scuttled back behind the vehicles and was now poised, ready for the brief scoot to the emergency exit.

'I do,' Ward said. 'I'm really sorry you've been inconvenienced.'

Another battering of the shutters by the wind, and Spiller moved. He caught the start of Enright offering a final ticking off before the door closed out the conversation. He headed up the stairs and waited at the top. Thirty seconds later, he heard the door below open.

'I'll head out this way,' Enright said to Ward. 'Save me a few minutes in the rain. You take care.'

Spiller peered over the rail and saw Enright start to ascend the stairs but halt as the raucous V8 fired up. Enright beckoned for Spiller to come back down. All Spiller wanted was to get the hell away from there, but, actually, what did he have on him now? Some cash. No crime in that. And he couldn't deny the morbid fascination in actually watching his nemesis get his comeuppance. He descended the stairs and they both put their faces to the grubby glass.

'Best seats in the house,' Spiller whispered. Enright ignored him.

The Maserati was deafening in the confined space. It grumbled up to the exit, then waited while the shutter rose and curled back along its roof tracks.

Enright pushed the door open a crack so they could hear what was imminently about to happen.

As the Maserati cleared the threshold, the ramp and the car were bathed in frantic, dancing beams of white light, which quickly converged as an amplified male voice called out.

'*Armed Police! Driver, stop your engine!*'

From their vantage point, Spiller and Enright couldn't see more than the Maserati and the ramp, and the pounding rain bouncing off every surface. The pavement was out of sight. They watched as the car stopped abruptly and its growling ceased.

Then there was another cry. A lone voice.

'*Gun gun gun!*'

Three rapid shots. Then a deafening hail of bullets Spiller couldn't even count. An armed officer appeared from the pavement, his carbine raised, and ran down the ramp to the passenger side of the car. He snatched the door open, gun at the ready, then immediately knelt down, obscuring himself from the street. Spiller watched him let go of his weapon so it hung on its sling, and lean into the Maserati. Ten seconds later, he backed out, holding the trigger guard of the Sig between his fingers.

'Weapon secured! Suspect down! Get an ambulance!'

And, with that, the curtain dropped on Dominic Ward.

'Fuck,' Spiller said. 'Fuck me.'

Enright tugged at Spiller's sleeve. 'Let's go. It's done.'

Spiller backed away and followed Enright up the concrete steps. An ambulance? A mop and bucket, more like. Enright pushed down on the bar and they exited onto the street. It seemed he had nothing more to say. He opened his umbrella above his head and set off briskly through the enlarging puddles and the end-of-day crowds.

Spiller watched him go for a few seconds, felt the rain permeate his cap and soak into his scalp. 'Hey!' he called suddenly, and ran after him.

'What?' Enright said, stopping. 'It worked perfectly.'

It seemed like the heavens were crying the pent-up tears for a thousand innocent deaths. Even in the shadow of the dripping brim of his trilby, Enright's eyes were gleaming with the moral certitude of a man who believed he'd just atoned for at least one of those poor souls.

Spiller held his arm tightly. 'No. What the fuck just happened there? The gun was under his seat. No way could that copper have seen it.'

'Let it go.'

'Was that Bartoli? Did he order it? *Is* he with you?'

'You think Bartoli could have persuaded a firearms officer to shoot an unarmed man? To put his career and his liberty on the line?'

'So, what happened?' Spiller asked, his features contorting in bafflement.

'Trust is everything. Nothing works without it.'

'Hey?'

'Go to Hollywood, Matthew. Have a nice life.'

Enright gave a sharp tug of his arm that broke Spiller's grip, and Spiller allowed him to turn and disappear into the throng, until his was just one more brolly bobbing away, shimmering darkly under the streetlamps.

After a minute of being barged and knocked by pedestrians, or being cursed as they detoured around his immobile form, Spiller realised he was in a slight fugue. He moved to the wall and set his case down and sat on it. A drainpipe gurgled beside him. Way above him an overhang provided some cover from the downpour, but he was wet through already. Gradually, he began to shiver. It was more than the cold; it was an emotional release. But it was more than shock. He'd killed people himself, so watching the cops shoot Ward wasn't it. This felt like... an exorcism. Of everything that had occurred since Christmas Eve. In fact, of the past twenty-five years. He could sense an exodus from every pore, and he knew it was a million times more cathartic than the tears he'd previously shed.

A five-pound note appeared under his downturned face.

'Here you go, young man, get yourself a hot drink and something to eat.'

Spiller looked up at the old lady, who was proffering a little charity to the sorry down-and-out. He smiled at her. She looked like she needed the money herself. He glanced down at her shoes, which were taped at the toes. He pushed to his feet, opened the pilot case and pulled out a wad of twenties. He thought it was five hundred. It could have been a thousand. It didn't matter.

'Thanks, sweetheart,' he said. 'But I'm fine. Here, you buy yourself some warm boots. And a brolly.'

She stared at the money for a moment like it was a cruel joke, so he placed it in her hand on top of the five-pound note, and gently closed her arthritic fingers around it.

'Put it away before someone sees,' he told her.

Her face came alive. 'Thank you,' she said, giggled, and pushed the bundle into her shopping bag.

Spiller picked up his case and wandered off in the direction of his car, feeling the strange unburdening continue.

Free and clear. Finally. Matt Spiller was free and clear.

Chapter Twenty-Eight

AS THE DAYS passed, Spiller realised his agreement with DCI Bartoli was solid. He'd been a little concerned that the detective might want to cap his success in solving the Ward case with a betrayal that would see his new Confidential Informant dragged into the station again. But Bartoli had evidently been happy with the outcome and wasn't keen to sully his last few days in Blighty by alerting his successor to a load of unanswered questions. He was going out on a high. The news channels disseminated his glorious contribution to British justice. A dogged New York detective, determined to crack one last case before resuming his career stateside.

The evidence had stacked up as Spiller and Enright had planned. Dominic Ward, jealous of his gangland brother, had organised his execution. Then, two of Callum Ward's most loyal retainers had also been killed, but this time by Dominic himself. Their bodies had been found dumped at the same spot where Callum was found, and ballistics had matched the rounds dug from their bodies to the gun found in Dominic Ward's car, with his prints all over it. The bagged drugs had been the cherry on top.

Until he heard about the prints, Spiller could only surmise exactly what had happened on the car-park ramp that dark afternoon. But Ward's prints on the gun meant only one thing: the copper who'd called *gun!* was one of Delaney's. He'd fired the first shots and had been the one who'd retrieved the weapon, and when he'd leaned inside the Maserati for ten seconds, it had been to clamp Ward's hand around the gun. The officer in question, who had not been named, was praised for his quick response, and his amazing observational skills in identifying a weapon in Ward's hand through a windscreen being battered by rain.

That's what Enright had meant about trust being everything. The firearms officer had to implicitly trust that, when Enright had told him a gun would be present, it was true. And Enright had equally needed to trust that Spiller could succeed in planting it without being spotted.

Of course, despite Bartoli's gloating, there remained a plethora of unanswered questions. Not just about Spiller's complicity, but more about why Dominic Ward would want to murder his own brother to take over a drug gang when he probably earned more as a barrister, and without any risks. No one was seriously looking to explain that enigma, though, because everyone knew the answer: people were just greedy. There was no such thing as enough. There were always higher highs, and a surprising number couldn't see them for what they really were: lower lows.

Spiller, however, was bucking the trend. His life was genuinely brimming. He did have enough. He had his family and they were all living together under one roof again, reunited, rejuvenated. He had money and more was on its way, because he now had the acting career he'd been chasing for decades.

Matt Spiller was happy. He kept mentally slapping himself to make sure, but, fuck yeah, he was happy. And he was sleeping well, and how blissful was that?

Returning home after the events of that afternoon, Spiller had destroyed all the evidence he'd secreted away on Charles Delaney. It was a matter of trust, and he didn't want to be the only one not honouring the code.

In the run-up to his departure for LA, no one called who he didn't want to hear from. There were no strange, vulgar cars outside his house—including his own. He sold the Audi within forty-eight hours at a hefty loss. It was an enjoyable beast but, even without the taxi plates, it would always remind him of a job he despised and a time he'd rather forget. The Fiesta went back to the hire company and he was content to pootle about in Helen's old Peugeot—at least for those remaining days. After he got paid, he'd take his pick. There wouldn't be anything he couldn't afford. Perhaps a nice Maserati. But not the Quattroporte. Maybe the more exclusive GranTurismo, or the GranCabrio if he stayed on in balmy LA, finished in metallic Rosso Trionfale.

He thought of Gibbo often. It was sad, he knew that. He felt bad—but not so much. His head had been rehabilitated. Previously he'd felt bad despite good things happening; now he felt good in spite of the bad. Maybe it was a little callous, but it was a welcome shift.

The girls had returned to education and both were now massively popular thanks to their soon-to-be-famous dad, although little Soph would still have preferred her dad was a cyclopic Minion. Sammy got on with her life as though nothing had happened, as though she'd not been tortured by a sadist her parents had then murdered and dumped in the hills. She declined offers to talk about it. She was stoicism incarnate.

On the surface, Helen was getting back to being the woman he'd met twenty years before, and seemed determined not to carry any of the recent wickedness forward with her. She never asked about Dominic Ward's demise, whether her husband had helped to orchestrate it, just as she'd never wanted to know where the gun or cash came from. And even when Gibbo's disappearance hit the news, Spiller had received only the slightest look of disdain—just once.

They were together again, but he had a heap of baggage he couldn't share with her. Emma, Delaney, Whittard, the Loughtys. That part of his life was his to bury alone. And, try as he might, he couldn't forget the other Helen he'd seen. Mrs Jekyll was back in charge, but, prior to the expanding foam incident, he hadn't even known there was a Mrs Hyde inside. Her emotional detachment prior to his first meeting with Delaney in the restaurant still niggled. The way she'd shrugged off the prospect of his death. He was terribly flawed, but his soul had perished when he thought he'd lost his family, and that included Helen. So he couldn't help but wonder if they construed the notion of love in starkly different ways. Time, so the saying went, would surely tell.

Spiller had his bags packed for LA four days before the flight, and knew his lines even before then. In fact, he could have recited the entire script, every word of every character.

He had a second chance and he wasn't going to screw it up.

Epilogue

THE DAY OF Spiller's departure was a weekday, so the girls were at school. He hugged them that morning as though he'd never see them again. Helen drove him to the airport, and left the Peugeot in the same section of the multi-storey where he'd parked on that fateful afternoon when he'd gone to pick up Brett Stutz in Gibbo's Lexus, with Gibbo dead in the boot.

She walked alongside him, linking his arm, as he pushed his trolley of luggage to the terminal building. Then, she oversaw his check-in as though he might fuck it up and end up on the wrong plane. He loved her for things like that.

They embraced for the longest time, and many times, parting only to be drawn back into a hug. They were like teenagers falling in love for the first time and never wanting to say goodbye.

'Thanks, darling,' Spiller said to her, amidst the bustle of the airport. People drifted by; singles, couples, families, weighed down or travelling light. He'd imagined this farewell so often over the years, the bitter-sweet moment when he would forsake a family he loved for a future he couldn't resist. It felt like the culmination of all that Napoleon Hill had promised. If anyone had asked, he'd have said there was no doubt in his mind he'd be back to reclaim them. But, in truth, there was a shard of doubt. This was the destiny he'd envisaged, but he'd never thought much beyond the achievement of fame. Would he be seduced by Hollywood? Would his fickle, needy soul guzzle down all the town had to offer—the drink, the drugs, the sycophants, the sex—and even more voraciously now he had two decades to make up for?

'You take care,' Helen said. 'Enjoy it all.' She pecked him one last time, then she turned, walked away, and didn't look back.

He watched her until she left the building, all the time praying for a glance over her shoulder, a wink or a blown kiss, something to help glue up the cracks in his character that he couldn't mend himself. He eyed the doorway for another minute, thinking she might return for one last hug, but she didn't.

What had she meant? *Enjoy it all.* Was she giving him permission to be wayward? Was she giving a shrug to the fates that had brought him to that moment? Acknowledging they had a plan for her husband that might not involve her? Or was she simply offering her best wishes? Enjoy your just mains, but don't partake of the desserts.

He grabbed his hand-luggage and checked the nearby board. He had over two hours until his flight to LAX. To be on the safe side, before he joined the long queue into the departures lounge, he decided to have a pee.

In the toilets, after relieving himself, he washed his hands and checked his reflection. His skin had recovered from the injuries he'd sustained that night at Delaney's restaurant. He looked good. He looked... younger. He'd told Whittard the loss of his parents had aged him ten years. Now he neither felt nor looked like that older person. He smiled at himself. He laughed.

He took his case and wheeled it out of the toilets, and thought he saw someone in the distance he knew. Was it an old friend? Perhaps an actor he recognised who was also heading out to be in Stutz's new movie—although in a lesser role, of course. As the man approached, Spiller offered him a puzzled smile, as any decent person would to avoid being rude. The man grinned back, and Spiller raised his hand in a little wave, still unsure.

As he drew nearer, it clicked. The beard was gone. Terry Loughty had shaved his beard off.

Spiller stuttered to a halt. He glanced over at a couple of armed cops, then back at Loughty, whose hand had reached inside his jacket.

'Oh, bloody hell...'

ACKNOWLEDGEMENTS

Thanks to Sean at Red Dog Press for his hard work, faith, superb editing, and continuing support.

A special shout-out to my brother Dave, my unofficial copy-editor, whose sharp eye catches the errors when I go text-blind after too many rewrites.

Love always to my wife and soul-mate, Jeannifer, and my kids, Tina, Carl, and Jade.